JUAN VALERA

Commander Mendoza

El Comendador Mendoza

ARIS & PHILLIPS HISPANIC CLASSICS

JUAN VALERA

Commander Mendoza

El Comendador Mendoza

Translated by

Robert M. Fedorchek

with an Introduction by

Susan M. McKenna

Aris & Phillips
is an imprint of
Oxbow Books, Oxford, UK

ISBN cloth 978-0-85668-859-1
ISBN paper 978-0-85668-858-4

A CIP record for this book is available from the British Library.

This book is available direct from

Oxbow Books, Oxford, UK
Phone: 01865-241249; Fax: 01865-794449

and

The David Brown Book Company
PO Box 511, Oakville, CT 06779, USA
Phone: 860-945-9329; Fax: 860-945-9468

or from our website

www.oxbowbooks.com

Printed by
Short Run Press, Exeter

CONTENTS

Translator's Preface   vii
Introduction   xi
  Susan M. McKenna
Selected Bibliography   xxii

El Comendador Mendoza (Commander Mendoza)   1

Notes   337

TRANSLATOR'S PREFACE

Juan Valera y Alcalá-Galiano (1824–1905) has been widely acclaimed by critics and students of literature as one of nineteenth-century Spain's foremost authors and literati. Well known inside his native country as a writer who cultivated virtually all genres, outside of it his fame rests on the novel and the short story, the lion's share of this fame on the former.

After the resounding success of his *Pepita Jiménez* (1874), the epistolary novel about a young seminarian who falls in love with a young widow, Valera published *Commander Mendoza* (*El Comendador Mendoza*, 1877), set at the close of the eighteenth century, which chronicles the life of the Commander in Spain, Peru, briefly in France during the French Revolution, and then, retired from the military, back in Spain for good. It contains a number of memorable characters, chief among them the commander himself, Don Fadrique López de Mendoza, an appealing deist; Doña Blanca Roldán de Solís, a staid, severe matron obsessed with guilt and driven by a corrosive religious fanaticism; and the congenial, down-to-earth Father Jacinto, friend of the commander and confessor to Doña Blanca, and perhaps the most sympathetic priest to appear in all of Valera's novels.

After the colorful preliminary chapters that give the commander's history from boyhood to manhood, the tale proper unfolds and the work is soon dominated by the presence – both perceived and actual – of Doña Blanca and the outcome of her long-ago, in time and place, affair with Don Fadrique. It is against this backdrop that Valera takes us on a journey of inquiry into the nature of sin and evil and fanaticism and redemption, even forgiveness. That he was pleased with the result can be seen in what he wrote to his friend Narciso del Campillo from Washington, DC (his diplomatic posting at the time), on November 18th, 1885: "What would please me would be to continue writing novels like *Pepita Jiménez* and *Commander Mendoza*" (Montesinos 75: *Lo que yo celebraría sería seguir escribiendo novelas como* Pepita Jiménez *y* El Comendador Mendoza).

The distinguished English-language translators of two of nineteenth-century Spain's greatest novels have summed up the challenges that

every literary translator faces. Agnes Moncy writes: "In *Fortunata and Jacinta*, language is rich. Metaphors, colloquialisms, neologisms, allusions, rhetorical devices, technical vocabulary, linguistic deformation – each could be considered at length" (xvii). And John Rutherford states: "Translation is a strange business, which sensible people no doubt avoid. By my calculation I have spent at least five times as many hours writing this English rendering of it as Alas spent writing *La Regenta*" (17).

I haven't spent quite as long a time with my English rendering of *El Comendador Mendoza*, which is much shorter than *La Regenta*, but surely at least one and a half times longer than the six months or so that it must have taken Valera to write it. The many, many months pile up because, like Agnes Moncy with Benito Pérez Galdós and John Rutherford with Leopoldo Alas, I was trying to get inside another person's head and weigh and consider meaning, for translation is nothing if not a continuous exercise in interpretation. To take but one common example, the Spanish adjective *fino* is often its cognate equivalent of *fine* in English, but depending on context it may also be expressed as *subtle, choice, delicate, select, acute, refined, shrewd, slender, well-bred, sharp, elegant, sheer*, and others.

There are numerous voices in *Commander Mendoza*, with consequent shifts in linguistic levels, levels that have to be reflected in the translation. They include: the elegant prose of the omniscient narrator; the conversational tones of dialogue, whether it be the severity of language in Doña Blanca, submissiveness in that of Don Valentín, untoward gravity in that of Clara, cheerfulness and expansiveness in that of Lucía, and an earthy sense of humor in Nicolasa's speech. Separate from the brief exchanges of the various characters are the long conversations between Father Jacinto and Doña Blanca, and between Don Fadrique and Doña Blanca, in which the registers range from lofty and eloquent to dismissive and haughty. And it is in these Jacinto/Blanca/Fadrique encounters that interpretation becomes the arbiter of nuance, as it does in the Commander's interior monologue concerning Doña Blanca, sin, and religion in chapter 25.

We find specialized vocabulary in the language of embroidery (Lucía), spices and dressing a hog (Doña Antonia), and the gustatory and olfactory delights of Valera's beloved Andalusian cuisine, for many of which there are no English equivalents.

Rhymed sayings and verse always compel a translator to make a

decision. Attempt to carry over an equivalent scheme from the source language to the target language or not? There are two sayings in *Commander Mendoza*, and because they are short I opt for rhyme in both (chapters 18 and 30) in order to preserve the playfulness or "punch," so to speak, but, in order to avoid a transfer that would result in stilted, artificial English, I render the two long idylls composed by young Don Carlos (chapters 7 and 30) into unrhymed prose and signal the lines of verse as I did in *Don Álvaro, or the Force of Fate*, my translation of the Duke of Rivas's *Don Álvaro o la fuerza del sino*, by setting the text in short lines in approximate measure with the original.

Most of the notes are intended for those who are unfamiliar with Spanish literature, Spanish history, and Spanish culture, while some are brief explanations of historical and mythological figures that may not be at readers' fingertips. Well read in a half dozen languages, Juan Valera's erudition never fails to impress as he cites works from ancient to modern times.

The Spanish editions used for the translation are those of 1881 (Madrid: Fernando Fe) and 2001 (Madrid: Biblioteca Castro), both of which follow the *El Campo* [periodical] version of 1876–77.

No translator functions in isolation, and for the help she has given me on numerous "*Mendozan*" occasions, I thank Consuelo García Devesa of Santiago de Compostela, friend and colleague, and professor emerita of Fairfield University. And I extend a special word of thanks to Dr. Jonathan Thacker, Series Editor of Aris & Phillips Hispanic Classics, and Clare Litt and Tara Evans of Oxbow Books, who made this publication possible.

Lastly, my introducer and I dedicate *Commander Mendoza* to our first – which is to say our most loyal and devoted – readers: Theresa Fedorchek and James Brophy.

INTRODUCTION

Susan M. McKenna

Aristocrat, diplomat, lawyer, poet, critic, playwright, novelist, and editor, Juan Valera is one of the great figures of nineteenth-century Spanish letters whose life and work not only span a tumultuous century but also defy simple classification.[1] Valera did not belong to any particular literary school, nor did his work fit readily into either / or categories. Rather, he represented a moderate position – a middle ground that reconciled the differences between the principal literary movements of his lifetime, including both realism and idealism. Valera considered himself neither realist nor idealist, opting instead to borrow elements and techniques from both, adjusting each to suit his writerly needs. Throughout his long, and at times, intermittent career, Valera, nonetheless, adhered to his own particular philosophy of art that effectively distinguished aesthetic standards from those of science, education, morality, or politics. Henry Thurston-Griswold has coined the term "synthetic idealism" – the harmonious synthesis of opposite postures – to capture the essence of Valera's life and works.[2] Consistent with this notion of synthesis, the artist uses reality to create the ideal. Without a base in reality art is false, and without the ideal, it is not art.

Before entering the novel itself, a brief examination of Valera's life and work is in order. Born October 18th, 1824 in Cabra, a sleepy Andalusian city of twenty-five thousand inhabitants located in the province of Córdoba, Valera was the son of Dolores Alcalá Galiano y Pareja, the Marquise of la Paniega, and José Valera y Viaña, a retired naval officer. The early years of his youth were divided between Cabra and the neighboring town of Doña Mencía, both of which provide inspiration for the setting in his five Andalusian novels. His father returned to active duty after the death of Fernando VII in 1833, and the family then moved to the larger cities of Córdoba, Madrid, and Málaga. In Málaga he attended the Seminario Conciliar for three years, and in 1841 he began to study law at the Colegio del Sacro Monte in Granada. The following year he transferred to the University of Granada where he earned his law degree in 1844.

Between the years 1844 and 1853, Valera enjoyed the privileges that youth, wealth, and family connections provided. He returned to Madrid intending to practice law, and quickly immersed himself in the social life of the metropolis, frequenting literary gatherings and cafés while dabbling in some writing. He soon realized that he needed to make a name for himself and to earn some money. The diplomatic corps seemed to him a profitable means towards fulfilling this goal. Over the next few years, Valera would serve as an attaché to the Duke of Rivas in Naples; and to his uncle in Lisbon, Antonio Alcalá Galiano, the famous orator and politician. After one short year in Lisbon, he was promoted to second secretary and transferred to Rio de Janeiro. He wrote little of consequence during this time with the exception of letters to family and colleagues, but his many experiences both at home and abroad would become fodder in future years for his novels and short stories.

Upon his return to Madrid in 1853 Valera began to dedicate himself seriously to writing literary criticism. Money, however, was always a consideration, so he continued his diplomatic service, traveling briefly to Dresden in 1855 and then to Russia (Moscow and St. Petersburg) in the winter and spring of 1856–57. He returned to Spain in 1857 and was elected deputy in the Cortes from the district of Archidona, in the province of Málaga. It is around this time (1859–1860) that Valera's proclivity and talent for critical and creative writing truly began to flourish. Throughout the next four decades, the symbiotic relationship between his theories and practices would provide a distinctive hallmark to his work. The palpable link between literary theory and artistic creation is best evinced in the eight novels he composed between 1874 and 1899.

Valera's novelistic output can be divided into two periods of intense literary activity separated by a hiatus of more than fifteen years. The first period (1874–1879) saw the publication of his masterpiece, *Pepita Jiménez* (1874), followed by *The Illusions of Doctor Faustino* (1875), *Commander Mendoza* (1877), *Don Braulio* [*Pasarse de listo*] (1878), and *Doña Luz* (1879). Three of these, *Commander Mendoza*, *The Illusions of Doctor Faustino*, and *Don Braulio* are somewhat autobiographical in nature: the first two are set in Valera's native Andalusia, and the third in his adopted Madrid. All three have protagonists modeled on certain aspects of Valera's own personality. Valera often drew upon personal experience for the settings, themes, and characters of his works, including the nostalgic reminiscences of local color, customs, foods, and

traditions so much a part of his Andalusian novels. Idealized versions of the real, they were, nonetheless, based on places and on people that he knew. The second period (1895–1899), brought forth *Juanita la Larga* (1895), *Genio y figura* (1897), and *Morsamor* (1899), the latter two not yet translated into English. In addition to these eight completed novels, there were several left unfinished, the most significant being *Mariquita y Antonio*, which was published serially in the newspaper *El Contemporáneo* during the spring of 1861. With the exception of *Morsamor* and several incomplete historical novels, *Commander Mendoza* is the only long work with a non-contemporary setting, taking place in the late 1700s. It is also an excellent example of the author's novelistic synthesis of theory and practice.

One of the earliest and most comprehensive expressions of Valera's conception of the nature and aims of art can be found in his 1860 essay, "On the Nature and Character of the Novel," (*De la naturaleza y carácter de la novela*), a response to Cándido Nocedal's inaugural address to the Royal Spanish Academy.[3] For Valera, the novel is akin to poetry, for it too is a creation of the poetic imagination. Whereas history attempts to portray things as they are, the novel paints them as they should be. The novel, nonetheless, must have a "true" basis and be logical (*i.e.*, possible within the fictional world) but it is not simply an imitation of reality. The novel must also entertain the reader and exalt the soul. In order to do so, the novelist uses a process of idealization that emphasizes the beautiful elements of an observable reality. A proponent of "art for art's sake," Valera argues against the doctrinal/dogmatic novels, favoring instead those whose thesis is implied, not openly expressed. Art, he believed, should be in harmony with good morals but should not be used to teach good morals – the objective of art is beauty. Finally, because the novel is, in many ways, a study of humans, their actions, and their motives, the novelist must try to present faithfully the interior world of his/her characters. Manuel Olguín succinctly summarizes Valera's philosophy of art: "Art is an imitation of nature, idealized through the imagination, and intended to produce delight and elevation of the mind to the world of ideals, where beauty, truth, and goodness prevail over the ugliness, falsity, and evil of daily reality" (27). Accordingly, all of Valera's novels, including *Commander Mendoza*, manifest these ideals.

Commander Mendoza was first published in the bimonthly *El Campo* during the winter and spring of 1876–77, and in book form a few months

later. Chronologically, it is Valera's third completed novel and scholars usually rank it third qualitatively as well, positioned behind *Pepita Jiménez* and *Juanita la Larga*. *Commander Mendoza* tells the story of a precocious young man, Don Fadrique de Mendoza, who establishes a career in the Royal Spanish Navy after leaving his small village of Villabermeja. Fadrique, known as the Commander in his later years, travels to Cuba, Peru, India, and France where he spends his youth enacting many exciting adventures – both military and amorous – before returning to Spain several decades later. Tired of these foreign exploits and then bored with life in the capital city, he returns to his ancestral village, books and memories in tow, to live out the rest of his days in a retired, orderly fashion. As fate will have it, however, a painful reminder of his decadent youth is there to greet him in the neighboring town, and the now more reflective Fadrique must come to terms with his past, and repair the damage done, before it is too late. Intertwined within this basic plot are the complicated interior voyages of the text's main characters, the Commander, Doña Blanca, Father Jacinto, and, to a somewhat lesser degree, Clara and Lucía, as they contend with the repercussions of decisions and actions, both past and present, in hopes of preserving a prosperous future.

The opening dedication to *Commander Mendoza* encapsulates many of Valera's aesthetic principals. It thus acts as an ironic introduction to the origins of his work. He begins by clarifying his position on eclectic interests and divergent productivity. The implied author who, as it turns out, is impossible to separate from the narrator, understatedly traces his unique literary trajectory: "First I was a lyric poet, then a journalist, then a critic, then I aspired to be a philosopher, then I had intentions and made attempts to be a composer of light opera or musical comedy, and lastly I tried to figure as a novelist in the lengthy catalogue of our authors." Rife with irony and multiple meaning, the opening sequence not only sets the stage for the novel's playful examination of Valera's ideas on art but also foregrounds the significance of the narrative act itself. At once theory and practice, *Commander Mendoza* can be read as a self-reflexive exploration of Valera's unique conceptualization of the nature and the aims of art.

In this brief, ironically rich dedication to "the most excellent Señora doña Ida de Bauer" that precedes the novel, Valera assumes the time-honored pose of the humble author seeking recognition from a discerning public. He first tells her that he never intended to become a popular

writer. Although he cannot discern why (in other words he doesn't see any problems), he has and will probably always have few readers. Even so, his love of writing is so strong that it overcomes both the public's indifference and his own disappointments. With ingenious precision, every instance of feigned humility introduced in the dedication is countered by an even stronger affirmation of the author's talent and genius. Reminiscent in structure, style, and tradition of Cervantes's ironic prologue to *El ingenioso hidalgo don Quijote de la Mancha* (1605), Valera's false modesty barely masks the author's exalted sense of self-worth. Fittingly, Valera's dedication provides the key to understanding the novel itself: the centrality of ironic discourse. As a result, the "fiction" begins before we turn the first page.[4]

The theme of self-reflexive fiction continues. Valera now explains to doña Ida the irregular circumstances under which he became a novelist. Indeed, he did not even know he wanted to be one – his first novel (*Pepita Jiménez*) "sprouted spontaneously" on its own. Others, he admits, he composed by design; "it is said," however, that he did a worse job of it. Evident from this phrasing, Valera does not agree with what "is said" about his second novel (*Las ilusiones del doctor Faustino*). So grave was his disenchantment, he reports, that he nearly gave up the entire enterprise. The Señora, however, stands out as one of his few true supporters. A woman of "rare discretion, refined taste, and profound and exquisite feeling," she alone applauded his modest efforts. This false modesty soon ends and the erroneous criticism of his detractors is now turned on its head. Because only beautiful people can perceive that which is truly beautiful, the Señora, he maintains, was one of the few privileged individuals to recognize the beauty of the novel. His critics lacked the necessary discernment, taste, and feeling and, therefore, were simply incapable of comprehending the novel's beauty.[5] In gratitude for her longstanding support, Valera dedicates his present novel, *Commander Mendoza*, to her. In the final paragraphs, the author imagines his character, the Commander, coming to pay his respects to the Señora and to place himself under her protection. Imitating one of Valera's former companions, the Commander "chooses" the Señora as his godmother. The dedication ends by requesting that the Señora not "disdain" her new godson, though he may not be as worthy as Pepita, and to always consider him as her "faithful, obedient servant."

Once again, the parallels to the *Quijote* are striking. The question of

literary authority or potency is one of the fundamental issues underlying Cervantes' Prologue to the first part of *Don Quijote*.[6] Cervantes makes use of the conventional metaphor depicting the text as the author's child but opts instead for the role of the step-father. Distancing himself somewhat ironically from his progeny, Cervantes is better able to critique his own work and to protect it from the uncertain reception of his critical audience. Valera, too, seeks protection for his progeny, affecting to allow his protagonist to choose his own guardian. In true Cervantine fashion, then, the Commander, a fictional character, elects doña Ida, a woman of flesh and blood, to be his godmother. Both Valera's dedication and Cervantes's prologue ironically invoke images of literary begetting to underscore the author's intimate relationship to the text. Both manifest a certain self-reflexivity in their discussions of narrative construction. Both blur the boundaries between fact and fiction by encouraging their characters to momentarily exit the novelistic world to interact with their projected audiences. According to the dedication, then, *Commander Mendoza* portends to be more than just a novel of regional customs and traditions; more than just a reflection on beauty, love, art, redemption, and sin. *Commander Mendoza* successfully illustrates Valera's conception of the inviolable link between theory and practice.

One fruitful approach to understanding Valera's work is to study the recurrent themes and motifs present in his novels.[7] With varying levels of success, all eight explore the inner workings of their characters' souls, and all are considered to be early manifestations of the twentieth-century psychological novel. *Commander Mendoza* is no exception. One of its predominant themes, love, can be explored through its diverse configurations such as the maternal, paternal, fraternal, spiritual, youthful, illicit, obsessive, and the May / December romance: a young woman courted by an older man. Such relationships produce unintended consequences, including amicable unions, discordant affairs, repentant lovers, guilty consciences, and illegitimate children. The problems created by this motif mark *Commander Mendoza*'s main plot line and determine the novel's thematic and structural unity. Accordingly, the reader is privy to the intimate world of its characters as they reexamine their principles, defend their actions, and work through possible solutions. External action plays a secondary role to the individual's internal drama. The principal action thus takes place within the characters' mind/soul. *Commander Mendoza* corresponds to Valera's view of art because it aims to present

faithfully the conflicted interior world of its protagonists. It is within the intimate regions of the soul, we remember, where an abundance of poetry resides. One function of the novel, then, is to set this poetry free.

Another narrative strategy initially proposed in the opening dedication and utilized throughout the novel is the deliberate intersection of fact and fiction. In Chapter One, for example, the narrator again enters his own text, converses with the fictional character Don Juan Fresco, and then defends his portrayal of him in a previous work of fiction – *The Illusions of Doctor Faustino*, which, of course, is a real novel written by a real author, Don Juan Valera. Juan Fresco not only "forgives" the narrator his indiscretion in this earlier novel but also goes on to praise him for writing novels based on "real" occurrences. This blurring of realities intensifies as the two begin to discuss the Commander and the different perceptions held of him by the citizens of Villabermeja. "The people say nothing clear and definitive," recounts Juan Fresco, "on the other hand they do tell a thousand confusing and apocryphal anecdotes." Thus it appears that multiple narrators holding multiple perspectives create multiple, and, at times, we are told, conflicting stories. Juan Fresco, however, says that he "knows" something about the Commander, and will now relay his own version to the narrator. The narrator, then, takes no credit for the creation of the story he is about to tell. Instead, he purports only to be the editor and scribe: "Gathering together now widespread and vague pieces of information, I'll set them down in summary form." Adding to the narrative confusion is the fact that several chapters later we learn that some of Juan Fresco's information concerning the Commander is itself second-hand. His version is based on the accounts of a Father Fernández, yet another fictional character whom most readers already met in Valera's second novel. Filtered through three different sets of fictional lenses, *Commander Mendoza* thus reminds us that all narrative perspectives are relative and every story has its multiple versions. There are no clear absolutes.

The self-reflexive examination of the narrator's role is a further integral component of the novelistic portrayal of narrative perspectives. Almost every chapter features at least one interruption on the part of the narrator. This intrusion disrupts narrative flow by interjecting the narrator's personal observations, interpretations, clarifications, and predictions. At times he assumes an omniscient position, underscoring his authority vis-à-vis the other characters: "It goes without saying that the commander did not hear what she said to him, but the novelist

knows everything and hears everything." Other times he acknowledges his limitations, admitting to his readers, "we do not know for sure" or "who knows what stirred in the commander's soul in these moments." Sometimes he simply uses his comments to propel the story forward: "... the subject of which will be made known to the curious reader at a later point." Similarly, the narrator exhibits an ambivalent relationship to his reader. At times he doubts the reader's ability and feels compelled to guide him/her directly, "... all of which merits a separate chapter, a chapter that will be one of the most important exchanges of this story." Other times he allows the reader to draw his/her own conclusions: "The chronicler of these events writes to recount, not to prove. He will not, therefore, decide whether Father Jacinto was right or wrong ... I leave that for the discreet reader to decide." Perhaps one of the most innovative narrative intrusions occurs when the narrator describes his and our own movement through the text as if we were physically following one of the characters, Father Jacinto, through the rooms of a house: "Thanks to the reverend's authority, and following him invisibly, all doors are open to us." Finally, the narrator comments on the structure of the narrative itself speaking directly to the reader, justifying the order of events, and defending his narrative prerogative: "The reader should not be surprised that we are going into these details. It was as well to cite them, but, distracted by the main story line, we had not gotten around to them." Again, the notion of narrative relativism is thoroughly underscored by the changing positions assumed by the narrator throughout the text.

As already evinced in *Pepita Jiménez* and *The Illusions of Doctor Faustino*, ambiguous narratives with multiple perspectives are very much a part of Valera's novelistic production.[8] *Commander Mendoza* further aims to vary its narrative focus by incorporating letters, multiple narrators, dialogue, a narrator who is sometimes omniscient and sometimes not, and intertextual references to other books, myths, poems, and songs directly into the text. In the absence of any absolute truths, everything becomes relative. Relativism not only affects the ways in which the story is told or how the characters view their respective conditions, but can also affect the ways in which the reader interprets the novel's themes themselves. Here again, ironic discourse plays an important role in delivering these messages. Without disclosing too much of the plot, the novel concludes by proposing alternative solutions to the conflicts that set the story in motion in the first place. Irony and a droll sense of humor help to

determine the final outcome of these conflicts, and to remind the reader once again of the shifting narrative perspectives of every situation. What is unacceptable in one situation is acceptable and perhaps preferable in others. It all depends on how one views the circumstances.

Intertextual references in *Commander Mendoza* also accentuate the fictionality of the text, calling attention to its artificial construction. Serving as the novel's two bookends are the idylls that both open and close the story. The idylls narrate opposing versions of a May-December romance – a familiar topic in Valera's fiction and in his own life. Of note are the differing perspectives offered by these poems – one positive, one negative – as well as their prominence in the overall structure of the novel itself. The second poem, "preserved in the archives of Villabermeja," is sent to the narrator from Juan Fresco, and serves as a palinode to the first. In addition, *Commander Mendoza* also incorporates biblical and mythical citations, lines from a Victor Hugo play, references to certain Spanish authors including Quevedo, Tirso, Calderón, María de Zayas, and the Duke of Rivas, and comparisons to the French writers and philosophers, Rousseau and Voltaire. Greek myths confer the truth behind certain well-kept secrets, and several letters are "transcribed" in full, including one from the Commander to Father Jacinto and two from Clara to her friend and confidante, Lucía, the Commander's niece. Juan Fresco was also the narrator in Valera's second novel, (and will resurface again in *Juanita la Larga*), and the Commander turns out to be the grandfather of its protagonist, Don Faustino. The novel's prominent intertextuality foregrounds the artificial construction of all narratives and highlights the significance of the narrative act itself.

It would be futile to discuss the synthesis of Valera's theories and practices without considering the ways in which *Commander Mendoza* exemplifies two of art's most important aims: delighting the reader and creating something of beauty. The two go hand in hand for, according to Valera, only something truly beautiful is powerful enough to entertain the soul. The novel's exploration of love – in all its many facets – readily incorporates this fusion of ideals. An important theme in all of Valera's works, the human reconciliation of the body and the spirit also takes thematic precedence in *Commander Mendoza*. Diverse examples of lovers in the text – some successful, others not – demonstrate the intrinsic need for measured equilibrium in any and all relationships. Despite some ironic diversion, the main thrust of this motif is that true love can only

flourish when the sensual is balanced against the spiritual. Commander Mendoza is a meditation on harmony in the form of human love. When balanced, this love is also one of the most exalted forms of expression for the soul's inner beauty. The synthesis of these two tendencies in the novel is a further example of Valera's syncretic blend of theory and practice. *Commander Mendoza*, then, entertains as it exalts the soul.

In *Commander Mendoza*, Valera has created some of his most evocative and memorable characters including the charming Commander, the beautiful but tragic Doña Blanca, and the endearing Father Jacinto. Several of the secondary characters, Lucía, Tío Gorico, and his daughter Nicolasa, also merit special attention: Tío Gorico for his detailed contribution of local manners and customs and the two women for occasionally transgressing their typecast roles. Optimistic by nature, the Commander's viewpoint is drawn mostly from eighteenth-century philosophers and somewhat mirrors Valera's own personality. A skeptic and a liberal, the Commander, nonetheless, respected others' religious beliefs. He admired Voltaire, was very much a sensualist, and believed in liberty, freedom, and the perfectibility of mankind. On the opposite end of the spectrum is Doña Blanca – the only character in the book, incidentally, whom Valera does not treat ironically. A tortured soul, she has lived under a self-imposed cloud of recrimination for close to two decades. Pious and exacting, she has allowed her guilt to transform itself into a fanatical mission that threatens to engulf those around her to atone for the sins of her past. In effect, some of the novel's most interesting chapters are those in which the fervent Doña Blanca verbally spars with the learned Father Jacinto or the arrogant Commander Mendoza. Finally, the intelligent and liberal-minded Father Jacinto plays an important role in facilitating not only plot development but also the psychological disclosures of the protagonists. We first encounter some of the Commander's inner thoughts, for example, in a letter addressed to Father Jacinto. Without reservation, the Commander openly reveals to him his world-weary disillusionment and then outlines his future domestic plans for retirement in Villabermeja. This is also the letter that provides an initial glimpse of Doña Blanca, filtered through the Commander's memory. Later we are privy to the doubts, the desires, and the obsessions that Doña Blanca and Clara reveal to Father Jacinto in his role as confessor and spiritual advisor. In all three cases, the end result is a complete portrait of the individual that includes both interior and exterior worlds.

The complex interlacing of multiple perspectives affects as well our reading of the metaphysical battle between Commander Mendoza and Doña Blanca that ultimately will determine Clara's fate. At first glance, religious intolerance and fanaticism appear to square off, with an enlightened Commander on one side and a fanatical Doña Blanca on the other. But in the emblematic absence of absolute truths so characteristic of Valera's novels, strict dividing lines begin to soften and blur, as do the seeming differences between the characters themselves. Instead, multiple and changing narrators afford the reader a more comprehensive understanding of both Fadrique and Doña Blanca, and, in turn, of their religious convictions. The enormous power – political, social, economic, and spiritual – wielded by the Catholic Church and the ensuing dialogue between religious tolerance and fanaticism is also the primary focus of Galdós's thesis novel, *Doña Perfecta*, written and published serially the same year as Valera's *Commander Mendoza*. Striking here are the different ways in which each novelist confronts the conservative, national milieu of the early years of the Restoration period. Tendentious, perhaps, but never didactic, *Commander Mendoza* underscores the notion that knowledge, truth, and morality exist in relation to culture, society, and historical context, and are, therefore, not absolute but rather relative. *Doña Perfecta*, on the other hand, juxtaposes the unyielding traditional authority of Doña Perfecta and the reactionary town of Orbajosa with the progressive liberalism of Pepe Rey and the city of Madrid. Valera's novel, then, is at once a beautiful, enjoyable work, and a nuanced reflection of the cultural problems and spiritual uncertainties plaguing society in late nineteenth-century Spain.

One cannot help but be struck by the modernity of the issues first presented in the opening dedication and then further developed in the text itself. Irony, literary authority, the role of the narrator, relativism, multi-perspectivism, reader response, and intertextuality are just some of the critical methods both examined and practiced in *Commander Mendoza*. The novel's ironic discourse, moreover, serves to distance the reader from the work by calling attention to the artifice of narrative construction. A self-reflexive treatise on the methods and the aims of art, *Commander Mendoza* imaginatively entertains at the same time that it exalts the soul. Valera desired to create something "worthy, complete, and beautiful" with his novels. In *Commander Mendoza* he reaches that goal and more.

SELECTED BIBLIOGRAPHY

First Editions of Valera's Novels

Pepita Jiménez. Madrid: Noguera, 1874.
Las ilusiones del doctor Faustino. Madrid: Noguera, 1875.
El Comendador Mendoza. Madrid: Ilustración Española y Americana, 1877.
El Comendador Mendoza. Madrid: Fernando Fé, 1881. (One of the two editions used for the translation.)
Pasarse de listo. Madrid: Perojo, 1878.
Doña Luz. Madrid: Perojo, 1879.
Juanita la Larga. Madrid: Fe, 1896.
Genio y figura. Madrid: Fe, 1897.
Morsamor. Madrid: Fe, 1899.

Modern Editions of Commander Mendoza

El Comendador Mendoza. Madrid: Biblioteca Nueva, 1925.
Obras completas, I. [novels]. 5th ed. Madrid: Aguilar, 1968.
Obras completas, II. Introductory note by Margarita Almela. Madrid: Biblioteca Castro, 2001. (One of the two editions used for the translation. Like the 1877 and 1881 editions, it follows the text of the periodical publication [*El Campo*] of 1886–87 cited in Valera's dedication. It became necessary to collate the two texts and compare because neither is free of typos and misattribution of dialogue.)

English Translations of Valera's Novels

Pepita Ximenez. Translated by Mary J. Serrano. New York: Appleton, 1886.
Pepita Jiménez. Translated by Harriet de Onís. Woodbury [N.Y.], Barron's Educational Series, 1964.
Doña Luz. Translated by Mary J. Serrano. New York: Appleton, 1891.
Doña Luz. Translated by Robert M. Fedorchek. Lewisburg: Bucknell University Press, 2002.
Don Braulio [*Pasarse de listo*]. Translated by Clara Bell. New York: Appleton, 1892.
Commander Mendoza. Translated by Mary J. Serrano. New York: Appleton, 1893.
Juanita la Larga. Translated by Robert M. Fedorchek. Washington: The Catholic University of America Press, 2006.

The Illusions of Doctor Faustino. Translated by Robert M. Fedorchek. Washington: The Catholic University of America Press, 2008

Secondary Sources

Alas, Leopoldo. *La Regenta*. Trans. John Rutherford. Athens: The University of Georgia Press, 1984.

Azorín. *De Valera a Miró*. Madrid: Afrodisio Aguado, 1959.

Araujo Costa, Luis. Introductory study to Volume I, 5th edition, of Juan Valera's *Obras completas*. Madrid: Aguilar, 1968.

Baquero Escudero, Ana. *"El perspectivismo cambiante en* El Comendador Mendoza *de Valera."* Alicante: Biblioteca Virtual Miguel de Cervantes, 2005.

Bermejo Marcos, Manuel. *Don Juan Valera, crítico literario*. Madrid: Editorial Gredos, 1968.

Bravo Villasante, Carmen. *Biografía de Don Juan Valera*. Barcelona: Editorial Aedos, 1959.

Camarero, Manuel. *Antología comentada de la literatura española, siglo XIX*. Madrid: Castalia, 1999.

Carnero, Guillermo. *Historia de la literatura española, siglo XIX*. Madrid: Espasa-Calpe, 1996.

DeCoster, Cyrus C., ed. *Correspondencia de Don Juan Valera, 1859–1905*. Madrid: Editorial Castalia, 1956.

DeCoster, Cyrus C. *Bibliografía crítica de Juan Valera*. Madrid: Consejo Superior de Investigaciones Científicas, 1970.

DeCoster, Cyrus C. Introductory study to the 1970 Castalia [Madrid] edition of *Las ilusiones del doctor Faustino*.

DeCoster, Cyrus C. *Juan Valera*. New York: Twayne Publishers, 1974. (The only book-length study in English of Valera's works [including not only the novels, but also his short stories, critical writings, and voluminous correspondence].)

Entrambasaguas, Joaquín de. "Juan Valera (1824–1905)," in *Las mejores novelas contemporáneas*, 1(1895–99). Barcelona: Planeta, 1957. Pages 514–24.

Eoff, Sherman. "The Spanish Novel of 'Ideas': Critical Opinion." *PMLA* 55 (1940): 531–558.

Franz, Thomas R. *Valera in Dialogue / In Dialogue with Valera*. New York: Peter Lang, 2000.

Jiménez, Alberto. *Juan Valera y la generación de 1868*. Oxford: Dolphin Book Co., 1956.

López-Morillas, Juan. *El krausismo español: perfil de una aventura intelectual*. México, D.F.: Fondo de Cultura Económica, 1956.

Marcus, Roxanne B. "Contemporary Life and Manners in the Novels of Juan Valera." *Hispania* 58 (1975): 454–66.

McKenna, Susan M. "Images of Paternity in the Quijote." *Hispanófila* 132 (2001): 43–52.

Montes Huidobro, Matías. "Sobre Valera. El estilo." *Revista de Occidente*, 2a época 35, No. 104 (1971): 168–91.

Montesinos, José F. *Valera o la ficción libre*. Madrid: Editorial Gredos, 1957. (2nd edition, revised, 1969.)

Olguín, Manuel. "Juan Valera's Theory of Art for Art's Sake." *Modern Language Forum* 35 (1950): 24–34.

Pardo Bazán, Emilia. *Retratos y apuntes literarios*. Madrid: Administración, n.d. "Don Juan Valera," pages 217–80.

Pérez de Ayala, Ramón. *Divagaciones literarias*. Madrid: Biblioteca Nueva, 1958. "Don Juan Valera o el arte de la distracción," pages 67–85; "Más sobre Valera," pages 87–111.

Pérez Galdós, Benito. *Fortunata and Jacinta: Two Stories of Married Women*. Trans. Agnes Moncy Gullón. Athens: The University of Georgia Press, 1986.

Romero Mendoza, Pedro. *Don Juan Valera. Estudio biográfico crítico*. Madrid: Ediciones Españolas, 1940.

Romero Tobar, Leonardo. "Recursos de la ficción en los relatos de Valera." *Congreso Internacional sobre Don Juan Valera* (1°, 1995. Cabra), Cabra: Ayuntamiento Córdoba, Diputación Provincial, 1997, pages 75–88.

Rubio Cremades, Enrique. *Biografía de Juan Valera*. Madrid: Castalia, 1992.

Saavedra, Ángel de, Duke of Rivas. *Don Álvaro, or the Force of Fate*. Trans. Robert M. Fedorchek. Washington, DC: The Catholic University of America Press, 2005.

Smith, Paul. "Juan Valera and the Illegitimacy Motif." *Hispania* 51 (1968): 803–811.

Taylor, Teresia Elizabeth Langford. *The Representation of Women in the Novels of Juan Valera: A Feminist Critique*. New York: Peter Lang, 1997.

Thurston-Griswold, Henry. *El idealismo sintético de don Juan Valera: teoría y práctica*. Potomac, Maryland: Scripta Humanistica, 1990.

Trimble, Robert G. *Chaos Burning on My Brow: Don Juan Valera in His Novels*. San Bernardino: The Borgo Press, 1995.

Valis, Noël. "The Use of Deceit in Valera's Juanita la Larga." *Hispanic Review* 49 (1981): 317–327.

Zaragüeta, Juan. "Don Juan Valera, filósofo." *Revista de Filosofía* 15 (1956): 489–518.

EL COMENDADOR MENDOZA

COMMANDER MENDOZA

A LA EXCELENTÍSIMA SEÑORA
DOÑA IDA DE BAUER

Nunca, estimada señora y bondadosa amiga, soñé con ser escritor popular. No me explico la causa, pero es lo cierto que tengo y tendré siempre pocos lectores. Mi afición a escribir es, sin embargo, tan fuerte, que puede más que la indiferencia del público y que mis desengaños.

Varias veces me di ya por vencido y hasta por muerto; mas apenas dejé de ser escritor, cuando reviví como tal bajo diversa forma. Primero fui poeta lírico, luego periodista, luego crítico, luego aspiré a filósofo, luego tuve mis intenciones y conatos de dramaturgo zarzuelero, y al cabo traté de figurar como novelista en el largo catálogo de nuestros autores.

Bajo esta última forma es como la gente me ha recibido menos mal; pero, aun así, no las tengo todas conmigo.

Mi musa es tan voluntariosa que hace lo que quiere y no lo que yo le mando. De aquí proviene que, si por dicha logro aplausos, es por falta de previsión.

Escribí mi primera novela sin caer hasta el fin en que era novela lo que escribía.

Acababa yo de leer multitud de libros devotos.

Lo poético de aquellos libros me tenía hechizado, pero no cautivo. Mi fantasía se exaltó con tales lecturas, pero mi frío corazón siguió en libertad y mi seco espíritu se atuvo a la razón severa.

Quise entonces recoger como en un ramillete todo lo más precioso o lo que más precioso me parecía de aquellas flores místicas y ascéticas, e inventé un personaje que las recogiera con fe y entusiasmo, juzgándome yo, por mí mismo, incapaz de tal cosa. Así brotó espontánea una novela, cuando yo distaba tanto de querer ser novelista.

Después me he puesto adrede a componer otras, y dicen que lo he hecho peor.

Esto me ha desanimado de tal suerte, que he estado a punto de no volver a escribirlas.

Entre las pocas personas que me han dado nuevo aliento, descuella usted, ora por la indulgencia con que celebra mis obrillas, ora por el valor

TO THE MOST EXCELLENT SEÑORA
DOÑA IDA DE BAUER

Never, esteemed lady and kind friend, did I dream about being a popular writer. I do not understand the reason, but the fact is that I have, and always will have, few readers. My love of writing, nonetheless, is so strong that it overrides the public's indifference and my disappointments.

Several times I acknowledged defeat and thought myself finished, but no sooner did I stop being a writer than I resurfaced as such in a different guise. First I was a lyric poet, then a journalist, then a critic, then I aspired to be a philosopher, then I had intentions and made attempts to be a composer of light opera or musical comedy, and lastly I tried to figure as a novelist in the lengthy catalogue of our authors.

It is in this latter category that I have been the least ill received, but even so, I am uneasy.

My muse is so willful that it does as it pleases and not what I order it to do. Which explains that, if by chance I garner applause, it is for want of foresight.

I wrote my first novel without realizing until the conclusion that what I was writing was a novel.

I had just finished reading a host of devotional books.

The poetic strain of those books enchanted me, but did not hold me captive. My imagination got carried away by such readings, but my hard heart retained its freedom and my indifferent spirit adhered to strict reason.

I then wanted to gather together, as in a bouquet, all of the most precious aspects, or what seemed to me the most precious aspects, of those ascetic and mystical flowers, and I invented a character who could gather them with faith and enthusiasm, considering myself, left to my own devices, incapable of such a thing. Thus did a novel sprout spontaneously, when I was such a long way from wanting to be a novelist.

Afterwards I set to composing others by design, and it is said that I did a worse job of it. This discouraged me to such an extent that I very nearly gave up writing novels again.

You stand out among the few people who have encouraged me to take heart, now because of the indulgence with which you applaud my

que los elogios de usted, si prescindimos por un instante de la bondad que los inspira, deben tener para cuantos conocen su rara discreción, su delicado gusto y el hondo y exquisito sentir con que percibe todo lo bello.

Aunque yo no hubiese seguido de antemano la sentencia de aquel sabio alejandrino que afirmaba que sólo las personas hermosas entendían de hermosura, usted me hubiera movido a seguirla, mostrándose luminoso y vivo ejemplo y gentil prueba de su verdad.

No extrañe usted, pues, que, lleno de agradecimiento, le dedique este libro.

Por ir dedicado a usted, quisiera yo que fuese mejor que *Pepita Jiménez,* a quien usted tanto celebra: pero harto sabido es que las obras literarias, y muy en particular las de carácter poético, sólo se dan bien en momentos dichosos de inspiración, que los autores no renuevan a su antojo.

En esto, como en otras mil cosas, la poesía se parece a la magia. Requiere la intervención del cielo.

Cuentan de Alberto Magno que, yendo en peregrinación de Roma a Alemania, pasó una noche a las orillas del Po, en la cabaña de un pescador. Agasajado allí muy bien, quiso el doctor probar su gratitud al huésped, y le hizo y le dio un pez de madera, tan maravilloso, que, puesto en la red, atraía a todos los peces vivos. No hay que ponderar la ventura del pescador con su pez mágico. Cierto día, con todo, tuvo un descuido, y el pez se le perdió. Entonces se puso en camino, fue a Alemania, buscó a Alberto, y le rogó que hiciera otro pez semejante al primero. Alberto respondió que lo deseaba (también deseo yo hacer otra *Pepita Jiménez),* mas que, para hacer otro pez que tuviese todas las virtudes del antiguo, era menester esperar a que el cielo presentase idéntico aspecto y disposición en constelaciones, signos y planetas, que en la noche en que el primer pez se hizo; lo cual no podía acontecer sino dentro de treinta y seis mil y pico de años.

Como yo no puedo esperar tanto tiempo, me resigno a dedicar a usted *El Comendador Mendoza.*

Este simpático personaje, antes de salir en público, no ya escondido y a trozos, sino por completo y por sí solo, pasa, con la venia de Lucía, a besar humildemente los lindos pies de usted y a ponerse bajo su amparo.

modest efforts, now – if we dispense for a moment with the kindness that inspires it – because of the weight that your praise should carry with all those who know your rare discretion, your refined taste, and the profound and exquisite feeling with which you judge all things beautiful.

Although I might not have accepted beforehand the maxim of that Alexandrian wise man who affirmed that only beautiful people understood beauty, you would have moved me to accept it, showing yourself to be a luminous, vibrant example and genteel proof of the truth of it.

Do not be surprised, then, that, as I am extremely grateful, I dedicate this book to you.

Because it is dedicated to you, I would like for it to be better than *Pepita Jiménez*, which you praise so highly, but it is well known that literary works, and very much in particular those of a poetic nature, are only conceived in felicitous moments of inspiration that authors cannot duplicate on impulse.

In this, as in a thousand other things, poetry has an affinity with magic. It requires the intervention of heaven.

The story is told about Albertus Magnus that, while going on a pilgrimage from Germany to Rome, he spent one night on the banks of the Po River, in a fisherman's cabin. As he was treated so hospitably there, the doctor wished to show his gratitude to his host, and he made for him and gave him a wooden fish, so marvelous that, placed inside the net, it attracted all the live fishes. You can imagine the fisherman's good fortune with his magic fish. One day, though, he was careless and the fish got lost. So he set off, went to Germany, found Albertus, and begged him to make another fish similar to the first one. Albertus responded that he wished he could (I also wish I could write another *Pepita Jiménez*), but that, in order to make another fish that had all the virtues of the original one, it was necessary for the heavens to present an identical appearance and arrangement of constellations, signs, and planets as on the night when the first fish was made, which would not occur for upwards of thirty-six thousand years.

Since I cannot wait such a long time, I resign myself to dedicating *Commander Mendoza* to you.

Before appearing in public, no longer hidden and in snippets,[9] but complete and by himself, this genial personage comes humbly now, with Lucía's consent, to pay his respects to you and to place himself under your protection. Imitating a former companion of mine, he chooses you

Remedando a un antiguo compañero mío, elige a usted por su madrina. No desdeñe usted al nuevo ahijado que le presento, aunque no valga lo que *Pepita,* y créame su afectísimo y respetuoso servidor.

1

A pesar de los quehaceres y cuidados que me retienen en Madrid casi de continuo, todavía suelo ir de vez en cuando a Villabermeja y a otros lugares de Andalucía, a pasar cortas temporadas de uno o dos meses.

La última vez que estuve en Villabermeja ya había salido a luz *Las ilusiones del doctor Faustino.*

Don Juan Fresco me mostró en un principio algún enojo de que yo hubiese sacado a relucir su vida y las de varios parientes suyos en un libro de entretenimiento; pero al cabo, conociendo que yo no lo había hecho a mal hacer, me perdonó la falta de sigilo. Es más: don Juan aplaudió la idea de escribir novelas fundadas en hechos reales, y me animó a que siguiese cultivando el género. Esto nos movió a hablar del comendador Mendoza.

–¿El vulgo– dije yo –, cree aún que el comendador anda penando, durante la noche, por los desvanes de la casa solariega de los Mendozas con su manto blanco del hábito de Santiago?

–Amigo mío– contestó don Juan –, el vulgo lee ya *El Citador* y otros libros y periódicos librepensadores. En la incredulidad, además, está como impregnado el aire que se respira. No faltan jornaleros escépticos; pero las mujeres, por lo común, siguen creyendo a pie juntillas. Los mismos jornaleros escépticos niegan de día, y rodeados de gente, y de noche y a solas, tienen más miedo que antes de lo sobrenatural, por lo mismo que lo han negado durante el día. Resulta, pues, que, a pesar de que vivimos ya en la edad de la razón y se supone que la de la fe ha pasado, no hay mujer bermejina que se aventure a subir a los desvanes de la casa de los Mendozas sin bajar gritando y afirmando a veces que ha visto al comendador, y apenas hay hombre que suba solo a dichos desvanes sin hacer un grande esfuerzo de voluntad para vencer o disimular el miedo. El comendador, por lo visto, no ha cumplido aún su tiempo de purgatorio, y eso que murió al empezar este siglo. Algunos

as his godmother. Do not disdain the new godson that I present to you, even though he may not be worth as much as *Pepita*, and always consider me your faithful, obedient servant.

1

Despite all the affairs and concerns that almost continually keep me in Madrid, I still journey now and then to Villabermeja and to other towns in Andalusia to spend brief periods of one or two months.

The last time that I was in Villabermeja *The Illusions of Doctor Faustino* had been published.[10]

At first Don Juan Fresco expressed some annoyance with me that I had depicted his life and that of several relatives of his in a book of entertainment, but, in the end, recognizing that I had not purposely done a bad thing, he forgave my lack of discretion. Furthermore, Don Juan applauded the idea of writing novels based on real occurrences and encouraged me to continue cultivating the genre. This prompted us to talk about Commander Mendoza.

"Do the townspeople," I asked, "still believe that the commander wanders, a soul in torment, through the attic of the Mendozas' ancestral home, in the white cloak of the habit of the Order of Saint James?"[11]

"My friend," answered Don Juan, "the people now read *El Citador*[12] and other books and freethinking newspapers. Besides, it's as though the air that we breathe were impregnated with unbelief. There's no lack of skeptical day laborers, but women for the most part still believe steadfastly. Those same skeptical day laborers deny faith during the day, while surrounded by people, but at night, when they're alone, they're more afraid of the supernatural than before, for the very reason that they denied being afraid during the day. It follows, then, that despite the fact that we now live in the age of reason and the assumption is that the age of faith has passed, there is no Villabermejan woman who ventures to go up to the attic of the Mendozas' house without coming down in a state, screaming and sometimes insisting that she has seen the commander, and there's scarcely any man who will go up alone to said attic without exercising great willpower in order to overcome or mask his fear. Apparently the commander has yet to complete his time in purgatory, in spite of the fact that he died at the beginning of this century. Some people

entienden que no está en el purgatorio, sino en el infierno; pero no parece natural que, si está en el infierno, se le deje salir de allí para que venga a mortificar a sus paisanos. Lo más razonable y verosímil es que esté en el purgatorio, y esto cree la generalidad de las gentes.

–Lo que se infiere de todo, ora esté el comendador en el infierno, ora en el purgatorio, es que sus pecados debieron de ser enormes.

–Pues mire usted– replicó don Juan Fresco –, nada cuenta el vulgo de terminante y claro con relación al comendador. Cuenta, sí, mil confusas patrañas. En Villabermeja se conoce que hirió más la imaginación popular por su modo de ser y de pensar, que por sus hechos. Sus hechos conocidos, salvo algún extravío de la mocedad, más le califican de buena que de mala persona.

–De todos modos, usted cree que el comendador era una persona notable.

–Y mucho que lo creo. Yo contaré a usted lo que sé de él, y usted juzgará.

Don Juan Fresco me contó entonces lo que sabía acerca del comendador Mendoza. Yo no hago más que ponerlo por escrito.

2

Don Fadrique López de Mendoza, llamado comúnmente el comendador, fue hermano de don José, el mayorazgo, abuelo de nuestro don Faustino, a quien supongo que conocen mis lectores.

Nació don Fadrique en 1744.

Desde niño dicen que manifestó una inclinación perversa a reírse de todo y a no tomar nada por lo serio. Esta cualidad es la que menos fácilmente se perdona, cuando se entrevé que no proviene de ligereza, sino de tener un hombre el espíritu tan serio, que apenas halla cosa terrena y humana que merezca que él la considere con seriedad; por donde, en fuerza de la seriedad misma, nacen el desdén y la risa burlona.

Don Fadrique, según la general tradición, era un hombre de este género: un hombre jocoso de puro serio.

think that he's not in purgatory, but in hell. It doesn't seem natural, though, that if he's in hell he would be allowed to leave there so that he could come to plague his fellow countrymen. The most reasonable and likely thing is that he's in purgatory, and this is what the majority of people believe."

"What can be deduced from all this, whether the commander be in hell, whether he be in purgatory, is that his sins must have been monstrous."

"As for that," replied Don Juan Fresco, "the people say nothing clear and definitive regarding the commander. On the other hand, they do tell a thousand confusing and apocryphal anecdotes. It's apparent that he captured popular imagination more for his way of living and thinking than for his deeds. And his known deeds, except for a few instances of youthful misconduct, prove him to be more of a good than a bad person."

"In any event, do you believe that the commander was a remarkable person?"

"Yes, I do, very much so. I'll relate to you what I know of him, and you'll be the judge."

Don Juan Fresco then recounted to me what he knew about Commander Mendoza. I am only setting it down in writing.

2

Don Fadrique López de Mendoza, commonly called the Commander, was the brother of Don José, the *mayorazgo* or heir by primogeniture, and grandfather of our Don Faustino, whom I expect is known to my readers.

Don Fadrique was born in 1744.

People say that from the time he was a child he displayed a perverse inclination to laugh at everything and to not take anything seriously. This trait is the one that is least easily forgiven when we suspect that it does not stem from frivolity, but from the fact that a man has such a serious nature that he scarcely encounters any human, earthly thing worthy of his serious consideration, so that as a result, scorn and mockery are born of that very same seriousness.

Don Fadrique, according to general belief, was a man of this sort: jocular out of sheer seriousness.

Claro está que hay dos clases de hombres jocosos de puro serios. A una clase, que es muy numerosa, pertenecen los que andan siempre tan serios que hacen reír a los demás, y sin quererlo son jocosos. A otra clase, que siempre cuenta pocos individuos, es a la que pertenecía don Fadrique. Don Fadrique se burlaba de la seriedad vulgar e inmotivada, en virtud de una seriedad exquisita y superlativa; por lo cual era jocoso.

Conviene advertir, no obstante, que la jocosidad de don Fadrique rara vez tocaba en la insolencia o en la crueldad, ni se ensañaba en daño del prójimo. Sus burlas eran benévolas y urbanas, y tenían a menudo cierto barniz de dulce melancolía.

El rasgo predominante en el carácter de don Fadrique no se puede negar que implicaba una mala condición; la falta de respeto. Como veía lo ridículo y lo cómico en todo, resultaba que nada o casi nada respetaba, sin poderlo remediar. Sus maestros y superiores se lamentaron mucho de esto.

Don Fadrique era ágil y fuerte, y nada ni nadie le inspiró jamás temor más que su padre, a quien quiso entrañablemente. No por eso dejaba de conocer y aun de decir en confianza, cuando recordaba a su padre, después de muerto, que, si bien había sido un cumplido caballero, honrado, pundonoroso, buen marido y lleno de caridad para con los pobres, había sido taínbién un *vándalo*.

En comparación con este aserto contaba don Fadrique varias anécdotas, entre las cuales ninguna le gustaba tanto como la del bolero.

Don Fadrique bailaba muy bien este baile cuando era niño, y don Diego, que así se llamaba su padre, se complacía en que su hijo luciese su habilidad, cuando le llevaba de visitas o las recibía con él en su casa.

Un día llevó don Diego a su hijo don Fadrique a la pequeña ciudad, que dista dos leguas de Villabermeja, cuyo nombre no he querido nunca decir, y donde he puesto la escena de mi *Pepita Jiménez*. Para la mejor inteligencia de todo, y a fin de evitar perífrasis, pido al lector que siempre que en adelante hable yo de la ciudad entienda que hablo de la pequeña ciudad ya mencionada.

Don Diego, como queda dicho, llevó a don Fadrique a la ciudad. Tenía don Fadrique trece años, pero estaba muy espigado. Como iba de visitas de ceremonia, lucía casaca y chupa de damasco encarnado con botones de acero bruñido, zapatos de hebilla y medias de seda blanca, de suerte que parecía un sol.

It is clear that there are two kinds of men who are jocular out of sheer seriousness. One kind, which is very numerous, is made up of those who always go around so serious that they make others laugh, and are jocular unintentionally. The other kind, which always numbers very few individuals, is the one that included Don Fadrique; Don Fadrique mocked baseless, ordinary seriousness, by virtue of his own superlative, exquisite seriousness, for which reason he was jocular.

We should note, nevertheless, that Don Fadrique's jocularity rarely reached the point of insolence or cruelty, nor did he delight in tormenting his fellow man. His gibes were innocuous and civil, and often laced with a certain gloss of gentle melancholy.

There can be no denying that the predominant feature of Don Fadrique's character pointed to a bad trait: the lack of respect. Since he saw the ridiculous and comical sides of everything, it followed that he respected nothing or almost nothing, without being able to help it. His teachers and superiors greatly deplored this shortcoming.

Don Fadrique was agile and strong, and no one thing or person ever inspired fear in him, except his father, whom he loved dearly. But not for that reason did he fail to acknowledge and even say in confidence, when reminiscing about his father after he had died, that although he had been a perfect gentleman, honorable and punctilious, a good husband and very charitable with the poor, he had also been a vandal.

As proof of this assertion, Don Fadrique told several anecdotes, his favorite of them all being the one about the bolero.

Don Fadrique did this dance very well when he was a child, and his father, Don Diego, delighted in having his son show off his ability whenever he took him on visits or received them in their home.

One day Don Diego took his son Don Fadrique to the town that is six miles away from Villabermeja, the name of which I have not wanted to disclose, and where I set the action of my *Pepita Jiménez*. For a clearer understanding of everything, and in order to avoid redundancy, whenever in future I speak of the "town" I ask the reader to understand that I speak of the town in question.

As has been said, Don Diego took Don Fadrique to the town. The boy was thirteen years old, but very tall and lanky. Since he would be paying formal visits, he sported a frock coat and a blood-red damask vest with polished steel buttons, buckle shoes and white silk stockings, which made him the very picture of a handsome child.

La ropa de viaje de don Fadrique, que estaba muy traída y con algunas manchas y desgarrones, se quedó en la posada, donde dejaron los caballos. Don Diego quiso que su hijo le acompañase en todo su esplendor. El muchacho iba contentísimo de verse tan guapo, y con traje tan señoril y lujoso. Pero la misma idea de la elegancia aristocrática del traje le infundió un sentimiento algo exagerado del decoro y compostura que debía tener quien le llevaba puesto.

Por desgracia, en la primera visita que hizo don Diego a una hidalga viuda, que tenía dos hijas doncellas, se habló del niño Fadrique y de lo crecido que estaba, y del talento que tenía para bailar el bolero.

–Ahora– dijo don Diego –, baila el chico peor que el año pasado, porque está en la *edad del pavo:* edad insufrible, entre la palmeta y el barbero. Ya ustedes sabrán que en esa edad se ponen los chicos muy empalagosos, porque empiezan a presumir de hombres y no lo son. Sin embargo, ya que ustedes se empeñan, el chico lucirá su habilidad.

Las señoras, que habían mostrado deseos de ver a don Fadrique bailar, repitieron sus instancias, y una de las doncellas tomó una guitarra y se puso a tocar para que don Fadrique bailase.

–Baila, Fadrique– dijo don Diego, no bien empezó la música.

Repugnancia invencible al baile, en aquella ocasión, se apoderó de su alma. Veía una contrariedad monstruosa, algo de lo que llaman ahora una *antinomia,* entre el bolero y la casaca. Es de advertir que en aquel día don Fadrique llevaba casaca por primera vez: estrenaba la prenda, si puede calificarse de estreno el aprovechamiento del arreglo o refundición de un vestido, usado primero por el padre y después por el mayorazgo, a quien se le había quedado estrecho y corto.

–Baila, Fadrique– repitió don Diego bastante amostazado. Don Diego, cuyo traje de campo y camino, al uso de la tierra, estaba en muy buen estado, no se había puesto casaca como su hijo. Don Diego iba todo de estezado, con botas y espuelas, y en la mano llevaba el látigo con que castigaba al caballo y a los podencos de una jauría numerosa que tenía para cazar.

–Baila, Fadrique– exclamó don Diego por tercera vez, notándose ya en su voz cierta alteración causada por la cólera y la sorpresa.

Era tan elevado el concepto que tenía don Diego de la autoridad paterna, que se maravillaba de aquella rebeldía.

Don Fadrique's travel clothes, threadbare and with a few stains and big tears, stayed at the inn where they left the horses. Don Diego wanted his son to accompany him in all his sartorial splendor. The boy was tickled pink at seeing himself look so smart in such a luxurious, lordly outfit. But the very idea of the aristocratic elegance of that attire instilled in him a somewhat exaggerated feeling as regards the decorum and composure that ought to be observed by the person wearing it.

Unfortunately, during the first visit that Don Diego made to a widowed noblewoman who had two maiden daughters, there was talk of the boy Fadrique and how much he had grown and the ability that he had to dance the bolero.

"Now," said Don Diego, "the lad dances worse than last year, because he's going through the awkward stage of adolescence – the insufferable stage, neither child nor man. You know, of course, that boys his age become very trying because they start assuming that they're grown up and they're not. Nevertheless, since you insist, the lad will demonstrate his ability."

The ladies, who had expressed a desire to see Don Fadrique dance, repeated their request, and one of the daughters took up a guitar and proceeded to play so that Don Fadrique would dance.

"Dance, Fadrique," said Don Diego as soon as the music began.

An insuperable repugnance toward the dance on that occasion seized his soul. He saw a monstrous disparity, somewhat like what nowadays is called antimony, between the bolero and the frock coat. It should be noted that Don Fadrique was wearing the frock coat for the first time that day, if we can call a "premiere showing" the use of that altered or modified garment, worn first by his father and afterwards by the *mayorazgo*, for whom it had gotten too tight and too short.

"Dance, Fadrique," repeated Don Diego, rather peeved.

Don Diego, whose country and travel clothes, in keeping with the dress of those parts, were in very good condition, had not donned a frock coat like his son. Don Diego wore an outfit of deerskin, had on boots and spurs, and carried in his hand the whip with which he drove his horse and the hounds of a numerous pack that he kept for hunting.

"Dance, Fadrique," ordered Don Diego for the third time, a certain change evident in his voice now, a change brought about by anger and surprise.

Don Diego's concept of paternal authority was so lofty that Fadrique's defiance astonished him.

–Déjele usted, señor Mendoza– dijo la hidalga viuda –. El niño está cansado del camino y no quiere bailar.

–Ha de bailar ahora.

–Déjele usted; otra vez le veremos– dijo la que tocaba la guitarra.

–Ha de bailar ahora– repitió don Diego –. Baila, Fadrique.

–Yo no bailo con casaca– respondió éste al cabo.

Aquí fue Troya. Don Diego prescindió de las señoras y de todo.

–¡Rebelde! ¡Mal hijo– gritó –: te enviaré a los Toribios: baila o te desuello; y empezó a latigazos con don Fadrique.

La señorita de la guitarra paró por un instante la música; pero don Diego la miró de modo tan terrible, que ella tuvo miedo de que la hiciese tocar como quería hacer bailar a su hijo, y siguió tocando el bolero.

Don Fadrique, después de recibir ocho o diez latigazos, bailó lo mejor que supo.

Al pronto se le saltaron las lágrimas; pero después, considerando que había sido su padre quien le había pegado, y ofreciéndose a su fantasía de un modo cómico toda la escena, y viéndose él mismo bailar a latigazos y con casaca, se rió, a pesar del dolor físico, y bailó con inspiración y entusiasmo.

Las señoras aplaudieron a rabiar.

–Bien, bien– dijo don Diego –¡Por vida del diablo! ¿Te he hecho mal, hijo mío?

–No, padre– dijo don Fadrique –. Está visto: yo necesitaba hoy de doble acompañamiento para bailar.

–Hombre, disimula. ¿Por qué eres tonto? ¿Qué repugnancia podías tener, si la casaca te va que ni pintada, y el bolero clásico y de buena escuela es un baile muy señor? Estas damas me perdonarán. ¿No es verdad? Yo soy algo vivo de genio.

Así terminó el lance del bolero.

Aquel día bailó otras cuatro veces don Fadrique en otras tantas visitas, a la más leve insinuación de su padre.

Decía el cura Fernández, que conoció y trató a don Fadrique, y de quien sabía muchas de estas cosas mi amigo don Juan Fresco, que don Fadrique refería con amor la anécdota del bolero, y que lloraba de ternura

"Let him be, Señor Mendoza," said the widowed noblewoman. "The boy's tired from traveling and doesn't want to dance."

"He will dance now."

"Let him be. We'll see him another time," said the daughter playing the guitar.

"He will dance now," repeated Don Diego. "Dance, Fadrique."

"I won't dance with a frock coat on," the boy finally responded.

Despite the presence of the ladies and the circumstances, Don Diego flew into a rage.

"You stubborn boy! You disobedient son!" he yelled. "I'll send you to the Toribios reformatory. Dance or I'll skin you alive."

And he started to whip Don Fadrique.

The girl with the guitar stopped playing for a moment, but Don Diego gave her such a terrible look that she feared he would make her play the way he wanted to make his son dance, and she resumed playing the bolero.

After receiving eight or ten lashes, Don Fadrique danced as well as he knew how.

At first tears spilled from his eyes, but then, considering that it was his father who had whipped him, appreciating that the entire scene had presented itself to his fancy in a comical manner, and seeing himself dance to lashes and with a frock coat on, he laughed, despite the physical pain, and he danced with inspiration and enthusiasm.

The ladies applauded effusively.

"Good, good," said Don Diego. "What the deuce! Did I hurt you, my son?"

"No, Father," said Don Fadrique. "It's pretty clear: I needed double accompaniment to dance today."

"Forgive me. But why are you so foolish? What reluctance could you have if the frock coat suits you to a T, and the classic, well-executed bolero is a very fine dance? These ladies will excuse me. Isn't that right? I'm somewhat hot-tempered."

Thus did the bolero incident end.

That day Don Fadrique danced another four times in as many visits at his father's merest indication.

Father Fernández, from whom my friend Don Juan Fresco learned many of these things, knew and had dealings with Don Fadrique, and he used to say that Don Fadrique would tell the bolero story lovingly, and

filial y reía al mismo tiempo, diciendo «mi padre era un vándalo», cuando se acordaba de él dándole latigazos, y retraía a su memoria a las damas aterradas, sin dejar una de ellas de tocar la guitarra, y a él mismo bailando el bolero mejor que nunca.

Parece que había en todo esto algo de orgullo de familia. El *mi padre era un vándalo* de don Fadrique casi sonaba en su labios como alabanza. Don Fadrique, educado en el lugar y del mismo modo que su padre, don Fadrique cerril, hubiera sido más vándalo aún.

La fama de sus travesuras de niño duró en el lugar muchos años después de haberse él partido a servir al rey.

Huérfano de madre a los tres años de edad, había sido criado y mimado por una tía solterona, que vivía en la casa, y a quien llamaban la chacha Victoria.

Tenía además otra tía, que si bien no vivía con la familia, sino en casa aparte, había también permanecido soltera y competía en mimos y en halagos con la chacha Victoria. Llamábase esta otra tía la chacha Ramoncica. Don Fadrique era el ojito derecho de ambas señoras, cada una de las cuales estaba ya en los cuarenta y pico de años, cuando tenía doce nuestro héroe.

Las dos tías o chachas se parecían en algo y se diferenciaban en mucho.

Se parecían en cierto entono amable y benévolo de hidalgas, en la piedad católica y en la profunda ignorancia. Esto último no provenía sólo de que hubiesen sido educadas en el lugar, sino de una idea de entonces. Yo me figuro que nuestros abuelos, hartos de la bachillería femenil, de las cultas latiniparlas y de la desenvoltura pedantesca de las damas que retratan Quevedo, Tirso y Calderón en sus obras, habían caído en el extremo contrario de empeñarse en que las mujeres no aprendiesen nada. La ciencia en la mujer hubo de considerarse como un manantial de perversión. Así es que en los lugares, en las familias acomodadas y nobles, cuando eran religiosas y morigeradas, se educaban las niñas para que fuesen muy hacendosas, muy arregladas y muy señoras de su casa. Aprendían a coser, a bordar y a hacer calceta; muchas sabían de cocina; no pocas planchaban perfectamente; pero casi siempre se procuraba que no aprendiesen a escribir, y apenas si se les enseñaba a leer de corrido en *El año cristiano* o en algún otro libro devoto.

Las chachas Victoria y Ramoncica se habían educado así. La diversa condición y carácter de cada una estableció después notables diferencias.

weep with filial tenderness and laugh at the same time, saying "My father was a vandal" when he remembered the lashes and recalled the terrified ladies, one of them playing the guitar without stopping, and pictured himself dancing the bolero better than ever.

It seems that in all of this there was a bit of family pride. Don Fadrique's "My father was a vandal" almost sounded like praise on his lips. Don Fadrique, educated in the town and in the same way as his father … Don Fadrique, uncouth, would have been even more of a vandal.

The fame of his childish pranks lasted in the town for many years after he had departed to serve the king.

Motherless at the age of three, Don Fadrique had been raised and spoiled by a spinster aunt who lived in the house and who was called Chacha Victoria.[13]

He had besides another aunt who, although she did not live with the family, but in a separate house, had also stayed a spinster and competed with Chacha Victoria in spoiling and indulging him. This other aunt was called Chacha Ramoncica. Don Fadrique was the apple of the eye of both ladies, each one of which was in her forties when our hero was twelve.

The two aunts or *chachas* were alike in some things and unalike in many others.

They were alike in a certain benevolent and kind hauteur as noblewomen, in Catholic piety, and in profound ignorance. This latter trait did not stem solely from having been educated in the town, but from a prevalent notion back then. I imagine that our grandparents, fed up with female prattle, with language larded with Latinisms, and with the pedantic freedom of the ladies that Quevedo, Tirso, and Calderón[14] depicted in their works, had gone to the opposite extreme of determining that women would learn nothing. Knowledge in a woman came to be seen as a source of perversion. Thus it was that in small towns, girls from well-to-do families, when they were religious and observed good customs, were raised to be very industrious, very proper, and very much the lady of the house. They learned to sew, to embroider, and to knit; many knew their way around a kitchen; not a few ironed perfectly; but it was almost always the case that they did not learn to write, and when it came to reading, they were scarcely taught enough to read fluently *The Christian Year* or some other devout book.

Both Chacha Victoria and Chacha Ramoncica had been raised in this manner. The diverse nature and character of each one gave rise afterwards to pronounced differences.

La chacha Victoria, alta, rubia, delgada y bien parecida, había sido y continuó siendo hasta la muerte, naturalmente sentimental y curiosa. A fuerza de deletrear, llegó a leer casi de corrido cuando estaba ya muy granada; y sus lecturas no fueron sólo de vidas de santos, sino que conoció también algunas historias profanas y las obras de varios poetas. Sus autores favoritos fueron doña María de Zayas y Gerardo Lobo.

Se preciaba de experimentada y desengañada. Su conversación estaba siempre como salpicada de estas dos exclamaciones, –¡Qué mundo éste! ¡Lo que ve el que vive!– La chacha Victoria se sentía como hastiada y fatigada de haber visto tanto, y eso que sus viajes no se habían extendido más allá de cinco o seis leguas de distancia de Villabermeja.

Una pasión, que hoy calificaríamos de romántica, había llenado toda la vida de la chacha Victoria. Cuando apenas tenía diez y ocho años, conoció y amó en una feria a un caballero cadete de infantería. El cadete amó también a la chacha, que no lo era entonces; pero los dos amantes, tan hidalgos como pobres, no se podían casar por falta de dinero. Formaron, pues, el firme propósito de seguir amándose, se juraron constancia eterna y decidieron aguardar para la boda a que llegase a capitán el cadete. Por desgracia, entonces se caminaba con pies de plomo en las carreras, no había guerras civiles ni pronunciamientos, y el cadete, firme como una roca y fiel como un perro, envejeció sin pasar de teniente nunca.

Siempre que el servicio militar lo consentía, el cadete venía a Villabermeja; hablaba por la ventana con la chacha Victoria, y se decían ambos mil ternuras. En las largas ausencias se escribían cartas amorosas, cada ocho o diez días; asiduidad y frecuencia extraordinarias entonces.

Esta necesidad de escribir obligó a la chacha Victoria a hacerse letrada. El amor fue su maestro de escuela, y la enseñó a trazar unos garrapatos anárquicos y misteriosos, que por revelación de amor leía, entendía y descifraba el cadete.

De esta suerte, entre temporadas de pelar la pava en Villabermeja, y otras más largas temporadas de estar ausentes, comunicándose por cartas, se pasaron cerca de doce años. El cadete llegó a teniente.

Hubo entonces un momento terrible: una despedida desgarradora. El cadete, teniente ya, se fue a la guerra de Italia. Desde allí venían

Chacha Victoria, tall, fair-haired, slender, and nice-looking, had been, and continued being until her death, naturally sentimental and curious. By dint of spelling out words, she almost came to read fluently when she was already long in the tooth, and she read not only hagiology, but also some secular histories and the works of several poets. Her favorite authors were Doña María de Zayas and Gerardo Lobo.[15]

She prided herself on being experienced and free of illusions. Her conversation was always as though sprinkled with these two exclamations: "What a world this is!" and "The things we see in life!" Chacha Victoria felt as if she were bored and wearied from having seen so much, in spite of the fact that her travels had taken her no further than fifteen or eighteen miles from Villabermeja.

A passion that today we would characterize as romantic had filled Chacha Victoria's entire life. When she was barely eighteen, she met a gentlemanly infantry cadet at a fair and fell in love with him. The cadet also fell in love with Chacha, who was not Chacha at the time, but the two lovers, who were as poor as they were noble, could not marry for lack of money. So they professed their resolute intention to continue loving each other; they swore eternal constancy to each other; and they decided to put off their marriage until the cadet became a captain. Unfortunately, in those days people progressed in their careers at a snail's pace, and there were no civil wars or military uprisings, and the cadet, stable like a rock and faithful like a dog, grew old without ever advancing higher than lieutenant .

Whenever military service permitted, the cadet would come to Villabermeja; he would talk at the window with Chacha Victoria, and both would say a thousand tender words to each other. During long absences they wrote loving letters every eight or ten days, a regularity and frequency that were extraordinary for the time.

This necessity to write obliged Chacha Victoria to become literate. Love was her schoolteacher, and it taught her to scratch out mysterious, anarchic scribbles that, by virtue of a revelation of love, the cadet read, deciphered, and understood.

In this fashion, between periods of amorous talk at the window in Villabermeja and other longer ones of absence, when they communicated by letter, close to twelve years went by. Then there was a terrible moment: a heartbreaking farewell. The cadet, a lieutenant now, went off to the war in Italy. Letters from there were few and far between, and at

las cartas muy de tarde en tarde. Al cabo cesaron del todo. La chacha Victoria se llenó de presentimientos melancólicos.

En 1747, firmada ya la paz de Aquisgrán, los soldados españoles volvieron de Italia a España: pero nuestro cadete, que había esperado volver de capitán, no parecía ni escribía. Sólo pareció, con la licencia absoluta, su asistente, que era bermejino.

El bueno del asistente, en el mejor lenguaje que pudo, y con los preparativos y rodeos que le parecieron del caso para amortiguar el golpe, dio a la chacha Victoria la triste noticia de que el cadete, cuando iba ya a ver colmados sus deseos, cuando iba a ser ascendido a capitán, en vísperas de la paz, en la rota de Trebia, había caído atravesado por la lanza de un croata.

No murió en el acto. Vivió aún dos o tres días con la herida mortal, y tuvo tiempo de entregar al asistente, para que trajese a su querida Victoria, un rizo rubio que de ella llevaba sobre el pecho en un guardapelo, las cartas y un anillo de oro con un bonito diamante.

El pobre soldado cumplió fielmente su comisión.

La chacha Victoria recibió y bañó en lágrimas las amadas reliquias. El resto de su vida le pasó recordando al cadete, permaneciendo fiel a su memoria y llorándole a veces. Cuanto había de amor en su alma fue consumiéndose en devociones y transformándose en cariño por el sobrino Fadriquito, el cual tenía tres años cuando supo la chacha Victoria la muerte de su perpetuo y único novio.

La pobre chacha Ramoncica había sido siempre pequeñuela y mal hecha de cuerpo, sumamente morena y bastante fea de cara. Cierta dignidad natural e instintiva, le hizo comprender, desde que tenía quince años, que no había nacido para el amor. Si algo del amor con que aman las mujeres a los hombres había en germen en su alma, ella acertó a sofocarlo y no brotó jamás. En cambio tuvo afecto para todos. Su caridad se extendía hasta los animales.

Desde la edad de veinticuatro años, en que la chacha Ramoncica se quedó huérfana y vivía en casa propia, sola, le hacían compañía media docena de gatos, dos o tres perros y un grajo que poseía varias habilidades. Tenía asimismo Ramoncica un palomar lleno de palomos, y un corral poblado de pavos, patos, gallinas y conejos.

Una criada, llamada Rafaela, que entró a servir a la chacha cuando ésta vivía aún en casa de sus padres, siguió sirviéndola toda la vida. Ama y criada eran de la misma edad y llegaron juntas a una extrema vejez.

length they stopped altogether. Chacha Victoria was overwhelmed with gloomy forebodings.

In 1747, the peace of Aachen having been signed,[16] all the Spanish soldiers returned from Italy to Spain, but our cadet, who had hoped to return as a captain, neither turned up nor wrote. The only one to turn up was his discharged orderly, who was a Villabermejan.

The loyal orderly, in the best language that he knew, and with the preparations and circumlocutions he deemed appropriate in order to cushion the blow, gave Chacha Victoria the sad news that the cadet, when he was about to see his wishes realized, when he was about to be promoted to captain, on the eve of peace, had fallen in the rout of Trebbia,[17] run through by a Croatian's lance.

He did not die immediately. He held out for two or three days with his mortal wound, and had time to hand over to his orderly, for him to take to his beloved Victoria, a blond curl of hers that he wore in a locket over his chest, the letters, and a gold ring with a pretty diamond.

The poor soldier faithfully carried out his mission.

Chacha Victoria received the dear relics and bathed them in tears. She spent the rest of her life treasuring the memory of the cadet, remaining faithful to it and now and then shedding tears for him. All the love in her soul was little by little consumed in religious devotions and transformed into affection for her nephew Fadrique, who was three years old when Chacha Victoria learned of the death of her perpetual and only fiancé.

Poor Chacha Ramoncica had always been on the small side, swarthy in the extreme, with a misshapen body, and a rather homely face. A certain natural, distinctive dignity made her understand, from the time that she was fifteen, that she had not been born for love. If something of the love with which women love men existed as a seed in her soul, she managed to quash it and it never sprouted. On the other hand, she had affection for everyone. Her charity extended even to animals.

From the age of twenty-four, when Chacha Ramoncica became an orphan and was living in her own house, alone, an assemblage of creatures kept her company: a half dozen cats, two or three dogs, and a rook that possessed several abilities. Ramoncica likewise had a dovecote full of pigeons, and a pen that held turkeys, ducks, hens, and rabbits.

A maidservant named Rafaela, who entered Chacha Ramoncica's service when Ramoncica still lived in her parents' house, continued serving her all her life. Mistress and servant were of the same age, and lived to a ripe old one together.

Rafaela era más fea que la chacha, y, hasta por imitarla, permaneció siempre soltera.

En medio de su fealdad, había algo de noble y distinguido en la chacha Ramoncica, que era una señora de muy cortas luces. Rafaela, por el contrario, sobre ser fea, tenía el más innoble aspecto, pero estaba dotada de un despejo natural grandísimo.

Por lo demás, ama y criada, guardando siempre cada cual su posición y grado en la jerarquía social, se identificaron por tal arte, que se diría que no había en ellas sino una voluntad, los pensamientos mismos y los mismos propósitos.

Todo era orden, método y arreglo en aquella casa. Apenas se gastaba en comer, porque ama y criada comían poquísimo. Un vestido, una saya, una basquina, cualquiera otra prenda, duraba años y años sobre el cuerpo de la chacha Ramoncica o guardada en el armario. Después, estando aún en buen uso, pasaba a ser prenda de Rafaela.

Los muebles eran siempre los mismos y se conservaban, como por encanto, con un lustre y una limpieza que daban consuelo.

Con tal modo de vivir, la chacha Ramoncica, si bien no tenía sino muy escasas rentas, apenas gastaba de ellas una tercera parte. Iba, pues, acumulando y atesorando, y pronto tuvo fama de rica. Sin embargo, jamás se sentía con valor de ser despilfarrada sino por empeño de su sobrino Fadrique, a quien, según hemos dicho, mimaba en competencia con la chacha Victoria.

Don Diego andaba siempre en el campo, de caza o atendiendo a las labores. Sus dos hijos, don José y don Fadrique, quedaban al cuidado de la chacha Victoria y del padre Jacinto, fraile dominico, que pasaba por muy docto en el lugar, y que les sirvió de ayo, enseñándoles las primeras letras y el latín.

Don José era bondadoso y reposado; don Fadrique, un diablo de travieso: pero don José no atinaba a hacerse querer, y don Fadrique era amado con locura de ambas chachas, del feroz don Diego y del ya citado padre Jacinto, quien apenas tendría treinta y seis años de edad cuando enseñaba la lengua de Cicerón a los dos pimpollos lozanos del glorioso y antiguo tronco de los López de Mendoza bermejinos.

Mientras que el apacible don José se quedaba en casa estudiando, o

Rafaela was uglier than her *chacha*, and, so as to imitate her, she too always remained single.

In the midst of her ugliness, there was something noble and distinguished about Chacha Ramoncica, who was very slow-witted. Rafaela, on the contrary, in addition to being ugly, had a most ignoble mien, but she was endowed with an abundance of native intelligence.

As to the rest, mistress and servant, each one always keeping her position and standing in the social hierarchy, identified with the other in such a way that you would think the two shared the same will, the same thoughts, and the same intentions.

Everything was order, method, and neatness in that house. Very little was spent on food, because mistress and servant ate next to nothing. A dress, a skirt, a petticoat or any other article of clothing lasted for years and years on Chacha Ramoncica's body or was stored away in the closet. Afterwards, as it was still in good condition, the item became Rafaela's.

The pieces of furniture never changed and were always preserved, as if by enchantment, with a cleanliness and a luster that gladdened the eye.

Although she had a meager income, living as she did Chacha Ramoncica scarcely spent one third of it. As a result, over the years she accumulated and hoarded money, and soon she gained a reputation for being wealthy. Nonetheless, she could never bring herself to be extravagant, except at the insistence of her nephew Fadrique, whom, as we have said, she pampered in competition with Chacha Victoria.

Don Diego was always out in the country, hunting or attending to the work of the land. His two sons, Don José and Don Fadrique, were left in the care of Chacha Victoria and Father Jacinto, a Dominican friar who had a reputation for great learning in the town and who served as their tutor, grounding them in the basics and teaching them Latin.

Don José was kind-hearted and gentle and Don Fadrique a mischievous devil, but Don José somehow could not make himself loved, whereas Don Fadrique was loved to distraction by both Chachas, by the fierce Don Diego, and by the abovementioned Father Jacinto, who had barely turned thirty-six when he was teaching Cicero's language to the two robust offshoots of the glorious and ancient trunk of the Villabermejan López de Mendozas.

While the peaceable Don José stayed at home studying, or went to

iba al convento a ayudar a misa, o empleaba su tiempo en otras tareas tranquilas, don Fadrique solía escaparse y promover mil alborotos en el pueblo.

Como segundón de la casa, don Fadrique estaba condenado a vestirse de lo que se quedaba estrecho o corto para su hermano, el cual, a su vez, solía vestirse de los desechos de su padre. La chacha Victoria hacía estos arreglos y traspasos. Ya hemos hablado de la casaca y de la chupa encarnadas, que vinieron a ser memorables por el lance del bolero; pero mucho antes había heredado don Fadrique una capa, que se hizo más famosa, y que había servido sucesivamente a don Diego y a don José. La capa era blanca, y cuando cayó en poder de don Fadrique recibió el nombre de la capa-paloma.

La capa-paloma parecía que había dado alas al chico, quien se hizo más inquieto y diabólico desde que la poseyó. Don Fadrique, cabeza de motín y de bando entre los muchachos más desatinados del pueblo, se diría que llevaba la capa-paloma como un estandarte, como un signo que todos seguían; como el penacho blanco de Enrique IV.

No era muy numeroso el bando de don Fadrique, no por falta de simpatías, sino porque él elegía a sus parciales y secuaces haciendo pruebas análogas a las que hizo Gedeón para elegir o desechar a sus soldados. De esta suerte logró don Fadrique tener unos cincuenta o sesenta que le seguían, tan atrevidos y devotos a su persona, que cada uno valía por diez.

Se formó un partido contrario, capitaneado por don Casimirito, hijo del hidalgo más rico del lugar. Este partido era de más gente; pero, así por las prendas personales del capitán, como por el valor y decisión de los soldados, quedaba siempre muy inferior a los fadriqueños.

Varias veces llegaron a las manos ambos bandos, ya a puñadas y luchando a brazo partido, ya en pedreas, de que era teatro un llanete que está por bajo de un sitio llamado el Retamal.

Siempre que había un lance de estos, don Fadrique era el primero en acudir al lugar del peligro; pero es lo cierto que no bien corría la voz de que *la capa-paloma iba por el Retamal abajo,* las calles y las plazuelas se despoblaban de los más belicosos chiquillos, y todos acudían en busca del capitán idolatrado.

La victoria, en todas estas pendencias, quedó siempre por el bando

the monastery to hear mass, or spent his time on other tranquil tasks, Don Fadrique usually stole off and raised one ruckus after another in the town.

As the second-born son in the family, Don Fadrique was condemned to wearing hand-me-downs or whatever got too tight or too short for his brother, who, in his turn, usually wore clothes cast off by their father. Chacha Victoria made these alterations and modifications. We have already spoken of the blood-red frock coat and vest, which turned into memorable garments owing to the bolero incident, but much earlier Don Fadrique had inherited a cape that became more famous and that had successively served Don Diego and Don José. The cape was white when Don Fadrique laid his hands on it, and he gave it the name "dove-cape."

It seemed that the dove-cape emboldened the boy, who turned more restless and devilish after he came into its possession. You could say that Don Fadrique, leader of the band of the most rebellious and reckless boys in the town, wore the dove-cape like a standard, like a sign that all followed, like the white plume of Henri IV.[18]

Don Fadrique's band was not very numerous, not for want of solidarity on the part of others, but because he chose his partisans and supporters by subjecting them to trials similar to those devised by Gideon[19] to select or reject his soldiers. In this way Don Fadrique ended up with fifty or sixty who followed him, so bold all of them and so devoted to him, that each one was worth ten.

An opposing party was formed and it was led by Don Casimirito, son of the town's richest nobleman. This party numbered more adherents, but both because of the personal qualities of the captain and the courage and resolve of the soldiers, it was always inferior to the Fadriquians.

Both bands came to blows on several occasions, now by fisticuffs, now with stone fights, the setting of which was a short stretch of level ground below a spot called Broom Field.

Whenever one of those encounters took place, Don Fadrique was the first one to arrive at the site of danger, but without fail as soon as word spread that "dove-cape was heading down below Broom Field," the streets and squares cleared of the most bellicose boys, and they all ran after their idolized captain.

Victory in these forays always belonged to Don Fadrique's band. Don

de don Fadrique. Los de don Casimiro resistían poco y se ponían en un momento en vergonzosa fuga; pero como don Fadrique se aventuraba siempre más de lo que conviene a la prudencia de un general, resultó que dos veces regó los laureles con su sangre, quedando descalabrado.

No sólo en batalla campal, sino en otros ejercicios y haciendo travesuras de todo género, don Fadrique se había roto además la cabeza otra tercera vez, se había herido el pecho con unas tijeras, se había quemado una mano y se había dislocado un brazo: pero de todos estos percances salía al cabo sano y salvo, merced a su robustez y a los cuidados de la chacha Victoria, que decía maravillada y santiguándose: –¡Ay, hijo de mi alma, para muy grandes cosas quiere reservarte el cielo, cuando vives de milagro y no mueres!

3

Casimiro tenía tres años más de edad que don Fadrique, y era también más fornido y alto. Irritado de verse vencido siempre como capitán, quiso probarse con don Fadrique en singular combate. Lucharon, pues, a puñadas y a brazo partido, y el pobre Casimiro salió siempre acogotado y pisoteado, a pesar de su superioridad aparente.

Los frailes dominicos del lugar nunca quisieron bien a la familia de los Mendozas. A pesar de la piedad suma de las chachas Victoria y Ramoncica, y de la devoción humilde de don José, no podían tragar a don Diego, y se mostraban escandalizados de los desafueros e insolencias de don Fadrique.

Sólo el padre Jacinto, que amaba tiernamente a don Fadrique, le defendía de las acusaciones y quejas de los otros frailes.

Éstos, no obstante, le amenazaban a menudo con cogerle y enviarle a los Toribios, o con hacer que el propio hermano Toribio viniese por él y se le llevase.

Bien sabían los frailes que el bendito hermano Toribio había muerto hacía más de veinte años; pero la institución creada por él florecía, prestando al glorioso fundador una existencia inmortal y mitológica. Hasta muy entrado el segundo tercio del siglo presente, el hermano Toribio y los Toribios en general han sido el tema constante de todas las amenazas para infundir saludable terror a los muchachos traviesos.

En la mente de don Fadrique no entraba la idea de la fervorosa

Casimiro's supporters would put up little resistance and would quickly be put to a shameful rout, but since Don Fadrique always risked more than befits a general's prudence, it turned out that on two occasions he "watered" his laurels with his blood, having cracked his head both times.

Not only in pitched battle, but also in other exercises and pranks of every kind, Don Fadrique had, in addition, broken his head a third time, wounded himself in the chest with scissors, burned a hand, and dislocated an arm, but he came away from all these mishaps safe and sound thanks to his toughness and to the care of Chacha Victoria, who used to say, amazed and crossing herself: "Ay, my precious boy, heaven must have great things in store for you when you live miraculously and don't die!"

3

Casimiro was three years older than Don Fadrique, and he was also huskier and taller. Vexed at always seeing himself bested as a captain, he wanted to pit himself against Don Fadrique in single combat. So they fought hand-to-hand using only their fists, and poor Casimiro came out for the worse, knocked down and stamped on, despite his apparent superiority.

The Dominican friars of the town never much cared for the Mendoza family. Notwithstanding the great piety of Chacha Victoria and Chacha Ramoncica and the humble devotion of Don José, they could not abide Don Diego and were scandalized by Don Fadrique's excesses and insolence.

Only Father Jacinto, who loved Don Fadrique tenderly, defended him against the accusations and complaints of the other friars. The latter, nevertheless, often threatened to lay their hands on him and send him to the Toribios reformatory, or to have Brother Toribio himself come for him and take him away.

The friars, of course, knew full well that their saintly Brother Toribio had died more than twenty years ago, but the institution created by him thrived, lending an immortal, mythological existence to the glorious founder. Until well into the second third of the present century, Brother Toribio and the Toribios in general were the constant bugaboo of all the threats to instill a salutary terror in mischievous boys.

The idea that did not make sense to Don Fadrique was the fervent

caridad con que el hermano Toribio, a fin de salvar y purificar las almas de cuantos muchachos cogía, les martirizaba el cuerpo, dándoles rudos azotes sobre las carnes desnudas. Así es que se presentaba en su imaginación el bendito hermano Toribio como loco furioso y perverso, enemigo de sí mismo para llagarse con cadenas ceñidas a los riñones, y enemigo de todo el género humano, a quien desollaba y atormentaba en la edad de la niñez y de la más temprana juventud, cuando se abren al amor las almas y cuando la naturaleza y el cielo deberían sonreír y acariciar en vez de dar azotes.

Como ya habían ocurrido casos de llevarse a los Toribios contra la voluntad de sus padres a varios muchachos traviesos, y como el hermano Toribio, durante su santa vida, había salido a caza de tales muchachos, no sólo por toda Sevilla, sino por otras poblaciones de Andalucía, desde donde los conducía a su terrible establecimiento, la amenaza de los frailes pareció para broma harto pesada a don Diego, y para veras le pareció más pesada aún. Hizo, pues, decir a los frailes que se abstuviesen de embromar a su hijo y mucho más de amenazarle, que ya él sabría castigar al chico cuando lo mereciese, pero que nadie más que él había de ser osado a ponerle las manos encima. Añadió don Diego que el chico, aunque pequeño todavía, sabría defenderse y hasta ofender, si le atacaban, y que además él volaría en su auxilio, en caso necesario, y arrancaría las orejas a tirones a todos los Toribios que ha habido y hay en el mundo.

Con estas insinuaciones, que bien sabían todos cuan capaz era de hacer efectivas don Diego, los frailes se contuvieron en su malevolencia; pero como don Fadrique (fuerza es confesarlo, si hemos de ser imparciales) seguía siendo peor que Pateta, los frailes, no atreviéndose ya a esgrimir contra él armas terrenas y temporales, acudieron al arsenal de las espirituales y eternas, y no cesaron de querer amedrentarle con el infierno y el demonio.

De este método de intimidación se ocasionó un mal gravísimo. Don Fadrique, a pesar de sus chachas, se hizo impío, antes de pensar y de reflexionar; por un sentimiento instintivo. La religión no se ofreció a su mente por el lado del amor y de la ternura infinita, sino por el lado del miedo, contra el cual su natural valeroso e independiente se rebelaba. Don Fadrique no vio el objeto del amor insaciable del alma, y el fin digno de su última aspiración, en los poderes sobrenaturales. Don Fadrique no vio en ellos sino tiranos, verdugos o espantajos sin consistencia.

charity with which Brother Toribio martyred the bodies and cruelly lashed the bare hides of all the boys that he caught so as to save and purify their souls. As a result the selfsame Brother Toribio appeared in his imagination as a perverse, raging madman, his own enemy as he self-inflicted wounds with chains encircling his lower ribs, and as an enemy of the entire human race, which he flayed and tormented in the childhood and early youth years, when souls open up to love and when nature and heaven should smile and caress instead of meting out lashes.

Since there had already been instances of several intractable boys being taken to the Toribios against the will of their parents, and since Brother Toribio, during his saintly life, had gone in pursuit of such boys not only in all of Seville, but in other Andalusian cities and towns as well, from which places he carted them off to his terrible establishment, the friars' threat, in Don Diego's eyes, seemed in very bad taste as a joke and in even worse taste as a truth. He made it known to the friars, therefore, that they should refrain from teasing his son, and especially from threatening him, as he would know how to punish the boy when he deserved it. Don Diego added that only he had the right to lay a hand on Fadrique, and that no one else should dare to touch him. He said too that the boy, although still young, would know how to defend himself, and even take the offensive if they attacked him, and that moreover he himself would fly to his son's aid, in the event it became necessary, and tear the ears off all the Toribios in the world, past and present.

With these warnings or quasi-threats of his own, which Don Diego was capable of carrying out, as everybody clearly understood, the friars held their ill will in check. But since Don Fadrique (it must be admitted, if we are to be impartial) continued behaving worse than the prince of darkness, the friars, no longer daring to wield temporal and worldly arms against him, had recourse to the arsenal of the spiritual and eternal ones, and did not cease trying to scare him with hell and the devil.

This method of intimidation occasioned a very grave wrong. Despite his Chachas, Don Fadrique became ungodly through an instinctive response, before thinking things over and reflecting. Religion did not instill in his mind feelings of love and infinite tenderness, but feelings of fear, against which his courageous and independent temperament rebelled. Don Fadrique did not see the object of the insatiable love of the soul, and the worthy end of his utmost aspiration, in supernatural powers; Don Fadrique saw in them only tyrants, executioners or elusive bogeymen.

Cada siglo tiene su espíritu, que se esparce y como que se diluye en el aire que respiramos, infundiéndose tal vez en las almas de los hombres, sin necesidad de que las ideas y teorías pasen de unos entendimientos a otros por medio de la palabra escrita o hablada. El siglo XVIII tal vez no fue crítico, burlón, sensualista y descreído porque tuvo a Voltaire, a Kant y a los enciclopedistas, sino porque fue crítico, burlón, sensualista y descreído, tuvo a dichos pensadores, quienes formularon en términos precisos lo que estaba vago y difuso en el ambiente: el giro del pensamiento humano en aquel período de su civilización progresiva.

Sólo así se comprende que don Fadrique viniese a ser impío sin leer ni oír nada que a ello le llevase.

Esta nueva calidad que apareció en él era bastante peligrosa en aquellos tiempos. Don Diego mismo se espantó de ciertas ideas de su hijo. Por dicha, el desenvolvimiento de tan mala inclinación coincidió casi con la ida de don Fadrique al Colegio de Guardias marinas, y se evitó así todo escándalo y disgusto en Villabermeja.

Las chachas Victoria y Ramoncica lloraron mucho la partida de don Fadrique; el padre Jacinto la sintió; don Diego, que le llevó a la Isla, se alegró de ver a su hijo puesto en carrera, casi más que se afligió al separarse de él; y los frailes, y Casimirito sobre todo, tuvieron un día de júbilo el día en que le perdieron de vista.

Don Fadrique volvió al lugar de allí adelante, pero siempre por brevísimo tiempo: una vez cuando salió del Colegio para ir a navegar; otra vez siendo ya alférez de navío. Luego pasaron años y años sin que viese a don Fadrique ningún bermejino. Se sabía que estaba ya en el Perú, ya en el Asia, en el Extremo Oriente.

IV

De las cosas de don Fadrique, durante tan larga ausencia, se tenía o se forjaba en el lugar el concepto más fantástico y absurdo.

Don Diego y la chacha Victoria, que eran las personas de la familia más instruidas e inteligentes, murieron a poco de hallarse don Fadrique

Each age has its spirit, which spreads and seems to be absorbed in the air that we breathe, perhaps penetrating the souls of men, without the necessity of ideas and theories passing from some minds to others by means of the spoken or written word. The eighteenth century perhaps was not critical, derisive, sensualist, and unbelieving because it had Voltaire, Kant, and the encyclopedists,[20] but rather because it was critical, derisive, sensualist, and unbelieving it had said thinkers, who formulated in precise terms what was vague and diffuse in the atmosphere: the course of human thought in that period of its progressive civilization.

Only in this way can it be understood that Don Fadrique should have become ungodly without reading or hearing anything that would point him in that direction.

This new quality that appeared in him was quite dangerous in those times. Don Diego himself was alarmed by certain of his son's ideas. Fortunately, the development of such an evil inclination almost coincided with Don Fadrique's entrance into the Spanish Naval Academy, and so all the scandal and unpleasantness were avoided in Villabermeja.

Chachas Victoria and Ramoncica wept copious tears over Don Fadrique's departure; Father Jacinto regretted it; Don Diego, who took him to La Isla,[21] rejoiced at seeing his son started on a career, almost more than he grieved at taking leave of him; and the friars, and most especially Casimirito, experienced a day of jubilation the day they saw the last of him.

Don Fadrique came back to the town in future, but always for very short stays: once when he left the Academy to sail the seas, another time when he was already a lieutenant junior grade. Then years passed without any Villabermejan seeing Don Fadrique. It was known that now he was in Peru, now in Asia, now in the Far East.

4

During such a long absence, people in the town had, or concocted, the most absurd and fantastic concept of Don Fadrique's comings and goings.

Don Diego and Chacha Victoria, who were the most well-educated and intelligent people in the family, died shortly after Don Fadrique

en el Perú. Y lo que es a la cándida Ramoncica y al limitado don José, no escribía don Fadrique sino muy de tarde en tarde, y cada carta tan breve como una fe de vida.

Al padre Jacinto, aunque don Fadrique le estimaba y quería de veras, también le escribía poco, por efecto de la repulsión y desconfianza que en general le inspiraban los frailes. Así es que nada se sabía nunca a ciencia cierta en el lugar de las andanzas y aventuras del ilustre marino.

Quien más supo de ello en su tiempo fue el cura Fernández, que, según queda dicho, trató a don Fadrique y tuvo alguna amistad con él. Por el cura Fernández se enteró don Juan Fresco, en quien influyó mucho el relato de las peregrinaciones y lances de fortuna de don Fadrique para que se hiciese piloto y siguiese en todo sus huellas.

Recogiendo y ordenando yo ahora las esparcidas y vagas noticias, las apuntaré aquí en resumen.

Don Fadrique estuvo poco tiempo en el Colegio, donde mostró grande disposición para el estudio.

Pronto salió a navegar y fue a La Habana en ocasión tristísima. España estaba en guerra con los ingleses, y la capital de Cuba fue atacada por el almirante Pocok. Echado a pique el navío en que se hallaba nuestro bermejino, la gente de la tripulación, que pudo salvarse, fue destinada a la defensa del castillo del Morro, bajo las órdenes del valeroso don Luis Velasco.

Allí estuvo don Fadrique haciendo estragos en la escuadra inglesa con sus certeros tiros de cañón. Luego, durante el asalto, peleó como un héroe en la brecha, y vio morir a su lado a don Luis, su jefe. Por último, fue de los pocos que lograron salvarse, cuando pasando sobre un montón de cadáveres y haciendo prisioneros a los vivos, llegó el general inglés, conde de Albemarle, a levantar el pabellón británico sobre la principal fortaleza de La Habana.

Don Fadrique tuvo el disgusto de asistir a la capitulación de aquella plaza importante y, contado en el número de los que la guarnecían, fue conducido a España en cumplimiento de lo capitulado.

Entonces, ya de alférez de navío, vino a Villabermeja y vio a su padre la última vez.

La reina de las Antillas, muchos millones de duros y lo mejor de nuestros barcos de guerra habían quedado en poder de los ingleses.

landed in Peru. And as for the naive Ramoncica and the slow-witted Don José, Don Fadrique very seldom wrote to them, and every letter was as short as an official document stating that an individual is still alive.

Although Don Fadrique esteemed and truly loved Father Jacinto, he also wrote infrequently to him, on account of the disgust and distrust that friars in general inspired in him. Thus it was that nothing for certain was known in the town about the adventures and deeds of the illustrious naval officer.

The person who at the time knew the most concerning him and his whereabouts was Father Fernández, who, as has been said, had had dealings with Don Fadrique and become somewhat friendly with him. Father Fernández then informed Don Juan Fresco, on whom the account of Don Fadrique's travels and adventures had so much effect that it influenced him greatly in becoming a first mate and following his footsteps in everything.

Gathering together now widespread and vague pieces of information, I'll set them down in summary form.

Don Fadrique spent little time at the Academy, where he exhibited a natural aptitude for study.

He soon struck out on his own to sail the seas and went to Havana at a most sad time. Spain was at war with England and the Cuban capital had been shelled by Admiral Pocock.[22] When our Villabermejan's ship sank, the crew, having been saved, was enlisted in the defense of Morro Castle[23] under the orders of the valiant Don Luis de Velasco.[24]

There Don Fadrique wreaked havoc on the English squadron with his well-aimed cannon fire. Then, during the assault, he fought in the breach like a hero and saw his superior Don Luis fall at his side. Lastly, he was one of the few who managed to escape when, passing over a pile of corpses and taking the living as prisoners, the English general, the Earl of Albemarle,[25] came and raised the British flag over Havana's primary fortress.

Don Fadrique experienced the displeasure of being present at the surrender of that important stronghold, and, as he found himself among those who manned it, was taken to Spain in accordance with the terms of surrender.

Back in his native country, a lieutenant now, he journeyed to Villabermeja and saw his father for the last time.

The Queen of the Antilles, many millions of *duros*, and the best part of our warships had been lost to the English.

Don Fadrique no se descorazonó con tan trágico principio. Era hombre poco dado a melancolías. Era optimista y no quejumbroso. Además todos los bienes de la casa los había de heredar el mayorazgo, y él ansiaba adquirir honra, dinero y posición.

Pocos días estuvo en Villabermeja. Se fue antes de que su licencia se cumpliese.

El rey Carlos III, después de la triste paz de París, a que le llevó el desastroso *Pacto de familia,* trató de mejorar por todas partes la administración de sus vastísimos estados. En América era donde había más abusos, escándalos, inmoralidad, tiranías y dilapidaciones. A fin de remediar tanto mal, envió el rey a Gálvez de visitador a Méjico, y algo más tarde envió al Perú, con la misma misión, a don Juan Antonio de Areche. En esta expedición fue a Lima don Fadrique.

Allí se encontraba cuando tuvo lugar la rebelión de Tupac-Amaru. En la mente imparcial y filosófica del bermejino se presentaba como un contrasentido espantoso el que su Gobierno tratase de ahogar en sangre aquella rebelión, al mismo tiempo que estaba auxiliando la de Washington y sus parciales contra los ingleses; pero don Fadrique, murmurando y censurando, sirvió con energía a su Gobierno, y contribuyó bastante a la pacificación del Perú.

Don Fadrique acompañó a Areche en su marcha al Cuzco, y desde allí, mandando una de las seis columnas en que dividió sus fuerzas el general Valle, siguió la campaña contra los indios, tomando gloriosa parte en muchas refriegas, sufriendo con firmeza las privaciones, las lluvias y los fríos en escabrosas alturas a la falda de los Andes, y no parando hasta que Tupac-Amaru quedó vencido y cayó prisionero.

Don Fadrique, con grande horror y disgusto fue testigo ocular de los tremendos castigos que hizo nuestro Gobierno en los rebeldes. Pensaba él que las crueldades e infamias cometidas por los indios no justificaban las de un Gobierno culto y europeo. Era bajar al nivel de aquella gente semisalvaje. Así es que casi se arrepintió de haber contribuido al triunfo, cuando vio en la plaza del Cuzco morir a Tupac-Amaru, después de un brutal martirio, que parecía invención de fieras y no de seres humanos.

Tupac-Amaru tuvo que presenciar la muerte de su mujer, de un hijo suyo y de otros deudos y amigos; a otro hijo suyo de diez años le

Don Fadrique did not get disheartened by such a tragic beginning. He was a man little given to melancholy and gloom. He was an optimist, not a complainer. Besides, the *mayorazgo* Don José was going to inherit all the family possessions, and he longed to acquire honor, money, and a position of his own.

Don Fadrique spent only a few days in Villabermeja, and left before his leave was up.

King Carlos III, after the sad peace of Paris, which resulted from the disastrous Family Pact,[26] attempted to improve the administration of his overseas possessions everywhere. But it was in America that there were the most abuses, scandals, immorality, tyranny, and waste. In order to remedy so much wrongdoing, the king sent Gálvez[27] to Mexico as inspector general, and shortly afterward he sent Don Juan Antonio de Areche[28] to Peru, also as inspector general. It was with the latter expedition that Don Fadrique went to Lima.

He was there when the rebellion of Tupac Amaru[29] broke out. In the philosophical and impartial mind of the Villabermejan it seemed like a shocking contradiction that his Government should try to suppress that rebellion in a sea of blood at the same time that it was aiding that of Washington and his followers against the English, but Don Fadrique, muttering and criticizing, served his Government effectively and contributed in large measure to the pacification of Peru.

Don Fadrique accompanied Areche on his march to Cuzco, and from there, commanding one of the six columns into which General Valle divided his forces, he carried on the campaign against the Indians, taking a glorious part in many skirmishes, steadfastly enduring privations, downpours, and cold snaps in the rugged heights of the Andes, and not stopping until Tupac Amaru was vanquished and taken prisoner.

To his great horror and dismay, Don Fadrique was an eyewitness to the barbarous punishments visited upon the rebels by our government. He thought that the cruelties and atrocities committed by the Indians did not justify paying them back in their own coin by a cultured European government. It was descending to the level of those semisavage people. Thus it was that he almost regretted having contributed to their victory when he saw Tupac Amaru die on the main square in Cuzco, following a brutal torture that seemed like the device of wild beasts and not of human beings.

Tupac Amaru had to witness the death of his wife, the death of one of his sons, and the deaths of other relatives and friends. Another of

condenaron a ver aquellos bárbaros suplicios de su padre y de su madre, y a él mismo le cortaron la lengua y le ataron luego por los cuatro remos a otros tantos caballos para que, saliendo a escape, le hiciesen pedazos. Los caballos, aunque espoleados duramente por los que los montaban, no tuvieron fuerza bastante para descuartizar al indio, y a éste, descoyuntado, después de tirar de él un rato en distintas direcciones, tuvieron que desatarle de los caballos y cortarle la cabeza.

A pesar de su optimismo, de su genio alegre y de su afición a tomar muchos sucesos por el lado cómico, don Fadrique, no pudiendo hallar nada cómico en aquel suceso, cayó enfermo con fiebre y se desanimó mucho en su afición a la carrera militar.

Desde entonces se declaró más en él la manía de ser filántropo, especie de secularización de la caridad, que empezó a estar muy en moda en el siglo pasado.

La impiedad precoz de don Fadrique vino a fundarse en razones y en discursos con el andar del tiempo y con la lectura de los malos libros que en aquella época se publicaban en Francia. El carácter burlón y regocijado de don Fadrique se avenía mal con la misantropía tétrica de Rousseau. Voltaire, en cambio, le encantaba. Sus obras más impías parecíanle ecos de su alma.

La filosofía de don Fadrique era el sensualismo de Condillac, que él consideraba como el *non plus ultra* de la especulación humana.

En cuanto a la política, nuestro don Fadrique era un liberal anacrónico en España. Por los años de 1783, cuando vio morir a Tupac-Amaru, era casi como un radical de ahora.

Todo esto se encadenaba y se fundaba en una teodicea algo confusa y somera, pero común entonces. Don Fadrique creía en Dios y se imaginaba que tenía ciencia de Dios, representándosele como inteligencia suprema y libre, que hizo el mundo porque quiso, y luego le ordenó y arregló según los más profundos principios de la mecánica y de la física. A pesar del *Cándido,* novela que le hacía llorar de risa, don Fadrique era casi tan optimista como el doctor Pangloss, y tenía por cierto que todo estaba divinamente bien y que nada podía estar mejor de lo que estaba. El mal le parecía un accidente, por más que a menudo se pasmase de que ocurriera con tanta frecuencia y de que fuera tan grande, y el bien le parecía lo sustancial, positivo e importante que había en todo.

his sons, a ten-year-old, was forced to watch the inhuman ordeal of his parents, and then he himself had his tongue cut out and both of his arms and legs tied to four horses so that, as they set off at a gallop, he would be drawn, torn to pieces. But the horses, although spurred ruthlessly by their riders, were not strong enough to tear the Indian into quarters, and so, dislocated after being pulled awhile in four different directions, his captors had to untie him and behead him.[30]

Despite his optimism, his cheerful nature, and his penchant for looking at the comical side of most incidents, Don Fadrique, unable to find anything comical in that one, fell ill with a fever and questioned his enthusiasm for making a career of the military.

From that point on, there became more pronounced in him the mania to be philanthropic, a kind of secularization of charity that began to be very fashionable in the last century.

Don Fadrique's precocious ungodliness came to be based on reasons and on discourses with the passage of time and with the reading of the baneful books that were being published in France in that period. Don Fadrique's jolly, irreverent character did not harmonize well with Rousseau's gloomy misanthropy. Voltaire, on the other hand, delighted him. His most ungodly works seemed to him echoes of his very own soul.

Don Fadrique's philosophy was the sensationalism of Condillac,[31] which he regarded as the *ne plus ultra* of human speculation.

With respect to politics, our Don Fadrique was an anachronistic liberal in Spain. Around 1783, when he saw Tupac Amaru die,[32] he was almost like one of today's radicals.

All this was linked to and based on a somewhat confusing and superficial theodicy, but one that was common back then. Don Fadrique believed in God and imagined that he had knowledge of him, seeing him in his mind's eye as a free, supreme intelligence who made the world because he wanted to, and then ordered it and arranged it according to the most profound principles of mechanics and physics. Despite *Candide*, a novel that reduced him to tears of laughter, Don Fadrique was almost as optimistic as Doctor Pangloss,[33] and was persuaded that everything was divinely right and that nothing could be better than it was. He thought evil an accident, for as much as he often marveled that it should occur with so much frequency and be so great, and he thought good the substantial, positive, and important element to be found in everything.

Sobre el espíritu y la materia, sobre la vida ultramundana y sobre
la justificación de la providencia, basada en compensaciones de eterna
duración, don Fadrique estaba muy dudoso; pero su optimismo era tal
que veía demostrada y hasta patente la bondad del cielo, sin salir de
este mundo sublunar y de la vida que vivimos. Verdad es que para ello
había adoptado una teoría, novísima entonces. Y decimos que la había
adoptado, y no que la había inventado, porque no nos consta, aunque
bien pudo ser que la inventase; ya que cuando llega el momento y suena
la hora de que nazca una idea y de que se formule un sistema, la idea
nace y el sistema se formula en mil cabezas a la vez, si bien la gloria de
la invención se la lleva aquel que por escrito o de palabra la expone con
más claridad, precisión o elegancia.

La idea, o mejor dicho, la teoría novísima, tal como estaba en la mente
de don Fadrique, era en compendio la siguiente:

Entendía el filósofo de Villabermeja que había una ley providencial
y eterna para la historia, tan indefectible como las leyes matemáticas,
según las cuales giran en sus órbitas los astros. En virtud de esta ley, la
humanidad iba adelantando siempre por un camino de perfectibilidad
indefinida; su ascensión hacia la luz, el bien, la verdad y la belleza,
no tenían pausa ni término. En esto, el humano linaje, en su conjunto,
seguía un impulso necesario. Toda la gloria del éxito era para el Ser
Supremo, que había dado aquel impulso; pero, dentro del providencial
movimiento que de él nacía, en toda acción, en toda idea, en todo
propósito, cada individuo era libre y responsable. El maravilloso trabajo
de la Providencia, el misterio más bello de su sabiduría infinita, consistía
en concertar con atinada armonía todos aquellos resultados de la libertad
humana a fin de que concurriesen al cumplimiento de la ley eterna del
progreso, o en tenerlos previstos con tan divina previsión y acierto que
no perturbasen lo que estaba prescrito y ordenado; así como, aunque
sea baja comparación, cuenta el inventor y constructor perito de una
máquina con los rozamientos y con el medio ambiente.

Tal manera de considerar los sucesos se avenía bien con el carácter
de don Fadrique, corroborando su desdén hacia las menudencias, y su
prurito de calificar de menudencias lo que para los más de los hombres
es importante en grado sumo, y transformando su propensión a la alegría
y a la risa en serenidad olímpica, digna de los inmortales.

About spirit and matter, about an ultramundane life, and about the justification of Providence, based on compensations of eternal duration, Don Fadrique was very dubious, but his optimism was such that he saw the goodness of heaven clearly demonstrated, and even made patent, without leaving this sublunary world and the life that we lead. It is true that to think as he did, he had adopted a theory, a very novel one at the time. And we say that he had adopted it and not that he had invented it because we do not know for sure, although it could well be that he *did* invent it, since when the moment arrives and the hour strikes for an idea to be born and for a system to be formulated, the idea is born and the system is formulated in a thousand heads all at once, although the glory of the invention belongs to the person who, in writing or verbally, explains it with greater clarity, precision or elegance.

What follows in brief is the idea, or rather, the novel theory, such as it was when it obtained in Don Fadrique's mind.

The philosopher from Villabermeja understood that there was an eternal, providential law for the sweep of human history, as indefectible as the mathematical laws, in accordance with which heavenly bodies revolve in their orbits. By virtue of this law, humanity progressed evermore along a path of indefinite perfectibility, its ascent toward light, goodness, truth, and beauty exhibiting neither interruption nor conclusion. In this, humankind as a whole followed a necessary impulse. All the glory of the outcome was for the Supreme Being, who had provided that impulse, but within the providential movement from which it sprang, in every action, in every idea, in every intention, each individual was free and responsible. The marvelous work of Providence, the most beautiful mystery of its infinite wisdom, consisted in reconciling with judicious harmony all those results of human liberty, so that they might come together in fulfillment of the eternal law of progress, or in having foreseen them with such prescience and good judgment that they would not disturb what was prescribed and ordained, just as, although the comparison may be inadequate, the inventor and expert builder of a machine makes allowances for the wear and tear of friction and the environment.

Such a way of regarding events harmonized with Don Fadrique's character, affirming his disdain for minutiae, and his desire to characterize as minutiae what for most men is important in the highest degree, and transforming his propensity to cheerfulness and laughter into Olympian serenity, worthy of immortals.

En su moral no dejaba de ser severo. No había borrado de sus tablas de la ley ni una tilde ni una coma de los mandamientos divinos. Lo único que hacía era dar más vigor, si cabe, a toda prohibición de actos que produzcan dolor, y relajar no poco las prohibiciones de todo aquello que a él se le antojaba que sólo traía deleite o bienestar consigo.

En aquella edad, pensar así en España y en sus dominios ya hemos dicho que era expuesto; pero don Fadrique tenía el don de la mesura y del tino, y sin hipocresía lograba no chocar ni lastimar opiniones o creencias.

Concurría a esto la buena gracia con que se ganaba las voluntades, no con inspirar trivial afecto a todo el mundo, sino inspirándole muy vivo a los pocos que él quería, los cuales valían siempre por muchos para defenderle y encomiarle.

En la primera mocedad, dotado don Fadrique de tales prendas, y siendo además bello y agraciado de rostro, de buen talle, atrevido y sigiloso, consiguió que lloviesen sobre él las aventuras galantes, y tuvo alta fama de afortunado en amores.

Después de terminada la rebelión de Tupac-Amaru ascendió a capitán de fragata, y su reputación de buen soldado y de sabio y hábil marino llegó a su colmo.

Casi cuando acababan de expirar en el Cuzco los últimos indios parciales de la independencia de su patria, siendo atenaceados algunos con tenazas candentes antes de ahorcarlos, llegó la nueva a Lima de que habíamos hecho la paz con Inglaterra, logrando la independencia de su colonia, en pro de la cual combatimos.

Don Fadrique pudo entonces obtener licencia para navegar a las órdenes de la Compañía de Filipinas, y salió para Calcuta mandando un navío cargado de preciosas mercaderías. Tres viajes hizo de Lima a Calcuta y de Calcuta a Lima, y como llevaba muy buena pacotilla y un sueldo crecido, y alcanzó ventas muy ventajosas, se halló en poco tiempo poseedor de algunos millones de reales.

En las largas temporadas que don Fadrique pasó en la India, se aficionó mucho a la dulzura de los indígenas de aquel país, y tomó en mayor aborrecimiento el fervor religioso y guerrero de otras naciones. Tippoo, sultán de Misor, se había empeñado en convertir al islamismo

In his morals he continued to be severe. He had not erased a dotted i nor a crossed t of the divine commandments from his tables of the law. The only thing he did was bring more energy, if possible, to the complete ban on acts that produce pain, and to relax in no small measure the bans on all undertakings or wishes that in his mind brought with them only pleasure or well-being.

As we have already said, to think that way in Spain and its dominions at that time was dangerous, but Don Fadrique had the gift of restraint and tact, and without hypocrisy he managed not to clash with nor to offend opinions and beliefs.

What contributed to this was his easy manner in winning people over, not by inspiring superficial affection in everybody, but by inspiring very strong feelings in the few whom he loved, who were always the equivalent of many when it came to defending him and singing his praises.

Endowed as he was with such qualities, and furthermore being bold, discreet, and handsome, and possessed of a comely face as well as a good figure, in his young days Don Fadrique enjoyed one chivalrous adventure after another, and had a well-deserved reputation for success in love affairs.

After the rebellion of Tupac Amaru was put down, he rose to the rank of frigate captain, and his fame as a good soldier and a wise and able naval officer reached its zenith.

Almost at the same time that the last Indian supporters of the independence of their homeland were dying in Cuzco, some of them having their flesh torn with white-hot pincers before being hanged, news reached Lima that we had made peace with England, thereby obtaining the independence of its colony, on behalf of which we had fought.[34]

Don Fadrique was then able to gain permission to sail under the orders of the Philippines Company, and he left for Calcutta in command of a ship loaded with valuable goods. He made three voyages from Lima to Calcutta and from Calcutta to Lima, and since he was making a nice profit together with a higher salary and profitable sales, in a short time he found himself the possessor of a few million *reales*.[35]

During the long periods that Don Fadrique spent in India he took a liking to the gentleness of the natives of that country and developed a greater abhorrence for the martial and religious fervor of other nations. Tippoo,[36] the sultan of Mysore, had been bent on converting all

a todos los indostaníes y en dilatar su imperio hasta el Cabo Comorín, a donde nunca habían penetrado las huestes de otros conquistadores musulmanes. La horrible devastación del floreciente reino de Travancor, en las barbas de los ingleses, fue la consecuencia de la ambición y del celo muslímico del sultán mencionado. El gobernador general de la India se resolvió al cabo a vengar y a remediar lo que hubiera debido impedir, y partió de Calcuta a Madrás con muchos soldados europeos y cipayos, y grandes aprestos de guerra. En aquella ocasión don Fadrique tuvo el gusto de ganar bastantes rupias, sirviendo una buena causa y conduciendo a Madrás en su navío, con la autorización debida, tropas, víveres y municiones.

Parece que poco tiempo después de este suceso, y aun antes de que el rajah de Travancor fuese restablecido en su trono, y el sultán Tippoo vencido y obligado a hacer la paz, don Fadrique, cansado ya de peregrinaciones y trabajos, con la ambición apagada y con el deseo de fortuna más que satisfecho, logró, de vuelta a Lima, obtener su retiro, y se vino a Europa, anhelante de presenciar la gran revolución que en Francia se estaba realizando, cuyos principios se hallaban tan en concordancia con los suyos, y cuya fama llenaba el mundo de asombro.

Don Fadrique, sin embargo, sólo estuvo en París algunos meses: desde fines de 1791 hasta septiembre de 1792. Este tiempo le bastó para cansarse y hartarse de la gran revolución, desengañarse un poco de su liberalismo y dudar de sus teorías de constante progreso.

En Madrid vivió, por último, dos años, y también se desengañó de muchísimas cosas.

Entrado ya en los cincuenta de su edad, aunque sano y bueno, y apareciendo en el semblante, en la robustez y gallardía del cuerpo, y en la serenidad y viveza del espíritu mucho más joven, le entró la nostalgia de que padecen casi todos los bermejinos, y tomó la irrevocable resolución de retirarse a Villabermeja para acabar allí tranquilamente su vida.

Las cartas que escribió a su hermano don José y a la chacha Ramoncica, que vivían aún, anunciándoles su vuelta definitiva y para siempre, fueron breves, aunque muy cariñosas. En cambio, escribió al padre Jacinto una extensa carta, que se conserva aún y que debe ser trasladada a este sitio. La carta es como sigue:

Hindustanis to Islam and extending his empire as far as Cape Comorin, where the armies of other Muslim conquerors had never penetrated. The horrible devastation of the flourishing kingdom of Travancore, right under the very noses of the English, was the consequence of the ambition and Muslim zeal of the aforementioned sultan. The Governor General of India finally resolved to avenge and remedy what he should have prevented, and he set out from Calcutta to Madras with a large contingent of sepoy and European soldiers ánd stocks of war matériel. On that occasion Don Fadrique had the pleasure of earning quite a few rupees, serving a good cause, and, with the necessary authorization, transporting troops, stores, and munitions.

It seems that shortly after these doings, and even before the rajah of Travancore was restored to his throne and sultan Tippoo vanquished and obliged to make peace, Don Fadrique – tired of travels and hardships, his ambition slaked and his desire for fortune more than satisfied – managed to secure his retirement upon his return to Lima. He then came back to Europe, eager to witness the great revolution that was unfolding in France, a revolution whose principles were so in accord with his, and whose fame held the world in thrall.

Nonetheless, Don Fadrique was in Paris only a few months, from the end of 1791 to September of 1792. This sojourn sufficed to tire him and give him his fill of the great revolution, to disillusion him a little with his liberalism, and cause him to doubt his theories of constant progress.

Lastly, he lived in Madrid for two years, and also became disenchanted with many, many things in our capital city.

In his fifties now, although hale and hearty, and looking much younger in facial appearance, in his vigorous and dashing figure, and in the serenity and liveliness of his spirit, Don Fadrique experienced the homesickness that nearly all Villabermejans suffer, and took the irrevocable decision of retiring to Villabermeja to end his days there in peace.

The letters that he wrote to his brother Don José and to Chacha Ramoncica, who were still alive, announcing his definitive return, to stay for good, were brief although very affectionate. On the other hand, he wrote a lengthy one to Father Jacinto, which has been preserved and which ought to be transcribed here. The letter reads as follows:

5

Mi querido padre Jacinto: Ya sabrá usted por mi hermano y por la chacha Ramoncica que estoy decidido a irme a ese lugar a acabar mi vida, donde pasé los mejores años y los más inocentes de ella (¡buena inocencia era la mía!), jugando al hoyuelo, a las chapas, al salto de la comba y algunas veces al cané, y andando a pedradas y a mojicones con mis coetáneos y compatricios.

Entonces estaba yo cerril; pero ya usted se hará cargo de que me he pulido bastante peregrinando por esos mundos, y de que ahora son otras mis aficiones y muy diversos mis cuidados. Los frailes compañeros de usted no tendrán ya necesidad de amenazarme con los Toribios.

Mi estancia en el lugar no traerá perturbación alguna; antes por el contrario, yo me lisonjeo de que reporte algunas ventajas. He hecho dinero y emplearé ahí mucha parte en fomentar la agricultura. El vino que ahí se produce es abominable y puede ser excelente. Trabajando se logrará hacerle potable y bueno.

Soñando estoy con las agradables veladas que vamos a pasar en el invierno, jugando a la malilla y al tute, disputando sobre nuestras no muy acordes teologías, y refiriendo yo a usted mis aventuras en el Perú, en la India y en otras apartadas regiones.

Sé que usted, a pesar de los años, está firme como un roble, por lo cual me prometo que ha de dar conmigo largos paseos a caballo y a pie, y ha de acompañarme a cazar perdices. Tengo dos magníficas escopetas inglesas, que compré en Calcuta, y con las cuales he cazado tigres, tan grandes algunos de ellos como borricos. Ya verá usted qué bien le va tirando con cualquiera de estas escopetas a las pacíficas y enamoradas perdices que acuden al reclamo en la estación del celo.

A pesar de nuestra edad, hemos de emplearnos todavía, si usted no se opone, en algunas cosas harto infantiles. Hemos de volver al Pozo de la Solana, como hace cuarenta años, a cazar colorines y otros pajarillos, ya con la red, ya con liga y esparto. Téngame usted preparado un buen par de cimbeles.

Todas las cosas de por ahí se me ofrecen a la memoria con el encanto de los primeros años. Entiendo que voy a remozarme al verlas y gozarlas.

5

My dear Father Jacinto:
I expect that you already know from my brother and from Chacha Ramoncica that I have decided to return home and end my days where I spent the best and most innocent years of my life (A fine innocence was mine!) pitching pennies or shooting marbles, tossing coins, skipping rope, and sometimes playing cards, and having stone fights and fistfights with my contemporaries and compatriots.

I was rough around the edges back then, but you'll understand that I have acquired some polish by traveling the world and that now my pursuits and my concerns are very different. Your friar comrades will no longer need to threaten me with the Toribios.

My presence in the town will not create a disturbance of any sort; on the contrary, I flatter myself to think that it will bring some advantages. I've made money and will use a substantial part of it to promote agriculture there. The wine that Villabermeja produces is abominable and could be excellent. With effort and industry we'll make it drinkable and good.

I'm dreaming of the pleasant evening socials that we are going to enjoy in the winter, playing *malilla*[37] and *tute*,[38] arguing over theology where we don't see eye to eye, and with me relating to you my adventures in Peru, India, and other distant countries.

I know that despite your age you are as solid as an oak tree, for which reason I expect you to take long horseback rides and walks with me, and to also go partridge hunting with me. I own two magnificent English shotguns that I bought in Calcutta, and with which I've hunted tigers, some of them as big as donkeys. You'll see how well you'll be able to shoot, with either of these shotguns, at the peaceable and lovesick partridges that come to the decoy during the mating season.

Despite our age, we'll still have it in us, if you don't object, to do a few rather childish things. We shall go to Solana Well, as we did forty years ago, to catch goldfinches and other small birds, either with a net or with birdlime and esparto. Get me a good pair of those lures that are tied to a stick with rope.

All sorts of things there are stirring in my memory with the enchantment of youth. I think I'm going to be rejuvenated on seeing them and enjoying them. I feel like eating many of our foods again, foods like

Tengo gana de volver a comer piñonate, salmorejo, hojuelas, gajorros, pestiños, cordero en caldereta, cabrito en cochifrito, empanadas de boquerones con chocolate, torta-maimón, gazpacho, longanizas y los demás primores de cocina y repostería con que suelen regalarse los sibaritas bermejinos. No por eso romperé con la costumbre contraída en otras tierras, sino que pienso llevar en mi compañía a un gabacho que he traído de París, el cual condimenta unos manjares que doy por cierto que han de gustar a usted, aunque tienen nombres imposibles casi de pronunciar por una boca de Villabermeja; pero ya usted se convencerá de que, sin pronunciarlos, los mastica, los saborea, se los traga y le saben a gloria.

Por más extraño que a usted le parezca, llevo también vino a esa tierra del vino. Yo recuerdo que usted era un excelente catador; que usted tenía un paladar muy fino y una nariz delicadísima. Espero, pues, que ha de comprender y estimar el mérito de los vinos de *extranjis* que yo lleve, y que no caerán en su estómago como si cayesen en el sumidero.

Estoy muy contento de que viva aún la chacha Ramoncica. Me han dicho que en su casa sigue todo como antes. Los mismos muebles, la misma criada Rafaela, y hasta el grajo, bien sea el mismo también, que por milagro de nuestro Santo Patrono vive aún, o bien sea otro que le reemplazó a tiempo, y parece el fénix renacido en sus cenizas.

Mucha gana tengo de dar un abrazo a la chacha Ramoncica, aunque, dicho sea entre nosotros, yo quería más a la pobre chacha Victoria. ¡Qué noble mujer aquella! Aseguro a usted que no he hallado igual mujer en el mundo. Si la hubiera hallado, no sería solterón.

En este punto he sido poco feliz. No he hallado más que mujeres ligeras, casquivanas, frívolas y sin alma. Una sola, allá en Lima, me quiso de veras: con amor fervoroso, pero criminal. Yo también la quise, por mi desgracia, porque tenía un genio de todos los diablos, y queriéndonos mucho, la historia de nuestros amores se compuso de una serie de peloteras diarias. Aquellos amores fueron pesadilla y no deleite. Ella era muy devota, había sido una santa y seguía en opinión de tal, porque procedimos siempre con cautela y recato. Sin embargo, en el fondo de su atribulada conciencia, en lo profundo de su mente, orgullosa y fanática a la vez, sentía vergüenza de haber humillado ante mí su soberbia y de haberse rendido a mi voluntad, y tenía miedo y horror de

candied pine nuts, *salmorejo*,[39] *gajorros*,[40] *pestiños*,[41] puff pastries, lamb stew, fricassee of kid, anchovy empanadas with chocolate, marzipan, gazpacho, pork sausages, and other culinary delights and confectionaries with which Villabermejan sybarites usually indulge themselves. Not for this reason, though, am I going to break with customs I've acquired in other lands, which means that I intend to bring along a Frenchy who has come with me from Paris. He whips up some dishes that I am certain you will like, although they have names that are almost impossible for a Villabermejan mouth to pronounce, but you'll soon be convinced that, without being able to pronounce them, you'll chew them, savor them, swallow them, and find that they taste heavenly.

For as strange as it may seem to you, I shall also bring some wine to that land of wine. I recall that you were an excellent judge of taste, that you had a fine palate and a keen sense of smell. So I hope you can understand and do justice to the foreign wines that I bring, and that they won't enter your digestive system as if they entered the sewer.

I am very pleased that Chacha Ramoncica is still alive. I've been told that everything in her house is the same as it always was. The same furniture, the same servant in Rafaela, and even the rook, be it the same one too, that through a miracle worked by our patron saint is still alive, or be it another one that replaced it in time and seems like the phoenix rising from the ashes.

I am very anxious to embrace Chacha Ramoncica, although, entre nous, I felt closer to poor Chacha Victoria. What a noble woman that one was! I assure you that I've not met her equal in the world, for if I had, I would not be a confirmed bachelor.

In this regard I've not been very fortunate. I have met only superficial, frivolous, scatterbrained, and heartless women. Just one, back in Lima, truly loved me. With a passionate, but criminal love. I also loved her, to my regret, because she had a devil of a temper, and even caring for each other deeply, our love affair developed into a series of rows. And that love turned into a nightmare, not a delight. She was very devout, and had been a saint and continued to be seen as one, because we always conducted ourselves with caution and circumspection. However, in the depths of her troubled conscience, in the recesses of her mind, which was at once haughty and fanatical, she felt shame at having humbled her pride before me and at having submitted to my will, and she lived in fear and horror at having deviated on my account from the straight

haber dejado por mí el buen camino, ofendiendo a Dios y faltando a sus deberes. Todo esto, sin darse ella mucha cuenta de que lo hacía, me lo quería hacer pagar, considerándome en extremo culpado. Lo que yo tuve que aguantar no tiene nombre. Créame usted, padre Jacinto, en el pecado llevé la penitencia. Así es que me harté de amores serios para años, y me dediqué desde entonces a los ligeros. ¿Para qué atormentarse en un asunto que debe ser todo de amenidad, regocijo y alegría?

Quizás por esta razón, y no porque apenas se dé *in rerum natura,* no alcancé nunca el amor de una chacha Victoria joven. Si le hubiera alcanzado, poco tierno soy de corazón, pero, no lo dude usted, hubiera muerto bendiciéndola, como murió el cadete, o hubiera conquistado por ella y para ella, no el grado de capitán, sino el mundo.

En fin, ya pasó la mocedad, y no hay que pensar en novelerías.

Yo estoy desengañado y aburrido, si bien con desengaño apacible y suave aburrimiento.

Se me acabó la ambición; no siento apetito de gloria; no aspiro a ser del vano dedo señalado; tengo más bienes de fortuna de los que necesito; estoy sediento de reposo, de oscuridad y de calma, y por todo esto me retiro a Villabermeja; pero no para hacer penitencia, sino para darme una vida regalada, tranquila, llena de orden y bienestar, cuidándome mucho y viendo lo que dura un comendador Mendoza bien conservado. Hasta ahora lo estoy. No parece que tengo cincuenta años, sino menos de cuarenta. Ni una cana. Ni una arruga. Todavía me llaman señorito, y no señor, y no faltan hembras de garbo que me califiquen de real mozo ofendiendo mi modestia.

Mi mayor desengaño ha sido el de mis ideas y doctrinas, si bien no ha sido bastante para hacerme variar.

Dios me perdone, si me equivoco a fuerza de creerle bueno. Yo, creyendo en él y figurándomele como persona, tengo que figurármele todo lo bueno que concibo que una persona puede ser. Por consiguiente, no completando mi concepto de su bondad la gloria de la otra vida por inmensa que sea, supongo en esta vida que vivimos, por más que sirva para ganar la otra, un fin y un propósito en sí, y no sólo el ultramundano. Este fin, este propósito es ir caminando hacia la perfección y sin alcanzarla aquí nunca, acercarse cada vez más a ella. Creo, pues, en el progreso;

and narrow, offending God and shirking her duties. Without being too aware of what she was doing, she wanted to make me pay for all this, figuring that I was blameworthy in the extreme. What I had to put up with cannot be described. Believe me, Father Jacinto, every sin carries its own punishment. So I had my fill of serious love affairs for years, and since then I have devoted myself to casual ones. What's the use of agonizing over a matter that should be nothing but amenity, delight, and joy?

Perhaps for this reason, and not because it scarcely occurs in *rerum natura*, I never did experience the love of a young Chacha Victoria. I am not very tender-hearted, but if I had experienced it, have no doubt that I would have died blessing her, as did the cadet, or because of her and for her I would have conquered not the rank of captain, but the world.

In short, my youth has passed and there is no point in dwelling on novelesque fantasies.

I am disillusioned and bored, although the disillusionment is gentle and the boredom mild.

Ambition has ended for me; I have no desire for glory; I do not aspire to call vain attention to myself; I have more material goods than I need; I am eager for calm, for obscurity, and for repose, and for all these reasons I am retiring to Villabermeja. Although not to do penance, but to lead a tranquil, pleasant life, one of order and well-being, taking good care of myself and seeing how long a well-preserved Commander Mendoza can last. Up till now I have been in good health. I don't look fifty, not even forty, for that matter. Not one gray hair. Not one wrinkle. I'm still called *Señorito*, not *Señor*,[42] and there is no lack of glamorous women who say I am a fine figure of a man, thus offending my modesty.

My greatest disillusionment has been in my ideas and principles, although not so great that it has caused me to change them.

God forgive me if I am mistaken because I believe him to be good. Believing in him and seeing him in my mind's eye as a person, I have to see him as possessed of all the goodness that I can expect a person to have. Consequently, while the glory of another life, great though it may be, does not complete my concept of his goodness, I presume in this earthly life that we live – for as much as it may serve to gain another – an end and a purpose in and of themselves, and not only their ultramundane ones. This end, this purpose is to continue along the road to perfection, and without ever reaching it here, to come as close to it as possible. I believe, then, in progress, that is, in the constant, gradual

esto es, en la mejora gradual y constante de la sociedad y del individuo, así en lo material como en lo moral, y así en la ciencia especulativa como en la que nace de la observación y la experiencia y da ser a las artes y a la industria.

El mejor medio de este progreso, y al mismo tiempo su mejor resultado en nuestros días, es, a mi ver, la libertad. La condición más esencial de esta libertad es que todos seamos igualmente libres.

Figúrese usted cuánto me encantaría la revolución francesa y su Asamblea Constituyente, que propendía a realizar estos principios míos: que proclamaba los derechos del hombre.

Pedí mi retiro, dejé mi carrera y vine lleno de impaciencia desde el otro hemisferio a bañarme en la luz inmortal de la gran revolución y a encender mi entusiasmo en el sagrado fuego que ardía en París, donde imaginé que estaban el corazón y la mente del mundo.

Pronto se desvanecieron mis ilusiones. Los apóstoles de la nueva ley me parecieron, en su mayor parte, bribones infames o frenéticos furiosos, llenos de envidia y sedientos de sangre. Vi al talento, a la virtud, a la belleza, al saber, a la elegancia, a todo lo que por algo sobresale en la tierra, ser víctima de aquellos fanáticos o de aquellos envidiosos. Las hazañas de los soldados de la revolución contra los reyes de Europa coligados no podían admirarme. No me parecían la defensa serena del que confía en su valor y en su derecho, sino el brío febril de la locura, excitada por la embriaguez de la sangre y por medio de asesinatos horribles. París se me antojaba el infierno, y no atino ahora a comprender cómo permanecí tanto tiempo en él. Todo estaba trocado: la brutalidad se llama energía; sencillez, el desaliño indecente; franqueza la grosería, y virtud el no tener entrañas para la compasión. Recordaba yo las épocas de mayor tiranía, y no hallaba época alguna peor, sobre todo si se considera que estábamos en el centro de Europa y que llevábamos tantos siglos de civilización y cultura. El tirano no era uno, eran varios, y todos soeces y sucios de alma y de cuerpo.

Huí de París y vine a Madrid. Otra desilusión. Si por allá creí presenciar una abominable y bárbara tragedia, aquí me encontré en un grotesco, asqueroso y lascivo sainete. Por allá sangre; por acá inmundicia.

No por eso apostaté de mi optimismo ni eché a un lado mi doctrina de

improvement of society and of the individual, in physical as well as in moral considerations, and in speculative knowledge as well as in the knowledge that springs from observation and experience, and gives rise to arts and industry.

The best means to achieve this progress, and at the same time its best result nowadays, is, in my view, freedom. The chief requirement of this freedom is that we all be *equally* free.

Imagine how delighted I was with the French revolution and its Constituent Assembly, which tended to make a reality of these principles of mine, which proclaimed the rights of man.

I put in for my retirement, I gave up my career, and I came, brimming over with impatience, from the other hemisphere to immerse myself in the immortal light of the great revolution and to kindle my enthusiasm in the sacred fire that was burning in Paris, where I imagined the world's heart and mind to be.

My illusions soon vanished. The apostles of the new rule struck me, in the main, as infamous rascals or raging demagogues, filled with envy and thirsty for blood. I saw talent, virtue, beauty, knowledge, elegance, and everything that stands out for some reason on Earth, fall victim to those fanatics or those envious miscreants. The exploits of the soldiers of the revolution against the allied kings of Europe could not excite my imagination. They did not seem to me the serene defense of the person who trusts in their bravery and in their rectitude, but rather the feverish spirit of madness, brought on by the intoxication of blood and by means of horrible assassinations. I thought Paris an inferno and fail to understand now why I stayed there so long. Everything was topsy-turvy: brutality was called energy; indecent slovenliness, simplicity; rudeness, frankness; and hardheartedness, virtue. I called to mind the ages of maximum tyranny and could not single out a time that was worse, especially if one considers that we were in the center of Europe and that we had a history of so many centuries of civilization and culture. There was not one tyrant; there were a number of tyrants, and all of them were foul and filthy in body and in soul.

I fled from Paris and came to Madrid. Another disenchantment. If in the City of Lights I thought I had witnessed an abominable and barbarous tragedy, here I found myself in a grotesque, repugnant, and lascivious farce. Blood there; squalor here.

Not for that reason did I commit apostasy, abandoning my optimism

indefinido progreso. Lo que hice fue reconocer mi error en cálculos de cronología, para los cuales no había contado yo con la feroz y desgreñada revolución de Francia.

En vista de esta revolución, el bien relativo, el estado de libertad y de adelantamiento para las sociedades, que yo fantaseaba como inmediato, se hundió hacia adentro, en los abismos del porvenir, lo menos dos o tres siglos.

Como para entonces no viviré yo, y como en el estado presente del mundo estoy ya harto de la vida práctica, he resuelto refugiarme en la contemplación; y a fin de gozar del espectáculo de las cosas humanas, mezclándome en ellas lo menos posible, voy a tomar asiento, como espectador desapasionado, en la propia Villabermeja.

Mi hermano, que tiene ya una hija casadera, a quien naturalmente desea que salte un buen novio, se va a vivir a la vecina ciudad, donde ya tiene casa tomada, y a mí me deja a mis anchas y solo en la casa solariega de los Mendoza, donde le daré albergue siempre que venga al lugar para sus negocios.

Yo me atengo al refrán que dice *o corte o cortijo;* y ya que me fugo de París y de Madrid, no quiero ciudad de provincia, sino aldea.

En la gran casa de los Mendoza bermejinos voy a estar como garbanzo en olla; pero se llenarán algunos cuartos con la multitud de libros que voy a llevar.

Vamos a tener una vida envidiable; y digo *vamos,* porque supongo y espero que usted me hará compañía a menudo.

Mi determinación es irrevocable, y me voy ahí, para no salir de ahí, salvo cuando vaya, como de paseo a caballo, a visitar a mi hermano y a su familia, en la ciudad cercana, la cual, a pesar de su pomposo título de ciudad, tiene también mucho de pueblo pequeño y rural, con perdón y en paz sea dicho.

Adiós, beatísimo padre. Encomiéndeme usted a Dios, con cuyo favor cuento para escapar de esta confusión ridícula de la corte, y poder pronto darle, en esa encantadora Villabermeja, un apretado abrazo.

and casting aside my doctrine of indefinite progress. What I did was recognize my error in calculations of chronology, for which I had not taken into account the ferocious and chaotic revolution in France.

As a result of this revolution, the relative good, the state of *liberté* and advancement for societies, which I fantasized as being immediate, sank inward, into the abysses of the future, for at least two or three centuries.

Since I won't be alive then, and since I am fed up with practical life in the present state of the world, I have resolved to take refuge in meditation, and so as to enjoy the spectacle of human affairs, involving myself in them as little as possible, I am going to take up residence, as a dispassionate spectator, right in Villabermeja.

My brother, who now has a marriageable daughter, for whom he very naturally hopes that a good husband will be found, is going off to live in the neighboring city, where he has already set up house, and is leaving me alone to do as I please in the Mendozas' ancestral home, where I shall always provide lodging for him whenever he comes to town on business.

I abide by the proverb that says, "Either live in the capital or in the country," and inasmuch as I am fleeing from Paris and from Madrid, I do not want a provincial city, but a village.

In the great house of the Villabermejan Mendozas I'm going to be like a duck in water,[43] but some rooms will fill up with the multitude of books that I'll bring with me.

We are going to live an enviable life, and I say "We" because I expect and hope that you will keep me company often.

My decision is irrevocable, and I'm going there, and will not leave there, except when I go horseback riding or visit my brother and his family in the neighboring city, which, in spite of its pompous title of city, also has much of a small country town about it, no offense intended or implied.

Good-bye, my saintly Father Jacinto. Commend me to God, on whose favor I rely in order to escape from this ridiculous confusion in the capital and to be able to give you soon, in that delightful Villabermeja, a big hug.

6

Veinte días después de recibida esta carta por el padre Jacinto, se realizó la entrada solemne en Villabermeja del ilustre comendador Mendoza.

Desde Madrid a la capital de la provincia, que entonces se llamaba reino, nuestro héroe vino en coche de colleras y empleó nueve días. En la capital de la provincia se encontró con su hermano don José, con el padre Jacinto y con otros amigos de la infancia, que le estaban aguardando. Entre ellos sobresalía el tío Gorico, maestro pellejero, hábil fabricador de corambres y notabilísimo en el difícil arte de echar botanas a los pellejos rotos. Éste había sido el muchacho más diabólico del lugar después de don Fadrique, y su teniente cuando las pendencias, pedreas y demás hazañas contra el bando de don Casimiro.

El tío Gorico no tenía más defecto que el de haberse entregado con sobrado cariño a la bebida blanca. El aguardiente anisado le encantaba. Y como al asomar la aurora por el estrecho horizonte de Villabermeja, el tío Gorico, según su expresión, mataba el gusanillo, resultaba que casi todo el día estaba calamocano, porque aquel fuego que encendía en su ser, con el primer fulgor matutino, se iba alimentando durante el día, merced a frecuentes libaciones.

Por lo demás, el tío Gorico no perdía nunca la razón; lo que lograba era envolver aquella luz del cielo en una gasa tenue, en un fanal primoroso, que le hacía ver las cosa del mundo exterior y todo lo interno de su alma y los tesoros de su memoria como al través de un vidrio mágico. Jamás llegaba a la embriaguez completa; y una vez sola, decía él, había tenido en toda su vida alferecía en las piernas. Era, pues, hombre de chispa en diversos sentidos, y nadie tenía mejores ocurrencias, ni contaba más picantes chascarrillos, ni se mostraba más útil y agradable compañero en una partida de caza.

En el lugar gozaba de celebridad envidiable por mil motivos, y, entre otros, porque hacía el papel de Abraham en el paso del Jueves Santo por la mañana tan admirablemente bien, que nadie se le igualaba en muchas leguas a la redonda. Con un vestido de mujer por túnica, una colcha de cama por manto, su turbante y sus barbas de lino, tomaba un aspecto venerable. Y cuando subía al monte Moria, que era un tablado cubierto de verdura, que se elevaba en medio de la plaza, adquiría la majestad patética de un buen actor. Pero en lo que más se lucía, arrancando

6

Twenty days after Father Jacinto received this letter, the illustrious Commander Mendoza made his solemn entry into Villabermeja.

From Madrid to the capital of the province, which back then was called a kingdom, our hero journeyed in a mule-drawn coach and took nine days. In the capital of the province he met up with his brother Don José, with Father Jacinto, and with other childhood friends, who were there waiting for him. One who stood out among them was Tío Gorico,[44] a master leather dresser, skillful worker with skins, and highly proficient in the difficult art of patching torn wineskins. He had been the rowdiest boy in town after Don Fadrique, and his lieutenant in the quarrels, stone fights, and other encounters with Don Casimiro's band.

Tío Gorico had only one fault: an excessive fondness for white alcoholic drinks, spirits, in a word. He especially loved aniseed-flavored brandy. And as the early light of dawn would streak over the narrow horizon of Villabermeja, Tío Gorico was already, in his expression, "taking his first nip of the morning," and it would result in the fact that he was tipsy nearly the whole day, because the fire that he lit inside him with that first sunbeam was fed throughout the day thanks to frequent libations.

As for the effects of his imbibing, Tío Gorico never took leave of his senses. What happened was that he would envelop that light from heaven in a fine gauze, in an exquisite beacon, that made him see the things of the exterior world and the entire inside of his soul, together with the treasures of his memory, as if through a magic glass. Never did he become completely inebriated, and he said that only once in his life had he had tremors in his legs. He was a lively sort in a number of respects, and nobody came out with wittier remarks, nor told more risqué stories, nor was a more useful and agreeable companion in a hunting party.

In the town he enjoyed enviable celebrity for a thousand different reasons, amongst others because he played the role of Abraham so admirably well on the float on Holy Thursday morning that nobody was his equal for many miles around. With a woman's dress for a tunic, a bedspread for a cloak, his linen turban and beard, he took on a venerable appearance. And when he climbed Mount Moriah, which was a greenery-covered stall erected in the middle of the square, he exuded the poignant majesty of a good actor. But the point at which he would be brilliant,

gritos de entusiasmo, era cuando ofrecía a Isaac al Todopoderoso antes
de sacrificarle. Isaac era un chiquillo de diez años lo menos. Con la
mano derecha el tío Gorico le levantaba hacia el cielo, y así, extendido
el brazo, como si no fuera de hueso y carne, sino de acero firmísimo,
permanecía catorce o quince minutos. Luego venía el momento de las
más firmes emociones: el terror trágico en toda su fuerza. Abraham ataba
al chiquillo al ara, y sacaba un truculento chafarote que llevaba al cinto.
Tres o cuatro veces descargaba cuchilladas con una violencia increíble.
Las mujeres se tapaban los ojos y daban espantosos chillidos, creyendo
ya segada la garganta del muchacho que prefiguraba a Cristo; pero el tío
Gorico paraba el golpe antes de herir, como no atreviéndose a consumar
el sacrificio. Al fin aparecía un ángel, con las alas de papel dorado, en el
balcón de las Casas Consistoriales, y cantaba el romance que empieza:

> Detente, detente, Abraham;
> no mates a tu hijo Isaac,
> que ya está Dios contento
> con tu buena voluntad.

El sacrificio del cordero en vez del hijo, con lo demás del paso, lo
ejecutaba el tío Gorico con no menos maestría.

En más de una ocasión trataron de ganarle, ofreciéndole mucho dinero
para que fuese a hacer de Abraham a otras poblaciones; pero él no quiso
jamás ser infiel a su patria y privarla de aquella gloria.

Don José, el padre Jacinto, el tío Gorico y los demás amigos, muy
contentos de haber abrazado a don Fadrique, contentísimo también de
verse entre los compañeros de su infancia, emprendieron a caballo el
viaje a Villabermeja, que con madrugar y picar mucho pudo hacerse en
diez horas, llegando todos al lugar al anochecer de un hermoso día de
primavera, en el año de 1794.

Doña Antonia, mujer de don José, y sus dos hijos, don Francisco,
de edad de catorce años, y doña Lucía, que tenía ya diez y ocho,
acompañados de la chacha Ramoncica, recibieron con júbilo, con
abrazos y otras mil muestras de cariño al comendador, quien ya tenía
por suya la casa solariega. Don José y su familia se habían establecido
en la ciudad, y sólo por dos días habían venido al pueblo para recibir al
querido pariente.

Este, como era de suyo muy modesto, se maravilló y complació en ver

eliciting shouts of enthusiasm, was when he offered Isaac to the Almighty before sacrificing him. Isaac was a little boy at least ten years old. With his right hand Tío Gorico would raise him toward heaven, and in this attitude – his arm outstretched, as if it were not of flesh and blood, but of the hardest steel – he would hold steady for fourteen or fifteen minutes. Then would come the moment of the strongest emotions: tragic terror in full force. Abraham tied the boy to the altar and from his sash withdrew a ferocious cutlass with which he delivered three or four slashes with unbelievable violence. Women covered their eyes and emitted frightful screams, thinking that the boy who foreshadowed Christ already had his throat slit, but Tío Gorico checked the blows before striking, as if not daring to consummate the sacrifice. Finally, an angel with wings of gilded paper would appear on the balcony of the town hall and sing the ballad that begins:

> "Stop, Abraham, stop;
> Do not kill your son Isaac,
> For my God is now well pleased
> With your honest intention."

The sacrifice of the lamb in place of the son, together with the rest of the staging of the float, was executed by Tío Gorico with no less mastery.

On more than one occasion he received offers of sizable amounts of money to play Abraham in other towns, but he refused to be unfaithful to his own and deprive it of that glory.[45]

Don José, Father Jacinto, Tío Gorico, and the rest of the friends, very happy at having embraced Don Fadrique, who was himself pleased as Punch to be reunited with his childhood companions, set out on horseback for Villabermeja. By rising early and riding hard they made the journey in ten hours, reaching the town at nightfall on a beautiful spring day in the year 1794.

Doña Antonia, Don José's wife, and their two children, Don Francisco, aged fourteen, and Doña Lucía, who was already eighteen, accompanied by Chacha Ramoncica, welcomed the commander with jubilation, with embraces, and with a thousand other tokens of affection. The Mendozas' ancestral home now belonged to Don Fadrique, and Don José and his family, who had taken up residence in the city, had returned to the town only for two days in order to welcome back their dear relative.

The latter, inasmuch as he was naturally very modest, was amazed and

que alcanzaba en Villabermeja más popularidad de lo que creía. Vinieron a verle todos los frailes, desde los más encopetados hasta los legos, el médico, el boticario, el maestro de escuela, el alcalde, el escribano y mucha gente menuda.

Al día siguiente de la llegada la chacha Ramoncica quiso lucirse, y se lució, dando un magnífico *pipiripao*. Don Fadrique, cuando oyó esta palabra, tuvo que preguntar qué significaba, y le dijeron que algo a modo de festín. En cambio, se cuentan aún en Villabermeja los grandes apuros en que estuvo aquella noche la chacha Ramoncica cuando volvió a su casa, cavilando qué sería lo que su sobrino le había pedido para el festín, y que ella ansiaba que le sirviesen, a fin de darle gusto en todo. El vocablo, para ella inaudito, con que su sobrino había significado la cosa que deseaba, casi se le había borrado de la mente. Por último, consultando el caso con Rafaela, y haciendo un esfuerzo de memoria, vino a recomponer el vocablo y a declarar que lo que su sobrino había pedido era *economía*.

–¿Qué es eso, Rafaela?– preguntó a su fiel criada. Y Rafaela contestó:

–Señora, ¿qué ha de ser? *¡Ajorro!*

No le hubo, sin embargo. La chacha Ramoncica echó aquel día el bodegón por la ventana.

Al siguiente le tocó lucirse al comendador, y a pesar de toda su filosofía gozó en el alma de que sus deudos y paisanos viesen maravillados su vajilla de porcelana, su plata y los demás objetos raros y bellos que de sus viajes había traído, y que había mandado por delante de él con su criado de más confianza. Hasta la extraña fisonomía de éste, que era un indio, pasmó a los bermejinos, con deleite y satisfacción de don Fadrique. Tuvo además un placer indescriptible en contar sus aventuras y en hacer descripciones de países remotos, de costumbres peregrinas y de casos singulares que había visto o en los que había tomado parte.

Nada de esto debe movernos a rebajar el concepto que del comendador tenemos. Por más que parezca pueril, tal vanidad es más común de lo que se cree. ¿A quién no le agrada, cuando vuelve al lugar de su nacimiento, darse cierto tono, sin ofender a nadie, manifestando cuán importante papel ha hecho en el mundo?

gratified to see that he enjoyed more popularity in Villabermeja than he believed. All the friars, from the most high and mighty to the lay brothers, came to visit him, as did the doctor, the druggist, the schoolteacher, the mayor, the notary, and much of the hoi polloi.

The day following his arrival, Chacha Ramoncica wished to outdo herself, and succeeded, giving a magnificent *pipiripao*. When he heard this word, Don Fadrique had to ask what it meant, and he was told that it was a kind of feast or banquet. He then spoke a word of his own to his aunt, a word that people in Villabermeja still cite when they reminisce about Chacha Ramoncica's great perplexity upon her return home that night. It seems that she tried to remember what it was that her nephew had requested of her for the feast, because she longed to serve him and please him in everything. The word, unknown to her, with which her nephew had signified the thing that he desired, had almost been erased from her mind. Finally, consulting the question with Rafaela and struggling to remember, she managed to reconstruct the word and say that what her nephew had asked for was *economy*.

"What is that, Rafaela?" she asked her faithful servant.

And Rafaela answered:

"Señora, what can it be? *Triftiness!*"[46]

There was none, however. That day Chacha Ramoncica rolled out the red carpet for Don Fadrique.

On the next one it was the commander's turn to put on a display, and despite all his philosophy it gladdened his heart to see his relatives and fellow Villabermejans looking with wonder at his chinaware, his silverware, and the other beautiful and rare objects that he had brought from his travels, and that he had sent ahead with his most trustworthy servant. Even the strange physiognomy of the latter, who was an Indian, astounded the townspeople, to Don Fadrique's delight and satisfaction. It gave him, in addition, unwonted pleasure to relate his adventures and to give descriptions of remote countries, exotic customs, and odd occurrences that he had witnessed or in which he had taken part.

None of this should cause us to lessen the high regard in which we hold the commander. Puerile though it may seem, such vanity is more common than is thought. Who does not take pleasure, when returning to one's birthplace, in putting on some airs, without offending anybody, by demonstrating what an important role he or she has played in the world?

Gente hay que no espera para esto ir a su lugar. Nacido en uno muy pequeño de Andalucía tuve yo cierto amigo que, como llegase a ser personaje de gran suposición y de muchas campanillas, cifraba su mayor deleite en mandar a su pueblo todos los años un ejemplar de la *Guía de forasteros,* con registro en las varias páginas en que estaba estampado su nombre. Un año fue la *Guía* con ocho registros, y el pasmo de los lugareños, participado por cartas a mi amigo, le dio un contento que casi rayaba en beatitud o bienaventuranza.

No es menor el gusto que se tiene en contar lances y sucesos y en describir prodigios. De aquí sin duda el reirán: *de luengas vías, luengas mentiras.* Baste, pues, decir, en elogio de don Fadrique, que el refrán no rezó con él nunca, porque era la veracidad en persona. Lo que no aseguraremos es que fuese siempre creído en cuanto refirió. Los lugareños son maliciosos y desconfiados; suelen tener un criterio allá a su manera; y a menudo las cosas más ciertas les parecen falsas o inverosímiles, y las mentiras, por el contrario, muy conformes con la verdad. Recuerdo que un mayordomo andaluz de cierto inolvidable y discreto duque, que estuvo de embajador en Nápoles, fue a su pueblo con licencia. Cuando volvió le embromábamos suponiendo que habría contado muchos embustes. Él nos confesó que sí, y aún añadió, jactándose de ello, que todo se lo habían creído menos una cosa.

–¿Qué cosa era esa?– le preguntamos.

–Que cerca de Nápoles– respondió –, hay un monte que echa chispas por la punta.

De esta suerte pudo muy bien nuestro don Fadrique, sin apartarse un ápice de la verdad, dejar de ser creído en algo, sin que sus paisanos se atreviesen a decirle, como decían al mayordomo del duque cuando hablaba del Vesubio: «¡Esa es grilla!»

Al día tercero después de la llegada de don Fadrique, su hermano don José y su familia se volvieron a la ciudad; y entonces, con más reposo, pudo entregarse el comendador a otro placer no menos grato: el de visitar y recordar los sitios más queridos y frecuentados de su niñez, y aquellos en que le había ocurrido algo memorable. Estuvo en el Retamal y en el Llanete, que está junto, donde le descalabraron dos veces; fue a la

There are people who do not want to return to their hometowns for this. I had a friend who was born in a hamlet in Andalusia, a man who, when he rose to be a personage of considerable standing and great importance, positively delighted in sending to his small village every year a copy of the *Strangers' Guide* with a bookmark for the several pages on which his name appeared. One year the *Guide* arrived with eight bookmarks, and the awe of the townspeople, which was made known to my friend in a letter, brought him joy that very nearly verged on exalted happiness or supreme bliss.

We derive no less pleasure from relating incidents and events and from describing marvels. Hence, no doubt, the proverb: "Long travels lead to long lies." Let it suffice, then, to say in praise of Don Fadrique, that the proverb never applied to him, because he was truthfulness personified. What we cannot say with certainty is that he was always believed when he recounted his experiences. People in small towns are suspicious and distrustful; they usually have their own yardstick by which to judge things, and often the most certain ones strike them as false and improbable, and lies, on the contrary, in keeping with the truth. I remember that the Andalusian majordomo of a certain unforgettable and discreet duke, who served as ambassador to Naples,[47] once went back to his hometown on leave. When he returned we teased him about the many fibs that we figured he must have told. He confessed that he had, and even added, boasting of it, that the people had believed all of what he had told them, except one thing.

"What thing was that?" we asked him.

"That near Naples," he answered, "there is a mountain that shoots sparks from its peak."

As a result of this attitude, it may well have been that our Don Fadrique, while not departing one iota from the truth, gave rise to disbelief, even though his fellow Villabermejans did not dare to say to him, as was said to the duke's majordomo when he spoke of the volcano of Mount Vesuvius: "That's a cock-and-bull story!"

The third day after Don Fadrique's arrival, Don José and his family returned to the city, and then the commander could more leisurely give himself over to another no less agreeable pleasure: visiting and remembering the most loved and frequented sites of his childhood, as well as those in which something memorable had happened to him. He went to Broom Field and nearby Llanete, where his head was broken

fuente de Genazahar y al Pilar de Abajo: subió al Laderón y a la Nava, y extendió sus excursiones hasta el cerro de Jilena y el monte de Horquera, poblado entonces de corpulentas y seculares encinas.

Tomó, por último, don Fadrique verdadera posesión de su vivienda, arrellanándose en ella, por decirlo así, poniendo en orden los muebles que había traído, colocando los libros y colgando los cuadros.

En estas faenas, dirigidas por él, casi siempre estaba presente el padre Jacinto; y al cabo don Fadrique quedó instalado, forjándose un retiro, rústico a par de elegante, y una soledad amenísima en el lugar donde había nacido.

7

Encantado estaba don Fadríque con su modo de vivir. Ya leyendo, ya de tertulia o de paseo con el padre Jacinto, ya de expediciones campestres y venatorias con el mismo padre y con el iluminado y ameno tío Gorico, el tiempo se deslizaba del modo más grato. Ningún deseo sentía don Fadrique de ir a otro pueblo, abandonando a Villabermeja; pero don José tenía cuarto preparado para recibirle en su casa de la ciudad, y sus instancias fueron tales, que no hubo más que ceder a ellas.

El comendador fue a la ciudad a pasar todo el mes de mayo. Llegó en la tarde del último día de abril, y como el viaje es un paseo, aquella noche estuvo de tertulia hasta cerca de las once, que en 1794 era ya mucho velar. Dos o tres hidalgos; otras tantas señoras machuchas; dos jóvenes amiguitas de Lucía, sobrina de don Fadrique; un respetable señor cura y un caballerito forastero y muy elegante componían la reunión de casa de don José, que empezó antes de que anocheciera.

Nadie llamó la atención de don Fadrique, que era harto distraído. Necesitaba que las personas le gustasen o le disgustasen para fijarse en ellas, y con gran dificultad acertaba la gente a gustarle, y mucho menos a disgustarle. Así es que, mostrándose muy urbano con todos, apenas si reparó en ninguno.

Al toque de oraciones sirvieron el refresco.

twice; he went to the fountain of Genahazar and to Pilar de Abajo; he climbed up to Laderón and to La Nava, and extended his excursions as far as Jilena Hill and Mount Horquera, at the time dotted with stout, age-old holm oaks.

At length, Don Fadrique took real possession of his abode, in effect making himself completely at home, arranging the furniture he had brought, shelving the books, and hanging the pictures.

During each of these tasks, all directed by him, Father Jacinto was almost always present, and finally Don Fadrique settled in, creating for himself a retreat at once rustic and elegant, and an ever so pleasant place of solitude in the town where he had grown up.

7

Don Fadrique was delighted with his way of life. Whether it was reading or attending a *tertulia*[48] or taking a stroll with Father Jacinto or going on country and hunting excursions with the selfsame priest and with the enlightened and likable Tío Gorico, time passed in the most agreeable manner. Don Fadrique had no desire to go off to some other place, abandoning Villabermeja, but Don José had a room ready to receive him at his house in the city, and his invitations were such that Don Fadrique could no longer refuse his brother.

The commander journeyed to the city to spend the entire month of May. He arrived the afternoon of the last day of April, and as the journey was a hop, skip, and a jump, that evening he stayed at the *tertulia* until close to eleven o'clock, which in 1794 was staying up very late. Two or three noblemen, as many elderly noblewomen, two young lady friends of Lucía's (Don Fadrique's niece), a respectable priest, and a very elegant young gentleman who was a stranger in the city, made up the gathering that began before nightfall at Don José's house.

Nobody attracted the attention of Don Fadrique, whose mind was elsewhere. In order to take notice of people he needed to like them or dislike them, and liking them did not come easily to him, and disliking them even less so. Thus it was that, being very polite to everybody, he scarcely took notice of anybody.

Refreshments were served when the prayer bell sounded.

Primero pasaron dos criadas repartiendo platos, servilletas y cucharillas de plata; luego entraron otras dos criadas, que traían sendas bandejas llenas de tacillas de cristal con almíbares diferentes. Cada tertuliano fue tomando en su asiento una tacilla del almíbar que más le gustaba. Las criadas de las bandejas pasaron de nuevo recogiendo las tacillas vacías, y rogando a los señores que tomasen otra de otro almíbar, como en efecto la tomaron muchos.

La historia, prolija en este asunto, cuenta que los almíbares eran de nueces verdes, de cabellos de ángel, de tomate y de hojas de azahar. Hubo también arrope de melocotón.

Las ninfas fregonas, muy compuestas y con muchas flores en el moño, sirvieron luego copitas de rosoli, del que sólo bebieron los caballeros; y por último trajeron el chocolate con torta de bizcocho, polvorones, pan de aceite y hojaldres. Terminó todo con el agua, que en vasos de cristal y en búcaros olorosos repartieron asimismo las criadas.

Duró esto hasta que dieron las ánimas.

El refresco se tomó con toda ceremonia y con pocas palabras. Las sillas pegadas a la pared, y todos sentados sin echar una pierna sobre otra, ni inclinarse de ningún lado ni recostarse mucho.

Después de tomado el refresco hubo alguna más libertad y expansión, y Lucía se atrevió a rogar al caballerito que recitase unos versos.

–Sí, sí– dijeron a coro todos los tertulianos –; que recite.

–Recitaré algo de Meléndez– dijo el joven.

–No; de usted– replicó Lucía –. Sepa usted, tío– añadió dirigiéndose al comendador –, que este señor es muy poeta y gran estudiante. Ya verá usted qué lindos versos compone.

–Usted es muy amable, señorita doña Lucía. La amistad que me tiene la engaña. Su señor tío de usted va a salir chasqueado cuando me oiga.

–Yo confío tanto en el fino gusto de mi sobrina– dijo el comendador –, que dudo de que se equivoque, por ferviente que sea la amistad que usted le inspire. Casi estoy convencido de que los versos serán buenos.

–Vamos, recítelos usted, don Carlos.

–No sé cuáles recitar que cansen menos, y que a usted que me fía, y a mí, que soy el autor, nos dejen airosos.

–Recite usted– contestó Lucía –los últimos que ha compuesto a Clori.

First, two maids entered handing out plates, napkins, and silver teaspoons; then two other maids came in, each one carrying a salver filled with small glass cups of various syrups. Each *tertuliano*, while remaining seated, took a cup of the syrup of his or her preference. The maids with the salvers circulated again, collecting the empty cups and urging people to take one of a different syrup, as many did.

The story, prolix on this point, is that the syrups were of green walnuts, angel hair,[49] tomato, and orange blossom. There was also peach syrup.

The scullery nymphs, nicely dressed and with a profusion of flowers in their chignons, then served glasses of rosolio, which only the gentlemen drank; and lastly, they brought in chocolate with sponge cake, sugar cookies, olive-oil bread, and puff pastries. It all ended with water, in glass tumblers and in fragrant clay beakers, likewise distributed by the maids.

This lasted until the evening prayer bell pealed, the hour to pray for the souls in purgatory.

The refreshments were taken very ceremoniously and in near silence. The chairs had been positioned against the walls, and everybody sat without crossing their legs and without leaning to either side or reclining too far back.

After they had had their refreshments, there was a bit more relaxation and expansiveness, and Lucía made bold to ask the young gentleman to recite some verses.

"Yes, yes," said all the *tertulianos* in chorus. "Do recite something."

"I'll recite something by Meléndez,"[50] said the young man.

"No, your own work," rejoined Lucía. "I'll have you know, Uncle," she said, speaking to the commander, "that this gentleman is a wonderful poet and a great student. You'll soon see what lovely verses he composes."

"You are most kind, Señorita doña Lucía. But friendship blinds you. Your esteemed uncle will be disappointed when he hears me."

"I trust so highly in my niece's good taste," said the commander, "that I doubt she is mistaken, no matter how fervent the friendship you inspire in her. I am almost convinced that the verses will be good."

"Come now, Don Carlos, recite them."

"I do not know which lines to recite that will be the least tiresome, and the ones that will do both of us credit, you as the friend who vouches for them and me as the author who wrote them."

"Recite the most recent ones that you composed to Chloris,"[51] said Lucía.

–Son largos.

–No importa.

Don Carlos no se hizo más de rogar, y con entonación mesurada y cierta timidez que le hubiera hecho simpático, aunque ya por sí no lo fuese, recitó lo que sigue:

El plácido arroyuelo
rompe el lazo de hielo,
y desatado en ondas cristalinas
fecunda la pradera.
Flora presenta sus galas a Chiprina;
reluce Febo en la celeste esfera,
y en la noche callada
la casta diosa a su pastor dormido,
con trémulo fulgor, besa extasiada.
Del techo antiguo a suspender su nido
ha vuelto ya la golondrina errante;
dulces trinos difunde Filomena;
el mar se calma, el cielo se serena;
sólo Céfiro amante,
oreando la hierba en los alcores.
Y acariciando las tempranas flores,
con música y aroma el aire agita.
En la rica estación de los amores
Amor en todo corazón palpita;
pero en el alma del zagal Mirtilo
halla perpetuo asilo.
Allí ingenioso el dios labra un dechado
de gracia encantadora,
donde con el fiel esmero ha retratado
a Clori bella, a la gentil pastora,
por quien Mirtilo muere.
Clori, en tanto, amistosa y compasiva,
quiere que el zagal viva,
mas amarle no quiere;
antes, dicen, que piensa dar su mano
a un rabadán anciano.

"It's a long poem."

"That's of no importance."

Don Carlos did not have to be asked again, and with a measured intonation and a certain diffidence that would have made him appealing were he not already viewed in this light, he recited the following lines:[52]

> Breaking free of its icy lock,
> The placid brook
> Renders the meadowland fertile
> In loosened, crystalline waves.
> Flora lends her trappings to Chiprina;
> Phoebus radiates light in the celestial
> Sphere, and in the silent night
> The chaste goddess, enraptured, kisses
> Her shepherd, asleep in a tremulous splendor.
> To suspend her nest from an ancient roof
> The migratory swallow has returned anew;
> Philomela emits her sweet warbles;
> The sea has calmed, the sky has cleared;
> Only loving Zephyr,
> Refreshing the grass on the hills
> And caressing the early flowers,
> Stirs the air with music and fragrance.
> In the rich season of romantic passion
> Love throbs in every heart,
> But in the breast of the young shepherd Myrtilus
> A perpetual haven does it find.
> There the ingenious god fashions a
> Model of enchanting grace,
> Wherein with exacting care he has depicted
> The lovely Chloris, the genteel shepherdess,
> For whom Myrtilus pines away.
> Chloris, meanwhile, friendly and compassionate,
> Wants the young shepherd to live,
> But not to love him;
> Rather, it is said, she intends to give her hand
> To an aged shepherd.

Con celos el zagal su pena aumenta,
y así en la selva oculto se lamenta:
—¡tú no sabes de amor, encanto mío!,
¡ah! Tu ignorancia virginal te engaña.
Seré merecedor de tu desvío,
mas no comprendo la ilusión extraña
que a dar tanta beldad te precipita,
inútil don, tesoro inmaculado,
a la vejez marchita.
La amapola del prado
no despliega la pompa de sus hojas,
de púdico amor rojas,
hasta que el sol derrama
en su velado seno estiva llama;
ni la rosa se atreve
a abrir el cáliz entre escarcha y nieve.
No censurara yo que Calatea
al cíclope adorase: la hermosura
bien en la fuerza y el valor se emplea:
bien con estrecho, cariñoso nudo,
la hiedra ciñe firme tronco rudo.
Mas nunca a quien apenas
sostener puede el peso de la vida
a llevar sus cadenas,
si dulces, graves, el amor convida.
Huyen del mustio viejo las Camenas;
si la flauta de Pan su labio toca,
allí perece el desmayado aliento,
sin convertirse en melodioso viento,
y la risa del sátiro provoca.
Con vacilante pie mal en el coro
de ninfas entra; y el alegre giro
y canto de las Ménades sonoro,
o con flébil suspiro,
o con dolientes ayes turba acaso;
que, en el misterio de la santa orgía,
ni el hierofante el tirso le confía,
ni él llega hasta la cumbre del Parnaso.

With jealousy does the youth his anguish increase,
And secreted in the forest does he thus lament:
"You do not know about love, my cherished one!
Your virginal innocence leads you astray.
Deserving I might be of your indifference,
But I do not understand the strange illusion
That entices you to present so much beauty,
A useless gift, a pure treasure,
To old age in decline.
The poppy of the meadow
Does not display the pomp of its petals,
Red as they are with chaste love,
Until the sun spills summer's warmth
Into its veiled bosom;
Nor does the rose dare to open
Its calyx in the midst of frost and snow.
Fault I would not find that Galatea
Should adore the Cyclops: beauty is
Well served in strength and valor, as is
Well girded the ivy that clings to the
Rough trunk with a close, loving tie.
But the one who can scarcely
Bear the weight of life is
Never invited by love to
Wear its sweet yet heavy chains.
The Muses flee from the wizened old man;
If his lip does Pan's flute touch,
On it does his faint breath die
Without turning into a melodious air,
Thereby provoking the satyr's laughter.
With faltering steps he struggles to enter
The chorus of nymphs, and perhaps disturbs
The Maenads' joyful dance and sonorous
Song, either with a mournful sigh or
With sorrowful laments, for in
The mystery of the sacred orgy the
Hierophant does not present him with the thyrsus
Nor does he reach the summit of Parnassus.

¡Ay Clori! Qué demencia te extravía?
Ya que por ti se pierde
mi tierno amor, mi juventud lozana,
de frescas rosas y de mirto verde
no ciñas ora una cabeza cana.
Trepa la vid al álamo frondoso,
y a la punzante ortiga
deja que adorne el murallón ruinoso.
¿Qué riesgo, qué fatiga
no aceptará mi amor por agradarte?
Por ti en el bosque venceré las fieras;
por ti el furor arrostraré de Marte;
y el rey de las praderas,
cuya bronceada frente
arma ostenta terrible, que figura
de nueva luna el disco refulgente,
de mi garrocha dura
sentirá en la cerviz la picadura.
El rabadán por la vejez postrado
tu solícito afán reclamaría,
¡oh, Clori! Mientras yo, por tu mandato,
al abismo del mar descendería
sus perlas para ver en tu garganta,
y acosaría al lobo carnicero,
su hirsuta piel con plomo y con acero
ganando para alfombra de tu planta.
Alucinada ninfa candorosa,
desecha ese delirio que te lleva
a ser del viejo rabadán esposa.
Pues qué ¿te he dado en balde tanta prueba
de amor? Ya ves que por seguirte dejo
el templo de Minerva y los vergeles
por do Betis copioso se dilata.
De mis padres me alejo,
y huyo también de mis amigos fieles
para sufrir crueldades de una ingrata.
No estriba tu desdén en mi pobreza,
que no oculta tan bajo sentimiento

Ah, Chloris! What dementia confounds you?
Since my tender love, my robust love,
Are lost on account of you,
Do not crown a gray head with
Fresh roses and green myrtle.
The vine climbs the leafy poplar,
But let the sharp, stinging nettle
Cling to the ruinous rampart.
What risk, what fatigue,
Will my love not accept to please you?
For you shall I vanquish wild beasts in the forest,
For you shall I brave the fury of Mars;
And the king of the meadowlands,
Whose bronzed brow flaunts
A terrible weapon, like the
Refulgent disk of the new moon,
Will on his neck feel the
Prick of my tempered spear.
The old shepherd, laid low by the years,
Would demand your solicitous zeal,
Oh, Chloris!, while I, at your command,
Would descend to the bottom of the ocean
To see pearls strung around your neck, and
Would pursue the bloodthirsty wolf
Taking its hirsute skin with lead or
Steel to be a carpet for you to tread.
Deluded, innocent nymph,
Set aside the delirium that leads you
To be the wife of the old shepherd.
Ask I must: Have I given you so much proof of love
In vain? You see that for your sake I have
Left Minerva's temple and the gardens
Watered by the copious Guadalquivir River.
My parents do I leave,
And from my faithful friends do I flee
Only to suffer the cruelties of an ingrate.
Your disdain does not lie in my poverty,
For such a base feeling your noble heart

tu noble corazón, y ni en riqueza
me vence el rabadán ni en nacimiento.
Sólo un funesto error, una locura,
¡oh, Clori! ¡Oh, rosa del pensil divino!,
te hará exhalar tu aroma y tu frescura
entre las secas ramas del espino;
te hará romper el broche delicado,
no para abril, para diciembre helado.
No así me hieras, si matarme quieres;
mira que así te matas cuando hieres.

No bien terminaron los versos, fueron estrepitosamente aplaudidos por el benévolo auditorio; pero, si hemos de decir la verdad, ni don José ni doña Antonia prestaron atención durante la lectura; las señoras mayores se adormecieron con el sonsonete; el señor cura halló la composición sobrado materialista y mitológica y un poco pesada, y las amiguitas de Lucía más se entusiasmaron con la buena presencia del poeta que con el mérito literario de su obra.

Don Carlos, en efecto, era un morenito muy salado de veintidós a veintitrés años. Sus vivos y grandes ojos resplandecían con el fuego de la inspiración. Su cabellera negra, ya sin polvos, lucía y daba reflejos azulados como las alas de un cuervo. Los movimientos de su boca al hablar eran graciosos. Los dientes que dejaba ver, blancos e iguales; la nariz, recta, y la frente, despejada y serena.

Iba don Carlos vestido con suma elegancia, a la última moda de París. Era todo un petimetre. Parecía el príncipe de la juventud dorada, transportado por arte mágica desde las orillas del Sena al riñon de Andalucía. El cuello de su camisa y el lienzo con que formaba lazo en torno de él estaban bastante bajos para descubrir la garganta y la cerviz robusta sobre que posaba airosamente la cabeza. La estatura, más bien alta que mediana, y el talle, esbelto. El calzón ajustado de casimir, la media de seda blanca y el zapato de hebilla de plata, daban lugar a que mostrase el galán la bien formada pierna y un pie pequeño, largo y levantado por el tarso.

Sin duda las niñas contemplaron más todas estas cosas, y se deleitaron más con la dulzura de la voz del señorito que con el que nos atrevemos a calificar de idilio, la mitad de cuyas palabras estaban en griego para ellas.

Don Fadrique había reparado en todo. Como la mayor parte de los distraídos, era muy observador, y prestaba atención intensa cuando se dignaba prestarla.

Does not harbor, nor in riches nor in
Birth does the old shepherd best me.
Only an ill-fated error, a madness,
– Oh Chloris! Oh, divine garden rose –
Will make you exhale your fragrance and your freshness
In the midst of the hawthorn's dry branches,
Will make you break the delicate clasp,
Not in April, but in frozen December.
If you wish to kill me, do not wound me thus,
For in so proceeding, yourself also do you kill."

As soon as the lines ended, they were loudly applauded by the benevolent audience, but, if we are to tell the truth, neither Don José nor Doña Antonia paid attention during the recitation. The older ladies dozed off with the singsong delivery; the priest found the composition exceedingly materialistic and mythological and a little tedious; and Lucía's girlfriends were more keen on the poet's impressive bearing than on the literary merit of his work.

Don Carlos was, as a matter of fact, a very handsome, dark-complexioned young man of twenty-two or twenty-three. His big, lively eyes gleamed with the fire of imagination. His unpowdered black hair glistened and gave off bluish flashes like a raven's wings. The movements of his mouth when he spoke were charming; his brow, clear and serene; his teeth, white and even; and his nose, straight.

Don Carlos dressed with the utmost elegance, in the latest Parisian fashion. A consummate dandy, he looked like the prince of gilded youth, transported by magic from the banks of the Seine to the heart of Andalusia. His shirt collar and the linen that formed a neck cloth around it were low enough to reveal his throat and the robust neck on which his head sat so gracefully. He was on the tall side and had a slender build. The tightfitting cashmere breeches, the white silk stockings, and the silver-buckled shoes allowed the young gallant to show off his nicely shaped legs and small feet, which were long and raised at the heel.

No doubt the girls took in all these details and delighted more in the sweetness of the *señorito*'s voice than in what we shall dare to call an idyll, half of whose words were Greek to them.

Don Fadrique had noticed everything about the youthful poet. Like most absent-minded people, he was very observant and paid very close attention when he deigned to pay any attention.

Los versos le parecieron regulares, no inferiores a los de Meléndez, aunque, ni con mucho, tan buenos como los de Andrés Chénier, que había oído en París. Lo que es el chico le pareció muy guapo.

Advirtió también, con cierto gusto mezclado de zozobra, que Lucía, su sobrina, había escuchado con ademán y gestos propios de quien entiende la poesía, y con cierta afición, que no atinaba él a deslindar si era meramente literaria, o reconocía otra causa más personal y más honda.

Por lo pronto, en consecuencia de tales observaciones, calificó a su sobrina, de quien hasta entonces apenas había hecho caso, de bonita y de discreta. Se puede decir que la miró concienzudamente por primera vez, y vio que era rubia, blanca, con ojos azules, airosa de cuerpo, y muy distinguida. De todos estos descubrimientos no pudo menos de alegrarse, como buen tío que era; pero hizo, o creyó haber hecho, otros descubrimientos, que le mortificaban algo. «Tal vez serán cavilaciones mías», decía para sí.

En punto de las diez se acabó la tertulia.

Sola ya la familia, doña Antonia convocó a los criados, y en compañía de todos, y en alta voz, se rezó el rosario.

Por último, no bastando el chocolate y el refresco, que pudiera pasar por merienda, para gente que comía entonces poco después de mediodía, se sirvió la indispensable cena.

Durante este tiempo don Fadrique buscó y encontró ocasión de tener un aparte con su sobrina, y le habló de este modo:

—Niña, veo que te gustan los versos más de lo que yo creía.

Ella, poniéndose muy colorada y más bonita desde la primera palabra que el tío pronunció, respondióle algo cortada:

—¿Y por qué no han de gustarme? Aunque criada en un lugar, no soy tan ruda.

—Basta con mirarte, hija mía, para conocer que no lo eres. Pero el que te gusten los versos no se opone a que puedan gustarte los poetas.

—Ya lo creo que me gustan. Fray Luis de León y Garcilaso son mis predilectos entre los líricos españoles— dijo Lucía con suma naturalidad.

Casi se disipó la sospecha de don Fadrique. Parecía inverosímil tanto disimulo en una muchacha de diez y ocho años, que rezaba el rosario todas las noches, iba a misa, y se confesaba con frecuencia.

He thought the verses middling, not inferior to those of Meléndez, although not nearly as good as those of André Chénier,[53] which he had heard in Paris. As for looks, the young man struck him as very handsome.

He also noticed, with a certain combination of pleasure and anxiety, that his niece Lucía had listened with the attitude and expression typical of someone who understands poetry, and clearly with a liking, but he could not decide whether it was merely literary or whether there was a deeper, more personal reason.

As a result of such observations, for the present he judged his niece, whom he had barely noticed until then, to be pretty and discreet. It could be said that he studied her carefully for the first time, and saw that she was fair-complected, blue-eyed, and blond, and that she had a graceful figure and a look of refinement. Like the good uncle that he was, the commander could not help rejoicing, but he made, or thought he had made, other discoveries that mortified him somewhat. "Perhaps they're misgivings of mine," he said to himself.

At ten o'clock sharp the *tertulia* ended.

As the family was alone now, Doña Antonia summoned the servants, and all together they recited the rosary.

Finally, because the chocolate and other refreshments could only be termed a snack and were insufficient for people who back then ate their main meal shortly after noon, the indispensable supper was served.

During this time Don Fadrique sought and found an opportunity to have a private word with his niece, and he spoke as follows:

"So, young lady, I see that you like poetry more than I thought."

Blushing deeply and looking prettier than ever from the first words spoken by her uncle, she responded, somewhat embarrassed:

"And why shouldn't I like it? Although I've been raised in a small town, I'm not that uncultured."

"All one has to do is look at you, my dear, to see that you are not. But the fact that you like poetry means that you can also like poets."

"I do indeed like them. Friar Luis de León and Garcilaso[54] are my favorites among Spanish lyric poets," said Lucía with the utmost naturalness.

Don Fadrique's suspicion nearly vanished. So much pretense seemed unlikely in a girl of eighteen, a girl who said the rosary every night, went to mass, and confessed frequently.

Don Fadrique no tenía tiempo para rodeos y perífrasis, y se fue bruscamente al asunto que le mortificaba.

—Sobrina, con franqueza: ¿Los versos que hemos oído los ha compuesto don Carlos para ti?

—¡Qué disparate!— respondió Lucía, soltando una carcajada.

—¿Y por qué había de ser disparate?

—Porque nada de aquello me conviene, porque yo no soy Clori.

—Bien pudieras serlo. El poeta no describe a Clori. Afirma vaga e indeterminadamente que Clori es bella, y tú eres bella.

—Gracias, tío; usted me favorece.

—No; te hago justicia.

—Sea como usted guste. Pero dígame usted, ¿de dónde sacamos a mi viejo rabadán? Porque yo no doy con él.

—Pues mira, yo creí haberle encontrado.

—¿Cómo, tío, si no estaba en la tertulia más que el señor cura?

—Y yo, ¿no soy nadie?

—¿Qué quiere usted decir con eso?

—Quiero decir que tengo cincuenta años, que te llevo treinta y dos, y que no estoy loco para aspirar a que me quieran; pero los poetas fingen lo que se les antoja, y el barbilindo de don Carlos puede haber levantado esa máquina de suposiciones absurdas para escribir su idilio. En tal caso, no está muy conforme con la verdad todo aquello de que el viejo rabadán no puede ya con sus huesos, ni baila, ni corre, ni guerrea, ni es capaz de cazar lobos como el zagal. Con mi medio siglo encima, me apuesto a todo con el tal don Carlitos. Todavía, si me pongo a bailar el bolero, estoy seguro de que he de bailarle mejor que cuando mi padre me hizo que le bailara a latigazos. Y en punto a pulmones y a resuello, no ya para encaramarme al Parnaso corriendo detrás de las Bacantes, no ya para tocar todas las flautas y clarinetes del mundo, sino para mover las aspas de un molino, entiendo que tengo de sobra.

—Pero tío, si don Carlos no ha soñado en usted ni ha pensado en mí.

—Vamos, muchacha, no seas hipocritilla. A mí se me ha metido en la cabeza que este chico te quiere, que ha sabido que yo venía a pasar aquí

Don Fadrique had no time for subterfuges and circumlocution, and therefore abruptly broached the matter that vexed him:

"Frankly now, niece, these verses that we've heard: did Don Carlos compose them for you?"

"What nonsense!" exclaimed Lucía as she burst out laughing.

"And why should it be nonsense?"

"Because nothing in those verses has to do with me. Because I am not Chloris."

"You certainly could be. The poet doesn't describe Chloris. He asserts in vague, hazy language that Chloris is beautiful, and you are beautiful."

"Thank you, Uncle. You flatter me."

"No, I do you justice."

"As you wish. But tell me: where are we to find my old shepherd? Because I don't see him."

"Well, look, I think I've found him."

"How is that, Uncle, since only the priest was present at the *tertulia*?"

"And me ... I'm no one?"

"What do you mean by that?"

"I mean that I am fifty years old, that I am thirty-two years older than you, and that I am not so mad as to aspire to be loved, but poets invent whatever they feel like and our dapper Don Carlos may have spun that tale of absurd suppositions in order to write his idyll. In such a case, everything that he said about the old shepherd is not much in keeping with the truth – that he is done in, that he can neither dance, nor run, nor put up a fight, nor hunt wolves like the young shepherd. With my half century on my back, I'm prepared to take on this Don Carlitos[55] in all these things. Still and all, if I decided to dance the bolero, I'm certain I would execute it better than when my father made me dance it to the cracks of his whip. And with regard to lungs and breathing, I believe I have more than enough capacity not only to climb up Parnassus running behind bacchantes, not only to play all the flutes and recorders in the world, but to move the arms of a windmill."

"But, Uncle, Don Carlos hasn't even dreamed of you nor has he thought of you."

"Come now, girl, don't be hypocritical. I've taken it into my head that that young man loves you, that he learned I was coming to spend a month

un mes, que ha oído decir que yo era viejo, y, con estos datos, el insolente ha supuesto lo demás.

Don Fadrique decía todo esto con risa, para embromar a su sobrina; y, aunque dudoso de su recelo, algo picado de la desvergüenza del poeta, que por otra parte no había dejado de caerle en gracia.

–Tío– dijo, por último, Lucía con la mayor gravedad que pudo –. Usted no es el viejo rabadán. El viejo rabadán es de Villabermeja como usted: hace dos años que está establecido aquí, y merece, en efecto, las calificaciones que le prodiga el poeta, porque está muy asendereado y estropeado. El viejo rabadán se llama don Casimiro. Usted debe de conocerle.

–¡Ya lo creo! ¡Y vaya si le conozco!– dijo el comendador recordando a su antiguo adversario y víctima de la niñez.

–Pero entonces, ¿quién es Clori?– añadió en seguida.

–Clori es una linda señorita, muy amiga mía. Su madre vive con gran recogimiento y no sale ni deja salir a su hija de noche. Por eso no ha estado Clori de tertulia; pero es mi vecina, y su madre consiente en que venga conmigo de paseo, en compañía de mi madre. Si mañana quiere usted ser nuestro acompañante, iremos a las huertas, a las diez, después del almuerzo, por sendas en que haya sombra. Clori vendrá, y usted conocerá a Clori.

–Iré con mucho gusto.

–¡Ah, tío! Por amor de Dios, que no se le escape a usted lo de que don Carlos está enamorado de mi amiga y lo de que ella es Clori. Mire usted que es un secreto. Nadie más que yo lo sabe en la población. Hay que tener mucho recato, porque los padres de ella no quieren más que a don Casimiro y nada traslucen del amor de don Carlos. Yo se lo he confiado a usted para que no fuese usted a creer que yo era Clori y que sin razón de ningún género habíamos convertido a usted en el viejo rabadán enclenque, a fin de dar motivo a los versos.

–Quedo satisfecho, muchacha, y no diré nada. Te aseguro que ya me interesa tu amiga Clori y que tengo curiosidad de verla.

De esta suerte, de improviso, vino don Fadrique a tener, apenas llegado, un secreto con su sobrina, y a figurar en intrigas y lances de amor.

Pensando en ello, se retiró a su cuarto, como los demás se retiraron, cada cual al suyo, y durmió hasta las ocho de la mañana, mejor que un mozo de veinte años.

here, that he heard I was old, and that in possession of this information, the insolent fellow thought up the rest."

Don Fadrique said all this with laughter in his voice, in order to pull his niece's leg, even though he was doubtful of his suspicion and somewhat annoyed at the brazenness of the poet who, notwithstanding his sentiments, had made a good impression on him.

"Uncle," Lucía finally said with all the gravity she could muster, "you are not the old shepherd. The old shepherd is from Villabermeja like you. He has been settled here for two years, and deserves, to be sure, the labels that the poet lavishes on him because he is sickly and feeble. The old shepherd's name is Don Casimiro. You must know him."

"I should think so! Of course I know him!" said the commander, remembering the one-time adversary and victim of his boyhood. "But then, who is Chloris?" he asked almost in the same breath.

"Chloris is a pretty *señorita*, a close friend of mine. Her mother lives in great seclusion and doesn't go out, nor does she let her daughter go out at night. That's why Chloris wasn't at the *tertulia*, but she's my neighbor, and her mother does allow her to come with me on walks, in the company of my mother. If you want to be our escort tomorrow, we'll go to the gardens, at ten o'clock, after breakfast, along the paths where there's shade. Chloris will come, and you'll meet Chloris."

"I'll go with much pleasure."

"Oh, Uncle! For the love of God, don't let any of this slip out – that Don Carlos is in love with my friend and that she is Chloris. Remember that it's a secret. Nobody here knows about it but me. Much caution is called for, because her parents want only Don Casimiro and have no inkling of Don Carlos's love. I've confided it to you so that you wouldn't go believing that I was Chloris, and that without any rhyme or reason we had converted you into a sickly old shepherd so as to be fit material for verses."

"I'm satisfied, Lucía, and I won't say anything. I assure you that your friend Chloris interests me now and that I am curious to see her."

In this way, unexpectedly and on the heels of his arrival, did Don Fadrique come to share a secret with his niece and to figure in intrigues and amorous adventures.

Thinking about all of it, he retired to his room, as did the others, each to his or her own, and slept until eight o'clock in the morning, better than a youth of twenty.

8

Doña Antonia amaneció con un tremendo jaquecazo, enfermedad a que era muy propensa. Tuvo, pues, que guardar cama y no pudo acompañar a paseo a su hija Lucía; pero, como el mal no era de cuidado, y ya Lucía tenía concertado el paseo con su amiga, se decidió que el comendador las acompañase.

La amiga de Lucía vivía en la casa inmediata. Un muro separaba los patios de una casa y otra. A la hora convenida, en punto de las nueve y media, pronta ya Lucía para salir y con su tío al lado, gritó desde el patio, al pie del muro:

—Clara (así se llamaba Clori en la vida real), ¿estás ya lista?

No se hizo aguardar la contestación.

Oyóse primero la voz de una criada que decía:

—Señorita, señorita, doña Lucía está llamando a su merced.

Un momento más tarde sonó en el patio contiguo una voz argentina y simpática que respondía:

—Allá voy; sal a la calle; ¿para qué he de entrar en tu casa?

Salieron don Fadrique y doña Lucía, y hallaron ya a doña Clara en la puerta.

El comendador, a pesar de sus distracciones, miró a doña Clara con extraordinaria curiosidad. Era una niña de poco más de diez y seis años. El color de su rostro, de un moreno limpio, teñido en las mejillas y en los labios del más fresco carmín. La tez parecía tan suave, delicada y transparente, que al través de ella se imaginaba ver circular la sangre por las venas azules. Los ojos, negros y grandes, estaban casi siempre dormidos y velados por los párpados y las largas y rizadas pestañas; si bien, cuando fijaban la mirada y se abrían por completo, brotaban de ellos dulce fuego y luz viva. Todo en doña Clara manifestaba salud y lozanía, y, sin embargo, en torno de sus ojos, fingiéndolos mayores y acrecentando su brillantez, se notaba un cerco oscuro, como de morado lirio.

Era doña Clara más alta que su amiga Lucía, bastante alta también, y, aunque delgada, sus formas eran bellas y revelaban el precoz y completo desenvolvimiento de la mujer. El cabello de doña Clara era negrísimo, las manos y el pie pequeños, la cabeza bien plantada y airosa.

8

Doña Antonia awoke with an awful migraine, an illness to which she was very susceptible. As a result, she had to keep to her bed and could not accompany her daughter Lucía on her walk. But inasmuch as her malady was not one of concern, and as Lucía had already arranged the walk with her friend, it was decided that the commander would accompany her.

Lucía's friend lived in the next house. A wall separated the patios of the two dwellings. At the agreed-upon hour, right at half past nine, ready to leave and with her uncle at her side, Lucía shouted from the patio by the wall:

"Clara (for such was Chloris's name in real life), are you ready yet?"

She did not have to wait long for an answer, but first the voice of a servant was heard saying:

"Señorita, Señorita, Doña Lucía is calling you."

A moment later a pleasant, silvery voice rang out from the adjoining patio:

"I'm coming. Meet me outside. There's no need for me to go into your house."

When Don Fadrique and Doña Lucía left, they found Doña Clara already at the doorstep.

Despite his inattentiveness, the commander eyed Doña Clara with acute curiosity. She was a girl little more than sixteen years old. The color of her face, a clear olive hue, was tinged on her cheeks and on her lips with the freshest carmine. Her skin seemed so soft, delicate, and transparent that through it you could imagine seeing her blood circulate in blue veins. Her eyes, big and black, were almost always half closed and veiled by lids and long, curly lashes, although when they opened up completely and fixed on something, a gentle fire and bright light radiated from them. Everything in Doña Clara proclaimed health and exuberance, and nevertheless, around her eyes, making them appear bigger and heightening their brilliance, there was a dark ring, like a purple iris.

Doña Clara was taller than her friend Lucía, who was herself rather tall, and although slender, her figure was beautiful and revealed the precocious and complete development of a woman. Doña Clara's hair was jet-black, her head graceful and nicely shaped, and her hands and feet small.

Ambas amigas iban vestidas de negro, con mantilla y basquiña y algunas rosas en el peinado.

Lucía dijo a su amiga la indisposición de su madre, y que su tío, el comendador, recién llegado de Villabermeja, las acompañaría de paseo. Salvos los cumplimientos y ceremonias de costumbre, no hubo en la conversación nada memorable, hasta que los tres que iban juntos salieron de la ciudad y llegaron al campo.

La pequeña ciudad está por todas partes circundada de huertas. Muchas sendas las cortan en diversas direcciones. A un lado y a otro de cada senda hay una cerca de granados, zarzamoras, mimbres y otras plantas. En muchas sendas hay un arroyo cristalino a cada lado; en otras un solo arroyo. Todas ellas gozan en primavera, verano y otoño, de abundante sombra, merced a los álamos corpulentos y frondosos nogales, y demás árboles de todo género que en las huertas se crían.

La tierra es allí tan generosa y feraz, que no puede imaginarse el sinnúmero de flores y la masa de verdura que ciñen las márgenes de los arroyos, esparciendo grato y campestre aroma. Campanillas, mosquetas, violetas moradas y blancas, lirios y margaritas, abren allí sus cálices y lucen su hermosura.

El sol radiante, que brilla en el cielo despejado y dora el aire diáfano, hace más espléndida la escena. Increíble multitud de pájaros la anima y alegra con sus trinos y gorjeos. En Andalucía, huyendo de la tierra de secano, buscando el agua y la sombra, se refugian las aves en estos oasis de regadío, donde hay frescura y tupidas enramadas.

Tales eran los sitios por donde paseaba el comendador con las dos bonitas muchachas. Apenas salieron de la población, tomaron la senda que llaman *del medio*. Ellas cogían flores, se deleitaban oyendo cantar los colorines o reían sin saber de qué. El comendador meditaba, sentía gran bienestar, gozaba de todo, aunque más tranquilamente que ellas.

Al llegar al sitio más ancho, no ya a otra senda, sino a un camino, los tres, que por ser la senda casi siempre estrecha habían ido uno en pos de otro, se pusieron en la misma línea. Clara estaba en el centro. Lucía dijo entonces, dirigiéndose a su tío:

—Vamos, ya habrá satisfecho usted su curiosidad. Ésta es Clori. ¿No es verdad que merece haber inspirado el idilio?

Doña Clara, que si bien más moza que Lucía, era más reflexiva y grave, sintió que su amiga hubiese confiado a su tío aquel secreto, y

Both friends were dressed in black, with mantillas and basquines, and a few roses in their hair.

Lucía told her friend of her mother's indisposition, and said that her uncle the commander, recently arrived from Villabermeja, would accompany them on their walk. Save for the usual courtesies and formalities, there was nothing memorable about their conversation until the three of them, keeping abreast, left the city and reached the country.

The small city is surrounded everywhere by gardens, and many paths cut through them in various directions. On either side of each path there is a hedge or fence of pomegranate trees, blackberry bushes, osiers, and other plants. Quite a few of the paths have a limpid brook on either side; some have a brook only on one side. All of them enjoy, in spring, summer, and autumn, abundant shade thanks to the stout poplars and leafy walnuts and other trees of every kind that grow in the gardens.

The soil there is so fertile and productive that one cannot imagine the multitude of flowers and the mass of greenery bordering the banks of the brooks, dispensing a pleasant, country smell. Harebells, dog roses, white and purple violets, irises, and daisies open their calyxes there and display their beauty.

The radiant sun, which shines in the cloudless sky and gilds the diaphanous air, makes it a more splendid scene. An incredible array of birds enliven and brighten it with their warbles and trills. In Andalusia, fleeing from dry land in search of water and shade, the birds take refuge in these irrigated oases where there is coolness and dense foliage.

Such was the site where the commander was strolling with the two pretty girls. As soon as they found themselves outside of the city, they took the path called the "Middle" one. The *señoritas* picked flowers, delighted in hearing the goldfinches sing, or laughed without knowing why. The commander meditated, experienced great well-being, and enjoyed everything, albeit more quietly than his companions.

When they reached a broader area, more like a road than a path, the three of them resumed walking abreast, whereas heretofore they had been walking single file because the path had almost always been narrow. Clara was in the middle. Turning to her uncle, Lucía then said:

"Well, you must have satisfied your curiosity by now. This is Chloris. Isn't it true that she's worthy of having inspired the idyll?"

Doña Clara, who, although younger than Lucía, was more reflective and serious, regretted that her friend had confided the secret to her

no pudo reprimir las muestras de su disgusto, frunciendo el entrecejo, poniéndose más seria y tiñéndose al mismo tiempo de grana sus mejillas con la vergüenza y el enojo.

Nada dijo doña Clara, a pesar de ello; pero Lucía advirtió su disgusto y prosiguió de esta suerte:

–No te ofendas, Clarita. No me motejes de parlanchina. Mi tío me puso anoche entre la espada y la pared y tuve que confesárselo todo. Tuve que disculparme y que disculpar a don Carlos. A mi tío se le metió en la cabeza que él era el viejo rabadán y que yo era Clori. Además, mi tío es muy sigiloso y no dirá nada a nadie. ¿No es verdad, tío?

–Descuide usted, señorita– respondió el comendador, encarándose con doña Clara, que se puso más encarnada aún –; nadie sabrá por mí quién ha inspirado el idilio, que es, por cierto, precioso.

El comendador advirtió que Clara se tranquilizaba, si bien no acertó, con la turbación, a pronunciar palabra alguna.

Doña Lucía continuó:

–¡Vaya si es precioso el idilio! Créame usted, tío: desde Vicente Espinel hasta nuestra edad, Ronda no ha producido más ingenioso poeta que nuestro amigo don Carlos de Atienza, ilustre mayorazgo de la mencionada ciudad, el cual vive en Sevilla con sus padres, trata de tomar en aquella Universidad la borla de doctor en ambos Derechos, y ahora descuida bastante los estudios por seguir a Clori, que, desde Sevilla, se ha venido aquí de asiento, con su familia, a quien usted sin duda conoce.

–Sobrina, yo no sé si tengo o no la honra de conocer a la familia de esta señorita, cuyo apellido no me has dicho. ¿Cómo un forastero recién llegado ha de adivinar la familia de quien sólo sabe que se llama Clori en poesía y Clara en prosa?

–¡Ay, es verdad! ¡Qué distraída soy! No había yo dicho a usted cómo se llamaba mi amiga. Pues bien, tío: esta señorita se llama doña Clara de Solís y Roldan. Y ahora, ¿qué dice usted? ¿Conoce usted o no conoce a su familia?

Al oír en boca de Lucía el nombre y apellidos de su amiga y la última inocente pregunta, el comendador se estremeció, se turbó: el color rojo que había teñido antes las mejillas delicadas de Clarita, se diría que había pasado con más fuerza a encender el rostro varonil de don Fadrique, curtido por el sol de la India y por los vientos de los remotos mares.

uncle and could not suppress signs of her displeasure, frowning and becoming solemn as her cheeks tinged scarlet with embarrassment and annoyance.

Nonetheless, Doña Clara said nothing, but Lucía noticed her displeasure and continued in this way:

"Don't take offense, Clarita.[56] And don't accuse me of being loose-tongued. Last night my uncle put me between a rock and a hard place, and I had to confess everything to him. I had to vindicate myself and Don Carlos too. My uncle had taken it into his head that he was the old shepherd and that I was Chloris. Besides, my uncle is very discreet and won't say a word to a soul. Isn't that right, Uncle?"

"Set your mind at ease, Señorita," answered the commander, speaking to Doña Clara, who blushed even more. "No one will learn from me who inspired the idyll, which, by the bye, is lovely."

The commander saw that Clara was calming down, although in her embarrassment she could not bring herself to speak a single word.

Doña Lucía continued:

"Of course the idyll is lovely! Believe me, Uncle: from the time of Vicente Espinel[57] to our own, Ronda has produced no more ingenious a poet than our friend Don Carlos de Atienza, an illustrious *mayorazgo* from that city who lives in Seville with his parents, wants to earn the doctor's degree in canon and civil law, and now neglects his studies so as to follow Chloris, who has come from Seville to settle here with her family, whom you no doubt know."

"My dear niece, I do not know whether I have or do not have the honor of knowing this young lady's family, whose name you have not told me. How is a recently arrived stranger supposed to divine the family of someone he knows only as Chloris in poetry and Clara in prose?"

"Oh, that's right! How absent-minded of me! I haven't told you my friend's surnames. Well, then, Uncle, this young lady is named Doña Clara de Solís y Roldán. So now what do you say? Do you know her family or not?"

When he heard from Lucía's lips her friend's first and last names and the last innocent question, the commander shuddered and became agitated; it was as if the redness that had earlier tinged Clarita's delicate cheeks had passed in a deeper hue to flush the manly face of Don Fadrique, which had been tanned by the sun of India and by the winds of distant seas.

Lucía, sin advertir la turbación de su tío, siguió diciendo:

–Pero ¿qué digo a su familia? A la misma Clara es posible que usted la conozca: sólo que ya no se acuerda. Cuando era ella chiquirritita, tal vez cuando ella nació, estaba usted en Lima. Clara es limeña.

Dominándose al cabo el comendador, contestó a su sobrina:

–Mal puedo acordarme y mal puedo haber olvidado a esta señorita, a quien nunca he visto. A quien sí he conocido y tratado mucho es a su señor padre; y también, a pesar de la vida retirada y austera que siempre ha hecho, tuve el gusto de tratar y ser amigo de mi señora doña Blanca Roldán. ¿Cómo está su señora madre de usted, señorita?

–Sigue bien de salud– contestó doña Clara –; pero, entregada como nunca a sus devociones, apenas se deja ver de nadie.

–¿Y el señor don Valentín, está bueno?

–Gracias a Dios, lo está– dijo Clara.

–Se ha retirado ya de la magistratura– añadió Lucía –; ha heredado los cuantiosos bienes de su hermano el mayor, que murió sin hijos; y vive aquí, donde tiene sus mejores fincas, de que Clarita es única heredera.

Como una nueva oleada de sangre subió entonces a la cara del comendador, enrojeciéndola toda. Reportándose luego, dijo de la manera más natural a su parlera sobrina:

–¿Conque esta señorita, además de ser tan guapa, es muy rica?

–Para estos lugares lo es. ¿No es verdad, tío, que es muy extraño que la quieran casar con don Casimiro? ¡Si viera usted qué viejo y qué feo está! Vamos, es ofender a Dios. Yo, si fuera el Papa, negaba la licencia que habrá que pedirle.

–Pues qué– exclamó don Fadrique –, ¿son ustedes parientes tan cercanos?

–Don Casimiro Solís es el pariente más cercano que tiene mi padre– contestó Clara.

–Sería su inmediato heredero si Clara no viviese– añadió Lucía, que no dejaba por contar nada de cuanto sabía, cuando se hallaba entre personas, como Clara y su tío, que le infundían tanta confianza y cariño.

Don Fadrique no llevó adelante la conversación. Quedó callado, y como pensativo y melancólico.

En silencio continuaron, pues, paseando hasta que llegaron al *nacimiento*. En mitad de un bosque de encinas y olivos, que pone término a las huertas, se alza un monte escarpado, formado de riscos y

Without noticing her uncle's agitation, Lucía continued:

"But, why am I saying her *family*? It's possible that you know Clara herself and just don't remember her. When she was a little bit of a thing, perhaps when she was born, you were in Lima. Clara's *limeña*."

Finally managing to control himself, the commander answered his niece:

"I can hardly remember, and can have hardly forgotten, this young lady, whom I've never seen. The one I have met and seen a lot of is her father, and, despite the withdrawn and austere life that she has always led, I had the pleasure of knowing and being friendly with Señora doña Blanca Roldán. How is your esteemed mother, Señorita?"

"She's in good health," answered Doña Clara, "but, given over to her devotions as never before, she sees scarcely anyone."

"And Señor don Valentín. Is he well?"

"Yes, he is, thanks be to God," said Clara.

"He's retired now from his judgeship," added Lucía. "He inherited the large estate of his older brother, who died without children, and lives here, where he has his best properties, of which Clara is the sole heiress."

Something like another surge of blood then rose to the commander's face, reddening it all over. Recovering his composure momentarily, he said to his talkative niece in the most natural manner:

"So this young lady, besides being beautiful, is wealthy?"

"For this neck of the woods she is. Isn't it true, Uncle, that it is very strange of them to want to marry her to Don Casimiro? If you saw how old and ugly he is! Really, it's offensive to God. If I were the pope, I would refuse the permission that will have to be sought."

"Why?" Don Fadrique asked Clara. "Are you such near relatives?"

"Don Casimiro is the nearest relative that my father has," she answered.

"He would be his immediate heir were Clara not alive," added Lucía, who never left unsaid anything of all that she knew when she was in the company of people like Clara and her uncle, who inspired so much trust and affection in her.

Don Fadrique chose not to carry on the conversation. He held his tongue, as though pensive and melancholy.

So they proceeded in silence, making their way to what people called the *nacimiento*, or source. In the middle of a wood of holm oaks and olive trees that delimit the gardens, there rises a steep mountain formed

peñascos enormes, que parecen como suspendidos en el aire, amenazando derrumbarse a cada momento.

Higueras bravías, jaras de varias especies, romero y tomillo, musgo, retama y otras mil hierbas, plantas y flores, nacen en las hendiduras de aquellas peñas o cubren los sitios en que no está pelada la roca viva, y hallan alguna capa vegetal donde fijar y alimentar las raíces.

Los peñascos horadados abren paso a diversas grutas o cuevas en no pocos sitios del cerro, a cuyo pie, más bajo aún que el nivel del camino, están como socavadas las piedras, formando una gruta mayor y de más grande entrada que las otras. En el fondo de esta gruta, que se ve todo sin penetrar allí, brota de una grieta, sin hipérbole alguna, un verdadero río. Por eso se llama aquel sitio el nacimiento del río, o sencillamente el *nacimiento*.

El agua que mana de entre las peñas cae con grato estruendo en un estanque natural, cuyo suelo está sembrado de blanquísimas y redondas piedrezuelas. Por aquel estanque se extiende mansa el agua, creando y desvaneciendo de continuo círculos fugaces; mas, a pesar de los círculos, son las hondas de tal transparencia, que al través de ellas se ve el fondo, aunque está a más de vara y media de profundidad, y en él pueden encontrarse las guijas todas.

En la margen del pequeño lago crecen juncos, juncia, berros y otras plantas acuáticas.

El estanque o lago llena la gruta y se dilata buen espacio fuera de ella, reflejando el cielo en su cristal. A derecha y a izquierda hay dos acequias por donde el agua corre, dividiéndose después en infinitos arroyuelos, y yendo a regar las mil y quinientas huertas que hacen del término de aquella pequeña ciudad un verde y florido paraíso.

Como todo por aquellas cercanías es terreno quebrado, el agua baja a las hondonadas con ímpetu brioso: a veces se precipita en cascadas, y a veces pone en movimiento aceñas, batanes y martinetes. No obstante, cerca del nacimiento del agua va por tierra llana, con sosegada corriente y apacible murmullo, sin que haya ruido mayor en aquella amena soledad que el que produce el nacimiento mismo; el golpe del agua que brota de la peña y cae dentro de la gruta.

A la orilla del estanque rústico hay varios sauces, y junto al tronco del más alto y frondoso, un poyo o asiento de piedra. Allí estaba sentado el

of cliffs and enormous rocks that seem to be as though suspended in air, threatening to collapse at any moment.

Wild fig trees, several species of dog rose, rosemary and thyme, moss, broom, and a thousand other herbs, plants, and flowers sprout in the crevices of those crags or blanket the places where the living rock is not bare, and they find a layer of soil or vegetation in which to sink and nourish roots.

The crags with gaps and breaches open onto various grottoes and caves here and there in the hillside, at whose base, which is even lower than the level of the road, the rocks are as though hollowed out, forming a larger grotto with a bigger entrance. At the far end of this grotto, which can be seen in its entirety without entering it, there springs from a fissure a veritable river, which by no manner of means is hyperbole. For this reason that site is called the source of the river, or simply the "source."

The water that flows from between the crags falls with a pleasant roar into a natural pool or pond, whose floor is strewn with round, milk-white pebbles. As it spreads gently in the pond, the water continually creates and disperses short-lived, concentric circles, but despite these circles the waves are so transparent that through them one can see the bottom, even though it is nearly five feet deep, and every pebble there can be counted.

Reeds, sedges, watercresses and other aquatic plants grow on the shore of the small lake.

The pond or lake fills the grotto and extends a good distance beyond it, reflecting the sky on its mirror surface. To the right and to the left there are two channels, along which the water flows, dividing afterwards into endless streams and brooks, and continuing on to irrigate the fifteen hundred or so gardens that make the outlying expanse of that small city into a green and floral paradise.

Since everything in that vicinity is uneven terrain, the water rushes down to gullies and ravines in a swift current, at times gushing in cascades, at times driving water mills, fulling mills, and drop hammers. However, near the source, the water runs on level ground, with a gentle flow and a quiet murmur, the only louder sound in that pleasant solitude being the one produced by the source itself as the water pours out of the fissure and falls inside the grotto.

On the bank of the rustic pond there are several willows, and next to the trunk of the tallest and leafiest is a stone bench or seat. Sitting there

poeta rondeño don Carlos de Atienza cuando llegaron el comendador, su sobrina y doña Clara.

Don Fadrique, como si anhelase apartar de sí tristes y enojosos pensamientos, impropios de su carácter y risueña filosofía, se pasó la mano por la frente, y creyendo que recobraba su serena y alegre condición, dijo en voz alta:

–Hola, ilustre poeta, ¿qué nuevo idilio compone usted en estas soledades?

Don Carlos se levantó del asiento, y yendo hacia los recién venidos, dijo:

–Buenos días, señor don Fadrique. Beso los pies de ustedes, señoritas.

El comendador le allanó el camino para que se viniese con él y con las niñas y los acompañase un rato en el paseo. Habló a don Carlos de sus estudios, le ponderó lo mucho que le agradaba la poesía, le encomió el idilio, y se le hizo repetir.

No podía haber dado mayor gusto a don Carlos, ni mayor satisfacción de amor propio; porque, como todos los que escriben, han escrito o escribirán versos en mundo, era don Carlos aficionadísimo a recitarlos en presencia de un benévolo y discreto auditorio, y siempre se inclinaba a calificarle de discreto, con tal de que fuese benévolo.

Don Fadrique miró con disimulo, pero con mucha atención, a Clarita mientras que don Carlos recitó el idilio. Si aún le hubiera quedado la menor duda de que Clara era Clori, la duda se hubiera disipado. A Clarita, valiéndonos de una expresión en extremo vulgar, si bien muy pintoresca, un color se le iba y otro se le venía mientras los versos duraron. Ya se ponía pálida, ya se cubrían de púrpura sus mejillas. Hasta cuando exclamó don Carlos recitando:

Pues ¡qué! ¿Te he dado en balde tanta prueba de amor?

Vio o imaginó ver don Fadrique que los párpados de doña Clara se contraían más de lo ordinario, como para recoger y ocultar indiscretas lágrimas que ansiaban por brotar de los hermosos ojos.

Después de recitados los versos, don Carlos, menos atrevido en prosa, apenas se acercó a Clara, y no le dijo palabra que todos no oyesen. Sólo con Lucía habló en voz baja y como en secreto.

Los cuatro se internaron, prosiguiendo el paseo y volviendo a la ciudad por otro camino, en medio de una frondosísima arboleda. Allí

when the commander, his niece, and Doña Clara arrived, was the poet from Ronda, Don Carlos de Atienza.

As if he longed to rid himself of gloomy and troublesome thoughts, unbecoming to his character and sunny philosophy, Don Fadrique ran his hand across his forehead and, believing that he was recovering his serene and cheerful disposition, said in a loud voice:

"Hello, illustrious poet. What new idyll are you composing in this wilderness?"

Don Carlos rose from the seat and, going to meet the three of them, replied:

"Good morning, Señor don Fadrique. At your service, Señoritas."

The commander smoothed the way for the poet to join him and the girls and to accompany them a while on their walk. He talked to Don Carlos about his studies, spoke warmly of how much poetry pleased him, praised his idyll, and had him repeat it.

He could not have given Don Carlos greater pleasure nor satisfied to a greater degree his *amour-propre*, because like all who write, have written or will write poetry in the world, Don Carlos was very keen on reciting his in the presence of a well-disposed and discriminating audience, and he was always inclined to consider it discriminating provided it was well-disposed.

Don Fadrique glanced furtively, but with much attention, at Clarita while Don Carlos recited. If he had harbored even the slightest doubt that Clara was Chloris, the doubt would have been dispelled. To use a very common expression, although a very colorful one, Clarita's cheeks turned every shade of red during his recitation, going from pale to purple. When Don Carlos exclaimed,

Ask I must: Have I given you so much proof of love
In vain?

Don Fadrique saw or imagined that he saw Doña Clara's eyelids close more than usual, as if to collect and conceal indiscreet tears that longed to spill from her beautiful eyes.

Having recited the verses, Don Carlos, less daring in prose, scarcely approached Clara, and did not say a word to her that the others could not hear. He spoke only to Lucía, in a low voice, as though in private.

The four continued to stroll a bit further, then turned around, returning to the city by another road, one that cut through a luxuriant poplar

Clara, o adelantándose o quedándose atrás y dejando al comendador con su sobrina, hubiera podido hablar a su placer con don Carlos; pero no parecía sino que le tenía miedo, que temblaba de oír su voz sin testigo, y que deseaba demostrar a los ojos del comendador que no quería pertenecer a don Carlos, sino a don Casimiro. Ello es que en los lugares más agrestes, Clara no se apartaba del lado de don Fadrique, como si temiese que saliese una fiera a devorarla y buscase en él su amparo y defensa.

¿Quién sabe lo que pasaba en aquellos instantes en el alma del comendador? Lo cierto es que casi no se atrevía a hablar a Clara; pero de repente, en una ocasión en que don Carlos y Lucía se adelantaron y se perdieron de vista entre los árboles, el comendador detuvo a Clara, la contempló de un modo extraño y dulce, y tomando su semblante una expresión solemne y en cierto modo venerable, exclamó:

–¡Hija mía! Es usted muy buena, muy hermosa... inocente de todo; Dios bendiga a usted y la haga tan feliz como merece.

Y diciendo esto, alzó las manos como para bendecir a la muchacha, tomó su cabeza entre ellas y le dio en la frente un beso.

Clara halló, sin duda, muy raro todo aquello, fuera del uso y del estilo común; pero la cara de don Fadrique estaba tan seria, y su expresión era tan simpática y noble, que, a pesar de las ideas con que personajes devotos habían manchado precozmente la conciencia de la niña, hablándole de pecados y faltas, Clara no pudo ver allí ningún atrevimiento liviano.

Más aún se afirmó en la idea de lo puro e impecable del extraño e inesperado beso, cuando le dijo el comendador:

–Don Carlos me parece un mozo excelente. ¿Le ama usted mucho?

Había en el acento de don Fadrique un suave imperio, al que Clara no supo resistir.

–Le he amado mucho– contestó –, pero yo acertaré a no amarle. He sido muy culpada. Sin que lo sepa mi madre le he querido. En adelante no le querré. Seré buena hija. Obedeceré a mi madre. Ella sabe mejor que yo lo que me conviene.

Don Fadrique no se atrevió a replicar ni a hacer un discurso subversivo de la autoridad materna.

grove. In that spot Clara, either by walking ahead or by lagging behind, might have been able to talk to Don Carlos at her pleasure, but it almost seemed that she was afraid of him, that she trembled to hear his voice without a witness, and that she wished to demonstrate in the eyes of the commander that she did not want to belong to Don Carlos but to Don Casimiro. The upshot of it was that in the most isolated stretches Clara did not leave Don Fadrique's side; it was as if she feared that a wild beast would materialize to devour her, and she sought in him refuge and defense.

Who knows what stirred in the commander's soul in those moments? The fact is that he almost did not dare to talk to Clara, but seeing that Don Carlos and Lucía had gone ahead and disappeared in a stand of trees, he abruptly stopped Clara and gazed at her with strange, gentle eyes. With his face having assumed a solemn and, in a manner of speaking, a venerable expression, he exclaimed:

"My dear girl! You are very good, very beautiful … innocent of everything. God bless you and make you as happy as you deserve to be."

And saying this, he raised his hands as if to bless the girl, took her head between them, and kissed her on the forehead.

Clara, no doubt, found all that behavior rather odd, not at all in keeping with the norm and common customs, but Don Fadrique's face was so serious, and his expression was so kind and noble that, despite the ideas with which devout individuals had precociously defiled the girl's conscience, talking to her about sins and misdeeds, Clara could see no lewd audacity there.

She became yet more convinced of the pious and sinless nature of the strange and unexpected kiss when the commander said to her:

"Don Carlos seems to me quite a fine young man. Do you love him very much?"

There was a gentle authority in Don Fadrique's voice that Clara could not resist.

"I have loved him very much," she answered, "but I'll find a way not to love him. I have been very much to blame. Keeping my mother in the dark, I have loved him. From now on I will not love him. I will be a good daughter. I will obey my mother. She knows what's best for me better than I do."

Don Fadrique did not dare to respond nor to deliver a subversive speech on maternal authority.

A poco volvieron a reunirse en un solo grupo los cuatro.

Antes de entrar de nuevo en la ciudad, don Carlos se despidió del comendador y de las dos señoritas, y se fue por otros sitios.

Apenas Lucía y su tío dejaron a Clara a la puerta de su casa, el tío preguntó a la sobrina:

—¿Qué te ha dicho don Carlos?

—¿Qué ha de decir? Que está desesperado; que Clara le desdeña, que le rechaza, y que, por obedecer a su madre, se casará con don Casimiro.

—Y don Valentín, ¿qué hace?

—Nada. ¿Qué quiere usted que haga? Pues qué, ¿ignora usted que don Valentín es un gurrumino? Una mirada de doña Blanca le confunde y aterra; una palabra de enojo de aquella terrible mujer hace que tiemble don Valentín como un azogado.

—De suerte que doña Blanca es quien ha decidido el casamiento de Clara con don Casimiro.

—Sí, tío: en esa casa doña Blanca es quien lo decide todo. Ella manda y los demás obedecen. No se atreven a respirar sin su licencia. No se puede negar que doña Blanca tiene mucho talento y es una santa. Sabe más de las cosas de Dios que todos los predicadores juntos. Reza muchísimo; lee y estudia libros piadosos; lleva una vida ejemplar y penitente, y hace muchas limosnas a los pobres y a la iglesia; pero, a pesar de tantas virtudes y excelentes prendas, nada tiene de amable. Antes al contrario, es terrible. A mí me pone miedo.

—No lo dudo, sobrina: ya era como tú la describes cuando yo la conocí.

—¡Ay, tío! ¿Y la veía usted con frecuencia?

—No con frecuencia, sobrina; pero al fin la traté algo.

—No extrañe usted que en una semana no venga a casa, ni para cumplir. Doña Blanca vive con la mente tan lejos de todo, y se resiste tanto a que le cuenten cosas del mundo exterior que distraigan su espíritu de la contemplación íntima en que vive, que de seguro ni ella ni su pobre marido sabrán que usted ha llegado. Don Valentín no creo que sea hombre muy interior, espiritual y contemplativo; pero como tiene tanto miedo a su mujer y quiere darle gusto siempre, vive también a lo místico, apartado del trato humano, y yo le juzgo capaz de azotarse con

Shortly afterwards the four came together again as a group.

Before they entered the city anew, Don Carlos said good-bye to the commander and the two young ladies and set out on a different path.

No sooner did Lucía and her uncle leave Clara at the door of her house than the uncle asked the niece:

"What did Don Carlos tell you?"

"What's he going to tell me? That he's desperate, that Clara disdains him, that she rejects him, and that, out of obedience to her mother, she will marry Don Casimiro."

"And Don Valentín, what does he do?"

"Nothing. What do you expect him to do? Why, don't you know that Don Valentín is a henpecked husband? A glance from Doña Blanca confounds and terrifies him. One angry word from that terrible woman makes Don Valentín shake like a leaf."

"So Doña Blanca is the one who decided on Clara's marriage to Don Casimiro."

"Yes, Uncle. In that house Doña Blanca is the one who decides everything. She commands and the others obey. It can't be denied that she's very intelligent and is a saint. She knows more about matters pertaining to God than all the preachers put together. She prays an awful lot; she reads and studies pious books; she leads an exemplary and penitent life; and she gives a great deal in alms to the poor and to churches. But, in spite of so many virtues and excellent qualities, there is nothing kind or nice about her. On the contrary, she's terrible. I'm scared of her."

"I don't doubt it, niece. She was as you describe her when I knew her a long time ago."

"Oh, Uncle! And did you see her often?"

"Not often, niece, but I did see her every now and then."

"Do not be surprised if they don't come to the house to visit for a week, not even to pay their respects. Doña Blanca lives with her mind so removed from everything, and is so unwilling to be told things about the outside world that might distract her spirit from the intimate meditation in which she lives, that for sure neither she nor her poor husband knows that you have arrived. I don't believe that Don Valentín is much of a contemplative, spiritual, inward-looking man, but since he's so afraid of his wife and always wants to please her, he too lives in a mystical manner, removed from human contact, and I think he is capable of

unas disciplinas, no tanto por amor de Dios, cuanto por amor y por miedo de doña Blanca.

Don Fadrique escuchaba y callaba. No tenía humor de despegar los labios. Lucía, que era aficionada a hablar, soltó la tarabilla y prosiguió diciendo:

—¡Pobre Clara! Figúrese usted lo divertida que estará. Yo no lo dudo; ella se irá al cielo; pero qué ¿no puede uno ir al cielo con menos trabajo? No acierto a ponderar a usted los prodigios de astucia, los portentos de habilidad, aunque esté mal que yo me alabe, que he tenido que hacer para ganarme un poco la voluntad y la confianza de doña Blanca y lograr que su hija se trate conmigo y salga a veces en mi compañía. Si no fuera por mí, Clara estaría como enterrada en vida, entre cuatro paredes. No sé cómo ha podido entenderse con don Carlos. Gracias a que él es muy listo y capaz de todo. Clara ha estado con él, no diré que en relaciones, sino casi en relaciones. Ello es que Clara le amaba. Luego ha tenido remordimientos de amar a un hombre a escondidas de su madre, y sobre todo cuando su madre la destina para otro. Así es que ahora rechaza al pobre don Carlos, y el infeliz zagal Mirtilo se muere de pena.

El comendador oía con interés a su sobrina, y no ponía en conversación ni una exclamación siquiera. Parecía que se había quedado mudo o que no sabía qué decir.

—Clara— prosiguió Lucía —, ahora que cree pecado amar a don Carlos, y que no halla posible oponerse a la voluntad de su madre, piensa a veces en ser monja; pero ni este deseo se atreve a confiar a su madre. Considera ella, en primer lugar, que no es buena su vocación; que quiere tomar el velo por despecho y como desesperada; y por otra parte, cree que decir a su madre que quiere ser monja es un acto de rebeldía, es oponerse a su voluntad de casarla con don Casimiro. ¿Qué piensa usted de la situación de mi desgraciada amiga?

Interrogado tan directamente el comendador, tuvo al cabo que romper el silencio; pero respondió con laconismo:

—Mala es, en verdad, la situación; pero, ¿quién sabe? Todo tiene remedio menos la muerte. Entre tanto— añadió don Fadrique, hablando con lentitud y bajo, dejando caer las palabras una a una, como si le

whipping himself with a scourge, not so much for love of God, as for love and fear of Doña Blanca."

Don Fadrique listened and kept his own counsel. He was not in the mood to say a word. Lucía, who liked to talk, picked up where she left off and talked a blue streak:

"Poor Clara! Imagine what an amusing life she must lead. I don't doubt that she'll go to heaven, but I ask you: can't one go to heaven with less suffering? You would not believe the marvels of cunning, the wonders of cleverness, although it may not seem fitting that I should pat myself on the back, that I have had to put into effect to earn some of the goodwill and trust of Doña Blanca and prevail upon her to let her daughter be my friend and go out now and then in my company. If it weren't for me, Clara would be buried alive inside four walls. I have no idea how she managed to have a secret understanding with Don Carlos. Thanks, I suppose, to the fact that he's very clever and capable of anything. Clara has maintained, I won't exactly say relations with him, but almost. The point is, though, that she loved him. Then she felt remorse for loving a man behind her mother's back, and especially when her mother intends that she should marry another. That's why she now rejects poor Don Carlos, and Myrtilus, the disconsolate young shepherd, is dying of grief."

The commander listened to his niece with interest, and did not so much as interject an exclamation. It seemed that he had lost his voice or that he did not know what to say.

"Clara," continued Lucía, "now that she believes it is a sin to love Don Carlos, and not seeing any possibility of opposing her mother's wishes, thinks sometimes of becoming a nun. She considers, on the one hand, that she does not of course have a true vocation, that she wants to take the veil out of spite and as though in desperation; and on the other, she believes that telling her mother that she wants to be a nun is an act of rebellion, that it's opposing her mother's wishes to marry her to Don Casimiro. Now then, what do you think of my unfortunate friend's situation?"

Questioned so directly, the commander finally had to break his silence, but he answered laconically:

"The situation, truth to tell, is bad … but who knows? Everything has a remedy except death. Meanwhile," added Don Fadrique, speaking slowly and softly, articulating his words clearly, as if it were a great effort

costasen grandes esfuerzos, y como si en vez de responder a su sobrina hablase consigo mismo y a sí propio se respondiese –; entre tanto, doña Blanca es discreta, es piadosa y es buena madre. Razones de mucho peso tiene... sin duda... para querer casar a su hija con don Casimiro. En fin, muchacha, sigue siendo buena amiga de Clara; pero no caviles ni formes juicios acerca de la conducta de doña Blanca. Voy, además, a hacerte otra súplica:

–Mande usted, tío.

–Es algo difícil lo que exijo de ti.

–¿Por qué?

–Porque te gusta hablar, y lo que exijo es que calles.

–¿Y qué he de callar? Ya verá usted cómo me callo. Yo no quiero que usted se disguste y forme mal concepto de mí,

–Pues bien; calla que me has puesto al corriente de los amores de don Carlos y doña Clara, y calla también cuanto sabes de estos amores.

–¡Tío, por amor de Dios! No me crea usted tan amiga de contarlo todo. El pícaro idilio tiene la culpa. Sin idilio, ni a usted le hubiera yo confiado nada.

Oído esto, sonrió el comendador a su sobrina; y como ya estaban en la casa, se apartó de la muchacha, yéndose algo meditabundo y ensimismado, cual si procurase resolver un difícil problema.

9

MIENTRAS el comendador y Lucía tenían el diálogo de que acabamos de dar cuenta, Clara había entrado en el cuarto de su madre.

Doña Blanca estaba sentada en un sillón de brazos. Delante de ella había un velador con libros y papeles. Don Valentín estaba allí, sentado en una silla, y no muy distante de su mujer.

El aspecto de doña Blanca era noble y distinguido. Vestida con sencillez y severidad, todavía se notaban en su traje cierta elegancia y cierto señorío. Tendría doña Blanca poco más de cuarenta años. Bastantes canas daban ya un color ceniciento a la primitiva negrura de sus cabellos. Su semblante, lleno de gravedad austera, era muy hermoso. Las facciones, todas de la más perfecta regularidad.

and as if, instead of answering his niece, he were speaking to himself and answering himself, "meanwhile, Doña Blanca is sensible, pious, and a good mother. She has sound reasons … no doubt … to want to marry her daughter to Don Casimiro. In short, girl, continue to be a good friend to Clara, but do not ponder or form judgments about Doña Blanca's conduct. In addition, I'm going to ask something else of you."

"Ask away, Uncle."

"What I'm going to ask of you is somewhat difficult."

"Why?"

"Because you like to talk, and what I ask is that you keep quiet."

"And what am I to keep quiet about? You'll see that I will. I don't want you to be displeased and form a poor opinion of me."

"All right. Keep quiet the fact that you have made me privy to Don Carlos and Doña Clara's love affair, and keep quiet too everything that you know about this love affair."

"Uncle, for the love of God! Do not think me so fond of spilling everything. It's the fault of that darned idyll. Without the idyll, I wouldn't even have told *you* anything."

Hearing this, the commander smiled at his niece, and since they were already in the house, he took leave of the girl, walking away from her in a somewhat pensive, self-absorbed mood, as if he were trying to resolve a thorny problem.

9

While the commander and Lucía were engaged in the conversation that we have just related, Clara had entered her mother's room.

Doña Blanca was sitting in an armchair, before a pedestal table with books and papers on it. Don Valentín was also there, sitting on a chair not very far from his wife.

Doña Blanca had a noble, distinguished appearance. Although she dressed simply and severely, you could still see a certain elegance and a certain stateliness in her attire. She looked to be in her early forties, with a number of gray hairs already lending an ashen color to the primary black. Her visage, which revealed an austere gravity, was stern and very beautiful, all the features of the most perfect regularity.

Era doña Blanca alta y delgada. Sus manos, blancas, parecían transparentes. Sus ojos, negros como los de su hija, tenían un fuego singular e indefinible, como si todas las pasiones del cielo y de la tierra y todos los sentimientos de ángeles y diablos hubiesen concurrido a crearle.

Don Valentín, tímido y pacífico, enamorado de su mujer en los primeros años de matrimonio, y lleno después de consideración hacia ella, no se atrevía a chistar en su presencia, si ella no le mandaba que hablase.

Era don Valentín un virtuoso caballero, pero débil y pusilánime. Había sido, por amor y respeto a su honra, un magistrado íntegro. Nada había podido apartarle del cumplimiento de su deber, y hasta había mostrado admirable entereza fuera de casa, donde la entereza, por grande que deba ser, basta con que dure un instante; pero en la casa, con la doméstica tiranía de una mujer dotada de voluntad de hierro, cuya presión era perpetua e incesante, don Valentín no había sabido resistir, y había abdicado por completo. La hacienda, los negocios, la educación de su hija, todo dependía y todo era dirigido y gobernado por doña Blanca.

El aspecto de don Valentín era insignificante y neutral.

Ni alto ni bajo, ni pelinegro ni rubio, ni flaco ni gordo. Parecía, con todo, un señor, por decirlo así, muy correcto en sus modales, en su continente y en su habla. La devota sumisión a su mujer añadía a dicha calidad de correcto una tintura de mansedumbre.

Don Valentín había sido en su mocedad muy buen católico, pero sin fervor penitente y sin inclinaciones místicas y contemplativas. Ahora, por no desazonar a su mujer, se esforzaba por remedar a San Hilarión o a San Pacomio.

Tenía don Valentín cerca de sesenta años de edad, pero parecía mucho más viejo, porque no hay cosa que envejezca y arruine más el brío y la fortaleza de los hombres que esta servidumbre voluntaria y espantosa, a que por raro misterio de la voluntad se someten muchos, cediendo a la persistencia endemoniada de sus mujeres.

No bien entró Clara en el cuarto, doña Blanca le preguntó:

–¿Dónde has estado, niña?

–Mamá, en el *nacimiento*.

–No sé cómo tiene pies mi señora doña Antonia para dar paseos tan disparatados. Con ir y volver, eso es andar cerca de una legua.

–Doña Antonia no ha estado hoy con nosotras– dijo Clara, no atreviéndose a mentir, ni siquiera a disimular.

Doña Blanca was tall and thin. Her hands, which were white, looked transparent. Her eyes, black like her daughter's, had a peculiar, indefinable fire, as if all the passions of heaven and earth and all the feelings of angels and demons had conspired to create it.

Don Valentín, timid and peaceable, in love with his wife during the early years of their marriage and afterwards full of consideration for her, did not dare to utter a word in her presence, except when she bade him speak.

Don Valentín was a virtuous gentleman, but weak and pusillanimous. He had been, out of love and regard for his honor, an honest, upright magistrate. Nothing had been able to keep him from fulfilling his duty, and he had shown admirable firmness outside of the home, where firmness – however great it ought to be – suffices even if it lasts a mere instant, but at home, in the face of the domestic tyranny of a woman endowed with an iron will, whose pressure was perpetual and incessant, Don Valentín had been unable to resist and had abdicated completely. Their properties, their finances, the education of their daughter, all these things depended on and were directed and managed by Doña Blanca.

Don Valentín's appearance was insignificant and unprepossessing.

Neither tall nor short, neither dark- nor light-haired, neither skinny nor fat. Nevertheless, he seemed, so to speak, like a man who was proper in his manners, in his demeanor, and in his speech. The devoted submissiveness to his wife added to said propriety a veneer of meekness.

In his youth Don Valentín had been a very good Catholic, but without penitential fervor, without contemplative and mystical inclinations. Now, so as not to upset his wife, he strove to be a Saint Hilarion or a Saint Pachomius.[58]

Don Valentín was nearing sixty, but he looked much older because there is nothing that ages and wrecks a man's spirit and fortitude more than this frightful and voluntary servitude, to which, out of some strange mystery of the will, many men subject themselves, giving in to the diabolical persistence of their wives.

No sooner did Clara enter the room than Doña Blanca asked her:

"Where have you been, child?"

"At the source, Mamá."

"I do not know how Señora doña Antonia has feet to take such unheard-of walks. There and back, that's close to a three-mile hike."

"Doña Antonia didn't go with us today," said Clara, not daring to lie, nor even to pretend.

El rostro de doña Blanca tomó cierta expresión de sorpresa y de notable desagrado.

–Entonces ¿quién os ha acompañado en el paseo?– preguntó doña Blanca.

–No se enoje usted, mamá: hemos ido bien acompañadas.

–Sí; pero ¿por quién? ¿Por alguna fregona? ¿Por alguna tía cualquiera?

–Mire usted, mamá, doña Antonia tenía la jaqueca y no pudo acompañarnos. En su lugar ha venido con nosotras el tío de Lucía.

–¿Y quién es ese tío?

–Un señor marino que estuvo en la India y en el Perú, que dice que conoce a usted, que hace poco ha venido a vivir a Villabermeja, y que anoche llegó aquí a pasar una temporada.

–Ése es el comendador Mendoza– dijo don Valentín, con cierto júbilo de saber que había llegado un antiguo amigo.

–Justamente, papá, así se llama: el comendador Mendoza; un señor muy fino, si bien algo raro.

–Oye, Blanca, será menester que vayamos a ver al comendador, que vive sin duda en casa de su hermano– exclamó don Valentín.

–Cumpliremos con ese deber que la sociedad nos impone– dijo doña Blanca con reposo y dignidad serena –; pero tú, Clara, no debes volver a salir de paseo ni tratarte con ese hombre, malvado e impío. Si la santa fe de nuestros padres no estuviera tan perdida; si las perversas doctrinas del filosofismo francés no nos hubiesen inficionado, ese hombre, en vez de vestir el honroso uniforme de la marina, vestiría el sambenito; en vez de andar libre por ahí, piedra de escándalo, fermento de impiedad, levadura del infierno, corrompiendo lo que aún en el cuerpo social se conserva sano, estaría en los calabozos de la Inquisición o ya hubiera muerto en la hoguera.

Clara se aterró al oír en boca de su madre aquella diatriba. Se representó en su mente al comendador como a un personaje endiablado; y, acordándose del tierno beso que de él había recibido, se llenó toda de espanto y de vergüenza.

Don Valentín, con el recuerdo del comendador, que le traía a la imaginación mejores tiempos, cuando él estaba menos viejo y menos sumiso, se sentía, contra su costumbre, con ánimo de contradecir y no someterse del todo. Así es que dijo:

–¡Válgame Dios, mujer, qué falta de caridad es ésa! Eres injusta con nuestro antiguo amigo. No te negaré yo que era algo *esprit fort* en su

Doña Blanca's face took on a certain expression of surprise and evident displeasure.

"Then who accompanied you on the walk?" asked Doña Blanca.

"Don't get angry, Mamá. We were in good hands."

"Yes, but whose? Some kitchen maid's? Those of some common woman?"

"Look, Mamá. Doña Antonia had a migraine today and couldn't accompany us. Lucía's uncle came with us in her place."

"And who is that uncle?"

"A naval officer who was in India and Peru, who says that he knows you, who not long ago went to live in Villabermeja, and who arrived here last night to visit for a spell."

"That's Commander Mendoza," said Don Valentín with a certain joy upon learning that an old friend had arrived.

"Precisely, Papá, that's his name: Commander Mendoza. A very refined gentleman, although a bit strange."

"Listen, Blanca, we'll have to go and see the commander, who no doubt is staying at his brother's house," interjected Don Valentín.

"We shall fulfill that duty, as required by society," said Doña Blanca, with calm and serene dignity, "but you, Clara, are not to go on another walk nor have anything to do with that impious, wicked man. If the faith of our ancestors were not so lost; if the perverse doctrines of French philosophism had not corrupted us, that man, instead of wearing the honorable uniform of the Spanish navy, would be wearing the sanbenito;[59] instead of walking around freely, a source of scandal, fountainhead of hell, perverting what is still kept sound in the social fabric, he would be in the dungeons of the Inquisition or would have already died at the stake."

Clara was horror-stricken to hear that diatribe from her mother's lips. She pictured the commander in her mind as a diabolical personage, and, remembering the tender kiss that she had received from him, was altogether filled with consternation and shame.

With the recollection of the commander, which brought to mind better times, when he was not as old and as submissive, Don Valentín felt himself, contrary to his custom, armed with the nerve to contradict his wife and not give in completely. Thus it was that he said:

"Good Lord, woman, what a lack of charity that is! I won't deny that he was somewhat of an *esprit fort* in his youth, but he must have mended

mocedad, pero ya se habrá enmendado. Por lo demás, siempre fue el comendador pundonoroso, hidalgo y bueno. ¿Qué tienes tú que decir contra su moralidad?

–Cállate, Valentín, que no dices más que sandeces. Y las llamo sandeces, por no calificarlas de blasfemias. ¿Qué moralidad, qué hidalguía, qué virtud puede haber donde falta la religión y las creencias, que son su fundamento? Sin el santo temor de Dios toda virtud es mentira y toda acción moral es un artificio del diablo para engañar a los bobos que presumen de discretos y que no subordinan su juicio a los que saben más que ellos. Ya lo he dicho y lo repito: el comendador Mendoza era un impío y un libertino, y seguirá siéndolo. Nosotros iremos a visitarle para no chocar, procurando no hallarle en casa y ver sólo a doña Antonia y a su bendito marido. En cuanto a Clarita, se buscará un pretexto cualquiera para que no salga más con Lucía, exponiéndose a ir en compañía de ese renegado, jacobino, volteriano y ateo. Primero confiaría yo a Clara al cuidado de la más vil pecadora de las mujeres. Esta mujer, con el auxilio de la religión, puede regenerarse y llegar a ser una santa; pero de quien niega a Dios o le aborrece, del empedernido de toda la vida, ¿qué esperanza es lícito concebir?

Clarita y don Valentín se compungieron y amilanaron con el sermón de doña Blanca, y nada supieron contestarle.

Quedó, pues, resuelto que Clarita, por culpa del comendador y para que no se contaminase, no volvería a pasear con Lucía.

10

Las resoluciones de doña Blanca Roldán eran irrevocables y efectivas. Ella sabía darles cumplimiento con calma persistente.

Una mañana, después de oír misa con don Valentín, estuvo doña Blanca a visitar a doña Antonia y a felicitarla por la venida de su cuñado; y fue con tal tino, que no se hallaba el comendador en casa.

Ni antes ni después de esta visita se dejaron ver doña Blanca y don Valentín de sus vecinos y amigos. Retirados siempre en el fondo del

his ways. As to the rest, the commander was always honorable, noble, and good. What do you have to say against his morality?"

"Be quiet, Valentín, because you are only speaking nonsense. And I call it nonsense so as not to characterize it as blasphemy. What morality, what nobility, what virtue can there be, absent religion and beliefs, which are their basis? Without the fear of God every virtue is a lie and every moral act is an artifice of the devil to deceive fools who pride themselves on being discreet and who do not subordinate their judgment to those who know more than they do. I have already said it and I will say it again: Commander Mendoza was an ungodly man and a libertine, and will continue being one. We will go to visit him so as not to be discourteous, but with the hope of not finding him at home, and then see only Doña Antonia and her saintly husband. As for Clarita, some sort of pretext will be found for her not to go out any more with Lucía, when she would only run the risk of being in the company of that apostate, that Jacobin, that Voltairean and atheist. I would sooner entrust Clara to the care of the most depraved of sinful women, one who, with the aid of religion, can reform and become a saint. But the man who denies God or who abhors him, a lifelong transgressor … what hope is it permissible to hold out for him?"

Clarita and Don Valentín, intimidated by Doña Blanca's sermon, felt remorse and found themselves at a loss to respond.

It was determined, therefore, that Clarita – because of the commander, and to keep her from being corrupted by him – would not go on walks again with Lucía.

10

Doña Blanca Roldán's decisions were irrevocable and effective. She knew how to enforce them with a persistent calm.

One morning, after hearing mass with Don Valentín, Doña Blanca went to visit Doña Antonia and congratulate her on the arrival of her brother-in-law, and she did so with such forethought in regard to the hour that the commander was not at home.

Neither before nor after this visit were Doña Blanca and Don Valentín seen by their neighbors and friends. Always in seclusion in the bosom of

antiguo caserón en que vivían, y pretextando enfermedades, no recibían visitas, a pesar de lo difícil y odioso que es negarse a recibir, estando en casa, cuando se vive en un pueblo pequeño.

En balde intentó repetidas veces Lucía sacar a paseo a Clara. Siempre que envió recado, le contestaron que Clara estaba mal de salud o muy ocupada y que le era imposible salir.

Lucía fue ella misma a ver a Clara, y sólo dos veces pudo verla, pero en presencia de su madre.

Estas pruebas de retraimiento y hasta de desvío estaban suavizadas por una extrema cortesía de parte de doña Blanca; aunque bien se dejaba conocer que si esta señora ponía de su parte cuantos medios le sugería su urbanidad a fin de no dar motivo de agravio, preferiría agraviar, si por agraviado se daba alguien, a cejar un punto en su propósito.

Fuera del día en que visitó a doña Antonia, no ponía doña Blanca los pies en la calle sino de madrugada, para ir a la iglesia, a misa y demás devociones. Don Valentín la acompañaba casi siempre, como un lego o doctrino humilde, y Clara la acompañaba siempre, sin osar apenas levantar los ojos del suelo.

Lucía, cavilando sobre las causas de aquella poco menos que completa ruptura de relaciones, llegó a temer que doña Blanca hubiese averiguado los amores de Clara con don Carlos de Atienza, la presencia de éste en la ciudad y la entrada y protección con que contaba en su casa.

Doña Clara no hablaba a solas ni escribía a su amiga; por los criados nada podía averiguarse, porque los de doña Blanca eran forasteros casi todos, y o no tenían confianza en la casa, o hacían una vida devota y apartada, imitando y complaciendo así a sus amos.

Sólo podía afirmarse que la única persona que entraba de visita en casa de don Valentín era su cercano pariente don Casimiro.

De esta suerte se pasaron diez días, que a don Carlos, a Lucía y al comendador parecieron diez siglos, cuando al anochecer, en una hermosa tarde, el comendador estaba en el patio de la casa solo con su sobrina. Esta traía con su tío una conversación muy animada, mostrándole las plantas y las flores que en arriates y en multitud de tiestos adornaban aquel patio, contiguo, como ya hemos dicho, al de la casa de don Valentín. Salvando el muro divisorio, la voz de ambos interlocutores podía llegar al patio inmediato. La voz llegó, en efecto, porque en medio de la conversación

the large, rambling old house in which they lived, and pleading illnesses, they received no visitors, in spite of how difficult and unpleasant it is to refuse to receive, being at home, when one resides in a small town.

In vain did Lucía try repeatedly to take Clara for a walk. Whenever she sent a message, a reply came back saying that Clara did not feel well or was very busy, which made it impossible for her to go out.

Lucía went herself to see Clara, but managed to do so only twice, and then in her mother's presence.

These proofs of withdrawal and even indifference were softened by an extreme courtesy on the part of Doña Blanca, although it was obvious that if this *señora* availed herself of all the means suggested by politeness not to give cause for offense, she would prefer to offend, were someone to take offense, rather than back down one iota in her designs.

Apart from the day that she visited Doña Antonia, Doña Blanca did not set foot in the street except to go to church very early in the morning, that is, to mass and other devotions. Like a lay brother or a humble orphan, Don Valentín almost always accompanied her, and Clara always did accompany her, scarcely daring to raise her eyes from the ground.

Reflecting on the causes of that nearly complete breaking-off of relations, Lucía came to fear that Doña Blanca had learned of Doña Clara's love affair with Don Carlos de Atienza, the presence of the latter in the city, and the entrée and protection that he enjoyed in her house.

Doña Clara did not speak alone with nor write to her friend. Nothing could be learned from the servants, because Doña Blanca's were almost all strangers there, and either they were not trusted in the house or they led a withdrawn, devout life, thus imitating and pleasing their mistress and master.

Just one thing could be affirmed: the only person who entered Don Valentín's house to pay a visit was his close relative Don Casimiro.

Ten days went by in this fashion, days that to Don Carlos, Lucía, and the commander seemed like ten centuries, when at the close of a beautiful afternoon, the commander was alone in the patio with his niece. The latter was carrying on a very animated conversation with her uncle, showing him the plants and the flowers that in beds and in a multitude of pots adorned that patio, which, as we have already said, was adjacent to that of Don Valentín's house. Despite the dividing wall, the voices of both speakers could be overheard next door, and proof of this reach soon came, because in the middle of their conversation Lucía and the

sintieron Lucía y el comendador el ruido de un pequeño objeto pesado que caía a sus pies. Lucía se bajó con prontitud a recogerle, y no bien le tuvo en la mano, dijo a su tío, toda alborozada y en voz baja:

—Es una carta de Clarita. ¡Qué buena es! Me quiere de veras. Menester es conocerla como yo la conozco, para estimar lo que vale esta fineza de su amistad. ¡Burlar por mí la vigilancia de su madre! ¡Escribirme furtivamente! Calle usted... tío... si parece imposible. ¡Por mí, esa infeliz, que es una santa, ha faltado a su deber de obediencia filial! ¿Y cómo, dónde, a qué hora habrá podido escribirme? Vamos... si le digo a usted que es un milagro de cariño. Y la picarita ¿con qué angustia habrá estado espiando la ocasión de echarme la carta, segura de que yo la recogería? ¡Benditas sean sus manos!

Y diciendo esto había desatado el papel de la china en que venía liado con un hilo, y se diría que quería comérsele a besos.

—Ven a leer esa carta— dijo el comendador –, donde haya luz y donde no vengan a interrumpirnos. En el despacho no hay nadie y ahora acaban de encender el velón. Ven, que ya es de noche y aquí no verás.

Lucía fue al despacho con su tío, y con acento conmovido, casi al oído del comendador, leyó lo siguiente:

«Mi querida Lucía: De sobra conoces tú lo mucho que te quiero. Considera, pues, cuánto me afligirá verte tan poco y no poder hablarte. Mi madre lo exige, y una buena hija debe complacer a su madre. No creas que mi madre ha sospechado nada de mis desenvolturas con don Carlos de Atienza. Me echo a temblar al representarme en la mente que hubiera podido sospecharlo. Nadie sabe más que tú, el comendador y yo, que don Carlos me pretende; pero Dios sabe mi pecado, del que estoy arrepentida. Ha sido enorme perversidad en mí dar alas a ese galán con miradas dulces y profanas sonrisas... casi involuntarias... te lo juro. No por eso me pesan menos en la conciencia. Algo he hecho yo, o arrastrada por mi maldad nativa, o seducida por el enemigo común de nuestro linaje, para alborotar a ese mozo, hacerle abandonar su Universidad y sus estudios, y moverle a venir aquí en persecución mía. En medio de todo, harto

commander distinguished the sound of a small, heavy object falling at their feet. Lucía quickly bent over to pick it up, and as soon as she had it in her hand, she said softly and all excited to her uncle:

"It's a letter from Clarita. How good she is! She really does love me. You have to know her as I do in order to appreciate what this token of her friendship means. To escape, for my sake, her mother's vigilance! To write to me furtively! I'm telling you, Uncle, it seems impossible! For my sake, that poor thing, who is a saint, has disregarded her duty of filial obedience! And how, where, when can she have written to me? Truly, Uncle, its's a miracle of affection. And with what anguish the sly girl must have been watching for a chance to throw me the letter, certain that I would pick it up! Blessed be her hands!"

And as she was saying this, she untied the letter from the pebble to which it was attached by a thread, and it seemed as though she wanted to devour it with kisses.

"Come to read that letter," said the commander, "where there's light and where nobody will interrupt us. The study is deserted and they've just now lit the oil lamp. Come, because it's dark already and you won't see here."

Lucía went to the study with her uncle and, in an emotional tone of voice, practically read in the commander's ear what follows:

My dear Lucía:

You know only too well how much I love you. Consider, then, how much it pains me to see so little of you and not be able to talk to you. My mother requires it, and a good daughter should oblige her mother. Don't think that my mother has suspected anything about my forwardness with Don Carlos de Atienza. I start trembling when I imagine that she might suspect it. Only you, the commander, and I know that Don Carlos courts me, but God knows my sin, of which I have repented. It was awful perversity on my part to encourage that suitor with sweet glances and immodest smiles – which were almost involuntary, I swear it. Not for that reason, though, do they weigh any less heavily on my conscience. I have done something, either prompted by my innate wickedness or seduced by the common enemy of our lineage, to agitate that young man, to make him abandon his university and his studies and to induce him to come here in pursuit of me. Nonetheless, in the midst of everything, I have much to be

tengo que agradecer a Jesús y a María Santísima, que se apiadan de mí, a pesar de lo indigna que soy, y disponen que no se solemnice mi falta con el escándalo. Favor sobrenatural del cielo es, sin duda, el que siga oculto el móvil que ha impulsado a don Carlos a venir aquí. La gente cree que vino y está aquí por ti. ¡Cuánto debo agradecerte que cargues con esta culpa! Si yo no hubiera sido atrevida, si yo no hubiera animado a don Carlos, si yo hubiera tenido la severidad y el recato convenientes, no me vería ahora en tan amargo trance. ¡Ay, mi querida Lucía! El corazón humano es un abismo de iniquidad... y de contradicciones. ¿Quieres creer que, si por un lado me desespero de haber dado ocasión para que don Carlos haya venido persiguiéndome, por otro lado me lisonjea, me encanta que haya venido, y advierto que si no hubiera venido sería yo más desgraciada? En medio de todo... no lo dudes... yo soy muy mala. Estoy avergonzada de mi hipocresía. Estoy engañando a mi madre, que es tan perspicaz. Mi madre me juzga demasiado buena... y vela por mí, como el avaro por su tesoro, cuando el tesoro está ya perdido. No acierto a decírtelo para que no te enojes, y, no obstante, quiero decírtelo. No cumpliría con un deber de conciencia si no te lo dijese. La causa de que mi madre me aparte de ti es tu tío. A mí me pareció un caballero muy fino y bueno; pero mi madre asegura, ¡qué horror!, que no cree en Dios. ¿Es posible ¡hija mía!, que hiera el demonio con tan abominable ceguedad los ojos de algunas almas? ¿Se comprende que la copia, la imagen, la semejanza, renieguen del original divino que les presta el único valor y noble ser que tienen? Si ello es cierto, si el comendador está obcecado en sus impiedades, ármate de prudencia y pide al cielo que te salve. Procura también traer a tu tío al buen camino. Tú tienes extraordinario despejo y don de expresarte con primor y entusiasmo. El Altísimo, además, se vale a menudo de los débiles para sus grandes victorias. Acuérdate de David mancebo, que era un pastorcillo sin fuerzas, y venció y derribó al gigante en el valle del Terebinto. ¿Cuántas hermanas, hijas, madres y esposas, no han logrado convencer a sus descarriados maridos, hermanos, hijos o padres? A gloria parecida debes aspirar tú, y Dios te premiará y te dará brío para alcanzarla. En cuanto a mí, aun siendo

grateful for to our Lord and to the Blessed Virgin Mary, who take pity on me, in spite of how unworthy I am, and who arrange not to let my fault be celebrated by scandal. The motive that drove Don Carlos to come here remains a secret, and this secret is without a doubt a supernatural favor. People think that he came and is here because of you. Oh, how much I should thank you for shouldering all this blame! If I had not been bold, if I had not encouraged Don Carlos, if I had had the opportune severity and caution, I would not find myself at such a bitter, critical juncture. Oh, my dearest Lucía! The human heart is an abyss of iniquity ... and of contradictions. Would you believe that if on the one hand I despair at having given occasion for Don Carlos to have come in pursuit of me, on the other it flatters me, it delights me that he has come, and I am sensible of the fact that if he had not come I would be more distraught? In the midst of everything ... have no doubts – I am a very bad person. I'm ashamed of my hypocrisy. I'm deceiving my mother, who is so clear-sighted. My mother thinks me too good, and she watches over me, like the miser over his treasure, when the treasure is already lost.

I'm not quite sure how to tell you this without upsetting you, and nevertheless I want to tell you. I would not be listening to my conscience if I didn't tell you. The reason my mother is keeping us apart is your uncle. He seemed to me a very refined gentleman and a good person, but my mother assures me – horrors! – that he does not believe in God. Is it possible, my friend, that the devil smites the eyes of some souls with such abominable blindness? Is it understandable that the copy, the image, the likeness should renounce the divine original that lends them the only worth and noble life that they have? If this is true, if the commander is stubbornly entrenched in his impieties, arm yourself with prudence and ask heaven to save you. Try also to put your uncle on the right path. You are extraordinarily clear-headed and blessed with the gift of expressing yourself eloquently and enthusiastically. Besides, the Almighty often avails himself of the weak to achieve his great victories. Remember David, a boy, who was a powerless young shepherd, and he defeated and brought down the giant in the Vale of the Terebinth. How many sisters, daughters, mothers, and wives have not succeeded in convincing their errant husbands, brothers, sons or fathers? You should aspire to a like glory, and God will reward you and give you the determination to attain it. As for me, even being so

tan niña, soy una miserable pecadora, y bastante tarea tengo con llorar mis locuras y apaciguar la tempestad de encontrados sentimientos que me destrozan el pecho. Dame la última y mayor prueba de amistad. Persuade a don Carlos de que no le amo. Dile que se vuelva a Sevilla y me deje. Convéncele de que soy fea, de que gusto de don Casimiro, de que mi ingratitud hacia él merece su desprecio. Yo debiera haberle hablado en este sentido: pero soy tan débil y tan tonta, que no hubiese atinado a decírselo, y tal vez le hubiera inducido estúpidamente a que creyese todo lo contrario. Por amor de Dios, Lucía de mi alma, despide por mí a don Carlos. Yo no puedo, no debo ser suya. Que se vaya; que no disguste por mí a sus padres; que no pierda sus estudios; que no motive un escándalo cuando se sepa que vino por mí y que yo soy una malvada, provocativa, seductora, quién sabe... Adiós. Estoy apuradísima. No tengo a nadie a quien confiar mis cosas, con quien desahogar mis penas, a quien pedir consejo y remedio. Espero con ansia la llegada del padre Jacinto, que es el oráculo de esta casa. Sé que lo que yo le diga caerá como en un pozo, y que sus consejos son sanos. Es el único hombre que tiene algún imperio sobre mi madre. ¿Cuándo vendrá de Villabermeja? Adiós, repito, y ama y compadece a tu Clara.»

11

Esta carta inocente, tan propia de una niña de diez y seis años, discreta y educada con devoción y recogimiento, gustó mucho al comendador; pero también le dio no poco que pensar. No entraremos nosotros en el fondo de su alma a escudriñar sus pensamientos, y nos limitaremos a decir que tomó tres resoluciones de resultas de aquella lectura.

Fue la primera buscar modo de ver y de hablar a la severísima doña Blanca; la segunda, sondear bien el ánimo de don Carlos para conocer hasta qué punto amaba de veras a la niña y merecía su amor, y la tercera tratar con el padre Jacinto y proporcionarse en él un aliado para la guerra que tal vez tendría que declarar a la madre de Clarita.

much a girl, I am a wretched sinner, and I have enough of a burden to bear with lamenting my folly and calming the tempest of conflicting feelings that are breaking my heart. Give me the ultimate and greatest proof of friendship. Persuade Don Carlos that I do not love him. Tell him to leave me and return to Seville. Convince him that I am ugly, that I like Don Casimiro, that my ingratitude toward him deserves his contempt. I myself should have said these things to him, but I am so weak and so foolish that I would have stupidly led him to believe just the opposite. For the love of God, my dear, dear Lucía, send Don Carlos away for me. I cannot, should not be his. Let him go home; let him not displease his parents because of me; let him not quit his studies; let him not give rise to scandal when it becomes known that he came on account of me and that I am an evil, provocative temptress of a girl … who knows. Good-bye. I am so distressed! I have nobody to whom to confide my affairs and to whom to unburden my troubles, nobody from whom to seek counsel and help. I anxiously await the arrival of Father Jacinto, who is the oracle of this house. I know that whatever I tell him will be kept in the strictest confidence, and that his advice is sound. He is the only man who has any sway over my mother. When will he come from Villabermeja? Good-bye a second time, and love and pity your,

Clara

11

This innocent letter, so typical of a discreet sixteen-year-old girl who was raised devoutly and led a secluded life, pleased the commander greatly, but it also gave him much to mull over. We shall not explore the depths of his soul in order to plumb his thoughts and will limit ourselves to saying that he made three decisions as a result of that reading.

The first was to look for a way of seeing and talking to the very severe Doña Blanca; the second, to probe Don Carlos's spirit in order to determine to what extent he really loved the girl and whether he deserved her love; and the third, to confer with Father Jacinto and gain in him an ally in the war that he would perhaps have to declare on Clarita's mother.

A fin de conseguir lo primero, en vez de escribir pidiendo una audiencia, que con cualquiera pretexto y muy políticamente se le hubiera negado, discurrió don Fadrique levantarse al día siguiente de madrugada, aguardar en la calle a doña Blanca cuando ella saliese para acudir a la iglesia, e ir derecho a hablarle, sin miedo alguno.

Así lo hizo el comendador. Doña Blanca, antes de las seis, apareció en la calle, con Clarita y don Valentín. Iba a misa a la Iglesia Mayor. Apenas los vio salir don Fadrique, se acercó muy determinado, y saludando cortésmente con sombrero en mano, dijo:

–Beso a usted los pies, mi señora doña Blanca. Dichosos los ojos que logran ver a usted y a su familia. Buenos días, amigo don Valentín. Clarita, buenos días.

Don Valentín, al verse llamar amigo tan blandamente y por una voz conocida y simpática, no se pudo contener; no reflexionó, se dejó llevar del primer ímpetu cariñoso y se fue hacia don Fadrique con los brazos abiertos. Por dicha, no obstante, don Valentín tenía la inveterada costumbre de no hacer la menor cosa sin mirar antes a su mujer para notar la cara que ponía y si le retraía de consumar o le alentaba a que consumase su conato de acción. A pesar, pues, de lo entusiasmado que iba a abrazar a don Fadrique, el instinto le indujo a que mecánicamente volviera la cara hacia doña Blanca antes de llegarse a dar el abrazo. Indescriptible es lo que vio entonces en los fulminantes ojos de su mujer. Casi no se puede describir el efecto que le produjo aquella mirada. Creyó don Valentín leer en ella el más profundo desdén, como si le acusase de una humillación estólida, de una bajeza infame; y creyó ver, al mismo tiempo, la ira y la prohibición imperiosa de que llevase a cabo lo que se había lanzado a ejecutar. El terror sobrecogió de tal suerte el ánimo de don Valentín, que se paró, se quedó inmóvil de súbito, como si se hubiera convertido en piedra. Sólo con voz apagada y apenas perceptible exhaló, por último, como lánguido suspiro, un:

–Buenos días, señor don Fadrique.

–Buenos días,– dijo también Clara, no con más aliento que su padre.

Doña Blanca miró de pies a cabeza al comendador, y con reposo y suave acento, sin alterarse ni descomponerse en lo más mínimo, le habló de esta manera:

–Caballero: Dios, que es infinitamente misericordioso, tenga a usted

So as to realize the first one, instead of writing to ask for a meeting, which with some pretext – and very politically – would have been refused him, Don Fadrique hit upon rising very early the next morning, waiting in the street for Doña Blanca when she left to go to church, and going right up to talk to her, without any hesitation whatsoever.

Which is what the commander did. Before six o'clock Doña Blanca, together with Don Valentín and Clarita, came out into the street. They were going to mass at the main church. No sooner did Don Fadrique spot them than he approached in a very determined fashion and, courteously greeting all three with a wave of his hat, said:

"At your service, Señora doña Blanca. What a pleasure to see you and your family. Good morning, Don Valentín, my friend. Clarita, good morning."

Upon hearing himself called "friend" so cordially, and by a genial, well-known voice, Don Valentín could not hold himself in check; he did not reflect and gave in to the first affectionate impulse, taking a step toward Don Fadrique with open arms. Fortunately, however – for his own good, as it turned out – Don Valentín had the inveterate habit of not doing the slightest thing without first glancing at his wife to see how she was reacting and whether she was discouraging him or encouraging him. So in spite of the enthusiasm with which he was going to embrace Don Fadrique, instinct induced him to turn mechanically toward Doña Blanca before actually giving the embrace. What he saw in his wife's fiery eyes beggars description. The effect produced in him by that withering look makes words seem inadequate. Don Valentín thought he read in it the most profound scorn, as if she were accusing him of a dimwitted humiliation, of an infamous act; and he thought he saw at the same time fury and an imperious prohibition against carrying through on what he had begun to effect. Terror seized Don Valentín's soul to such an extent that all of a sudden he froze, as if he had been turned into stone. Only in a very weak, barely audible, voice did he finally utter, like a languid sigh, a muted:

"Good morning, Señor don Fadrique."

"Good morning," said Clara, with no more spirit than her father.

Doña Blanca eyed the commander from head to toe, and in a calm, collected tone, without becoming agitated, without getting worked up in the slightest, said to him:

"Sir: May God, who is infinitely merciful, keep you in his holy

en su santa guarda. No por amor suyo, de que usted carece, sino por el mundano honor de que usted se jacta y por los respetos y consideraciones que todo hombre bien nacido debe a las damas, ruego a usted que no nos distraiga del camino que llevamos, ni perturbe nuestra vida retirada y devota.

Y dicho esto, hizo doña Blanca al comendador una ceremoniosa y fría reverencia, y echó a andar con sosegada gravedad, siguiéndola don Valentín y llevando delante a Clara.

Don Fadrique pagó la reverencia con otra; se quedó algo atolondrado, y dijo entre dientes:

—Está visto: es menester acudir a otros medios.

No bien la familia de Solís se hubo alejado treinta pasos del comendador, vio éste que doña Blanca se volvía a hablar con su marido.

Es evidente que el comendador no oyó lo que le decía; pero el novelista todo lo sabe y todo lo oye. Doña Blanca, que trataba siempre de usted y con el mayor cumplimiento a su señor marido, cuando le echaba un sermón o reprimenda, le habló así mientras Clara iba delante:

—Mil veces se lo tengo dicho a usted, señor don Valentín. Ese hombre, que usted se empeñó en introducir en casa, allá en Lima, es un libertino, impío y grosero. Su trato, ya que no inficione, mancha o puede manchar la acrisolada reputación de cualquier señora. Yo tuve necesidad poco menos que de echarle de casa. Motivos hubo, en su falta de miramientos y hasta de respeto, para que en otras edades bárbaras, olvidando la ley divina, alguien le hubiera dado una severa lección, como solían darla los caballeros. Esto no había de ser: era imposible... Nada que más repugne a mi conciencia; nada más contrario a mis principios; pero hay un justo medio... Delito es matar a quien ha ofendido... pero es vileza abrazarle. Señor don Valentín, usted no tiene sangre en las venas.

Todo esto lo fue soltando, despacio y bajo, casi en el oído de don Valentín, su tremenda esposa doña Blanca.

Fueron tan duras y crueles las últimas frases, que don Valentín estuvo a punto de alzar bandera de rebelión, armar en la calle la de Dios es Cristo y contestar a su mujer lo que merecía; pero el olor de mil flores regalaba el olfato; la gente pasaba con alegre aspecto; el día estaba hermosísimo; la paz reinaba en el cielo; un fresco vientecillo primaveral oreaba y calmaba las sienes más ardorosas; la familia de Solís iba al incruento sacrificio de la misa; Clara marchaba delante tan linda y

embrace. Not out of love for him, which you lack, but out of the worldly honor of which you boast and out of the respect and consideration that every well-bred man owes to ladies, I entreat you not to divert us from the path that we are following, nor to disturb our devout and quiet life."

And having said this, Doña Blanca made a stiff, cold curtsy to the commander and resumed walking with sedate gravity, Clara going ahead and Don Valentín following behind.

Don Fadrique returned her curtsy with a bow, found himself somewhat bewildered, and muttered:

"So now we know: Other measures are called for."

No sooner had the Solís family taken some thirty steps than the commander saw that Doña Blanca turned around to talk to her husband.

It goes without saying that the commander did not hear what she said to him, but the novelist knows everything and hears everything. Doña Blanca, who always used the *usted*,[60] or formal, level of address, and with the greatest politeness, when she lectured or rebuked her husband, spoke to him as follows while Clara walked on ahead:

"I have told you a thousand times, Señor don Valentín. That man, whom you insisted on inviting into our home back in Lima, is a rude, ungodly libertine. His acquaintance, while it may not contaminate, stains or could stain the impeccable reputation of any lady. I was nearly forced to turn him out of the house. There were reasons – his lack of courtesies and even of respect – that in other, barbarous ages would have caused someone, forgetting the divine law, to give him a severe lesson, as gentlemen were wont to do. This, of course, could not be; it was impossible. I find nothing more repugnant to my conscience, nothing more contrary to my principles, but there is a just means ... It is a crime to kill someone who has given offense ... , but it is vileness to embrace him. Señor don Valentín, you have no blood in your veins."

All this did his tremendous wife Doña Blanca slowly and softly speak almost into his ear.

The last words were so callous and cruel that Don Valentín was on the verge of raising the flag of rebellion, creating a terrible row in the street, and answering his wife as she deserved, but the fragrances of a thousand flowers delighted the sense of smell; people passed by with cheerful expressions; the day was glorious; peace reigned in the sky; a fresh spring breeze refreshed and soothed the most feverish temples; the Solís family was on their way to the bloodless sacrifice of the mass; and Clara, so pretty

tan serena. ¿Cómo turbar todo aquello con una disputa horrible? Don Valentín apretó los puños y se limitó a exclamar con acento un sí es no es colérico:

—¡Señora!...

Luego añadió para sí, cuidando mucho de que no lo oyese doña Blanca:

—¡Maldita sea mi suerte!

Y no bien lanzada la exclamación, se asustó don Valentín de la blasfema rebeldía contra la Providencia que su exclamación implicaba, y se tuvo un instante por primo hermano del propio Luzbel.

Como se ve, el éxito del comendador en este primer intento de reanudar relaciones amistosas con la familia Solís, no pudo ser más desgraciado.

12

No se arredró por eso nuestro héroe. Aguardó un rato en medio de la calle a fin de que no pudiese decir ni pensar doña Blanca que él la seguía, y al cabo se fue a la Iglesia Mayor, a donde sabía que la familia Solís se había encaminado.

Don Fadrique no iba allí, sin embargo, con el intento de acercarse a doña Blanca otra vez y de sufrir nueva repulsa, sino a fin de hallar a don Carlos, quien, a su parecer, no podía menos de estar en la iglesia, ya que no había otro medio de ver a Clara.

En efecto, don Fadrique entró en la iglesia y se puso a buscar al poeta a la sombra de los pilares y en los sitios donde menos se nota la presencia de alguien. Pronto le halló, detrás de un pilar y no lejos del altar mayor. Parecía don Carlos tan embebecido en su oraciones o en sus pensamientos, que nada del mundo exterior, salvo Clara, podía distraerle ni llamarle la atención.

Llegó, pues, don Fadrique hasta ponerse a su lado. Entonces advirtió que Clara estaba no muy lejos, de rodillas, al lado de su madre, que don Carlos la miraba, y que ella, si bien fijos casi siempre los ojos en su libro de rezos, los alzaba de vez en cuando rápidamente, y miraba

and so serene, was walking ahead. How could he disturb all that with a horrible argument? Don Valentín clenched his fists and limited himself to exclaiming in a tone of voice with some asperity in it:

"*Señora* … !"

Then he added to himself, taking care to ensure that Doña Blanca would not hear what he said:

"My fate be damned!"

And no sooner did he utter this exclamation than Don Valentín got frightened of the blasphemous defiance of Providence that his exclamation implied, and for a moment believed he was a first cousin of Lucifer himself.

As can be seen, the commander's success in this first attempt to renew friendly relations with the Solís family could not have been more unfortunate.

12

Not on this account did our hero lose heart.

He waited for a while in the middle of the street so that Doña Blanca could neither say nor think that he was following her, and then he too headed for the main church, where he knew that the Solís family had gone.

Don Fadrique was not going there, however, with the intention of approaching Doña Blanca again and suffering another rebuff, but in order to find Don Carlos, who in his view could not help being in the church, since he had no other way of seeing Clara.

So Don Fadrique also entered the church and set about looking for the poet in the shadows of the pillars and in places where someone's presence was least likely to be noted. He soon spotted him behind a pillar not far from the main altar. Don Carlos seemed so engrossed in his prayers or in his thoughts that nothing of the external world except Clara could distract him or attract his attention.

Don Fadrique then walked over and stood at his side. From that vantage point he noticed that Clara, not very far away, was kneeling beside her mother, that Don Carlos had his eyes peeled on her, and that she, although she kept hers fixed on her prayer book, would very quickly raise them from time to time and glance with alarm and tenderness in

con sobresalto y ternura hacia donde estaba el galán, declarando así que le veía, que se alegraba de verle, y que tenía miedo y cierto terror de profanar el templo y de pecar gravemente engañando a su madre y alentando a aquel hombre, de quien decía que no podía ser esposa.

No ha de extrañarse que todo esto se viera en las miradas de Clarita. Eran miradas transparentes, en cuyo fondo fulguraba el alma como diamante purísimo que por maravilla ardiese con luz propia en el seno de un mar tranquilo.

El comendador estuvo un rato observando aquella escena muda, y se convenció de que ni doña Blanca ni don Valentín recelaban nada de los amores de la niña. Calculó, no obstante, que su presencia allí podría atraer hacia él la mirada de doña Blanca, excitar de nuevo su ira, hacerle reparar en el gentil mancebo que estaba a su lado y darle a sospechar lo que no había sospechado todavía.

Entonces, si bien con pena de interrumpir aquellos arrobos y éxtasis contemplativos, tocó en el hombro a don Carlos y le dijo casi a la oreja:

—Perdóneme usted que le distraiga de sus devociones y que turbe la visión beatífica de que sin duda goza; pero me urge hablar con usted. Hágame el favor de venir conmigo, que tengo que hablarle de cosas que le importan muchísimo.

Sin aguardar respuesta echó a andar don Fadrique, y don Carlos, si bien con disgusto, no pudo menos de seguir sus pasos.

Ya fuera de la iglesia, salió don Fadrique al campo; don Carlos fue en pos de él; y cuando se hallaron en sitio solitario, donde nadie podía oírlos ni interrumpir la conversación, don Fadrique se explicó en estos términos:

—Vuelvo a pedir a usted perdón de mi atrevimiento en obligarle a abandonar la iglesia, y más aún en mezclarme en asuntos de usted sin título bastante para ello. Apenas conozco a usted. Ésta es la séptima o la octava vez que le hablo. A Clarita la he visto hoy por segunda vez en mi vida. Sin embargo, el bien de Clarita y el de usted me interesan mucho. Atribúyalo usted a un absurdo sentimentalismo; al afecto que profeso a mi sobrina Lucía, que llega a ustedes de rechazo: a lo que usted quiera. Lo que le ruego es que me crea un hombre leal y franco y no dude de mi buena voluntad y mejores propósitos. Quiero y puedo hacer mucho en favor de usted. En cambio, aspiro a que oiga usted mis consejos y a que los siga.

the direction of her suitor, thus declaring that she saw him, that she rejoiced at seeing him, and that she was afraid and maybe even terrified of profaning that temple and of sinning gravely, deceiving her mother and encouraging that man, whose wife she said she could not be.

It should come as no surprise that all this could be seen in Clarita's glances. They were transparent glances, in whose depths her soul glittered like the purest of diamonds, a gem that by virtue of some marvel glowed with its own light in the bosom of a calm sea.

The commander observed that silent scene for some moments and became convinced that neither Doña Blanca nor Don Valentín suspected anything of the girl's love affair. He reasoned, nonetheless, that his presence there might attract a glance from Doña Blanca, arouse her wrath once again, cause her to take notice of the genteel youth at his side, and get her to suspect what she had not yet suspected.

Then, although he regretted interrupting those raptures and contemplative ecstasies, he touched Don Carlos on the shoulder and practically whispered in his ear:

"Forgive me for distracting you from your devotions and disturbing the beatific vision that you no doubt are enjoying, but I must talk to you. Please come with me, because I have to talk to you about things that are of the utmost importance to you."

Without waiting for a response, Don Fadrique began to walk away, and Don Carlos, although against his will, could not help following him.

Once outside the church, Don Fadrique made for the country, with Don Carlos at his heels, and when they came to a lonely spot where no one could hear them or interrupt their conversation, Don Fadrique stated his purpose:

"Again I ask you to forgive my boldness in obliging you to leave the church, and still more for meddling in your affairs when I have no call to do so. I hardly know you. This is the seventh or eighth time that I've spoken to you. I have seen Clarita today for only the second time in my life. Nonetheless, I am very interested in Clarita's welfare and in yours. Attribute this interest to an absurd sentimentality, to the affection that I profess for my niece Lucía, which is coming to you two on the rebound, to … any number of reasons. What I ask is that you believe me to be a loyal and candid person and that you not question my good will and better intentions. I want to and can do a great deal to benefit you. In exchange, I am hoping that you will listen to my advice and follow it."

Don Carlos oyó al comendador atentamente y con muestras de respeto y deferencia. Luego le contestó:

–Señor don Fadrique, por usted y por ser usted el tío de la señorita doña Lucía, tan bondadosa y excelente, estoy dispuesto a oír a usted y hasta a obedecerle, en cuanto esté de mi parte, sin considerar el provecho que por mi obediencia usted me promete.

–No me he explicado bien– replicó don Fadrique –. Yo no prometo premios en pago de obediencia: lo que quiero significar es que de seguir usted ciertos consejos míos se ha de alcanzar naturalmente lo que de otra suerte se malogrará acaso, con gran pesar de todos.

–Aclare usted su pensamiento– dijo don Carlos.

–Quiero decir– prosiguió don Fadrique –, que este modo que tiene usted de enamorar a Clarita no va, hace días, por buen camino. Hasta ahora nadie sospecha en esta pequeña ciudad sus amores de usted, gracias a mi sobrina. Como ella estuvo, dos meses ha, en Sevilla, donde usted la conoció, y usted ha venido luego aquí, y usted va a su casa de tertulia todas las noches, y habla usted mucho con ella, y no pocas veces en secreto; y como mi sobrina es joven y graciosa y linda, si el amor de tío no me engaña, todos creen que ha venido usted por ella, que usted la enamora, que usted es su novio. ¿Quién había de imaginarse que chica tan mona y en tan verdes años se limitaría a hacer el triste y poco airoso papel de confidenta? Por eso, pues, se desorientan los curiosos, y sus amores de usted siguen secretos: pero Lucía lo paga. Confiese usted que es mucha generosidad.

–Yo... señor don Fadrique...

–No se disculpe usted. No hablo de ello para que usted se disculpe, sino para narrar los sucesos como son en sí. En este lugar creen todos que usted ha venido, abandonando a sus padres, su casa y sus estudios, para pretender a Lucía; pero este engaño no puede durar. Imagine usted el alboroto, los chismes, las hablillas a que dará usted ocasión y motivo el día en que se sepa, como no podrá menos de saberse, que usted pretende a Clarita, a quien todos creen ya prometida esposa de don Casimiro Solís.

–Esto no será nunca mientras yo viva– exclamó don Carlos con grandes bríos.

–Tratemos de impedirlo– continuó con calma don Fadrique –. Yo le ayudaré a usted cuanto pueda, y repito que algo puedo; pero toda

Don Carlos listened attentively to the commander, and with signs of respect and deference. He then said:

"Señor don Fadrique, because you are who you are and because you are the uncle of Señorita doña Lucía, who is so kind and good-hearted, I am prepared to listen to you and even to obey you insofar as I am able, without looking to the advantage that you promise me for my obedience."

"I haven't explained myself well," responded Don Fadrique. "I'm not promising rewards in return for obedience. What I mean is that by following my advice you should be able to attain in the natural course of things what might otherwise fall through, much to everybody's regret."

"Can you be more clear?"

"I mean," continued Don Fadrique, "that the manner in which you are pursuing Clarita is not heading – has not for some time been heading – in the right direction. Up till now nobody in this small city has suspected your love affair, thanks to my niece. Since she was in Seville two months ago, where you met her, and since you then came here and you go to the *tertulia* at her house every evening, and talk to her a great deal and often in great secrecy; and since my niece is young and charming and pretty, if an uncle's love is not playing tricks on me, everybody believes that you have come because of her, that you are wooing her, that you are *her* suitor. Who would imagine that such a young and attractive girl would consent to play the sad and not very distinguished role of confidante? So for this reason the busybodies are thrown off track and your love affair remains a secret, but Lucía pays the price. And you have to admit that she's being very generous."

"Señor don Fadrique, I ..."

"Don't apologize. I'm not speaking of this for you to apologize, but to recount events and put them into perspective. Everybody in this place thinks that you have come here, forsaking your parents, your home, and your studies, in order to court Lucía, but this deception cannot last. Imagine the commotion, the gossip, the chatter you will stir and occasion the day it becomes known, as it inevitably will, that you are courting Clarita, whom everybody believes is Don Casimiro Solís's intended."

"She'll never be his wife while I'm alive," exclaimed Don Carlos heatedly.

"Let's try to prevent that," Don Fadrique calmly continued. "I will help you as much as I can, and I repeat that there are things that I can do,

la energía de usted y toda la prudencia que yo emplee serán inútiles si desoye usted mis advertencias y consejos.

–Ya he dicho a usted que deseo seguirlos.

–Pues bien, amigo don Carlos, es menester que usted se persuada de que Clarita, de cuyo amor hacia usted estoy convencido, está criada con tan santo temor de Dios y con tan grande, y hasta si usted quiere exagerado e irracional respeto a su madre, que por obedecerla, por no darle un disgusto, por no rebelarse, será capaz de casarse con don Casimiro, aunque se muera de amor por usted al día siguiente de casada, aunque su vestido de boda sea la mortaja con que la entierren.

–Pero si Clara dice a su madre que no ama a don Casimiro...

–Clara no se atreverá a decirlo.

–Si declara a su madre que me ama...

–Antes morirá que confesar a su madre ese amor.

–Y si tanto miedo tiene a su madre, ¿no podrá huir conmigo?

–No creo que dé jamás tan mal paso. De todos modos, aunque tan mal paso fuese posible, no se debía apelar a él sino apurados antes otros medios más prudentes y juiciosos. Reitero, con todo mi afirmación. Creo capaz a Clarita de morir de dolor; pero no la creo capaz de prestarse al escándalo de un rapto.

–Entonces, ¿qué quiere usted que yo haga?

–Lo primero, volver a Sevilla con sus señores padres, y dejar a doña Clara tranquila con los suyos.

–Bien se conoce que usted no ama. A su edad de usted...

–Dale... con la tontería... Caballerito poeta... yo no soy viejo ni rabadán... ni me parezco en nada al del idilio. Váyase usted a Sevilla hoy mismo. Salga usted de esta ciudad antes de que doña Blanca se percate de que hay moros en la costa. Yo velaré aquí por los intereses de usted. Y si peligran; si es menester apelar a medios violentos, cuente usted también conmigo... hasta para el rapto. A poco me aventuro prometiéndoselo a usted, porque doy por firme que no se dejará robar doña Clarita.

–¿Y por qué, para qué he de irme a Sevilla?

–¿Pues no se lo he dicho a usted ya? Porque aquí no hace usted sino perjudicarse, sin gusto y sin ventaja. Estoy seguro de que no logrará usted más que ver a Clara en la iglesia, con más angustia que deleite por

but all your energy and all the prudence I exercise will be futile if you turn a deaf ear to my counsel and advice."

"I've already told you that I wish to follow your advice."

"All right, then, Don Carlos, my friend, it is essential that you understand that Clarita – who, I am convinced, does indeed love you – has been raised with such a holy fear of God and with such a great and, we might even say, exaggerated and irrational respect for her mother, that to obey her, not to displease her, not to rebel, she would be capable of marrying Don Casimiro, even if she were to die of love for you the day after her marriage, even if her wedding dress were the shroud used for her burial."

"But if Clara tells her mother that she doesn't love Don Casimiro…"

"Clara wouldn't dare to say such a thing."

"If she tells her mother that she loves me…"

"She would rather die than confess that love to her mother."

"And if she's so afraid of her mother, can't she run off with me?"

"I don't believe that she would ever take such a risky step. In any case, even if such a step were possible, you shouldn't have recourse to it before all other prudent and judicious measures have been exhausted. So I restate my view of how things stand: I believe that Clarita is capable of dying of heartache, but I do not believe that she is capable of consenting to the scandal of an abduction."

"Then, what do you want me to do?"

"The first thing, go back to Seville to be with your parents and leave Doña Clara in peace with hers."

"It's clear that you do not love a woman. At your age – "

"There you go … with your foolishness. My poet friend, I am neither an old man nor a head shepherd, nor do I at all resemble the old shepherd in your idyll. Return to Seville today. Leave this place before Doña Blanca realizes that the coast is not clear. I'll look out for your interests here. If they are in danger, if it becomes necessary to have recourse to violent measures, again, count on me … even for an abduction. I do not run much of a risk by promising this to you, because I am certain that Clarita will not consent to being carried off."

"And why, for what reason should I go back to Seville?"

"Haven't I already told you that? Because here you are doing nothing but hurting yourself, with no pleasure, no gain. I know for a fact that you will only manage to see Clara in church, causing the poor girl more

parte de la pobre muchacha. Y esto mientras doña Blanca no descubra nada. El día en que descubra doña Blanca su juego de usted, será para Clarita un día tremendo y usted no volverá a verla. Váyase usted, pues, a Sevilla.

—¿Y qué ganaré con irme?

—Que yo trabaje con tranquilidad en favor de usted. Usted me estorba para mis planes. Si usted se queda, precipitará la boda de don Casimiro y hará que se envíe a escape por la licencia a Roma. Si usted se va, no afirmo yo que evitaré la boda de Clara con el viejo rabadán y conseguiré que sea para Mirtilo; pero, o yo he de valer poco, o he de lograr que se nos dé tiempo y... quién sabe... Nada prometo. Sólo ruego a usted que se vaya. Váyase usted hoy mismo.

El interés que el comendador le mostraba, su empeño de que se fuese, la decisión con que se entrometía en sus asuntos, todo chocaba a don Carlos y le tenía desconfiado y descontento.

El comendador apuró todas las razones, empleó todos los tonos, pero singularmente el de la súplica; don Carlos le contestó varias veces de mal humor, y fue menester la prudente superioridad del comendador para calmar y contener a don Carlos y evitar que llegase a ofender a quien le aconsejaba y casi le mandaba.

Por último, tanto rogó, prometió y dijo don Fadrique, que don Carlos hubo de someterse y salir aquel mismo día para Sevilla, si bien ofreciendo sólo ausencia de poco más de un mes: hasta que llegasen las vacaciones de verano. En cambio, exigió y obtuvo de don Fadrique que le había de escribir dándole noticias de Clara, y avisándole del menor peligro que hubiese, para volar en seguida donde estaba ella.

Don Carlos, aunque no era tímido ni torpe, no había obtenido jamás que Clara recibiese carta suya, y menos aún que le escribiese. Pero ¿qué mucho, si ni siquiera de palabra Clara le había dado a entender que le amaba? Clara le amaba, sin embargo. Bien sabía el galán que era falso, de puro modesto, aquello de que

> ...Amistosa y compasiva,
> quiere que el zagal viva,
> mas amarle no quiere.

Clara le amaba, y a su despecho, contra su voluntad, había declarado su

anguish than delight. And as long as Doña Blanca does not discover anything, you'll keep coming. But the day that she does discover your game, it will be an awful day for Clarita, and you'll not see her again. So go back to Seville."

"And what will I gain by leaving?"

"My working quietly on your behalf. Your presence hinders my plans. If you stay here you will hasten the marriage to Don Casimiro and bring about a speedy application to Rome for a dispensation. If you leave, I'm not assuring you that I can prevent Clara's marriage to the old shepherd and that I can arrange one to Myrtilus, but either I'm a man of little consequence or I'll manage to buy some time and ... who knows. I am promising nothing. I am only imploring you to leave. Leave this very day."

The interest shown to him by the commander, his insistence that he leave, the decisiveness with which he meddled in his affairs ... all this took Don Carlos aback and made him distrustful and disgruntled.

The commander exhausted every argument, used every tone of voice, but especially that of entreaty; several times Don Carlos retorted in a bad temper and the commander's judicious superiority was needed to calm and satisfy Don Carlos and to keep him from offending the person he was advising and almost ordering.

At length, so much did Don Fadrique implore, promise, and cajole that Don Carlos had to give in and agree to set out that very day for Seville, although committing himself to an absence of just a little over a month, until the summer vacation. In exchange, he insisted on and obtained Don Fadrique's word that the commander would write giving him news of Clara and warning him if there was the least danger, so that he could fly to her side.

Although he was neither timid nor awkward, Don Carlos had never managed to have Clara receive a letter of his, and still less to have her write to him. But can that come as a surprise if Clara had never, in so many words, given him to understand that she loved him? And nonetheless Clara loved him. Well did the gallant know the falseness, out of sheer modesty, of the lines that read,

> Chloris ... friendly and compassionate,
> Wants the young shepherd to live,
> But not to love him.

Clara did love him, and in spite of herself, against her will, she had

amor; pero sólo con los ojos, por donde se le iba el alma en busca del bizarro y gracioso estudiante, sin que todos sus escrúpulos religiosos y filiales fuesen bastante poderosos para detenerla.

Don Fadrique pudo convencerse, en el largo coloquio que tuvo con don Carlos, de que su pasión por Clara era verdadera y profunda. Del amor de Clara por el poeta rondeño estaba más convencido aún. Con este doble convencimiento, de que se alegraba, precipitó más la partida de don Carlos, y antes de mediodía consiguió que saliese del pueblo con dirección a Sevilla.

Don Carlos salió a caballo con un su criado; y don Fadrique, a caballo también, se unió con él en el ejido, y le acompañó más de una legua, dándole esperanzas y hablándole de sus amores. Al llegar a una encrucijada, don Fadrique se despidió cariñosamente del joven, y tomó el camino de Villabermeja con el intento de conferenciar con el padre Jacinto.

La sencillez y la modestia de este santo varón no habían dejado ver a don Fadrique la inmensa importancia que durante su larga ausencia había adquirido.

Como predicador, gozaba el padre de extraordinaria nombradía por toda aquella comarca. Era igualmente celebrado por los tres estilos que tenía de predicar. En el estilo llano o de homilía encantaba a la gente rústica y ponía la religión y la moral a su alcance, amenizando tan graves lecciones con chistes y jocosidades que un severo crítico condenaría, pero que eran muy del caso para que los zafios campesinos se aficionasen a oírle y se deleitasen oyéndole. En sermones de empeño, en días de gran función, el padre Jacinto era otro hombre: echaba muchos latines, ahuecaba la voz y esmaltaba su discurso de un jardín de flores, de un verdadero matorral de adornos exuberantes, que también gustaban a los discretos y finos de aquellos lugares. Y tenía, por último, el estilo patético de la Semana de Pasión y de la Semana Santa, durante las cuales los sermones, más que hablados, eran en Villabermeja, y siguen siendo aún, cantados, sin que gusten de otra manera. Sermón de Semana Santa, sin lo que llaman allí el *tonillo,* no gusta a nadie ni se tiene por sermón. Cuando en el día va a Villabermeja un cura forastero, tiene que aprender el *tonillo.* En este *tonillo* fue el padre Jacinto un dechado de perfección, que nadie ha superado hasta ahora. Al oírle, aunque sea reminiscencia

declared her love, but only with her eyes, through which her soul went in search of the dashing and charming student, all her filial and religious scruples not sufficiently powerful to rein it in.

Don Fadrique became convinced, in the long conversation that he had with Don Carlos, that the youth's passion for Clara was genuine and profound. Of Clara's love for the poet from Ronda he was still more convinced. Having come to this twofold conviction, at which he rejoiced, the commander urged Don Carlos to depart even sooner, and shortly before noon succeeded in getting him to leave for Seville.

Don Carlos left the city on horseback with his servant, and Don Fadrique, also on horseback, joined up with him on the commons and accompanied him for more than three miles, nourishing his hopes and talking to him about his love affair. When they reached a crossroads, Don Fadrique said a warm good-bye to the youth and took the highway to Villabermeja with the intention of conferring with Father Jacinto.

The simplicity and modesty of this holy man had not allowed Don Fadrique to see the immense importance that he had acquired during his long absence.

As a preacher the priest enjoyed extraordinary renown throughout that entire region. He was equally celebrated for the three styles of preaching that he had. In his plain or homily style he delighted country folk and put religion and morality on their level, enlivening grave lessons with jokes and jests that a severe critic would condemn, but which were very appropriate to engage coarse peasants and make them want to hear him and to delight in hearing him. In his lofty sermons, on feast days and other holy days, Father Jacinto was another man altogether: he sprinkled Latin phrases here and there, he deepened his voice and embellished his discourse with a garden of flowers, with a veritable thicket of exuberant adornments, which then pleased the refined and discriminating individuals in those environs. And he had, lastly, the pathetic style of Passion Week[61] and Holy Week, during which the sermons, more than spoken in Villabermeja, were chanted, and to this day still are, no other manner winning favor. A sermon in Holy Week without what people call the *tonillo*, or singsong kind of delivery,[62] pleases nobody and is not considered a sermon. Even nowadays, when a priest from some other town goes to Villabermeja, he has to learn the *tonillo*. In this *tonillo* Father Jacinto was a model of perfection and no one has ever surpassed him. Although it may be a heathenish comparison, it is said that when

gentílica, dicen que se comprendía cómo Cayo Graco se hacía acompañar por un flautista cuando pronunciaba en el Foro sus más apasionadas arengas. El padre Jacinto predicaba también en el Foro, o dígase en medio de la plaza pública, durante la Semana Santa. Allí se hacían todos los pasos a lo vivo, y el padre los explicaba en el sermón conforme iban ocurriendo. Así, había sermón que duraba tres horas, y siempre sin dejar el *tonillo,* lo cual no obstaba para que el padre expresara los más vivos afectos, como piedad, dolor y cólera. Cuando aparecía el pregonero en el balcón de las Casas Consistoriales y leía la sentencia de muerte contra Jesucristo, ha quedado en la memoria de los bermejinos el furor con que el padre se volvía contra él, gritando:

«Calla, falso, ruin, necio y miserable pregonero, y oirás la voz del Ángel que dice:»

Y entonces salía un ángel muy vistoso por otro balcón de la plaza, y cantaba el inefable misterio de la Redención, empezando:

«Ésta es la sentencia que manda cumplir el Eterno Padre...» y lo demás que tantas veces hemos oído los que somos de por allí.

Pero, volviendo al padre Jacinto, diré que su mérito como predicador era quizás lo de menos. Su gran valer fue como director espiritual. Se pasaba horas y horas en el confesonario. Desde el convento bermejino tenía con frecuencia que ir al convento de la ciudad cercana, donde tenía no pocas hijas de confesión entre el señorío. Era además hombre de consejo y tino en los negocios mundanos, y acudían todos a consultarle cuando se hallaban en tribulación, apuro o dificultad. En suma, el padre Jacinto era un gran médico de almas, aunque duro y feroz a veces en los remedios. Gustaba de aplicarlos heroicos, como suelen hacer los demás médicos de los lugares, que tal vez recetan a un hombre el medicamento que convendría recetar a un caballo. A pesar de esto, tenía el padre tal autoridad y discreción; era tan ameno en su trato y tan resuelto valedor y defensor de las mujeres, que gozaba de inmensa popularidad entre ellas, y era fervorosamente reverenciado, así de las jornaleras humildes, como de las encopetadas hidalgas.

Aunque tocaba en los setenta años, estaba firme y robusto aún, si bien había perdido ciertos ímpetus juveniles, que le habían hecho

people listened to him they understood how it was that Caius Gracchus[63] could have had himself accompanied by a flutist when he delivered his impassioned speeches in the Forum. Father Jacinto also preached in the Forum, that is, in the middle of the public square during Holy Week. All the floats depicting the passion of Christ passed by there and he would explain them in his sermon as they were being enacted. As a result, there were sermons that lasted three hours, and given in the *tonillo* the whole time, which did not prevent the priest from expressing the strongest emotions, like compassion, sorrow, and anger. When the town crier appeared on the balcony of the town hall and read the sentence of death for Jesus Christ, Father Jacinto would turn toward him, and there remains in the collective memory of Villabermejans the fury in his voice as he shouted:

"Be silent, you false, contemptible, foolish, and despicable town crier and you will hear the voice of the Angel saying:"

And the Angel, in very colorful dress, would come out on another balcony of the square and sing the ineffable mystery of the redemption, beginning:

"This is the sentence that the Eternal Father has decreed ..." and then the rest of it, words that those of us who are from that part of Andalusia have heard so many times.

But coming back to Father Jacinto, I will say that his merit as a preacher was perhaps the least of his priestly virtues. His great worth was as a spiritual director. He spent hours on end in the confessional. He frequently had to go from the Villabermejan monastery to the monastery of the neighboring city, where there were a number of women among the upper crust who regularly confessed to him. He was, furthermore, a man of counsel and good judgment in worldly affairs, and all the people went to consult him when they found themselves in dire straits, distress or difficulty. In short, Father Jacinto was a great physician of souls, although tough and fierce at times in his remedies. He liked to apply heroic ones, as do other small-town doctors, who may be inclined to prescribe for a man a medication strong enough for a horse. Despite those remedies, the priest had such authority and discretion, was such agreeable company and such a resolute protector and defender of women, that he enjoyed immense popularity among them, and was fervently revered both by humble workingwomen and high-and-mighty noblewomen.

Although he was nearing seventy, Father Jacinto was still hale and hearty, notwithstanding the loss of certain youthful impulses that

famoso, llevándole en ocasiones a imitar al Divino Redentor, más que en la mansedumbre, en aquel arranque que tuvo cuando hizo azote de unos cordeles y echó a latigazos a los mercaderes del templo. El padre Jacinto había sido un jayán y había sacudido el polvo a algunos desalmados y pecadores contumaces, sobre todo cuando eran maridos que se emborrachaban, gastaban el dinero en vino y juego y daban palizas a sus mujeres.

Con esta clase de hombres había sido duro de veras el padre Jacinto. Ya no tenía aquellos arrestos de la mocedad; pero su virtud y su fuerza moral, unida al recuerdo de la física, infundían gran respeto entre los rústicos.

Tales eran las calidades principales y la brillante posición del antiguo maestro del comendador, con quien éste iba ahora a consultar y tratar negocios arduos, y de quien esperaba obtener poderoso auxilio.

13

No bien llegó el comendador a Villabermeja y dejó el caballo en su casa, se dirigió al convento, que distaba pocos pasos, y como era la hora de la siesta, halló en su celda al padre Jacinto, el cual no dormía, sino estaba leyendo, sentado a la mesa.

Mis lectores deben de formarse ya, por lo expuesto hasta aquí, cierta idea bastante aproximada de la condición del mencionado fraile. Fáltame añadir, para que sea completo el retrato, que era alto y seco; que veía y oía bien; que tuteaba a todo el género humano, y que se preciaba de no tener pelillos en la lengua, esto es, de decir cuanto se le ocurría, con una franqueza que tocaba y hasta pasaba a menudo de sus límites, entrando con banderas desplegadas por la jurisdicción y término de la desvergüenza. Sólo con don Fadrique se mostraba el padre respetuoso y deferente, suponiendo que él tenía, sin poderlo remediar, un afecto por su antiguo discípulo, que le hacía sobrado débil:

—Muchacho— dijo a don Fadrique, apenas le vio entrar –, ¿qué buen viento te trae por aquí de improviso?

—Maestro— contestó el comendador –, he venido expresamente para consultar a usted.

had made him famous, leading him on occasion to imitate the Divine Redeemer, more than in meekness in that outburst of righteous anger when he made a whip of some cords and used it to drive the merchants from the temple.

Father Jacinto had been a big, powerful man, and he had thrashed a number of cruel and wayward sinners, especially when they were husbands who got drunk, spent their money on wine and gambling, and beat their wives. With men of this sort he had been truly severe. He no longer had the ardor of youth, but his virtue and his moral strength, together with the recollection of his physical strength, instilled great respect in the peasants.

Such were the chief qualities and brilliant position of the commander's former teacher, the man with whom he was going to consult and discuss difficult matters, and from whom he hoped to obtain powerful assistance.

13

No sooner did the commander arrive at Villabermeja and leave the horse at his house than he headed for the monastery, which was only a stone's throw away; and as it was the siesta hour, he found Father Jacinto in his cell, not sleeping, but seated at the table and reading.

From what has been said of him so far, my readers must have formed a pretty good, or approximate, idea of the makeup of this friar. But in order for the picture to be complete I need to add that he was tall and thin, that his vision and hearing were good, that he used the familiar you or *tú* with the entire human race, and that he prided himself on not mincing words, that is, saying everything that occurred to him with a frankness that verged on, and even exceeded on occasion, the limits of candor, when he entered, full steam ahead, the jurisdiction and confines of impudence. Only with Don Fadrique was Father Jacinto respectful and deferential, and he assumed that such was the case because, unable to help it, he had formed an attachment to his old pupil that made him overly weak.

"Well, well," he said to Don Fadrique as soon as he saw him, "what brings you here unexpectedly?"

"Master," answered the commander, "I have come expressly to consult you."

–¿Para consultarme a mí? ¿Y sobre qué? ¿Qué hay, que tú no sepas mejor que yo y mejor que nadie?

–Mi consulta es de suma importancia.

–Vamos... ¿de qué se trata?

–Se trata... se trata... nada menos que de un caso de conciencia.

Al oír *caso de conciencia,* el padre miró fijamente al comendador con aire de incredulidad y de recelo, y exclamó al cabo:

–Mira, hijo mío, si es que te aburres en estos lugares y quieres chancearte y divertirte, toma una tabla y dos cuernos, y no te diviertas ni te chancees conmigo. Ya está duro el alcacer para zampoñas.

–¿Y de dónde infiere usted que me chanceo o que me burlo? Hablo con formalidad. ¿Por qué no he de exponer yo a usted formalmente un caso de conciencia?

–Porque todo hombre de cierta educación, criado en el seno de la sociedad cristiana, aunque haya perdido la fe en Nuestro Señor Jesucristo, tiene la conciencia tan clara como yo, y no hay caso que no resuelva por sí, sin necesidad de consultarme. Si tuvieses fe, podrías acudir a mí en busca de los consuelos que da la religión. No acudiendo para esto, ¿qué podré yo decirte, que ignores? La moral tuya es idéntica a la mía, aunque en sus fundamentos discrepe. Y al fin, harto lo conoces tú, no hay caso de conciencia, meramente moral, cuya solución no sea llana para todo entendimiento un poco cultivado. Sin duda que Dios, para ejercitar nuestra actividad mental y aguzar nuestro ingenio, o para dar precio a nuestra fe, ha circundado de tinieblas los grandes problemas metafísicos: los ha envuelto en misterios, impenetrables a veces; pero no en lo tocante a la moral, en lo que atañe al cumplimiento de nuestros deberes, no hay misterio alguno: todo está claro como el agua. El soberano Señor, en su infinita bondad y misericordia, no ha querido, a pesar de nuestras maldades, que nadie tenga que ser un Séneca para ver perfectamente cuál es su obligación, ni mucho menos que nadie tenga que ser un héroe estupendo para cumplirla. Ni para conocerla te falta entendimiento, ni para cumplir con ella debe faltarte voluntad. ¿Qué es lo que buscas, pues, en mí?

–Mucho pudiera argumentarse contra lo que usted dice: pero no quiero disputar, sino consultar. Quiero convenir en que la moral no es ninguna reconditez y en que no es tan arduo cumplir con ella.

"To consult me? And about what? What is there that you do not know better than I and better than anybody?"

"My consultation is of the greatest importance."

"All right ... what's it about?"

"It's about ... it's about nothing less than a matter of conscience."

Upon hearing *matter of conscience*, the priest stared at the commander with a look of disbelief and suspicion, and finally exclaimed:

"Listen, my son, if you are getting bored around here and want to crack jokes and amuse yourself, find a piece of wood and two horns[64] and do not amuse yourself and crack jokes with me. I'm past the age for this kind of business."

"And what makes you think that I'm joking or poking fun? I'm speaking seriously. Why shouldn't I present a matter of conscience to you in all seriousness?"

"Because every man of a certain kind of education – raised in the bosom of Christian society, although he may have lost faith in Our Lord Jesus Christ – has a conscience as clear as mine, and there is no matter that he cannot resolve for himself, without the necessity of consulting me. If you had faith, you could come to me seeking the consolations that religion gives. Not coming for such a thing, what can I tell you that you do not know? Your morals are identical to mine, even though they may differ in their bases. In short, and well do you know it, there is no matter of conscience – no merely moral matter – whose solution is not straightforward for a person of some intellect. No doubt, God, in order to exercise our mental activity and to sharpen our wits, or in order to lend value to our faith, has surrounded the great metaphysical problems with darkness, has enveloped them in mysteries that at times are impenetrable, but with respect to morals or morality, in what concerns the fulfillment of our duties, there is no mystery whatsoever: everything is as clear as water. The sovereign Lord, in his infinite goodness and mercy, has not wanted any of us, despite our wicked ways, to have to be a Seneca[65] to know perfectly what our obligation is, and much less that anyone has to be a stupendous hero to fulfill it. And you lack neither the intellect to know what it is, nor should you be lacking in the will to fulfill it. What is it, then, that you seek from me?"

"Much could be argued to refute what you say, but I do not wish to debate, but to consult. I will agree that morality is no recondite matter and that it is not so hard to fulfill its precepts."

–Se entiende– interrumpió el padre– , para todos aquellos pueblos donde la luz del Evangelio ha penetrado. Tú imaginas que el natural discurso ha bastado a los hombres para formar la ley moral: yo creo que han necesitado de la revelación; pero tú y yo convenimos en que, una vez presentada esa ley, la razón humana la acepta como evidente. Es gran bellaquería suponer esa ley oscura y vaga, y forjarse casos terribles, conflictos espantosos entre los sentimientos naturales y el sencillo cumplimiento de un deber. Esto equivaldría a suponer la necesidad de ser un pozo de ciencia y de sentirse capaz de sobrehumanos esfuerzos para ser persona decente. Ya tú comprendes que esto sería disculpar y dar casi la razón a los tunos. Al fin y al cabo, no todos los hombres son sabios ni tienen las fibras de hierro y el corazón de diamante. Realzar así la moral es hacerla poco menos que imposible, salvo para algunos seres privilegiados y de primera magnitud, más profundos que Crisipo y más constantes que Régulo.

–Mucho tiene que ver el caso que quiero presentar con todo lo que usted está diciendo. No es curiosidad ociosa, sino interés muy respetable el que me induce a resolver una duda.

–Imposible... tú no puedes dudar.

–Déjeme usted que acabe. Yo no dudo sobre el caso... Tengo formado mi juicio... que me parece de no menor certidumbre que este otro: dos y tres son cinco. Mi duda está en si usted, por razones que se fundan en la inexhausta bondad divina, tiene la manga más ancha que yo, o si por razones de la ley positiva, en que cree, la tiene más estrecha. ¿Me entiende usted ahora?

–Te entiendo muy bien, y desde luego te declaro que no he de tener la manga ni más ancha ni más estrecha que tú. Lo mismo calificaremos ambos un pecado, una falta, un delito; y lo mismo marcaremos y determinaremos la obligación que de él nazca. Las razones teológicas tienen que ver con la penitencia, con la expiación, con el perdón, con la gloria o el infierno, allá en el otro mundo; y en esto para nada tienes tú que meterte ahora. Veamos, pues, ese caso, ya que quieres consultarme.

–Desde luego, usted convendrá en que lo robado debe devolverse a su dueño.

–Indudable.

–Y cuando por efecto de un engaño, algo que pertenece a uno viene a pertenecer a otro, ¿qué debemos hacer?

"Meaning," interrupted the priest, "in all those places where the light of the gospel has penetrated. You think that natural reasoning has sufficed for men to shape the moral law; I believe that they have needed revelation, but you and I agree that, once this law has been introduced, human reason accepts it as evident. It's a vile thing indeed to suppose that this law is obscure and vague, and to dream up terrible cases, conflicts between natural feelings and the simple fulfillment of a duty. This would be equivalent to supposing that one needs to be a well of knowledge and to feel capable of superhuman efforts in order to be a decent person. You understand of course that this would be excusing and almost absolving villains. When all is said and done, not all men are sages, nor do they have iron sinews nor diamond hearts. To elevate morality in such a way is to make it just short of impossible, except for a few privileged beings of the first magnitude, more profound than Chrysippus[66] and more steadfast than Regulus."[67]

"The matter that I want to present to you has much to do with what you are saying. It's not idle curiosity, but a considerable interest that moves me to resolve a doubt."

"Impossible … you cannot doubt."

"Let me finish. I have no doubt about this matter. I have formed my judgment … which seems to me no less certain than the other one: that two and three add up to five. My doubt is whether you, for reasons founded on inexhaustible divine goodness, are more broad-minded than I am, or whether for reasons of the positive law, in which you believe, you are less so. Do you understand me now?"

"I understand you very well, and of course I say outright that I will be neither more nor less broad-minded than you. Both of us, I expect, shall regard in like manner a sin, a shortcoming, a crime, and in like manner shall indicate and determine the obligation that may spring from it. The theological reasons have to do with penance, with expiation, with forgiveness, with glory or hell, in the other world, and there is no need for you to involve yourself in any of this now. So let's hear that matter, since you wish to consult me."

"Naturally you'll agree that what has been stolen should be returned to its owner."

"Certainly."

"And when, as a result of deception, something that belongs to one person ends up belonging to another, what should we do?"

–Debemos poner fin al engaño para que lo que posee alguien sin derecho pase a manos de su señor legítimo.

–¿Y si al poner fin al engaño resultan males evidentemente mayores?

–Aquí importa distinguir. Si tú tienes que hablar, no debes decir jamás mentira por inmensos que sean los males que de decir la verdad resulten. Condenada está la mentira oficiosa, como la perniciosa. No debes mentir ni por salvar la vida del prójimo, ni por salvar la honra de nadie, ni por el bien de la religión; pero yo me atrevo a sostener que debes callar la verdad cuando nadie la inquiere de ti y cuando de decirla resultan más males que bienes. Pensar algo en contra es delirio. Lo sostengo sin vacilación. Voy a explanar mi doctrina en breves palabras. Tú cometes un pecado. Eres, por ejemplo, mentiroso. Los males que nazcan de tu pecado debes remediarlos hasta donde te sea posible y lícito, esto es, sin cometer pecado nuevo para remediar el antiguo. Dios, para hacernos patente la enormidad de nuestras culpas, consiente a veces en que nazcan de ella males cuyos humanos remedios son peores. Tratar tú de evitarlos o de remediarlos entonces no es humildad, sino soberbia, orgullo satánico; es luchar contra Dios; es tomar el papel de la Providencia; es dar palo de ciego; es querer enderezar el tuerto que tú mismo hiciste, torciendo y ladeando lo que está recto y tirando a trastornar el orden natural de las cosas.

–Hablando con franqueza– dijo el comendador –, la doctrina de usted me parece muy cómoda. Veo que tiene usted la manga más ancha de lo que yo pensaba.

–Vete a paseo, comendador– repuso el padre, bastante enojado –. En ninguna ocasión pasé yo por complaciente. Me diriges la acusación más dura que a un confesor puede dirigirse. Un santo ha dicho: *Non est pietas, sed impietas, tolerare peccata,* y yo disto mucho de ser impío. Todo proviene, sin duda, de que tú confundes las cosas. Aquí no hablamos de penitencia, de expiación, de castigo de la culpa. Sobre este punto no tengo que decirte yo lo que exigiría de un penitente para absolverle. Aquí hablamos sólo de la obligación de satisfacer el agravio que nace del pecado o del delito. Ya esto he respondido con sencillez. El pecador o delincuente debe ir hasta donde le sea posible y lícito. Si ha de cometer nuevos pecados, si ha de hacer nuevas maldades y desatinos,

"We should put an end to the deception so that what the 'one person' possesses unjustly will be restored to its rightful owner."

"And if by putting an end to the deception patently greater evils could ensue?"

"Here it is important to draw distinctions. If you have to talk, you should never tell a lie no matter how great the evils that may result from telling the truth. The white lie must be condemned as much as the pernicious one. You should not lie even to save the life of your fellow man, nor to save anyone's honor, nor for the good of religion, but I daresay you should keep back the truth when no one asks it of you and when by telling it more evil than good might result. To think otherwise is madness. I say so without hesitation. I am going to explain my stance in brief. You commit a sin. You are, for example, untruthful. The evils that may arise from your sin should be remedied to the extent that it is possible and licit for you to do so, that is, without committing a new sin in order to rectify the old one. In order to make clear to us the enormity of our faults, at times God allows evils to stem from them, evils whose human remedies are worse. For you to try to avoid them or remedy them is not humility, then, but arrogance, satanic pride; it is struggling against God; it is assuming the role of Providence; it is lashing out wildly; it is wanting to right the wrong that you yourself committed, twisting and bending what is straight and tending to upset the natural order of things."

"Speaking frankly," said the commander, "your stance seems very convenient to me. I see that you are more broad-minded than I thought."

"Go jump in the lake, Commander," responded the priest, rather hot under the collar. "Nobody ever considered me complacent. You level at me the harshest accusation that can be leveled at a confessor. A saint has said: *Non est pietas, sed impietas, tolerare peccata*,[68] and I am a long way from being impious. It all stems, no doubt, from the fact that you are confusing things. We are not speaking here of penance, of expiation, of punishment of sin. On this point I do not have to tell you what I would require of a penitent in order to grant absolution. Here we are speaking only of the obligation to make amends for the injury that results from a sin or a crime. And I have given a simple response to this. The sinner or delinquent should go as far as it is possible and licit for him to go. If he is to commit new sins, if he is to carry out new iniquities, new follies,

mejor es que lo deje y no se meta a remediar el mal que ha hecho. Pues qué, ¿estaría bien, por ejemplo, que tú hirieses a uno, y luego, sin saber de cirugía, tratases de curarle y le acabases de matar? Dices tú que la tal doctrina es cómoda. ¿Dónde está la comodidad? Aunque yo te excuse de poner el remedio, no te libro de la penitencia, del remordimiento y del castigo. Antes al contrario, lo cómodo es lo otro: remediar el mal de mala manera, creerse ya horro y darse ya por absuelto. Así un criado torpe te romperá un día el vaso más precioso de los que has traído de la China, le pegará luego chapuceramente con cola, y se quedará tan fresco como si no te hubiese causado el menor perjuicio. Lo que debe hacer el criado es andar siempre muy cuidadoso para no romper el vaso, y si le rompe, sentir mucho su falta, y, ya que no puede ni componer el vaso, ni comprarte otro nuevo e igual, sufrir con humildad la reprimenda que tú le eches.

—Me complazco en ver que estamos de acuerdo en lo general de la doctrina. En la explicación a casos particulares es en lo que veo que cabe mucha sutileza. Contra la opinión de usted, el buen camino se presenta muy anublado y confuso. ¿Cómo determinar a veces hasta dónde es posible y lícito lo que quiero hacer para reparar el daño?

—Es muy sencillo. Si para repararle causas otro daño mayor, deja subsistir el primero, que es más pequeño; y esto aunque en el segundo daño que causes no haya pecado de tu parte. Habiendo nuevo pecado, nueva infracción de la ley moral en el remedio, aunque este segundo pecado sea menor que el primero que cometiste, no debes cometerle. Dios, si quiere, remediará el mal causado.

—De suerte que no hay más que cruzarse de brazos; dejar rodar la bola.

—No hay más que dejarla rodar, ya que deteniéndola puedes hacer que todo ruede. Las Sagradas Letras vienen en mi apoyo con no pocos textos. David dijo: *Abyssus abyssum invocat;* Salomón, *Est processio in malis;* el profeta Amos, *Si erit malum quod Dominus nonfecerit?* Con lo cual da a entender que Dios permite u ordena el mal como pena del pecado y escarmiento de las criaturas; y el mismo Salomón, antes citado, dice, de modo más explícito, que no podemos añadir ni quitar de lo que Dios hizo para ser temido: *Non possumus quidquam addere nec auferre, quae fecit Deus ut timeatur.*

it is better that he leave things be and not attempt to remedy the evil he has done. Let us suppose, by way of example, that you injure someone. Would it not be a fine thing if afterward, without knowing anything about surgery, you tried to treat him and finished killing him? You say that my stance is convenient. Where is the convenience? Although I may excuse you from making amends, I will not exempt you from penance, from remorse, and from punishment. On the contrary, the convenient way is the other way: to remedy the wrong in the wrong manner, and to think yourself free and consider yourself absolved. In like fashion a clumsy servant might one day break the most precious of the vases that you brought from China, then shoddily put it back together with glue and be blithely unconcerned, as if he had not caused you the slightest damage. What the servant ought to do is always exercise great care not to break the vase, and if he does break it, be sorry for his blunder, and since he can neither mend the vase properly nor buy a new one just like it, suffer humbly your reprimand."

"I am pleased to see that we are essentially in agreement with respect to your stance or thinking. It is in the application to particular cases that I see the possibility of such subtlety. Unlike you, I believe that the right path looks clouded and indistinct. How do I determine at times to what extent it is possible and licit to do what I want to do in order to remedy the wrong?"

"It is very simple. If in order to remedy it you cause a greater wrong, leave the first one in place, as it is the lesser, despite the fact that in the second wrong that you cause you commit no sin. Now, there being the possibility of a new sin, a new infraction of the moral law in the remedy, even though this second sin is not as great as the first one that you committed, you must not commit it. God, if he so wishes, will remedy the wrong that has been caused."

"So all we can do is fold our arms, let the ball roll?"

"All we can do is let it roll, since by stopping it we might make everything roll. Scripture supports me with a few examples. David said: *Abyssus abyssum invocat*; Solomon, *Est processio in malis*; the prophet Amos, *Si erit malum quod Dominus non fecerit?*,[69] with which he gives us to understand that God permits or ordains evil as punishment for sin and as a lesson to mankind; and the very same Solomon says in the most explicit manner that we can neither add nor take away from what God did in order for him to be feared: *Non possumus quidquam addere nec auferre, quae fecit Deus ut timeatur.*"[70]

–A pesar de los textos, a pesar de los latines, me repugna esa cobarde resignación.

–¿Cómo cobarde? ¿Dónde viste tú que para con Dios haya cobardía? La resignación a su voluntad no implica, por otra parte, el que te aquietes y te llenes de contentamiento de ti propio. Sigue llorando tu culpa; desuéllate el alma con el azote de la conciencia y el cuerpo con unas disciplinas crueles; haz de tu vida en el mundo un durísimo purgatorio; pero resígnate y no trates de remediar lo que sólo de Dios debe esperar remedio. Hasta el sentido común está de acuerdo en esto, miradas las acciones humanas por el lado de la utilidad y conveniencia, las cuales, bien entendidas, concuerdan con la moralidad y con la justicia. ¡Qué atinado es el refrán que reza: *No siento que mi hijo pierda, sino que quiera desquitarse!* Si malo es jugar, peor es aún volver a jugar; reincidir en el pecado para remediar el mal del pecado. Pero a todo eso, tú no hablas sino de generalidades, y el caso de conciencia no parece.

–Voy al caso– dijo el comendador.

–Soy todo oídos– repuso el fraile.

–¿Qué debe hacer el que no es hijo de quien pasa por su padre, según la ley, y usurpa nombre, posición y bienes que no son suyos?

–¡Hombre... tú eres famoso! ¿Después de tanto preámbulo te vienes con una preguntilla tan baladí? Prescindo ahora de la dificultad o imposibilidad en que ese hijo postizo estaría de probar el delito de su madre. Yo no sé de leyes; pero la razón natural me dicta que contra la fe de bautismo, contra la serie de actos y documentos oficiales que te han hecho pasar hasta hoy por hijo de un determinado y conocido López de Mendoza, no pueden valer testimonios sino de un orden excepcional y casi imposible. Doy, con todo, de barato que posees tales testimonios. Creo, decido que no debes valerte de ellos. ¿Sabes los mandamientos de la ley de Dios? ¿Sabes que el orden en que están no es arbitrario? Pues bien: ¿qué dice el séptimo?

–No hurtar.

–¿Y el cuarto?

–Honrar padre y madre.

–Es, pues, evidente que para quitarte de encima el pecado contra el séptimo ibas a pecar contra el cuarto, deshonrando a tu madre y a tu

"Despite the quotes, the Latin tags, I find that cowardly resignation repugnant."

"Cowardly how? Where did you come up with the notion that there is cowardice in dealing with God? Resignation to his will does not imply, moreover, that you are to be at ease and filled with self-satisfaction. Continue to feel remorse for your sin; flay your soul with the whip of conscience and your body with a cruel scourge; make of your life in the world a harsh purgatory; but resign yourself and do not endeavor to remedy what can be remedied only by God. Even common sense is in accord with this, because as you look at human actions from the perspective of usefulness and expediency, you see that when they are properly understood they are in line with morality and with justice. How apt is the saying, 'I am not sorry that my son loses money gambling, but that he wants to win it back.' If it is bad to gamble, it is even worse to try to recoup losses, to relapse into sin in order to remedy the evil of sin. But all this time you have spoken only in generalities, and I have yet to hear this matter of conscience."

"Here goes," said the commander.

"I'm all ears," said the friar.

"What should someone do who is not the offspring of the man who passes for his father in the eyes of the law, and who usurps a name, position, and wealth that are not his?"

"Well, I'll be ... that takes the cake! After this long preamble you come up with such a trivial question? I will overlook now the difficulty or impossibility that said false offspring or son would have in proving his mother's transgression. I do not know about laws, but innate reason suggests to me that to override the baptismal certificate, to override the series of acts and official documents that have made you pass up to the present for a son of a certain and well-known López de Mendoza, only testimony of an exceptional and almost impossible type would carry the day. I believe, and determine, that you ought not to avail yourself of it. You know God's commandments? You know that the order they're in is not arbitrary? All right. What does the seventh say?"

"You shall not steal."

"And the fourth?"

"Honor your father and your mother."

"Well, it is evident that in order to cast off the sin against the seventh you were going to sin against the fourth, dishonoring your mother and

padre, que padre sería siempre el que te tuvo por hijo, te crió, te alimentó y te educó, aunque no te engendrara.

—Tiene usted razón, padre Jacinto. Y, sin embargo, los bienes que no son míos, ¿cómo sigo gozando de ellos?

—¿Y quién te dice que goces de ellos? Pues qué, ¿es tan difícil dar sin expresar la causa por qué se da? Dalos, pues, a quien debes. Ya los tomarán... En tomar no hay engaño. Y si, por extraño caso, hallares a alguien en el tomar inverosímilmente escrupuloso, ingéniate para que tome. Lejos de oponerme, pido, aplaudo la reparación, siempre que para llevarla a cabo no sea menester hacer mayor barbaridad que la que remedie.

—Está bien... pero si no es el hijo, sino la madre culpada... ¿qué debe hacer la madre culpada?

—Lo mismo que el hijo... no deshonrar públicamente a su marido... no amargarle la vida... no desengañarle con desengaño espantoso... no añadir a su pecado de fragilidad el de una desvergüenza cruel y sin entrañas.

—La madre, no obstante, no tiene medios de devolver bienes que por su culpa van a pasar o han pasado a quien no corresponden.

—Y si no los tiene, ¿qué se le ha de hacer? Ya lo he dicho, que se resigne. Que se someta a la voluntad de Dios. Todo eso lo debió prever antes de pecar, y no pecar. Después del pecado, no le incumbe el remedio si implica pecado nuevo, sino la penitencia. ¿Has expuesto ya todo el caso?

—No, padre; tiene otras complicaciones y puntos de vista.

—Dilos.

—¿Qué piensa usted que debe hacer el hombre pecador, cómplice de la mujer, en aquel delito cuya consecuencia es el hurto, la usurpación de que hemos hablado?

—Lo mismo que he dicho del hijo y de la madre.

—¿Y si posee bienes para subsanar el daño causado a los herederos?

—Subsanar ese daño, pero con tal recato, discreción y sigilo, que no se sepa nada. En el libro de los *Proverbios* está escrito: *Melius est nomen bonum quam divitiae multae.* Así es que por cuestión de intereses no se debe perjudicar a nadie en su buen nombre.

your father, because your father would always be the one who looked upon you as his son, who raised you, who fed you and educated you, even though he did not beget you."

"You're right, Father Jacinto. Nonetheless, the wealth that is not mine … how do I continue to enjoy it?"

"And who tells you to enjoy it? What? It's so difficult to give without explaining the reason behind what is given? Give it away, then, to whom you should. It will be accepted. There is no deceit in accepting. And if, by some strange chance, you deal with an individual who is improbably scrupulous in accepting, find a way to change his mind. Far from being opposed, I require, I applaud the reparation, provided that in order to carry it out it shall not be necessary to engage in a greater atrocity than the one you wish to remedy."

"Fine … but what if the mother is the guilty party and not the son? What should the guilty mother do?"

"The same as the son. Not dishonor her husband publicly, not embitter his life, not disillusion him with a frightful disillusionment, not add to her sin of frailty one of cruel, cold-blooded shamelessness."

"The mother, though, does not have the wherewithal to return the wealth that through her fault is going to pass or has passed to someone wrongfully."

"And if she does not have the wherewithal, what can be done about it? I have already said what: she must be resigned, she must submit to the will of God. She should have foreseen all that before sinning, and not have sinned. After the sin, restitution is not incumbent upon her if it involves another sin, but penance is. Have you laid out the entire matter?"

"No, Father. It has other complications and factors."

"Let's hear them."

"What do you think the man should do, the woman's sinner accomplice in that crime whose consequence is theft, the usurpation of which we have spoken?"

"The same thing I've said the son and the mother should do."

"And what if he possesses the means, the wealth to make restitution for the injury done to the heirs?"

"Then he should make restitution for that injury, but with such circumspection, discretion, and secrecy that nothing becomes known. In the Book of Proverbs it is written: *Melius est nomen bonum quam divitiae multae.*[71] So no one's name should be disgraced over a question of money."

El historiador de estos sucesos escribe para narrar, y no para probar. No decide, por lo tanto, si el padre Jacinto estaba atinado o no en lo que decía; si hablaba guiado por el sentido común o por la doctrina moral cristiana, o por ambos criterios en consonancia completa; y no se inclina tampoco a creer que dicho padre tenía una moral burda y grosera y el atrevimiento y la confianza de un rústico ignorante. Quédese esto para que lo resuelva el discreto lector. Baste apuntar aquí que el comendador mostraba una satisfacción grandísima de ver que su maestro, como él le llamaba, pensaba exactamente lo que él quería que pensase.

El padre Jacinto, desconfiado como buen lugareño, no advertía el interés vivísimo con que su antiguo discípulo le interrogaba, y temiendo siempre una burla, una especie de examen hecho por el comendador para pasar el rato, volvió a hablar un tanto picado, diciendo:

—Me parece que estoy archicándido. ¿A dónde vas a parar con tanta preguntilla? ¿Quieres examinarme? ¿Piensas retirarme la licencia de confesar si no me crees bien instruido?

—Nada de eso, maestro. Yo ignoro si está usted o no de acuerdo con sus librotes de teología moral; pero está usted de acuerdo conmigo, lo cual me lisonjea, y lo está también con mis propósitos, lo cual me llena de esperanza. Yo buscaba en usted un aliado. Contaba siempre con su amistad, pero no sabía si podía contar también con su conciencia. Ahora comprendo que su conciencia no se me opone. Su amistad, por consiguiente, libre de todo obstáculo, vendrá en auxilio mío.

El padre Jacinto conoció al fin que se trataba de un caso práctico, real, y no imaginado, y se ofreció a auxiliar al comendador en todo lo que fuese justo.

Aguardando, pues, una revelación importante, quiso tomar aliento haciendo una pausa, y trató de solemnizar la revelación yendo a una alhacena, que no estaba lejos, y sacando de ella una limeta de vino y dos cañas, que puso sobre la mesa, llenándolas hasta el borde.

—Este vino no tiene aguardiente, ni botica, ni composición de ninguna clase– dijo el padre al comendador –. Es puro, limpio y sin mácula. Está como Dios le ha hecho. Bebe y confórtate con él, y cuéntame luego lo que tengas que contar.

—Bebo al buen éxito de mis planes– contestó el comendador, apurando el vino de su caña.

The chronicler of these events writes to recount, not to prove. He will not, therefore, decide whether Father Jacinto was right or wrong in what he said; whether he spoke guided by common sense or the moral doctrine of Christianity, or by both criteria in complete accord; nor is he inclined either to believe that said priest had a crude, clumsy sense of morality and the daring and presumption of an ignorant rustic. I leave that for the discreet reader to decide. Suffice it to note here that the commander exhibited tremendous satisfaction on seeing that his master, as he called him, thought exactly what he wanted him to think.

Distrustful like a good villager, Father Jacinto did not notice the intense interest with which his former pupil was questioning him, and, always fearing a joke, a kind of examination dreamed up by the commander to pass the time, he went on to say:

"It seems to me that I've been downright ingenuous. What are you getting at by asking me one question after another? Do you wish to examine me? Do you intend to have my faculty to hear confessions revoked if you do not find me sufficiently well-educated?"

"Nothing of the sort, Master. I have no idea whether you are or are not in agreement with your tomes of moral theology, but you are in agreement with me, which flatters me, and you are also in agreement with my intentions, which fills me with hope. I was looking for an ally in you. I always counted on your friendship, but I did not know if I could also count on your conscience. Now I know that your conscience does not oppose me. Your friendship, consequently, free of any drawbacks, will come to my aid."

Father Jacinto realized at last that they were talking about a real, practical case, not a hypothetical one, and he offered to assist the commander in everything that was just.

Then, expecting an important revelation, he wanted to take a breather, and so, pausing to solemnize the revelation, he stepped over to a nearby closet and took out a bottle of wine and two glasses, which he set on the table, filling the glasses to the brim.

"This wine has neither eau-de-vie added, nor potion, nor adulteration of any kind," the priest said to the commander. "It's pure, unblended, and clean-tasting, just as God made it. Drink and fortify yourself with it, and then tell me what you have to tell."

"I drink to the good success of my plans," responded the commander, draining his glass.

–Así sea, si Dios lo quiere– replicó el fraile, bebiendo también, y se dispuso a atender a don Fadrique con sus cinco sentidos.

14

La celda no tenía mucho que llamase la atención. Sobre la mesa o bufete, que era de nogal, había recado de escribir, el *Breviario* y otros libros. Dos sillones de brazos, frente el uno del otro, con la mesa de por medio, y donde se sentaban nuestros interlocutores, eran de nogal igualmente. A más de los dos sillones, había cuatro sillas arrimadas a la pared. Los asientos todos eran de enea. Un *Ecce Homo*, al óleo, a quien cuadraba el refrán de *a mal Cristo mucha sangre,* era la única pintura que adornaba los muros de la celda. No faltaban, en cambio, otros más naturales adornos. En la ventana, tomando el sol, se veían dos floridos rosales; dentro del cuarto, cuatro macetas de brusco, y colgadas en la pared cinco jaulas, dos con perdices cantoras, y tres con colorines, excelentes reclamos. Otro bonito colorín, diestro cimbel, asido a la varilla saliente que estaba fija a una tabla de pino, volaba a cada momento hasta donde lo consentía el hilo largo que le aprisionaba, y volvía con mucho donaire a posarse en la varilla.

Los jilgueros cantaban de vez en cuando y animaban la habitación.

Arrimadas a un ángulo había dos escopetas de caza.

Y, por último, en una alcobita que apenas se descubría, por hallarse la pequeña puerta casi tapada del todo por una cortina de bayeta verde, estaba la cama del buen religioso. La alhacena de donde éste sacó el vino y que era bastante capaz, servía de bodega, ropero, despensa, caja o tesoro y biblioteca a la vez.

Todo, aunque pobre, parecía muy aseado.

El padre Jacinto, con el codo sobre la mesa, la mano en la mejilla y los ojos clavados en don Fadrique, aguardaba que hablase.

Don Fadrique, en voz baja, habló de este modo:

–Aunque yo no soy un penitente que vengo a confesarme, exijo el mismo sigilo que si estuviese en el confesonario.

El padre, sin responder de palabra, hizo con la cabeza un signo de afirmación.

Entonces prosiguió don Fadrique:

"May it be so, God willing," said the friar, also drinking as he prepared to give Don Fadrique his undivided attention.

14

Not much in the cell caught the eye. On the table or desk, which was made of walnut, there were writing materials, the breviary, and other books. There were also two walnut armchairs, in which our principals sat, one across from the other, with the table in between. In addition to the two armchairs, four straight chairs, all with rush bottoms, were arranged against one wall. An *Ecce Homo* in oil, which epitomized the saying "For a Christ with little art, much blood,"[72] was the only painting that adorned the walls of the cell. On the other hand, there was no lack of other more natural adornments. At the window, drinking in the sun, were two rosetrees in flower; inside the cell were four pots of butcher's broom; and hanging on the walls, five cages, two with singing partridges and three with goldfinches, which were excellent lures. Another pretty goldfinch and deft decoy, tied to a rod that was affixed to a pine board and projected from it, flew continuously as far as the long string that imprisoned it would allow, only to return and alight anew on the rod with great panache.

From time to time the goldfinches would sing and gladden the room.

Leaning against a wall in one corner were two hunting shotguns.

And, lastly, in a recess that could scarcely be seen, because the small door was almost completely covered by a green baize curtain, was the good priest's bed. The closet from which the latter had taken the wine, and which was quite roomy, served at the same time as a wine cellar, wardrobe, pantry, cashbox or secret hoard, and library.

Everything, although poor, looked very tidy and clean.

Father Jacinto, with his elbow on the table, his cheek in his hand, and his eyes riveted on Don Fadrique, waited for his old pupil to begin.

Don Fadrique, in a low voice, spoke as follows:

"Although I am not a penitent come to make my confession, I insist on the same secrecy of the confessional."

Without saying a word, the priest nodded his head in assent.

Don Fadrique then continued:

–El hombre de que he hablado a usted, el pecador causa del pecado y del hurto, soy yo mismo. La ligereza de mi carácter me ha hecho olvidar mi delito y no pensar en las fatales consecuencias que de él habían de dimanar. El acaso... ¿qué digo el acaso?... Dios providente, en quien creo, me ha vuelto a poner en presencia de mi cómplice y me ha hecho ver todos los males que por mi culpa se originaron y amenazan originarse aún. Dispuesto estoy a remediarlos y a evitarlos, de acuerdo con la doctrina de usted, hasta donde me sea posible y lícito. Es un consuelo para mí el ver que usted está en concordancia conmigo. Yo no he de buscar remedio peor que la enfermedad; pero hay una persona que le busca, y es menester oponerse a toda costa a que le halle. Sería una abominación sobre otra abominación.

–¿Y quién es esa persona?

–Mi cómplice,– contestó el comendador.

–¿Y quién es tu cómplice?

–Usted la conoce. Usted es su director espiritual. Usted debe de tener grande influjo sobre ella. Mi cómplice es... Cuenta, maestro, que jamás he hecho a nadie esta revelación. Al menos nadie pudo jamás tildarme de escandaloso. Pocas relaciones han sido más ocultas. La buena fama de esta mujer aparece aún, después de diez y siete años, más resplandeciente que el oro.

–Acaba: ¿quién es tu cómplice? Haz cuenta que echas tu secreto en un pozo. Yo sé callar.

–Mi cómplice es doña Blanca Roldán de Solís.

El padre Jacinto se llenó de asombro, abrió los ojos y la boca y se santiguó muy de prisa media docena de veces, soltando estas piadosas interjecciones:

–¡Ave María Purísima! ¡Alabado sea el Santísimo Sacramento! ¡Jesús, María y José!

–¿De qué se admira usted tan desaforadamente?– dijo el comendador, pensando que el padre extrañaba que tan virtuosa y austera matrona hubiese nunca sucumbido a una mala tentación.

–¿De qué me admiro?... Muchacho... ¿De qué me admiro?... Pues, ¿te parece poco? Bien dicen... Vivir para ver... El demonio es el mismo demonio. Miren... y no lo digo por ofender a nadie... ¡miren con qué ramillete de claveles te acarició y te sedujo nuestro enemigo común!... Como un manojo de aulagas. Suave flor trasplantaste al jardín de tus

"The man of whom I have spoken, the sinner who is the cause of the deception and the theft, is me. The frivolity or levity of my character had made me forget my offense and not think about the fatal consequences that would stem from it. Chance ... why am I saying chance? Provident God, in whom I believe, has again put me in the presence of my accomplice and has made me see all the evils that resulted from my fault and that still do threaten to result from it. I am prepared to make amends for them, in accordance with your views, and to avoid other evils, to the extent that it is possible and permissible for me to do so. I find much consolation in the fact that our thinking is identical. I will not seek a remedy that is worse than the illness, but there is a person who does seek such a one, and we must keep that person from finding it, and do so at any cost. It would be one abomination on top of another abomination."

"And who is that person?" asked the priest.

"My accomplice," answered the commander.

"And who is your accomplice?"

"You know her. You are her spiritual director. You must have great influence over her. My accomplice is ... Bear in mind, Master, that I have never revealed this to anyone. At least no one could ever criticize me for scandalous behavior. Few relationships have been more secret. The good name of this woman still appears, after seventeen years, more resplendent than gold."

"Enough already. Who is your accomplice? Remember that your secret is perfectly safe with me. I know how to keep quiet."

"My accomplice is Doña Blanca Roldán de Solís."

Father Jacinto, struck with amazement, opened his eyes and mouth wide and rapidly crossed himself a half dozen times, uttering these pious exclamations:

"By the holy Virgin! Praised be the most Blessed Sacrament! Jesus, Mary, and Joseph!"

"What astonishes you to such an extreme?" asked the commander, thinking that the priest marveled that such a virtuous and austere matron had ever succumbed to an evil temptation.

"What astonishes me? My son ... What astonishes me? You think it's a small thing? It's true ... Live and learn ... The devil is the very devil. Look ... and I don't say this to offend anyone ... look with what a bouquet of carnations you were enticed and seduced by our common enemy! With a handful of gorse. A soft, sweet flower you transplanted to the garden of

amores... ¡Un cardo ajonjero! Hermosa debe haber sido doña Blanca... todavía lo es; pero ¡hombre!, ¡si es un erizo! Yo... perdóneme su ausencia... no la creía impecable, pero no la creía capaz de pecar por amor.

Don Fadrique respondió sólo con un suspiro, con una exclamación inarticulada, que el padre creyó descifrar como si dijese que diez y siete años antes doña Blanca era muy otra, y que además, la misma dureza de su carácter y la briosa inflexibilidad de su genio hacían más vehemente en ella toda pasión, incluso la del amor, una vez que llegaba a sentirla.

Repuesto un poco de su pasmo, dijo el padre Jacinto:

—Y dime, hijo, ¿qué trata de hacer doña Blanca para remediar el mal? ¿Qué proyectos son los suyos, que tanto te asustan?

—¿Quién sería el inmediato heredero de su marido si ella no tuviese una hija?– preguntó el comendador.

—Don Casimiro Solís,– fue la respuesta.

—Pues por eso quiere casar a su hija con don Casimiro.

—¡Pecador de mí! ¡Estúpido y necio!– exclamó el padre, todo lleno de violencia y dando en la mesa unos cuantos puñetazos. –¿Quieres creer que soy yo tan egoísta que el egoísmo me había cegado? Yo no había visto en el plan de doña Blanca ninguna mala traza. Me parecía natural que casase a Clarita con su tío. Yo no miraba sino a mi pícaro interés; a que nadie se llevase a Clarita lejos de estos lugares. Es menester que lo sepas... Clarita me tiene embobado. Por ella, no más que por ella, aguanto a su madre. Lo que yo quería, como un bribón de siete suelas, es que se quedase por aquí... para ir a verla y para que ella me agasajase, como me agasaja ahora, cuando voy a casa de su madre, sirviéndome, con sus blancas y preciosas manos, jícaras de chocolate y tacillas de almíbar. Se me antojó que Clarita era una muñeca para mi diversión. Yo no caí en nada... no me hice cargo... pensé sólo en que, ya casada, haría una excelente señora de su casa, y me recibiría al amor de la lumbre, y yo le llevaría flores, frutas y pajaritos de regalo. ¡Si vieses qué corza he hecho venir para ella de Sierra Morena! Es un primor. La tengo abajo en el corral... y se la iba a llevar mañana. Nada... ¿has visto qué bárbaro?... sin dar la menor importancia a lo del casamiento. Ahora lo comprendo todo. ¡Qué monstruosidad! ¡Casar aquel dije con semejante estafermo!

your love. A carline thistle! Doña Blanca must have been beautiful ... , and she still is, but, Fadrique, my boy, she's a bad-tempered sort! I ... not to speak ill of one who is absent ... I didn't think her incapable of sinning, but I did think her incapable of sinning out of love."

Don Fadrique responded only with a sigh, with an inarticulate exclamation, which the priest understood as his way of saying that seventeen years before Doña Blanca was a very different woman, and moreover that the very harshness of her character and the resolute inflexibility of her nature made every passion, including love, that much more vehement in her when she came to feel each one.

Somewhat recovered from his astonishment, Father Jacinto asked:

"And tell me, my son, what is Doña Blanca trying to do to remedy the wrong? What is this scheme of hers that has you so alarmed?"

"Who would be her husband's immediate heir if she did not have a daughter?" asked the commander.

"Don Casimiro Solís," was the answer.

"Well, that's why she wants to marry her daughter to Don Casimiro."

"A stupid, foolish old man am I, and blind to boot!" exclaimed the priest, forcefully banging the table a number of times with his fist. "Would you believe that I am so egoistic that my egoism had blinded me? It seemed natural to me that she should marry Clarita to her uncle. I was looking only at my blasted self-interest, watching that no one would take Clarita away from these parts. You need to know this: I am positively captivated by Clarita. For her sake, and only for her sake, I put up with her mother. What I wanted, like a proper rogue, was for her to remain here ... so that I could go to see her and so that she could shower attention on me, as she does now, when I go to her mother's house, serving me, with her exquisite white hands, cups of chocolate and small bowls of syrup. I figured that Clarita was a doll for my amusement. I didn't realize... I didn't understand... I thought only that once she was married, she would make an excellent lady of the house, and that she would receive me by the fireside, and that I would take her gifts like flowers, fruits, and birds. If you saw the doe that I've had brought down from the Sierra Morena[73] for her! She's a beauty. I have her out in the corral and was going to take her to Clarita tomorrow. Anyhow ... what a turn of events. And here I was, not attaching the slightest importance to the marriage. Now I see it only too clearly. What a monstrous design! To marry that gem to such a nonentity. Naturally ... she doesn't find

Ya se ve... ella no lo repugna... no lo entiende... ¿quién diablo sabe?... pero yo lo entiendo... y me espeluzno... me horrorizo.

—Tiene razón usted de horrorizarse... Ella lo repugna... lo entiende... pero cree que no debe resistir a la autoridad materna.

—Eso será lo que tase un sastre. ¡Pues no faltaba más! Obedecerá a su madre; pero antes obedecerá a Dios. *Diligendus est genitor, sed praeponendus est Creator.* Es sentencia de San Agustín.

—Además,— dijo el comendador —, Clarita ama a otro hombre.

—¿Cómo es eso? ¿Qué me cuentas? ¿Qué mentira, qué enredo te han hecho creer? Si amase a un galán, Clara me lo hubiera confesado.

—Ella misma ignora casi que le ama; pero me consta que le ama.

—Vamos, sí, ya doy en ello: ciertas miradas y sonrisas de un estudiantillo... Me las ha confesado. Está arrepentida... ¡Con un estudiantillo!... ¿Pues se había de ir Clarita a correr la tuna?

—Padre Jacinto, usted chochea.

—¡Desvergonzado! ¿Cómo te atreves a decir que chocheo?

—El estudiantillo no es de esos que van con el manteo roto y con la cuchara puesta en el sombrero de tres picos, pidiendo limosna, sino que es un caballero principal, un rico mayorazgo.

—¿De veras? Ya eso es harina de otro costal. De eso no me había dicho nada aquella cordera inocente. Oye... ¿y es buen mozo?

—Como un pino de oro.

—¿Buen cristiano?

—Creo que sí.

—¿Honrado?

—A carta cabal.

—¿Y la quiere mucho?

—Con toda el alma.

—¿Y es discreto y valiente?

—Como un Gonzalo de Córdoba. Además es poeta elegantísimo, monta bien a caballo, posee otras mil habilidades, es muy leído y sabe de torear.

—Me alegro, me alegro y me realegro. Le casaremos con Clarita, aunque rabie doña Blanca.

it disgusting ... she doesn't understand ... who the devil does? But I understand ... and it makes my hair stand on end ... it horrifies me."

"You have reason to be horrified. She does find it disgusting, she does understand, but she believes that she should not resist maternal authority."

"A fine state of affairs. That's all we needed. Obey her mother, yes, but first she will obey God: *Diligendus est genitor, sed praeponendus est Creator*. It's a saying of Saint Augustine's."

"Besides," said the commander, "Clarita loves another man."

"How's that? What are you telling me? What lie, what love entanglement have you been made to believe? If she loved a gallant, Clara would have confessed that to me."

"She herself is practically ignorant of the fact that she loves him, but I know that she does."

"All right, yes, now I get it. Certain glances and smiles for a young student. She confessed[74] them to me. She has repented. A student! Would we have Clarita leading a vagrant existence, singing and asking for alms?"

"Father Jacinto, you're turning senile."

"What cheek! How do you dare to say I'm turning senile?"

"This student isn't one of those that go around in a torn cloak and with a spoon in a three-cornered hat[75], begging money, but a young gentleman of some standing, a rich heir."

"Really? Well, that's a horse of a different color. Our innocent lamb has not said a thing to me about this. So tell me, Fadrique: is he a handsome youth?"

"As fine-looking as they come."

"A good Christian?"

"I think so."

"Honorable?"

"In every respect."

"And he truly loves her?"

"With his whole heart."

"And is he discreet and brave?"

"Like a Gonzalo de Córdoba.[76] Moreover, he is a most elegant poet, sits a good horse, possesses a thousand other abilities, is well-read, and knows about bullfighting."

"I'm glad, I'm glad, I'm very glad. We'll marry him to Clarita, even if Doña Blanca rants and raves."

–Sí, querido maestro, le casaremos... pero es menester que seamos muy prudentes.

–*Prudentes sicut serpentes...* Pierde cuidado. Harto sé yo quién es doña Blanca. Es omnímodo el imperio que ejerce sobre su hija. El respeto y el temor que le infunde exceden a todo encarecimiento. Y luego, ¡qué brío, qué voluntad la de aquella señora! A terca nadie le gana.

–No soy yo menos terco... y no consentiré que Clara sea el precio del rescate de nadie; que sobre ella, que no tiene culpa, pesen nuestras culpas; que doña Blanca la venda para conseguir su libertad. Sin embargo, importa mucho la cautela. Doña Blanca, llevada al extremo, pudiera hacer alguna locura.

Después de esta larga conversación, y perfectamente de acuerdo el comendador y el padre Jacinto, el primero se volvió a la ciudad en aquel mismo día para que su ausencia no se extrañase.

El padre Jacinto quedó en ir a la ciudad al día siguiente de mañana.

Los pormenores y trámites del plan que habían de seguir se dejaron para que sobre el terreno se decidiesen.

Sólo se concertó el mayor sigilo y circunspección en todo y disimular en lo posible la íntima amistad que entre el fraile y el comendador había, a fin de no hacer sospechoso y aborrecible al fraile a los ojos de doña Blanca.

Se convino, por último, en que, a pesar de la gravedad de la situación, no era ninguna salida de tono, ni tenía una inoportunidad cómica o censurable, que el padre Jacinto llevase a Clarita la corza y se la regalara.

15

Al volver aquella noche a la ciudad, el comendador tuvo que sufrir un interrogatorio en regla de su sobrina, que era la muchacha más curiosa y preguntona de toda la comarca. Tenía además un estilo de preguntar, afirmando ya lo mismo de que anhelaba cerciorarse, que hacía ineficaz la doctrina del padre Jacinto de callar la verdad sin decir la mentira. O había que mentir o había que declarar: no quedaba término medio.

–Tío– dijo Lucía apenas le vio a solas –, usted ha estado en Villabermeja.

"Yes, dear master, we'll marry him. But we must be very prudent."

"*Prudentes sicut serpentes* ...[77] Don't worry. I know full well who Doña Blanca is. The authority that she exercises over her daughter is absolute. The respect and fear that she inspires in Clarita boggle the mind. And then, what determination, what willpower that woman has! Nobody beats her when it comes to obstinacy."

"I am no less obstinate, and I will not allow Clara to be the price of anyone's redemption, nor permit our sins to be visited upon her, as she's not to blame, nor let Doña Blanca sell her in order to obtain her own freedom. Nonetheless, it behooves us to be very cautious. Pushed to an extreme, Doña Blanca might do something crazy."

After this long conversation, which ended with the commander and Father Jacinto being in complete agreement, the former returned to the city that very same day so that his absence would not cause people to wonder where he was.

Father Jacinto agreed to go to the city the following morning.

The details of the plan, and steps to be taken, were left to be determined on the spot. However, they did acknowledge the necessity of maintaining great secrecy and circumspection in everything and of concealing, as far as possible, the close friendship that existed between the friar and the commander, so as not to make the former suspect and abhorrent in the eyes of Doña Blanca.

It was agreed, lastly, that, despite the gravity of the situation, it was not unseemly, nor comically nor reprehensibly inappropriate for Father Jacinto to take the white doe to Clarita and give it to her as a gift.

15

Upon his return to the city that night, the commander had to suffer a detailed interrogation on the part of his niece, who was the most curious and inquisitive girl in the entire region. She had, furthermore, a manner of questioning that consisted in affirming the very thing that she longed to ascertain, which challenged the effectiveness of Father Jacinto's views of holding back the truth without telling the lie. Either he had to lie or he had to state the truth: there was no middle ground.

"Uncle," Lucía said to him as soon as they were alone, "you have been in Villabermeja."

–Sí... he estado.

–¿A qué ha ido usted por allí? ¡Si le traerán a usted entusiasmado los divinos ojos de Nicolasa!

–No conozco a esa Nicolasa.

–¿Que no la conoce usted?... ¡Bah!... ¿Quién no conoce a Nicolasa? Es un prodigio de bonita. Muchos hidalgos y ricachos la han pretendido ya.

–Pues yo no me cuento en ese número. Te repito que no la conozco.

–Calle usted, tío... ¿Cómo quiere usted hacerme creer que no conoce a la hija de su amigo el tío Gorico?

–Pues digo por tercera vez que no la conozco.

–Entonces, ¿qué hay que ver en Villabermeja? ¿Ha estado usted para visitar a la chacha Ramoncica?

El comendador tuvo que responder francamente.

–No la he visitado.

–Vamos, ya caigo. ¡Qué bueno es usted!

–¿Por qué soy bueno?... ¿Por qué no he visitado a la chacha Ramoncica que me quiere tanto?

–No, tío. Es usted bueno... En primer lugar porque no es usted malo.

–Lindo y discreto razonamiento.

–Quiero decir que es usted bueno, porque no es como otros caballeros, que por más que estén ya con un pie en el sepulcro, de lo que dista usted mucho, a Dios gracias, andan siempre galanteando y soliviantando a las hijas de los artesanos y jornaleros. Ahora no... por el noviazgo; pero antes... bien visitaba don Casimiro a Nicolasa.

–Pues yo no la he visitado.

–Pues ésa es la primera razón por la que digo que es usted bueno. Nicolasa es una muchacha honrada... y no está bien que los caballeros traten de levantarla de cascos...

–Apruebo tu rigidez. Y la segunda razón por la cual soy bueno, ¿quieres decírmela?

–La segunda razón es, que no habiendo ido usted a ver a Nicolasa ni a ver a la chacha Ramoncica, ¿a qué había usted de haber ido tan a escape como no fuese a ver al padre Jacinto y a tratar de ganarle en favor de Mirtilo y de Clori? Vaya, ¿a que ha ido usted a eso?

"Yes, I have."

"And why did you go there? Is it because you are taken with Nicolasa's divine eyes?"

"I don't know that Nicolasa."

"You don't know her? Bah! Who doesn't know Nicolasa? She's as pretty as can be. Many hidalgos and well-heeled men have already courted her."

"Well, I don't count myself among them. I repeat that I do not know her."

"None of that, Uncle. How do you expect me to believe that you don't know the daughter of your friend Tío Gorico?"

"Well, I'm saying for the third time that I don't know her."

"Then, what is there to see in Villabermeja? Did you go to visit Chacha Ramoncica?"

The commander had to answer honestly.

"I did not visit her."

"All right, now I understand. How good you are!"

"Why am I good? Because I didn't visit Chacha Ramoncica, who loves me so much?"

"No, Uncle. You are good … in the first place because you are not bad."

"A nice, sensible piece of reasoning."

"I mean that you are good because you are not like some other gentlemen who, for as much as they already have one foot in the grave, which does not at all apply to you, thank God, are always flirting with and leading on the daughters of craftsmen and workmen. Not now … on account of the engagement, but before … Don Casimiro visited Nicolasa for sure."

"Well, I didn't visit her."

"Well, that's the first reason I say you are good. Nicolasa is a decent girl, and it's not right that gentlemen should try to fill her with false hopes."

"I approve of your strict view. And the second reason that I am good: are you going to tell me what it is?"

"The second reason is that, not having gone to see Nicolasa or Chacha Ramoncica, what could you have gone off to do in such a rush if not to see Father Jacinto and try to gain his support on behalf of Myrtilus and Chloris? Am I not right?"

–No puedo negártelo.

–Gracias, tío. No es usted capaz de encarecer bastante lo orgullosa que estoy.

–¿Y por qué?

–Toma... porque, por muy afectuoso que sea usted con todos, al fin no se interesaría tanto por dos personas que le son casi extrañas, si no fuese por el cariño que tiene usted a su sobrinita, que desea proteger a esas dos personas.

–Así es la verdad– dijo el comendador, dejando escapar una mentira oficiosa, a pesar de la teoría del padre Jacinto.

Lucía se puso colorada de orgullo y de satisfacción, y siguió hablando:

–Apostaré a que ha ganado usted la voluntad del reverendo. ¿Está ya de nuestra parte?

–Sí, sobrina, está de nuestra parte; pero por amor de Dios, calla, que importa el secreto. Ya que lo adivinas todo, procura ser sigilosa.

–No tendrá usted que censurarme. Seré sigilosa. Usted, en cambio, me tendrá al corriente de todo. ¿Es verdad que me lo dirá usted todo?

–Sí– dijo el comendador, teniendo que mentir por segunda vez. Luego prosiguió:

–Lucía, tú has dicho una cosa que me interesa. ¿Qué clase de amoríos das a entender que hubo o hay entre don Casimiro y esa bella Nicolasa?

–Nada, tío... ¿No lo he dicho ya? Fueron antes del noviazgo con Clarita. Don Casimiro no iba con buen fin... y Nicolasa le desdeñó siempre; pero de esto informará a usted mejor que yo el padre Jacinto. Yo lo único que añadiré es que el tal don Casimiro me parece un hipocritón y un bribón redomado.

–No es malo saberlo– pensó el comendador.

–¡Ah! Diga usted, tío. Ya sé que se fue a Sevilla don Carlos. Envió recado despidiéndose y excusándose de no haberlo hecho en persona por la priesa. Es evidente que usted le ha hablado al alma y le ha convencido para que se vaya, asegurándole que esto convenía al logro de nuestro propósito. ¿No es así, tío?

–Así es, sobrina– respondió el comendador –. Veo que nada se te oculta.

"I can't deny it."

"Thank you, Uncle. You can't begin to imagine how proud I am."

"And why is that?"

"Why? Because for as kind as you may be to everybody, nevertheless you wouldn't take so much interest in two people who are practically strangers to you if it weren't for the affection you feel for your dear niece, who wishes to protect those two people."

"That's the truth," said the commander, letting slip a white lie, despite Father Jacinto's theory.

Lucía blushed with pride and satisfaction, and continued:

"I bet you have won over his reverence's goodwill. Is he on our side now?"

"Yes, niece, he's on our side, but for the love of God, keep this to yourself because secrecy is very important. Since you've guessed everything, try to be discreet."

"You won't have to reproach me. I'll be discreet. You, on the other hand, will keep me apprised of everything. You will tell me everything, will you not?"

"Yes," said the commander, having to lie a second time. Then he went on:

"Lucía, you've said something that interests me. What kind of relationship or affair are you implying there was or is between Don Casimiro and that lovely Nicolasa?"

"It's nothing, Uncle. Haven't I already told you? It was before the engagement to Clarita. Don Casimiro did not have a good end in mind, and Nicolasa always scorned him, but Father Jacinto can give you a better account than I can. The only thing I'll add is that this Don Casimiro fellow strikes me as a big hypocrite and an out-and-out scoundrel."

"*Not a bad thing to know*," thought the commander.

"Oh, on a related point, Uncle. I know that Don Carlos has gone back to Seville. He sent a message saying good-bye and apologizing for not having done so in person as he was in a hurry. It's evident that you spoke to him in earnest and convinced him to leave, assuring him that this would be best for the success of our objective. Isn't that right, Uncle?"

"That's right, niece," answered the commander. "I see that nothing escapes you."

16

Cuando ocurrían los sucesos que vamos refiriendo, no había tantas carreteras como ahora. Desde Villabermeja a la ciudad puede hoy irse en coche. Entonces sólo se iba a pie o a caballo. El camino no era camino, sino vereda, abierta por las pisadas de los transeúntes racionales e irracionales. Cuando había grandes lluvias, la vereda se hacía intransitable; era lo que llaman en Andalucía un camino real de perdices.

Poseía el padre Jacinto una borrica modelo por lo grande, mansa y segura. En esta borrica iba y venía siempre, como un patriarca, desde Villabermeja a la ciudad y desde la ciudad a Villabermeja. Un robusto lego le acompañaba a pie. En el viaje que hizo a la ciudad, al día siguiente de su largo coloquio con el comendador, le acompañó, a más del lego, un rústico seglar o profano, para que cuidase la corza.

Seguido, pues, de su lego, de la corza y del rústico, y caballero en su gigantesca borrica, el padre Jacinto entró sano y salvo en la ciudad a las diez de la mañana. Como el convento de Santo Domingo está casi a la entrada, no tuvo el padre que atravesar las calles con aquel séquito. En el convento se apeó, y, apenas se reposó un poco, se dirigió a la casa de don Valentín Solís, o más bien a casa de doña Blanca. El cuitado de don Valentín se había anulado de tal suerte, que nadie en el lugar llamaba a su casa la casa de don Valentín. Sus viñas, sus olivares, sus huertas y sus cortijos eran conocidos por de doña Blanca, y no por suyos. Aquella anulación marital no había llegado, con todo, hasta el extremo de la de algunos maridos de Madrid, a quien apenas los conoce nadie sino por sus mujeres, cuya notoriedad y gloria se reflejan en ellos y los hacen conspicuos.

Pero dejemos a un lado ejemplos y comparaciones, que pueden tomar ciertos visos y vislumbres de murmuración, y sigamos al padre Jacinto, y penetremos con él en casa de doña Blanca, donde tan difícil era entrar para el vulgo de los mortales.

Merced a la autoridad del reverendo, y siguiéndole invisibles, todas las puertas se nos franquean.

Ya estamos en el salón de doña Blanca. Clara borda a su lado. Don Valentín, a respetable distancia y sentado junto a una mesa, hace paciencias con una baraja. Don Casimiro habla con la señora de la casa y con su hija.

16

When the events that we are relating took place there were not as many highways as there are now. Today you can go by coach from Villabermeja to the city; in those times you could only go on foot or on horseback. The road was not a road, but a path, opened up by the passage of rational and irrational travelers. When there were heavy rains, the path became impassable: it was what in Andalusia people call a "highway for partridges."

Father Jacinto had a nonpareil donkey for how big, gentle, and surefooted it was. He rode like a patriarch on this donkey, back and forth from Villabermeja to the city and from the city to Villabermeja. A lusty lay brother would accompany him on foot. On the journey that he made to the city the day after his long conversation with the commander, he was accompanied, in addition to the lay brother, by a secular or non-religious peasant who tended the doe.

Followed, then, by his lay brother, the doe, and the peasant, and astride his gigantic donkey, Father Jacinto entered the city safe and sound at ten o'clock in the morning. Inasmuch as the monastery of Santo Domingo is very near the entrance, he did not have to cross streets with that entourage. He dismounted at the monastery, and as soon as he rested a little he headed for Don Valentín Solís's house, or rather for Doña Blanca's house. The spineless Don Valentín had lost his identity to such a degree that no one there called his house Don Valentín's house. His vineyards, his olive groves, and his farms were known as Doña Blanca's, not his. That marital nullification had not, however, reached the extreme of some Madrid husbands, who are hardly known by anyone except through their wives, whose notoriety and whose glory are reflected on them and make them conspicuous.

But let us set aside examples and comparisons that can take on certain appearances and glimmers of malicious gossip, and follow Father Jacinto and with him enter Doña Blanca's house, which was so difficult for ordinary mortals to penetrate.

Thanks to the cleric's authority, and following him invisibly, all doors are opened to us.

We are now in Doña Blanca's drawing room. Clara is embroidering at her side. Don Valentín, at a respectful distance and seated at a table, is playing solitaire with a deck of cards. Don Casimiro is talking with the lady of the house and her daughter.

Los lectores conocen ya a don Casimiro, como si dijéramos de fama, de nombre y hasta de apodo, pues no ignoran que para don Carlos, Lucía, Clara y el comendador, era el *viejo rabadán*. Veamos ahora si logramos hacer su corporal retrato.

Era alto, flaco de brazos y piernas y muy desarrollado de abdomen; de color trigueño, poca barba, que se afeitaba una vez a la semana, y los ojos verde-claros y un poquito bizcos. Tenía ya bastantes arrugas en la cara, y el vivo carmín de sus narices no armonizaba con la palidez de los carrillos. En su propia persona se notaba poco esmero y aseo; pero en el traje sí se descubrían el cuidado y la pulcritud que en la persona faltaban, lo cual denotaba desde luego que don Casimiro más se cuidaba la ropa por ser ordenado, económico y aficionado a que las prendas durasen, que por amor a la limpieza. Iba vestido muy de hidalgo principal, si bien a la moda de hacía quince o veinte años. Su casaca, su chupa, sus calzones y medias de seda, no tenían una mancha, y, si tenían alguna rotura, ésta se hallaba diestra y primorosamente zurcida. Gastaba peluca con polvos y coleta, y lucía muchos dijes en las cadenas de sendos relojes que llevaba en ambos bolsillos de la chupa. Su caja de tabaco, que él mostraba de continuo, pues no cesaba de tomar rapé, era un primor artístico, por los esmaltes y las piedras preciosas que le servían de adorno. Al hablar usaba don Casimiro de cierta solemnidad y pausa muy entonada; pero su voz era ronca y desapacible, asegurándose provenir esto en parte de que no le desagradaba el aguardiente, y más aún de que, en su casa y despojado de las galas de novio o de pretendiente amoroso, fumaba mucho tabaco negro.

La expresión de su semblante, sus modales y gestos, no eran antipáticos: eran insignificantes; salvo que no podía menos de reconocerse por ellos en don Casimiro a una persona de clase, aunque criada en un lugar.

Se advertía, por último, en todo su aspecto, que don Casimiro debía padecer no pocos achaques. Su mala salud le hacía parecer más viejo.

Dado a conocer así somera, y no favorablemente, por desgracia, podemos ya lisonjearnos de conocer a cuantas personas ocupaban la sala cuando entró en ella el padre Jacinto.

Doña Blanca, Clarita, don Valentín y don Casimiro se levantaron para recibirle, y todos le besaron humildemente la mano. El padre estuvo

Readers already know Don Casimiro, so to speak, by reputation, by name, and even by nickname, since they are not unaware that for Don Carlos, Clara, and the commander, he was the *old shepherd*. Let us see if we can manage to draw his physical portrait.

He was tall, with thin arms and legs and a bulging abdomen; he had a dark complexion and not much of a beard, which he shaved once a week, and light green and somewhat squinty eyes. There were already a goodly number of wrinkles on his face, and the vivid carmine of his nose did not harmonize well with the paleness of his cheeks. His person itself showed little neatness and attention, but in his dress you could see the care and smartness missing in his person, which of course indicated that Don Casinmiro took care of his clothes more out of being orderly, economical, and keen on having his clothes last than out of love of cleanliness. He was dressed very much like an illustrious hidalgo, although in the fashion of fifteen or twenty years past. His frock coat, his vest, his breeches, and his silk stockings were spotless, and if they had any tears they were skillfully and exquisitely mended. He wore a wig complete with powder and queue, and displayed numerous charms on the chains of timepieces that he wore on each of the two pockets of his vest. His snuffbox, which he brought out continually, as he was always taking a pinch of tobacco, was a lovely work of art owing to the enamels and precious stones that adorned it. In his speech Don Casimiro adopted a certain solemnity and used modulated pauses, but his voice was husky and unpleasant, and this stemmed from the fact that he did not dislike brandy, and even more from the fact that, at his house and stripped of his finery as a fiancé or loving suitor, he smoked a lot of black tobacco.

The expression on his face, his manners, and his gestures were not disagreeable, they were insignificant, except that one could not help recognizing in them that Don Casimiro was a person of standing, although brought up in a small town.

You could tell, lastly, from his entire appearance, that Don Casimiro must have suffered from not a few ailments. His poor health made him look older.

Having thus described him superficially and not favorably, more's the pity, we can now compliment ourselves on knowing all the people who occupied the drawing room when Father Jacinto entered it.

Doña Blanca, Clarita, Don Valentín, and Don Casimiro all rose to receive him and all humbly kissed his hand. The priest, a smile on his

sonriente y amabilísimo con ellos; y a Clarita le dio, como si no fuese ya una mujer, como si fuese una niña de ocho años, y con la respetabilidad que setenta bien cumplidos le prestaban, dos palmaditas suaves en la fresca mejilla, didendole:

–¡Bendito sea Dios, muchacha, que te ha hecho tan buena y tan hermosa!

–Su merced me favorece y me honra– contestó Clarita.

Doña Blanca se lamentó del mucho tiempo que el padre había estado sin venir de Villabermeja, y todos le hicieron coro. Se trató de que el padre tomase algo hasta la hora de comer, y el padre no quiso tomar nada, salvo asiento cómodo. Desde su asiento habló de mil cosas con animada y alegre conversación, resuelto a aguardar allí a que don Casimiro se fuese y a que don Valentín y doña Clara despejasen, para hablar a solas con doña Blanca.

Doña Blanca adivinó la intención del fraile, entró en curiosidad, y pronto halló modo de despedir a don Casimiro y de echar de la sala a don Valentín y a Clarita.

Verificado ya el despejo, dijo doña Blanca:

–Supongo y espero que, después de tan larga ausencia, honrará usted nuestra mesa comiendo hoy con nosotros.

El padre Jacinto aceptó el convite, y doña Blanca prosiguió:

–He creído advertir que estaba usted impaciente por hablarme a solas. Esto ha picado mi curiosidad. Todo lo que usted me dice o puede decirme me inspira el mayor interés. Hable usted, padre.

–No eres lerda, hija mía– contestó éste –. Nada se te escapa. En efecto, deseaba hablarte a solas. Y lo deseaba tanto, que dejo para después de tu comida, que acepto gustoso, dejo para sobremesa, la aparición de un objeto que traigo de presente a nuestra Clarita, y que le va a encantar. Figúrate que es una lindísima corza, tan mansa y doméstica, que come en la mano y sigue como un perro. Pero vamos al caso: vamos a lo que tengo que decirte. Por Dios, que no te incomodes. Tú tienes el genio muy vivo, eres una pólvora.

–Es verdad; yo soy muy desgraciada, y los desgraciados no es fácil que estén de buen humor. Usted, sin embargo, no tiene derecho a quejarse del mío. ¿Cuándo estuve yo, desde que nos tratamos, desabrida y áspera con usted?

–Eso es muy verdad. Convendrás, con todo, en que yo no he dado motivo. Yo no soy como otros frailes, que se meten a dar consejos que

face, was very affable with them, and he gave Clarita – as if she were not a young woman, as if she were a little girl of eight, and with the respectability that his good seventy years lent him – two light pats on her fresh cheek, saying:

"Blessed be God, girl, who made you so good and so beautiful!"

"Your reverence favors me and honors me," responded Clarita.

Doña Blanca expressed regret that Father Jacinto had spent so much time in Villabermeja without coming to visit them, and they all echoed his sentiments. Offered something to drink before the main meal hour, the priest refused everything except a comfortable seat. From his chair he spoke animatedly and cheerfully about a thousand things, resolved to wait for Don Casimiro to take his leave and for Don Valentín and Doña Clara to go elsewhere in order to speak alone to Doña Blanca.

Doña Blanca, having guessed the friar's intention and finding her curiosity piqued, soon hit upon a way to get rid of Don Casimiro and to send Don Valentín and Clara out.

With the drawing room cleared, Doña Blanca said:

"I assume and expect that, after such a long absence, you will honor our table by dining with us today."

Father Jacinto accepted the invitation, and Doña Blanca continued:

"I thought I noticed that you were impatient to speak to me alone. This has piqued my curiosity. Everything that you say to me or can say to me awakens the greatest interest in me. So go ahead, Father."

"You're not slow, my dear," said Father Jacinto. "Nothing escapes you. I did in fact want to speak to you alone. And so much did I want to, that I will leave for after the meal, which I gladly accept, that I will leave better yet for dessert time, the appearance of something that I've brought as a present for our Clarita, and which she is going to love. You wait and see: the prettiest white doe, so gentle and tame that she eats out of your hand and follows you around like a dog. But let's get down to brass tacks; let's take up what I have to say to you. And for heaven's sake, do not be put out, because you have a very short fuse and a sharp tongue."

"That's true. I am most unfortunate, and it's not easy for unfortunates like me to be in a good humor. You, however, have no right to complain about mine. Since we have known each other, when have I been surly and gruff with you?"

"That's very true. You'll grant, though, that I have never given cause. I am not like other friars, who take it upon themselves to dispense advice

no les piden, y quieren gobernar lo temporal y lo eterno, y dirigirlo todo en cada casa donde entran. ¿No es así?

–Así es. Más bien tengo yo que lamentarme de que usted me aconseja poco.

–Pues hoy no te quejarás por ese lado. Tal vez te quejes de que te aconsejo mucho y de que me meto en camisón de once varas.

–Eso nunca.

–Allá veremos. De todos modos, tengo disculpa. Tú sabes que Clarita es mi encanto. Me tiene hecho un bobo. ¿Quién ignora mi predilección hacia las mujeres? Menester ha sido de toda mi severidad para que allá cuando mozo no me quitaran el pellejo los maldicientes. Hoy, hija mía (alguna ventaja ha de tener el ser viejo), con treinta y cinco años en cada pata, puedo, sin temor de censura, quereros a mi modo y trataros con íntima familiaridad que me deleita. Te confieso que para querer a los hombres tengo que acordarme a menudo de que son prójimos y quererlos por amor de Dios. A las mujeres, por el contrario, las quiero, no ya sin esfuerzo, sino por inclinación decidida. Sois dulces, benignas, compasivas y muchísimo más religiosas que los hombres. Si no hubiera sido por vosotras, lo doy por cierto, hubiérase perdido hasta la huella de la primitiva cultura y revelación del paraíso, y los hombres jamás hubieran salido del estado salvaje. Si yo fuera un sabio había de componer un libro demostrando que todo este ser de la Europa del día, que todos estos adelantamientos sociales, de que el mundo se jacta, se deben, en lo humano, principalmente a las mujeres. Calcula, pues, cuán alto y lisonjero es el concepto que tengo de vosotras. Pues bien; en los últimos años de mi vida, tu hija Clara ha venido a sublimar mucho más aún este concepto de mi mente. En mi mente tenía yo como un tipo soñado de perfección, al cual ninguna de las mujeres que he conocido se acercaba ni en diez leguas. Clarita ha ido más allá, ¡Qué inocencia la suya, tan rara por su enlace con la discreción y el despejo! ¡Qué fe religiosa tan sana y atinada! ¡Qué amor a su madre y qué sumisión a sus mandatos! Clara es una santita en este mundo, y al verla hay que alabar a Dios, que la ha criado, a fin de dejarnos rastrear y columbrar por ella lo que serán en el cielo los angelitos y las bienaventuradas vírgenes.

–Mucho lisonjean mi orgullo de madre– interpuso doña Blanca –, esos encomios de Clarita que oigo en boca de usted; pero mi amor a la

that is not asked of them, and want to control the temporal and the eternal, and direct everything in every house that they enter. Isn't that right?"

"Yes, it is. On the contrary: I have to regret the fact that you advise me too little."

"Well, today you won't complain in that regard. You might even complain that I advise you too much and that I'm meddling in a matter that doesn't concern me."

"That, never."

"We shall see. In any event, I have an excuse. You know that Clarita is my joy. She has me eating out of her hand. Who doesn't know of my predilection for women? It took every ounce of my severity as a youth to keep the backbiters from skinning me alive. Today, my dear (being old has some advantages), with thirty-five years chalked up on each leg, I can, without fear of censure, love all of you in my own way and treat all of you with the close familiarity that delights me. I will admit to you that in order to love men I often have to remember that they are fellow creatures and love them for the love of God. Women, on the contrary, I love not just effortlessly, but from a decided inclination. You women are sweet, kind, compassionate, and very much more religious than men. If it had not been for you, I take for granted that even the trace of primitive culture and revelation of paradise would have been lost, and man never would have emerged from the savage state. If I were a learned person, I would write a book showing that all of this life in present-day Europe, that all these social advances of which the world boasts are due, in human respects, mainly to women. Imagine, then, what a lofty and flattering concept I have of you. So you will understand that in the last few years of my life your Clara has elevated this concept of my mind to an even more exalted level. In my mind I had conceived of something like an ideal type of perfection, which none of the women I have known ever approached, not for thirty miles around. Clarita has gone much further. What innocence hers is, so rare combined as it is with discretion and intelligence! What a sound and wise religious faith! What love for her mother and what submission to her commands! Clara is a young saint walking this earth, and on seeing her you have to praise God, who created her so that we might discover and surmise through her what kinds of angels and blissful virgins there will be in heaven."

"My maternal pride," interjected Doña Blanca, "is very flattered hearing you speak all this praise for Clarita, but my love of justice inclines

justicia me induce a creerlos exagerados. Yo me los explico de cierto modo, que voy a tener la sinceridad de declarar a usted. En el puro amor que en general profesa usted a las mujeres, hay algo de antiguo caballero andante, algo del hechizo que tiene para todo ser fuerte dar protección a los débiles y desvalidos. En el concepto superior a la realidad que de las mujeres usted forma, hay gran bondad e instintiva poesía. Todos estos nobles sentimientos de usted se han empleado, durante una larga y santa vida, en lugareñas, jornaleras unas, e hidalgas o ricachas otras, pero toscas las más, en comparación con Clara, criada en grandes ciudades, con otro barniz, con otra más elevada cultura, con mayor delicadeza y refinamiento. Ventajas tales, meramente exteriores y debidas a la casualidad, han sorprendido y alucinado a usted, y le han hecho pensar que lo que está en la superficie está en el fondo; que modales más distinguidos, mayor tino y mesura en el hablar, y ciertas atenciones y miramientos que nacen de más esmerada educación, y que llegan a tenerse maquinalmente, gracias a la costumbre, son virtudes y excelencias que brotan del centro mismo de un alma que se eleva sobre las otras.

–No, hija mía; nada de eso basta para explicar mi predilección por Clarita.

–¿Cómo que no basta? Sea usted franco. ¿No quiere usted y estima casi tanto a Lucía?

–Las comparaciones son odiosas, y las del cariño más. Supongamos, a pesar de todo, que estimo y quiero a Lucía casi tanto. Eso probaría sólo que Lucía vale casi tanto como Clara.

–Y que ambas están educadas con más esmero.

–Bueno... ¿Y qué?... Concedo que así sea. ¿Quién te ha negado el poder de la educación? Lo que yo niego es que la educación valga hasta ese punto sobre un espíritu estéril e ingrato; y lo que niego también es que su influjo no pase de la superficie y penetre en el fondo, y no mejore el ser de las personas. Es, pues, evidente, que Clara debe mucho a Dios, y luego a ti, que la has educado bien; pero esto que debe a ti no es superficial y externo; los modales, las palabras, las atenciones y los miramientos no son signos vanos. Cuando no hay en ellos afectación, es porque brotan del alma misma, mejor criada por Dios o por los hombres que otras almas sus hermanas. Cierto que yo no he visto ni conocido más gente en mi vida que la de esta ciudad y la de Villabermeja; pero

me to believe that it is exaggerated. I understand this praise in a certain way, and I am going to be honest in explaining it to you. In the pure love that you profess in general for women, there is something of the knights-errant of old, something of the charm that prompts any strong person to give protection to the weak and the helpless. In the concept, superior to reality, that you have formed of women, there is great kindness and instinctive poetry. All these noble sentiments of yours have been directed, during a long and holy life, toward village women, workingwomen some of them, and noblewomen or rich women some others, but most of them coarse in comparison with Clara, who was brought up in big cities, with another polish, with another more elevated culture, with greater delicacy and refinement. Such advantages, merely external and due to chance, have surprised and deluded you, and have made you think that what is on the surface is what is beneath it, and that more distinguished manners, greater tact and moderation in speech, and certain attentions and considerations that stem from a more careful education, and which are acquired mechanically, thanks to habit, are virtues and excellences that spring from the very core of a soul that rises above others."

"No, my dear, none of that is sufficient to explain my predilection for Clara."

"What do you mean it's not sufficient? Be frank. Don't you love and esteem Lucía almost as much?"

"Comparisons are odious, and more so when discussing affection. Let us suppose, nonetheless, that I esteem and love Lucía almost as much. That would only prove that Lucía is worth almost as much as Clara."

"And that both have been more carefully educated."

"Fine. What of it? I grant that such is the case. Who has denied to you the power of education? What I deny, am denying, is that education has that degree of worth over a sterile and ungrateful spirit, and what I also deny is that its influence does not pass from the surface and does not penetrate beneath it and does not improve people's lives. It is evident, therefore, that Clara owes much to God, and then to you, for you have raised her well. But what she owes you is not superficial and external: manners, attentions, considerations, and speech are not meaningless signs. When there is no affectation in them it is because they spring from the soul itself, better nurtured by God or by man than other kindred souls. It's true that never in my life have I seen or known people outside of this city and Villabermeja, but I imagine and expect that there must

adivino y veo claramente que ha de haber duquesas y hasta princesas cuyo barniz no me engañaría ni me alucinaría. Yo conocería al momento que era falso y de relumbrón y que en el fondo eran aquellas damas más vulgares que tu cocinera. Conste, por consiguiente, que no me alucino al encomiar a Clarita.

—¿Y no provendrá la alucinación— dijo doña Blanca —, de la cándida y espontánea propensión de Clarita a hacerse agradable?

—Sin duda que provendrá; pero esa misma propensión, siendo espontánea y cándida, prueba la bondad de alma de quien la tiene.

—¿Y usted no sabe, padre, que eso se califica con un vocablo novísimo en castellano, y que suena mal y como censura?

—¿Qué vocablo es ése?

—Coquetería.

—Pues bien; si la coquetería es sin malicia, si el afán de agradar y el esfuerzo hecho para conseguirlo no traspasan ciertos límites, y si el fin que se propone una mujer agradando no va más allá del puro deleite de infundir cordial afecto y gratitud, digo que apruebo la coquetería.

Doña Blanca y el padre Jacinto se tenían mutuamente miedo. Ella temía la desvergüenza del fraile, y el fraile el genio violentísimo de ella. De este miedo mutuo nacía el que se tratasen por lo común con extremada finura y con el comedimiento más exquisito y circunspecto, a fin de no terminar cualquier coloquio en pelea o disputa.

Llevada de esta consideración, doña Blanca no impugnó la defensa de la coquetería; dio por satisfecha su modestia de madre, y acabó por aceptar como justos y merecidos los encomios de su hija Clara.

Luego añadió:

—En suma, mi hija es un prodigio. En las alabanzas de usted no toma parte sino la justicia. Me alegro. ¿Qué mayor contento para una madre? Imagino, con todo, que tan lisonjero panegírico bien se podía haber pronunciado en presencia de testigos. Lo que sigilosamente tenía usted que decirme no ha salido aún de sus labios.

El padre Jacinto se paró a reflexionar entonces, al verse tan directamente interrogado, y casi se arrepintió de haber venido a tratar del asunto de la boda de Clarita, dejándose llevar de un celo impaciente, sin ponerse antes de acuerdo con el comendador, según habían concertado; pero el padre Jacinto no era hombre que cejaba una vez dado el primer paso, y después de un instante de vacilación, que no dejó percibir a ojos tan linces como los de su interlocutora, dijo de esta manera:

be duchesses and even princesses whose polish would not deceive nor delude me. I would recognize at once that it was false and a sham, and that at bottom those ladies were more ordinary than your cook. It follows, consequently, that I am not deluding myself when I praise Clarita."

"And can't the delusion," asked Doña Blanca, "stem from Clarita's innocent and spontaneous tendency to make herself agreeable?"

"It no doubt does, but that same tendency or propensity, being spontaneous and innocent, proves the goodness of the soul of whoever possesses it."

"Do you not know, Father, that such behavior is characterized by a new word in Spanish, which sounds bad and like a reproach?"

"What word is that?"

"Coquetry."

"Well now, if the coquetry is without malice, if the desire to please and the effort that is made do not exceed certain limits, and if the end that a woman has in mind by pleasing someone does not go beyond the pure delight of inspiring cordial affection and gratitude, I say that I approve of coquetry."

Doña Blanca and Father Jacinto were afraid of each other. She feared the friar's outspokenness, and the friar her violent temper. It was because of this mutual fear that they generally treated each other with extreme politeness and with the most circumspect and exquisite courtesy, so as not to conclude any conversation with a quarrel or an argument.

Swayed by this consideration, Doña Blanca did not refute his defense of coquetry; she deemed her maternal modesty satisfied, and in the end she accepted the encomiums of her daughter Clara as just and deserved.

Then she added:

"In short, my daughter is a wonder. Your words of praise only do her justice. I am pleased. What greater contentment is there for a mother? I imagine, however, that such a flattering panegyric could just as easily have been delivered in the presence of witnesses. What you had to tell me privately has yet to be said."

Father Jacinto, on finding himself questioned so directly, then stopped to reflect and almost regretted having come to take up the matter of Clarita's marriage, allowing himself to be carried away by an impatient zeal, without first having touched base with the commander, as they had arranged. But Father Jacinto was not a man who backed down once the first step had been taken, and after a moment's hesitation, which he concealed from his lynx-eyed interlocutor, he broached the subject:

–Allá voy, hija; ten calma que todo se andará. Mi encomio de Clarita estaba muy bien en su lugar, porque de Clarita voy a hablarte. Me consta, como su director espiritual que soy, que te obedecerá en todo; pero dime, ¿no consideras tú que para algunas cosas, de la mayor importancia, convendría consultar su voluntad?

–¿Y quién ha informado a usted de que yo no la consulto cuando conviene?

–¿Has preguntado, pues, a Clara si quiere casarse tan niña?

–Sí, padre, y ha dicho que sí.

–¿Le has preguntado si aceptará por marido a don Casimiro?

–Sí, padre, y también ha dicho que sí.

–¿Y no serán parte el temor y el respeto que inspiras a tu hija en esas respuestas?

–Creo que no merezco sólo inspirar a mi hija respeto y temor, sino también cariño y confianza. Prevaliéndose, pues, mi hija del cariño y de la confianza que debo inspirarle, hubiera podido contestar que no quería casarse con don Casimiro. Nadie la ha violentado para que diga que quiere. Querrá cuando lo dice.

–Es cierto: querrá cuando lo dice. No obstante, para que una decisión de la voluntad sea válida, importa que la voluntad esté previamente ilustrada por el entendimiento acerca de aquello sobre lo cual decide. ¿Crees tú que Clarita sabe lo que quiere y por qué lo quiere?

–Acaba usted de hacer el encomio más extremado de mi hija, y ahora me induce a pensar que la tiene por tonta, por incapaz de sacramento. ¿Cómo quiere usted que una mujer de diez y seis años ignore los deberes que el santo matrimonio trae consigo?

–No los ignora... Pero no me vengas con sofismas... una niña de diez y seis años no sabe toda la trascendencia del sí que va a dar en los altares.

–Por eso tiene a su madre para iluminarla, aconsejarla y dirigirla.

–¿Y tú la has iluminado, aconsejado y dirigido según tu conciencia?

–La menor duda sobre eso, la mera pregunta que me hace usted es una ofensa terrible y gratuita. ¿Cómo presumir, sospechar, ni por un instante, que había yo de aconsejar a mi hija en contra de lo que mi conciencia me dictase? ¿Tan mala me cree usted?

"I will come to the point. But be calm. Everything in due course. My praise of Clarita was very fitting, because it is about Clarita that I am going to talk to you. I know, since I am her spiritual director, that she will obey you in everything, but tell me: don't you think you should consult her in some matters, of the greatest importance, to learn her wishes?"

"And who has told you that I do not consult her when it is appropriate?"

"So you have asked Clara whether she wishes to marry so young?"

"Yes, Father, and she said yes."

"Have you asked her whether she will accept Don Casimiro as a husband?"

"Yes, Father, and she said yes again."

"And is it not possible that part of those answers lie in the fear and respect that you inspire in your daughter?"

"I believe that I deserve to inspire not only fear and respect in my daughter, but also affection and trust. Availing herself, then, of the affection and trust I ought to inspire in her, my daughter could have answered that she did not want to marry Don Casimiro. No one forced her to say that she wants to. She must, though, since she says she does."

"That's true. She must want to since she says she does. Nevertheless, for a decision of the will to be valid, it is important that the will be enlightened beforehand by understanding with respect to the matter to be decided. Do you believe that Clarita knows what she wants and why she wants it?"

"You have just enthusiastically sung my daughter's praises, and now you cause me to think you consider her a fool, a half-wit. How do you expect a woman of sixteen to be ignorant of the duties that holy matrimony brings with it?"

"She's not ignorant of them, but let's not have any of your sophistry. A girl of sixteen does not know all the consequences of the yes she is going to say at the altar."

"That's why she has her mother to enlighten her, advise her, and guide her."

"And have you enlightened, advised, and guided her according to your conscience?"

"The slightest doubt on this point, the mere question that you ask me is a terrible, gratuitous offense. How can you presume, suspect, even for an instant, that I would advise my daughter contrary to the dictates of my conscience? You think me so evil?"

–Perdona; me expliqué con torpeza. Yo no creo, ni puedo creer que hayas aconsejado a tu hija contra tu conciencia; pero sí puedo creer que en tu entendimiento cabe error, y que, llevada tú de algún error, induces a tu hija a dar un paso deplorable.

–Extraño muchísimo los razonamientos de usted en el día de hoy. ¡Qué diferentes de lo que eran antes! ¿Qué cambio ha habido en usted? Seré yo víctima de un error, y en virtud de ese error daré malos consejos y tomaré funestas resoluciones; pero usted lo sabía, tiempo ha, y nada había dicho en contra cuando no había aún compromiso alguno contraído. ¿Cómo ha venido de pronto a hacerse patente a los ojos de usted ese error, que antes no percibía? ¿Qué luz del cielo le ha ilustrado a usted el alma? ¿Qué santo o qué ángel bendito ha bajado a la tierra a descubrir a usted lo bueno y a distinguirlo de lo malo?

Doña Blanca, según se ve, iba ya perdiendo su aplomo y su dificultosa dulzura. El padre Jacinto empezaba también a amostazarse, pero hizo un esfuerzo heroico, y en vez de seguir adelante y de excitar la tempestad, procuró calmarla por cuantos medios se le ocurrieron.

–Tienes razón que te sobra– contestó con mucha humildad –. Yo debí disuadirte a tiempo de que concertaras esa boda. Del error que noto en ti, confieso que he participado. Por lo menos, ha sido en mí un descuido atroz, una ligereza imperdonable, el no hablarte antes, como te estoy hablando hoy. Pero si yo erré, con reconocerlo ya y con apartarme del error, te induzco a que me imites, aunque te dé armas en contra mía. Lo que afirmas probará mi inconsecuencia, mas no prueba nada contra mi consejo.

–¿Cómo que no prueba nada? Quita a su consejo de usted toda la autoridad que de otra suerte hubiera tenido. Consejo dado tan de repente... hasta pudiera sospecharse... que no se funda en pensamiento propio del consejero.

Doña Blanca, al pronunciar esta última frase, lanzó al padre una penetrante y escrutadora mirada. El padre, que no era tímido, se cortó un poco y bajó los ojos. Serenándose al instante, repuso:

–No se trata aquí de más autoridad que de la autoridad de la razón. Para darte el consejo, válganme la amistad y el cariño que tengo a tu

"Forgive me. I have done a poor job of explaining myself. I do not believe, nor can I believe, that you advised your daughter contrary to the dictates of your conscience, but I can believe that there is room for error in your understanding, and that, affected by some error, you are prompting your daughter to take a deplorable step."

"I am shocked by your reasoning today. How different from what it was earlier! What change has taken place in you? I might be the victim of an error, and by reason of this error I might give bad advice and make ill-fated decisions, but you knew that some time ago, and yet you said nothing in opposition when no commitment of any sort had been entered into. How has this error suddenly become obvious in your eyes when you did not perceive it earlier? What heavenly brilliance has enlightened your soul? What saint or what blessed angel has come down to earth to reveal to you the good and distinguish it from the bad?"

Doña Blanca, as can be seen, was already beginning to lose her aplomb and her off-putting sweetness, while Father Jacinto for his part was beginning to get peeved, but he made a heroic effort, and instead of raising a tempest, he endeavored to calm it by all the means that occurred to him.

"You couldn't be more right," he answered very humbly. "I should have dissuaded you in time to prevent the arrangement of this marriage. I admit that I have partaken in the error that I see in you. At the very least for me it was an atrocious instance of negligence, an unforgivable disregard, not having spoken to you earlier as I am speaking to you today. But if I erred, by acknowledging this error and putting it behind me, I urge you to do the same, even though I am giving you arms to use against me. What you state will demonstrate my inconsistency, but it takes nothing away from my advice."

"What do you mean it takes nothing away? It takes away from your advice all the authority that it otherwise would have had. Advice given so unexpectedly … one might even suspect … that it is not based on the adviser's own thought."

As she spoke these last words, Doña Blanca shot a sharp, penetrating glance at the priest. The latter, who was not timid, became a little embarrassed and cast his eyes downward. But regaining his composure at once, he replied:

"The only authority we're talking about here is the authority of reason. Let the friendship and affection that I have for you and your family be

persona y a los de tu familia: para que le aceptes o le deseches, no pretendo que valga sino el ingenio, que pido a Dios me conceda, para llevar el convencimiento a tu alma.

–Está bien. ¿Quiere usted decirme qué razones hay para que Clara no se case con don Casimiro? Usted es el confesor de Clara, ¿ama Clara a otro hombre?

–Por lo mismo que soy su confesor, si Clara amase a otro hombre y ella me lo hubiese confiado, no te lo diría, sin que ella me diese su venia, que yo sabría pedir y exigir en caso necesario. Por dicha, para nada tiene que entrar aquí la cuestión de si Clara ama o no a otro hombre.

–No me venga usted con rodeos y sutilezas. Yo he educado a mi hija con tal rigidez y con tal recogimiento, que no tengo la menor duda de que no ha tenido amoríos. Clara no ha mirado jamás con malicia a hombre alguno.

–Así será. Pero ¿no podrá mirarle el día de mañana? ¿No podrá amar, si no ama aún?

–Amará a su marido. ¿Por qué no ha de amarle?

–Vamos, señora– dijo el padre Jacinto, ya con la paciencia perdida –, no amará a su marido, porque su marido es feo, viejo, enfermizo y fastidioso.

–Quiero suponer– contestó doña Blanca con el reposado entono que tomaba cuando más tremenda se ponía –, quiero suponer que las caritativas calificaciones de usted cuadran perfectamente al sujeto, a la persona de mi familia, a quien usted honra con ellas. Su exquisito gusto de usted en las artes del dibujo halla feo a don Casimiro; sus conocimientos de usted en la medicina le han hecho comprender que está el pobre mal de salud, y la amenidad y discreción que en usted campean, es natural que le induzcan a fastidiarse de todo ser humano que no sea tan ameno y tan ingenioso como usted, cosa, por desgracia, rarísima; pero usted no me negará que mi hija, menos instruida en las proporciones y bellezas de la figura del hombre, puede no hallar feo a don Casimiro, como no le halla; menos docta en ciencias médicas, puede creerle más sano, y menos chistosa que usted, puede muy bien hallar en don Casimiro algún chiste y no aburrirse de su conversación. Y por otra parte, aunque mi hija viese en don Casimiro los defectos que usted señala, ¿por qué no había de amarle? Pues qué, ¿una mujer de honor, una buena cristiana, ha de amar sólo la hermosura física, y el desenfado en el hablar? ¿Será menester buscarle para marido, no a un caballero de

my justification for giving advice. For you to accept it or reject it will be a question of the light of reason, which I implore God to grant me, which I need in order to make conviction penetrate your soul."

"All right. Will you tell me what reasons there are for Clara not to marry Don Casimiro? You are Clara's confessor. Does Clara love another man?"

"For the very reason that I am her confessor, if Clara loved another man and had confided that to me, I wouldn't tell you without her consent, which I would indeed request, and demand, were it necessary. Fortunately, however, the question of whether Clara loves or does not love another man is not a factor here."

"Don't start with your subterfuges and subtleties. I've raised my daughter with such strictness and in such seclusion that I do not have the least doubt that she has not had love affairs. Clara has never looked at any man provocatively."

"Granted. But what about tomorrow? Will she not be able to love, even if she does not yet?"

"She will love her husband. Why shouldn't she love him?"

"Come now, Señora," said Father Jacinto, having lost his patience, "she won't love her husband because the man is ugly, old, sickly, and irksome."

"I want to suppose," responded Doña Blanca, in the quiet manner that she assumed whenever she got her considerable dander up, "I want to suppose that your charitable labels suit perfectly the individual, the member of my family, whom you honor with them. Your exquisite taste in the drawing arts deems Don Casimiro ugly; your medical knowledge has made you understand that the poor man is in ill health; and the pleasantness and discretion that stand out in you naturally incline you to find irksome every human being who is not as pleasant and witty as you, something that, unfortunately, is extremely rare. But you won't deny that my daughter, less instructed in the proportions and beauties of a man's figure, may not find Don Casimiro ugly, as is the case; less learned in medical sciences, she may think him more healthy and amusing than you, may well find some wit in Don Casimiro and not be bored by his conversation. And on the other hand, even if my daughter were to see in Don Casimiro the defects that you single out, why shouldn't she love him? What? Is a woman of honor, a good Christian woman, to love only physical beauty and smooth speech? Will it be necessary to find her a

su clase, honrado, temeroso de Dios, virtuoso y lleno de atenciones y buenos deseos para hacerla dichosa, sino a algún saltimbanquis robusto, a algún truhán divertido, que provoque en ella con sus chocarrerías una risa indecorosa y un regocijo poco honesto?

–Mira, doña Blanca– dijo el fraile que jamás abandonaba su tuteo, aunque se incomodara –, no creas que se necesita ser un Apeles o un Fidias para conocer que es feo don Casimiro. Su fealdad es tan patente y somera que no hay que ahondar mucho para descubrirla. Y en cuanto a su ruin salud y escasa amenidad te aseguro lo mismo. Sin haber cursado medicina, sin ser un Hipócrates ve cualquiera que don Casimiro está por demás estropeado. Y sin haber estudiado el *Examen de ingenios* de Huarte, se descubre en seguida que el de don Casimiro es romo y huero. Yo no pretendo que busques para Clarita a Pitágoras y a Milón de Crotona en una pieza; pero ¿qué diablura te lleva a darle por marido a Tersites?

El padre Jacinto se abstenía de echar latines cuando hablaba a las mujeres; pero no podía menos de citar en romance, siempre que se dirigía a damas de distinción, hechos, personajes y sentencias de la antigüedad clásica y de las Sagradas Escrituras. Por lo demás, era tan claro el sentido de lo que decía, que doña Blanca, aunque no hubiera sabido más o menos confusamente la condición de los personajes citados, no hubiera tenido la menor duda sobre lo que el fraile quería significar. Así es que le respondió:

–Reverendo padre, ésos son insultos y no consejos; pero jamás me enojaré con usted. Lo único que afirmo es que todos los defectos que pone usted a mi futuro yerno han de estar menos al descubierto de lo que usted supone ahora, cuando antes de ahora no los ha conocido usted. Y si los conocía, ¿por qué antes no me los dijo? Repito que alguien ha venido a ilustrar su claro entendimiento de usted. Alguien le induce a dar este paso. No hay que disimular. Sea usted leal y franco conmigo. Usted ha hablado con alguien acerca de la proyectada boda de Clarita. Sus consejos de usted no son consejos, sino un mensaje solapado.

El padre Jacinto era fresco de veras; pero con doña Blanca no había frescura que valiese. El pobre fraile estaba sofocado, rojo hasta las orejas. Por él hubiera podido inventarse aquella frase con que se denotaba que a alguien le han dado una buena descompostura: *tenía encarnadas las orejas como fraile en visita.*

husband who is not a gentleman of her class, honorable, God-fearing, virtuous, and possessed of attentions and good wishes to make her happy, but some robust charlatan, some amusing buffoon to arouse indecorous laughter and unseemly gaiety in her with his clownishness?"

"Look, Doña Blanca," said the friar, still using the familiar tú, which he never abandoned, no matter how miffed he might have been, "don't go thinking that one needs to be an Apelles[78] or a Phidias[79] in order to know that Don Casimiro is ugly. His ugliness is so evident and superficial, that you don't have to probe deeply to discover it. And as for his inferior health and scant pleasantness, I assure you that the same thing can be said. Without having studied medicine, without being a Hippocrates, anyone can see that Don Casimiro is, moreover, a broken down man. And without having studied Huarte's *Examination of Creative Faculties*[80] one discovers immediately that Don Casimiro's ingenuity is addled and sterile. I'm not advocating that you seek a Pythagoras[81] and a Milo of Crotona[82] all in one for Clarita, but what in the devil prompts you to give her a Thersites[83] for a husband?"

Father Jacinto refrained from using Latin quotes when he spoke to women, but he could hot help citing in Spanish, whenever he addressed ladies of distinction, deeds, personages, and sayings of classical antiquity and Holy Scripture. As to the rest, the sense of what he said was so clear that Doña Blanca, even if she had not known in a more or less vague way the character of the cited personages, would not have had the least doubt about what the friar meant. Thus it was that she said:

"Those are insults and not advice, Reverend Father, but I will never get angry with you. The only thing I shall say is that all the defects you ascribe to my future son-in-law must be less apparent than you suppose at present, since they weren't known to you earlier. And if they were known to you, why did you not mention them to me? I repeat that someone has come to enlighten your clear understanding. Someone has encouraged you to take this step. There's no point pretending it isn't so. Be honest and frank with me. You have spoken with someone about Clarita's planned marriage. Your advice is not advice, but an underhanded message."

Father Jacinto was truly self-possessed, but with Doña Blanca there was no self-possession to stand him in good stead. The poor friar, embarrassed and discomfited, was flushed all the way to his ears. The saying that expresses one's pronounced discomposure, "His ears were as red as a friar's on a visit," might have been invented for him.

Hasta su lengua, que por lo común estaba tan suelta, se le había trabado un poco y no atinaba a contestar.

Doña Blanca, notando aquel silencio, le excitaba a que se explicase y añadía:

–No me cabe duda. Está usted convicto y casi confeso. Usted desaprueba hoy lo que ayer aprobaba, porque un enemigo mío le ha llenado la cabeza de ideas absurdas. Atrévase usted a negar la verdad.

Interpelado, acusado con tan desmedida audacia y con tan ruda serenidad, el padre Jacinto sacó fuerzas de flaqueza; puso a un lado la causa de su inusitada timidez, que era sólo el recelo de perjudicar los intereses de Clara y de su amigo y antiguo discípulo; y ya libre de estorbos, contestó tan enérgica y sabiamente, que su contestación, la réplica a que dio lugar y todo el resto del diálogo tomaron un carácter distinto y solemne, por donde merecen capítulo aparte, el cual será de los más importantes de esta historia.

17

El padre Jacinto, sin alterarse, imitando el entonado reposo de su ilustre amiga, contestó lo que sigue:

– Ya he confesado con ingenuidad que debí aconsejarte antes. No lo hice, no porque aprobase tu plan, sino porque llevado de ligereza vergonzosa y de indiferencia villana y grosera, no advertí todo el horror de la boda que tienes concertada. ¿Debo el advertirlo ahora a mi propio espíritu, o bien al de otra persona que me ha ilustrado? Punto es éste que podrá interesarte sabe Dios por qué, y que podrá afectar mi reputación de hombre entendido; pero en nada altera el valor de mis consejos. No quiero ni puedo justificar mi inconsecuencia. Puedo y debo, con todo, mitigar un poco la rudeza de tu acusación, y lo haré al exponer las razones en que fundo mis consejos de ahora. Sentiré expresarme con impropiedad, aunque espero de tu buena fe que no me armes disputa sobre las palabras, si entiendes la idea y la sana intención con que la expreso. Tal vez está educada Clara con rigidez que raya en extremos peligrosos. Temiendo tú

Even his tongue, which was usually so loose, failed him at that moment, and he found himself unable to respond.

Taking note of his silence, Doña Blanca urged him to explain and added:

"I have no doubt. You are guilty and almost self-convicted. You disapprove today of what you approved yesterday, because an enemy of mine has filled your head with absurd ideas. Dare to deny the truth."

Asked to explain himself, and accused with such boundless audacity and with such steely serenity, Father Jacinto made a supreme effort; he put aside the cause of unwonted timidity, which was only the fear of compromising Clara's interests and those of his friend and one-time pupil; and free now of hindrances, he answered so energetically and wisely that his reply, the response that it occasioned, and the rest of the conversation took on a solemn and different character, all of which merits a separate chapter, a chapter that will be one of the most important exchanges of this story.

17

Father Jacinto did not get upset; imitating the haughty repose of his illustrious friend, he answered as follows:

"I have already candidly admitted that I should have advised you before. I did not, not because I approved of your plan, but because, influenced or affected by a shameful apathy and by a gross, base indifference, I did not take account of all the horror of the marriage you have arranged. Do I owe taking account of it now to my own intelligence or to that of another person who has enlightened me? This is a point that might interest you, and that might affect my reputation as a clever man, but in no respect does it alter my advice. I do not wish to justify nor can I justify my inconsistency. I can and ought, however, to mitigate somewhat the harshness of your accusation, and I will do so by stating the reasons on which I now base my advice. I'll be sorry to express myself with infelicitous language, although I'm banking on your good faith and hoping that you won't argue with me over words if you understand the idea and the sound intention behind it.

"Perhaps Clara has been raised with a strictness that borders on dangerous extremes. Fearing that one day she could fall, you have

que un día pueda caer, le has exagerado los tropiezos. Temiendo tú que
la nave pueda zozobrar e irse a pique, has ponderado los escollos y bajíos
que hay en el mar del mundo, el ímpetu y violencia de los vientos que
combaten la nave y hasta su fragilidad y desgobierno. Esto tiene también
sus peligros. Esto infunde una desconfianza en las propias fuerzas que
raya en cobardía. Esto nos hace formar un concepto de la vida y del
mundo mucho peor de lo que debe ser. ¿Cómo ha de negar un creyente
que de resultas de nuestros pecados el mundo es un valle de lágrimas;
que el demonio tiende su red de continuo para perdernos; que nuestra
flaca condición es propensa al mal, y que es necesario el favor del cielo
para no caer en las tentaciones? Todo esto es innegable, pero conviene no
exagerarlo. Una vez muy exagerado, o hay que huir al desierto y hacer la
vida ascética de los ermitaños, y entonces todo va bien, porque la belleza
y la bondad que no se ven en la tierra, se esperan, se presienten y casi se
ven ya en el cielo, en éxtasis y arrobos, o hay que dar, faltando el amor
divino, faltando la caridad fervorosa, en un desesperado desprecio de uno
mismo y en tal desdén y odio a todo lo creado y a nuestros semejantes, que
hacen a quien así vive odioso y enojoso a sí y a los demás seres. Hija, no
sé si me explico, pero tú eres perspicaz y me irás entendiendo. Otro grave
peligro nace también de tu método de educar. La conciencia se halla con
él más apercibida y precavida para la lucha; pero al mancharlo todo, se
mancha; al inficionarlo todo, se inficiona; al presentir en todo un delito,
una impureza, provoca y hasta evoca las impurezas y los delitos. Clarita
tiene un entendimiento muy sano, un natural excelente; pero, no lo dudes,
a fuerza de dar tormento a su alma para que confiese faltas en que no ha
incurrido, pudiera un día torcer y dislocar los más bellos sentimientos
y convertirlos en sentimientos pecaminosos; pudiera concebir del
escrúpulo de su conciencia, inquisidora del pecado, el pecado mismo que
antes no existía. No tengo que asegurarte que yo por mil motivos no he
procurado relajar la rigidez de los principios que has inculcado a Clarita,
si bien mi modo de ser me lleva, por el contrario, a la indulgencia: a ver
en todo el lado bueno, y a tardar muchísimo en ver el lado malo, y a no
descubrirle sino después de larga meditación. Así es que al principio,
contrayéndonos al asunto de la boda, no vi sino el lado bueno. Vi que

exaggerated the obstacles for her. Fearing that the ship could capsize and sink, you have pondered the reefs and shoals in the world, the impetus and violence of the winds that batter the ship and even its fragility and its damaged steerage. This has its dangers. This instills a lack of confidence in one's strength that borders on cowardice. This makes us form an idea of life and of the world that is much worse than what it ought to be. How is a believer to deny that as a result of our sins the world is a vale of tears? That the devil continually spreads his net to entrap us? That our weak nature is prone to evil? And that God's grace is necessary not to fall into temptation? All this is undeniable, but it is as well not to exaggerate it. Once it has been exaggerated, either you must flee to the desert and lead the ascetic life of hermits, and then all goes well – because the beauty and goodness that are not seen on earth are hoped for, discerned, and almost glimpsed already in the heavens, in ecstasies and raptures – or, lacking divine love and fervent charity, you must fall – fall into a desperate self-contempt and into such scorn and hatred of everything in creation, including our fellow human beings, that it makes such a person living such a life odious and vexatious to himself or herself and to everyone else too. I don't know whether I am explaining myself clearly, but you're perceptive and will understand me.

"Another grave danger also arises from your method of educating. As a consequence of it the conscience becomes more wary, more forewarned, but on tarnishing everything in this struggle, it tarnishes itself; on foreseeing in everything an offense, an impurity, it provokes and even evokes impurities and offenses. Clarita has a very good mind and an excellent disposition, but – and have no doubts on this score – by dint of tormenting her soul to have it confess faults that it has not committed, she might one day distort and warp the most beautiful feelings and transform them into sinful feelings; she might conceive from the scrupulousness of her conscience, which is so inquisitive as to sin, sin itself, when it did not exist before. I do not need to assure you that for a thousand reasons I have not attempted to relax the strictness of the principles that you have instilled in Clarita, although my temperament is such that it inclines me, on the contrary, toward indulgence, leads me first to see the good side in everything and then to be as slow as a snail in seeing the bad side, and at that not to discover it except after long meditation. Which explains why in the beginning, restricting ourselves to the subject of the marriage, I saw only the good side. I saw that Don

don Casimiro es un caballero de tu clase, honrado, religioso, prendado de Clarita y deseando hacerla feliz. Vi que, casándose con ella, seguiría ella aquí y no se la llevarían lejos de su madre y de nosotros, que la queremos tanto. Vi que con su mucha hacienda y con la de su marido haría un bien inmenso a estos lugares, empleándose en obras de caridad. Y vi en la misma austeridad con que está educada la garantía de que para Clarita no podía ser el matrimonio el medio de satisfacer y aun de santificar, merced a un lazo sagrado e indisoluble, una pasión violenta, profana y algo impía, ya que consagra al hombre cierta adoración y culto que a sólo Dios debe, y una ilusión caduca, efímera, que se disipa tanto más pronto cuanto más vivo y ardiente es el resplandor con que la fantasía la finge y colora. Todo esto vi, y por haberlo visto trato de cohonestar, ya que no disculpe, el no haberme opuesto antes a la boda. Imaginaba yo, además, que Clarita no la repugnaba. Clarita nada me ha dicho después; pero mis ojos se han abierto, y ahora comprendo que la repugna con repugnancia invencible, allá en el fondo de su alma. Ahora comprendo que Clarita no ve solo en el matrimonio un voto de devoción y sacrificio. Clarita quiere amar y que el matrimonio sancione y purifique su amor. El matrimonio, por lo tanto, no puede ser para ella el mero cumplimiento de un deber social, un acto de abnegación, un padecimiento a que hay que resignarse, una penitencia, una prueba, un castigo. El profundo respeto que te tiene, la ciega obediencia con que se somete a tu voluntad, la creencia de que casi todo es pecado, no consentirán que ella confiese nunca ni a sí misma lo que te digo; pero yo no dudo ya que lo siente. Ahora bien; ¿es merecedora Clarita de esa penitencia? ¿Es digna de ese castigo? ¿Qué derecho tienes para imponérsele? Y si es prueba, ¿quién te da permiso para poner a prueba su bondad? ¿Por qué, si lo grave y lo áspero de un deber, como es el del matrimonio, puede mezclarse y combinarse con lícitos contentos que aligeren la cruz y con satisfacciones y gustos que suavicen las asperezas del camino, quieres tú sólo para tu hija la aspereza del camino y la pesadumbre de la cruz, y no también la permitida dulzura?

Doña Blanca escuchó impasible, y al parecer muy sosegada, todo el sermón del buen fraile. Al ver que no seguía, dijo, después de un instante de silencio:

—Aun conviniendo en que casarse con un hombre de bien, lleno de

Casimiro is a gentleman and your social equal, that he is honorable, religious, captivated by Clarita, and desirous of making her happy. I saw that by marrying him she would stay here and would not be taken far from her mother and from the rest of us, who love her so much. I saw that with her possessions and income and those of her husband she would do all kinds of good in these parts with numerous works of charity. And I saw in the very austerity with which she has been raised the guarantee that for Clarita marriage would not be the means of satisfying and even sanctifying, thanks to a sacred, indissoluble bond, a violent, profane, and somewhat impious passion, since it devotes to man a certain adoration and worship which is due only to God, and an ephemeral, fleeting illusion that vanishes all the more quickly when the splendor with which fantasy imagines and colors it is so vivid and ardent. All this did I see, and because I saw it, I try to justify, if not excuse, not having opposed the marriage before. I assumed, furthermore, that Clarita did not find it repugnant. Clarita said nothing to me about this afterwards, but my eyes have since been opened, and now I understand that she finds it repugnant, insuperably repugnant, in the depths of her soul. Now I understand that Clarita does not see in marriage only a vow of devotion and sacrifice. Clarita wants to love and wants marriage to sanction and purify her love. Marriage, therefore, cannot be for her the mere fulfillment of a social duty, an act of abnegation, a suffering to which one has to be resigned, a penance, a trial, a punishment. The profound respect that she has for you, the blind obedience with which she submits to your will, the belief that almost everything is a sin, will not ever allow her to confess, even to herself, what I am saying to you, but I do not at all doubt that she feels it. Now then: does Clarita deserve that penance? Does she deserve that punishment? What right do you have to impose it on her? And if it is a trial, who has given you permission to put her goodness to the test? If the gravity and the asperity of a duty, as is the case with marriage, can be mixed and combined with legitimate pleasures that lighten the cross and with satisfactions and enjoyments that ease the ruggedness of the way, why do you want for your daughter only the ruggedness of the way and the sorrow of the cross and not the permissible sweetness too?"

Doña Blanca listened impassively and, to all appearances, very calmly to the good friar's sermon. When she saw that he was not going to continue, she said after a moment of silence:

"Even admitting that marriage to a good man, one of much affection

afecto y de juicio, fuese una penitencia, fuese una cruz, Clarita la debiera llevar y resignarse. La mujer no ha venido al mundo para su deleite y para satisfacción de su voluntad y de su apetito, sino para servir a Dios en esta vida temporal, a fin de gozarle en la eterna. Y usted convendrá conmigo, si en estos días no ha tratado con gentes que han perturbado su razón y le han apartado del camino recto, que el modo mejor de servir a Dios es, en una hija, el obedecer a sus padres. Usted mismo reconoce que el santo sacramento del matrimonio no fue instituido para santificar devaneos. Cierto que es mejor casarse que quemarse; pero aún es mejor casarse sin quemarse, a fin de ser la fiel compañera de un varón justo y fundar o perpetuar con él una familia cristiana, ejemplar y piadosa. Este concepto puro, cristiano y honestísimo del matrimonio no es fácil de realizar; mas para eso he educado yo tan severamente a Clarita: para que con la gracia de Dios tenga la gloria de realizarse, en vez de buscar en el casamiento un medio de hacer lícito y tolerable el logro de mal regidos deseos y de impuras pasiones. Más pudiera decir en mi abono acerca de este asunto, pero no se trata aquí de una discusión académica. Yo carezco de estudios y de facilidad de palabra para discutir con usted sobre la cuestión general de si el matrimonio ha de ser un estado tan difícil y estrecho como otro cualquiera que se toma para servir a Dios, y no un expediente mundanal para disimular liviandades. Aquí debemos concretarnos al caso singular de Clarita, y para ello vuelvo a lo dicho: necesito, exijo que sea usted leal y sincero. ¿Quién envía a usted a que me hable? ¿Quién le aconseja para que me aconseje? ¿Quién le ha abierto los ojos, que tenía usted tan cerrados, y le ha hecho ver que Clarita, si no ama, amará? Vamos, respóndame usted. ¿Por qué disimularlo o callarlo? Hay un hombre que ha hablado a usted de todo esto.

—No lo negaré, ya que te empeñas en que lo declare.

—Ese hombre es el comendador Mendoza.

—Es el comendador Mendoza– repitió el fraile.

Tal declaración, aunque harto prevista, dejó silenciosos y como en honda meditación a ambos interlocutores durante un largo minuto que les pareció un siglo.

Doña Blanca, aunque sin precipitar sus palabras, mostrando ya en lo trémulo de la voz y en el brillo de los ojos, viva y dolorosa emoción mal reprimida, habló luego así:

and a sense of judgment, were a penance, were a cross, Clarita ought to carry it and be resigned. Woman has not come into the world for her pleasure and for the satisfaction of her will and her desires, but to serve God in this temporal life so as to enjoy him in the eternal one. And you will agree, if you have not consorted lately with people who have distorted your reason and turned you away from the straight path, that the best way for a daughter to serve God is to obey her parents. You yourself recognize that the holy sacrament of marriage was not instituted to sanctify the flames of short-lived passion. True, it is better to marry than to burn, but it is better still to marry without burning, so as to be the faithful companion of a just man and found or perpetuate with him a pious and exemplary Christian family. This pure, Christian, and most honorable concept of marriage is not easy to realize, but with such an aim in mind have I raised Clarita as strictly as I have, so that with God's grace she will indeed have the glory of realizing it, instead of seeking in marriage a means of making the achievement of ill-controlled desires and impure passions permissible and tolerable. I could say more on this subject to justify my means, but we are not engaged in an academic discussion here. I lack the formal studies and fluency of speech to argue with you the general question of whether marriage is to be as difficult and austere a state as any other that one chooses in order to serve God, and not a worldly expedient to disguise lustful urges. Here we must restrict ourselves to Clarita's particular case, and to do so I come back to what I said earlier: I need, I entreat you to be loyal and sincere. Who has sent you to speak to me? Who has advised you to advise me? Who has opened your eyes – eyes that were unseeing – and made you see that Clarita, if she does not presently love, will in future love? Come now, answer me. Why hide it or hush it up? There is a man who has spoken to you about all this."

"I won't deny it, since you are being so insistent."

"That man is Commander Mendoza."

"That man is Commander Mendoza," repeated the friar.

Such a declaration, although it had clearly been anticipated, left both interlocutors silent and as though in profound meditation for a long minute, which to them seemed like a century.

Without rushing her words, but betraying an intense and ill-repressed emotion in her tremulous voice and in her brilliant eyes, Doña Blanca spoke as follows:

–Todo lo sabe usted y me alegro. Quizás hice mal en no decírselo yo misma la primera vez que me arrodillé ante usted en el tribunal de la penitencia. Sírvame de excusa que ya mi mayor delito había sido varias veces confesado, y la consideración de que cada vez que me confieso de nuevo hago sabedora a una persona más del deshonor de quien me ha dado su nombre. Todo lo sabe usted sin que yo se lo haya dicho. Bendito sea Dios, que me humilla como merezco, sin que yo, tan culpada, cometa la nueva culpa de infamar a mi pobre marido. Pues bien: sabiéndolo usted todo, ¿cómo se atreve a aconsejarme lo que me aconseja? ¿Cómo quiere apartarme del camino que llevo, único posible para una reparación, aunque incompleta? Si contra su parecer de usted, si contra la ley del decoro, manchásemos la conciencia de Clara, descubriéndole su origen, ¿qué piensa usted que haría ella? ¿No la despreciaría usted si no buscase la reparación? Y para ello, sin hacer pública la infamia de su madre y de aquel a quien debe venerar como a padre, ¿qué otro recurso tiene Clara sino entrar en un convento o dar la mano a don Casimiro? ¿Por qué, dirá usted, ha de pagar Clara la falta que no cometió? Harto la pago yo, padre. Los remordimientos, la vergüenza me asesinan. Pero Clara también debe pagarla. Si esto parece a usted inicuo, vuélvase usted impío y blasfemo contra la Providencia y no contra mí. La Providencia, en sus designios inescrutables, con ocasión de mi culpa, ha puesto a mi hija en la alternativa o de sacrificarse o de ser falsaria y poseedora indigna de riquezas que no le pertenecen.

–No he de ser yo, por cierto– interrumpió el fraile –, quien disimule o atenúe lo difícil de la situación y la verdad que hay en lo que dices. Convengo contigo. Sé la nobleza de alma de Clara. Si ella supiera quien es... pero no, mejor es que no lo sepa.

–¿Qué piensa usted que haría si lo supiese?

–Sin vacilar... Clara se retiraría a un convento. Tu plan de casarla con don Casimiro le parecería absurdo, malo, no ya siendo feo y viejo don Casimiro, sino aunque fuese precioso y estuviese ella prendada de él. Con este casamiento ni se remedia el mal nacido del embuste o la falsía, ni se despoja tu hija de bienes que no son suyos.

–Es, sin embargo, la única reparación posible, aunque incompleta,

"You know everything and I'm glad. Perhaps I was wrong not to tell you the whole story myself the first time I knelt before you in the confessional. The only excuse I have is that my greatest misdeed had been confessed several times already, and each time I confess it anew I make yet another person privy to the dishonor of the man who has given me his name. You know everything without my having told you. Blessed be God, who humiliates me as I deserve, because, for as blameworthy as I am, I shall not have to commit the additional offense of discrediting my poor husband. Now then, given that you know everything, how is it that you dare to advise me as you do? How can you expect me to deviate from the course I am following, the only possible one for reparation, albeit incomplete? If, contrary to your inclination, if, contrary to the law of decency, we were to tarnish Clara's conscience by revealing to her the circumstances of her birth, what do you think she would do? Wouldn't you despise her if she did not seek to make reparation? And in order to do so, without making public her mother's infamy and the disgrace of the man she ought to venerate as a father, what other recourse does Clara have except to enter a convent or give her hand to Don Casimiro? Why, you will ask, must Clara pay for the sin she did not commit? I pay for it in abundance, Father. The remorse, the shame, they take a mortal toll on me. But Clara should also pay for it. If this seems wicked to you, become irreverent and blasphemous and rail against Providence and not against me. Providence, in its inscrutable designs, on the occasion of my offense, has presented my daughter with the alternative of either sacrificing herself or of being a swindler and unworthy possessor of riches that do not belong to her."

"I will certainly not be the one," interrupted the friar, "who overlooks or minimizes the difficulty of the situation and the truth of what you say. I agree with you. I know Clara's nobility of soul. If she knew who she is ... but no, it's better that she not know."

"What do you think she would do if she did?"

"Without wavering, Clara would retire to a convent. Your plan to marry her to Don Casimiro would strike her as absurd, pernicious, even if Don Casimiro wasn't ugly but handsome, and even if he was not old and she was in love with him. With that marriage you remedy neither the evil nor the duplicity born of the fraud, nor does your daughter relinquish the possessions that are not hers."

"It is, nonetheless, the only reparation possible, even though

ignorando Clara el motivo que hay para la reparación. Convengo en que entrando Clara en un claustro el mal se remediaría mejor; menos incompletamente. Pero ¿cómo la hija de un ateo ha de tener vocación para esposa de Jesucristo?

Al pronunciar estas últimas palabras, el rostro de doña Blanca tomó una expresión sublime de dolor; sus mejillas se tiñeron de carmín ominoso como el de una fiebre aguda; dos gruesas lágrimas brotaron de repente de sus ojos.

El padre Jacinto vio a doña Blanca transfigurada; reconoció en ella un corazón de mujer que antes no había sospechado siquiera bajo la aspereza de su mal genio; y le tuvo lástima, y la miró con ojos compasivos. Ella prosiguió:

–He meditado en largas noches de insomnio sobre la resolución de este problema, y no veo nada mejor que el casamiento de Clara con don Casimiro. No piense usted que me falte valor para otra cosa. No me falta valor; me sobra piedad. Mil veces, ansiosa de que me matase, he estado a punto de revelar mi pecado al hombre a quien ofendí cometiéndole. Yo misma hubiera puesto gustosa el puñal en su mano; pero, le conozco, ¡infeliz!, hubiera llorado como un niño; yo le hubiera muerto de pena, en vez de recibir el merecido castigo; él, con mansedumbre evangélica, me hubiera perdonado, y mi duro pecho y mi diabólico orgullo, lejos de agradecer el perdón, hubiera despreciado más aún al hombre que me le otorgaba. Manso, pacífico, benigno, Valentín hubiera apurado un cáliz de hiel y veneno al oír mi revelación; no hubiera sido mi juez inexorable, sino hubiera acabado de ser mi víctima, y yo, réproba, llena de satánica soberbia, hubiera ahogado el manantial de la compasión y de la ternura con desdén, hasta con asco, de una resignación santa, que el demonio mismo me hubiera pintado como enervada flaqueza. Mi deber era, pues, callar: hacer lo menos amarga posible la vida de este débil y dulce compañero que el cielo me ha dado, disimular, ocultar, hasta donde cabe..., mi falta de amor..., mi injusta, impía, irracional, involuntaria falta de estimación. Así se explican el engaño y la persistencia en el engaño; pero la vileza del hurto no cabe en mí. Mi alma no la sufre. ¿Pretende quizás ese ateo malvado que me envilezca yo con el hurto? ¿Qué razón, qué derecho, qué sentimiento paternal invoca quien tan olvidado tuvo durante años el fruto de su amor... y de la cólera divina? Usted dice bien: lo mejor sería que Clara se sepultase en un claustro: se consagrase

incomplete, and this way Clara remains ignorant of the reason for the reparation. I agree that were Clara to enter a cloister the evil would be remedied better, less incompletely. But how is the daughter of an atheist going to have the vocation to become a bride of Christ?"

As she spoke these last words, Doña Blanca's face took on a sublime expression of sorrow; her cheeks showed a tinge of the ominous carmine of an acute fever; and two fat tears suddenly spilled from her eyes.

Father Jacinto saw a transfigured Doña Blanca; he recognized in her a womanly heart that he had not even suspected beneath the asperity of her bad temper, and he pitied her, and he contemplated her with compassionate eyes. She continued:

"During long nights of insomnia I have pondered the solution of this problem, and I see nothing better than Clara's marriage to Don Casimiro. Do not think that I lack the courage for another course of action. I do not lack courage; I have an excess of pity. A thousand times, eager to have him kill me, I was on the verge of revealing my sin to the man whom I offended by committing it. I myself would have gladly placed the dagger in his hand, but I know him, poor man! He would have cried like a child. I would have killed him with grief instead of receiving the deserved punishment myself. With his evangelical meekness he would have forgiven me, and my hard heart and my diabolical pride, far from being grateful for the forgiveness, would have scorned still more the man who was granting it to me. Meek, peaceable, kind, Valentín would have drained a cup of gall and venom upon hearing my revelation. He would not have been my inexorable judge, rather he would have finished being my victim, and I, reprobate, full of satanic arrogance, would have stifled the fountain of compassion and tenderness with scorn, even with loathing, would have trampled a saintly resignation, which the devil himself would have represented to me as ingrained weakness. My duty, therefore, was to hold my tongue, to make as little bitter as possible the life of this frail and gentle companion that heaven sent me; to conceal, to hide to the extent that I am able, my lack of love … my unjust, impious, irrational, involuntary lack of regard. In this way can deception, and persistence in deception, be explained, but I draw the line at the villainy of theft. What reason, what right, what paternal feeling can be invoked by a man who for so many years had forgotten the fruit of his love … as well as divine wrath? You are right: the best thing would be for Clara to shut herself up in a cloister, to devote herself to God. I have done my

a Dios. Yo he hecho lo posible por disgustarla del mundo, pintándosele horroroso; pero en ella han podido, más que mis palabras, la confianza juvenil, el brío maldito de la sangre, el deleite y la exuberancia de la vida. ¿Qué arbitrio me queda sino casarla con don Casimiro? ¿Por qué la compadece usted? Pues qué, ¿no sale ganando? La hija del pecado no debiera tener bienes, ni honra, ni nombre siquiera, y todo esto conservará y de todo podrá gozar sin remordimientos, sin sonrojo.

En la última parte de su discurso doña Blanca estuvo hermosa, sublime como una pantera irritada y mortalmente herida. Se había puesto de pie. Al fraile se le figuraba que había crecido y que tocaba con la cabeza en el techo. Hablaba bajo, pero cada una de sus palabras tenía punta acerada como una saeta.

El padre Jacinto conoció que había confiado por demás en su serenidad y en su elocuencia. Se hizo un lío y no supo decir nada. Se encontró tan apurado, que la vuelta de Clarita al salón le quitó un peso de encima y le dio tregua para poder replicar en momento más propicio y después de meditarlo.

Doña Blanca, no bien entró su hija, supo dominarse y recobrar su calma habitual.

Un poco más tarde vino el benigno don Valentín, y todos fueron a comer como si tal cosa.

El padre Jacinto echó la bendición al empezar la comida, y rezó al sentarse y al levantarse.

Ya de sobremesa, tuvo efecto la grata sorpresa de la corza. Clarita la halló encantadora. La corza se dejó besar por Clarita en un lucero blanco que tenía en la frente, y se comió cuatro bizcochos que ella misma le dio con su mano.

Don Valentín se maravilló, simpatizó y hasta se enterneció con la mansedumbre de aquel lindo animalejo.

Cuando, terminado todo, salió el padre Jacinto de casa de doña Blanca, se apresuró a ir a ver al comendador, quien le aguardaba impaciente, no habiéndole visto al llegar de Villabermeja, porque el fraile había adelantado más de una hora su venida a la ciudad. Excusándose de esto y de su precipitación en dar pasos sin consultar al comendador, el padre Jacinto le relató cuanto había pasado.

Don Fadrique López de Mendoza no era de los que condenan todo

utmost to alienate her from the world, depicting it as horrible, but other things have had a more powerful effect on her than my words, things like youthful confidence, the accursed spirit of blood, and the joy and exuberance of life. What choice is left to me except to marry her to Don Casimiro? Why do you pity her? Does she not come out ahead? The child of sin should not have wealth or honor or even a name, and yet she will retain them all and be able to enjoy them all without remorse, without shame."

In this last part of her discourse Doña Blanca looked beautiful, sublime like an angry, mortally wounded female panther. She had stood up. The friar fancied that she had grown and that she was touching the ceiling with her head. She had been speaking softly, but each of her words had a steel-tipped point like an arrow.

Father Jacinto recognized that he had relied too much on his calmness and eloquence. He had made a mess of the meeting and now words eluded him. He found himself so beleaguered that Clarita's return to the drawing room took a weight off his mind and afforded him a respite in order to respond at a more propitious moment and after thinking things over.

As soon as her daughter came in, Doña Blanca took hold of herself and regained her habitual calm.

A little later the kindly Don Valentín also returned, and they all went to eat as if nothing had happened.

Father Jacinto blessed the food, and said a prayer at the beginning of the meal and at the end of it.

After dinner, the friar sprang the pleasant surprise of the doe. The animal let the delighted Clarita kiss the white spot on her forehead and then ate four biscuits from her new mistress's hand.

Don Valentín marveled at that pretty animal, and took to it and was even moved by its gentleness.

When, at the conclusion of his after-dinner presentation, Father Jacinto left Doña Blanca's house, he hastened to go and see the commander, who was impatiently awaiting him, not having seen the priest since his arrival from Villabermeja because Father Jacinto had reached the city more than an hour sooner. Apologizing for this and for having impetuously taken steps without consulting the commander, the priest related to him all that had transpired.

Don Fadrique López de Mendoza was not one of those people who

lo que se hace cuando no se les consulta. Halló bien lo hecho por su maestro, y lo aplaudió. Hasta la turbación y mutismo final del fraile le parecieron convenientes, porque no habían traído compromiso, porque no se había soltado prenda. Ya hemos dicho que el comendador era optimista por filosofía y alegre por naturaleza.

18

Después de haberse enterado de la conversación entre el fraile y doña Blanca, el comendador se abstuvo de tomar una resolución precipitada. Se contentó con rogar a su maestro que no se volviese a Villabermeja, que siguiese frecuentando la casa de doña Blanca y que tratase de desvanecer todo recelo en dicha señora, prometiéndole no hablar con Clarita de la proyectada boda ni decirle nada en contra de los deseos de su madre.

El comendador quería meditar, y meditó largamente, sobre el asunto. Sus meditaciones (ya hemos dicho que el comendador era descreído) no podían ser muy piadosas. Era también el comendador alegre, frío y sereno, y nada podían tener de apasionadas sus meditaciones. Su espíritu analítico le presentaba, sin embargo, todas las dificultades del caso.

No cabía la menor duda. La criatura lindísima y simpática que a él debía el ser, estaba condenada o a vivir como usurpadora indigna de lo que no le pertenecía, o a casarse con don Casimiro, o a ser monja. Uno de estos tres extremos era inevitable, a no causar un escándalo espantoso o a no realizar un difícil rescate.

Doña Blanca tenía razón, salvo que para tenerla no era menester mostrarse tan hosca y tan poco amena con todo el género humano, empezando por su infeliz marido.

Para don Fadrique había un ideal económico más fundamental que el político. Este ideal era que toda riqueza, todos los bienes de fortuna llegasen a ser un día, cuando la sociedad tocase ya en la perfección deseada, signo infalible de laboriosidad, de talento y de honradez en quien los había adquirido: que el ser rico fuese como innegable título de nobleza, ganado por uno mismo o por el progenitor que ha dejado los bienes.

condemn everything that is done when they are not consulted. He approved of what his master had done, and applauded it. Even the friar's concern and silence at the end of his account seemed like a positive sign to him, because they signaled that he had made neither a promise nor a pledge. And we have already said that it was the commander's philosophy to be optimistic and his nature to be cheerful.

18

After being informed of the conversation between the friar and Doña Blanca, the commander refrained from making a hasty decision. He contented himself with entreating his master not to return to Villabermeja, to continue frequenting Doña Blanca's house, and to try to dispel all of that lady's suspicions by promising her that he would not speak to Clarita of the projected marriage nor say anything to her contrary to her mother's wishes.

The commander wanted to reflect, and he reflected on the subject for a long time. His reflections (we have already said that the commander was an unbeliever) could not have been very pious. The commander was also cheerful, cool, serene, and there could not have been anything impassioned about his reflections. His analytical mind, nonetheless, considered all the difficulties of the case.

There was not the slightest doubt. The lovely, charming creature who owed her existence to him was condemned either to live as unworthy usurper of what did not belong to her, or to marry Don Casimiro, or to be a nun. One of these three extremes was inevitable, short of causing a frightful scandal or not effecting a difficult rescue.

Doña Blanca was right, which did not mean, though, that she needed to be so surly and ill-tempered with the entire human race, beginning with her unfortunate husband.

For Don Fadrique there was an economic ideal more fundamental than the political one. This ideal was that all wealth, all possessions would one day, when society attained the desired perfection, be the infallible sign of industry, of talent, and of honesty in whoever had acquired them; that being wealthy would be like an undeniable title of nobility, earned by the holder or by the ancestor who has left him or her the possessions.

Bien sabía don Fadrique que este término estaba aún remotísimo, pero
sabía además que el mejor modo de acercarse a él era el de hacer todo
negocio suponiéndole ya llegado; esto es, como si no hubiese riqueza
mal adquirida en la tierra. Lo contrario sería conspirar a que prevaleciese
el villano refrán de que *quien roba a un ladrón tiene cien años de perdón,*
y contribuir a que la vida, la historia, el desenvolvimiento civilizador de
la sociedad sean una trama inacabable de bellaquerías.

Fundado en estos principios, desechaba de sí don Fadrique el
pensamiento de que en cada lugar del mundo habría de seguro un
enjambre de madres en el caso de doña Blanca y una multitud de hijas o
de hijos en el caso de Clarita, para los cuales el problema moral de tan
difícil solución que atormentaba a doña Blanca era como si no fuese,
dejándolos disfrutar de la hacienda que la suerte y la ley les otorgaban,
sin el menor escrúpulo y con la mayor frescura. Desechaba también la
idea, algo cómica, pero más que posible, de que el mismo don Casimiro,
por circunstancias análogas, podría tener menos derecho que Clarita
a la herencia, aunque toda fuese vinculada; de que don Valentín, su
padre o su abuelo podrían también no haber tenido derecho, y de que
sólo Dios sabe, aunque tal vez el diablo no lo ignore, por qué arcaduces
subterráneos y por qué intrincados caminos ha venido a cada cual lo que
por herencia disfruta. En estos casos la fe debe salvar; pero en el caso de
doña Blanca no había fe que valiese contra la evidencia que ella tenía.
Cerrar los ojos, vendárselos y remedar fe, era una infamia. Don Fadrique,
condenando en su corazón y en su inteligencia serena los furores de
doña Blanca, la aplaudía y ensalzaba de que pensase con rectitud y con
nobleza. Vaya a quien vaya, merézcale o no, tenga derecho o no le tenga
aquel a quien un bien se destina, son cosas que importan poco ante la
superior consideración de que ese bien me consta que no es mío y de que
sólo le gozo por engaño, por delito y por mentira.

Como don Fadrique era persona de mucho seso y sentido común,
aunque se hallaba en época de reformas, sistemas y ensueños de toda
clase, no pensó en condenar la herencia. Sin el grandísimo deleite de
dejar ricos a nuestros hijos, se perdería el mayor estímulo para el trabajo,
para el buen orden, para la aplicación y para aguzar y ejercitar el ingenio.
Don Fadrique reconocía, no obstante, que si estaba lejos aún el día en
que sea casi imposible adquirir mal lo que uno mismo adquiere, estaba

Don Fadrique knew full well that this period in time was still very distant, but he also knew that the best way to approach it was to deal with every piece of business by supposing that it had already arrived, that is, as if there were no ill-gotten gains or wealth in the world. The contrary would be to conspire to give currency to the popular proverb, "To the robber of a thief, a century of relief,"[84] and to contribute to making life, history, and the civilizing development of society an endless chain of vile deeds.

Based on these principles, Don Fadrique dismissed the thought that in every town in the world there would surely be a swarm of mothers in Doña Blanca's circumstances and a multitude of daughters or sons in Clarita's circumstances, for whom the moral problem, so difficult to resolve, that tormented Doña Blanca, was as though it did not exist, allowing them to enjoy the wealth that fate and the law granted them, without the least scruple and completely unconcerned. He also dismissed the idea, somewhat comical but more than possible, that Don Casimiro himself, because of analogous circumstances could perhaps have even less right to it either; and that only God knows, although the devil may perhaps not be in the dark, by what subterranean channels and by what tangled paths has come to every person what he or she enjoys through inheritance. In these cases faith must be the saving grace, but in Doña Blanca's case there was no faith that stood a chance against the evidence that she cited. To close your eyes, blindfold them, and feign faith was an infamous act. Although Don Fadrique condemned Doña Blanca's fits of rage in his heart and in his serene mind, he applauded her and praised her for thinking with rectitude and integrity. No matter to whom a bequest goes, whether the person is deserving or not, whether the person has a right or not, are matters of little import in light of the higher consideration when I know that this bequest is not mine and that I enjoy it only because of deception, a crime, and a falsehood.

Inasmuch as Don Fadrique was a person of considerable intelligence and common sense, he did not think of condemning the inheritance, even though he lived in a period of reforms, systems, and dreams of all kinds. Without the profound pleasure of leaving our children wealthy, we would lose the primary stimulus for work, for good order, for application, and for sharpening and exercising our wits. Don Fadrique recognized, nonetheless, that if the day was still far off when it will be nearly impossible to acquire wrongfully what one does acquire, the

aún mucho más lejos el día en que sea casi imposible heredar mal lo que
se hereda. El modo de no empujar hacia más hondo porvenir la aurora de
ese día, era dar buen ejemplo en contra. La razón de doña Blanca salía
siempre triunfante de cada laberinto de reflexiones en que don Fadrique
se abismaba.

Había un mal moral que pedía remedio. Hasta aquí iba don Fadrique
de acuerdo con la idea de doña Blanca. ¿Era el remedio peor que el mal?
El remedio era duro; pero don Fadrique comprendía que no era peor que
la enfermedad, y que era menester aplicarle no habiendo otro.

El remedio podía aplicarse de dos maneras. O casando a Clarita con
don Casimiro, y esto era fácil, o haciéndola tomar el velo. Esto segundo,
a pesar de lo mundano, impío y antirreligioso que era don Fadrique, le
parecía mil veces mejor. Comprendía, no obstante, que para que Clarita
entrase en un convento sin saber ella por qué, era necesario que alguien
le infundiese la vocación. Tal trabajo no podía tomarle su madre. Sólo el
padre Jacinto podría persuadir a Clarita a que se retirase al claustro.

Para un hombre lleno del espíritu del siglo XVIII, alimentado con la
lectura de los enciclopedistas, creyente en Dios, pero hablando siempre
de la naturaleza, no hay que exponer aquí cuán horrible aparecía el
sacrificio de la hermosura, de la vida, del brío juvenil, sintiendo ya sin
duda fervorosamente el amor y reclamándole, en aras de un sentimiento
misterioso, de un objeto, a su ver, impalpable y hasta incomprensible.
Al comendador se le antojaba esto una nefanda monstruosidad, pero la
prefería a ver, a imaginar a Clara entre los secos brazos de don Casimiro;
y en su orgullo de hidalgo, y en su afán de no verse él mismo mentiroso
y fullero y de no pensar menos noblemente que una mujer fanática y
desatinada, lo prefería todo a que Clarita se alzase en su día con los
bienes de don Valentín.

El punto final de las meditaciones de don Fadrique era siempre el
mismo, por cuantas sendas y rodeos tratase de llegar a él. No quería a
Clara poseedora de lo que le constaba que no era suyo; no la quería mujer
de don Casimiro; no la quería monja tampoco, y no quería dar escándalo
ni amargar la vida de don Valentín con afrentoso desengaño. Era, pues,
indispensable que él fuese el libertador, el rescatador de Clarita.

day was still that much further off when it will be nearly impossible to inherit wrongfully what one inherits. The way not to push the dawn of that day into an even more distant future was to give a good example to the contrary. Doña Blanca's reasoning always emerged triumphant from each labyrinth of reflections into which Don Fadrique plunged himself.

There was a moral evil that cried out for a remedy. On this point Don Fadrique found himself in agreement with Doña Blanca's idea. Was the remedy worse than the evil? The remedy was stiff, but Don Fadrique understood that it was not worse than the malady, and that it was necessary to bring it into effect, there being no other.

The remedy could be effected in two ways: either by marrying Clarita to Don Casimiro, and this was easy, or by making her take the veil. This second way, despite how worldly, impious, and antireligious Don Fadrique was, seemed a thousand times better to the commander. He understood, nevertheless, that for Clarita to enter the convent without knowing why, it was necessary that someone should instill a vocation in her. Only Father Jacinto could persuade Clarita to retire to the cloister.

For a man infused with the spirit of the eighteenth century and nurtured by the works of the encyclopedists, a believer in God but one who was always talking about nature, there is no need to explain here how horrible the sacrifice of beauty, life, and youthful spirit appeared to him. And the sacrifice would take place while Clara was doubtless already fervently experiencing love and demanding love, for the sake of a mysterious feeling, an object, in her view, that was impalpable and even incomprehensible. The commander considered that such a thing was an unspeakable monstrosity, but he preferred it to seeing, to imagining Clara in the skinny arms of Don Casimiro; and in his pride as an hidalgo, and in his desire not to see himself as a liar and a cheat, and not to think less nobly than a fanatic, deranged woman, he preferred everything rather than witnessing Clarita's rise in the world one day thanks to Don Valentín's wealth.

The final point of Don Fadrique's reflections was always the same, however many paths and roundabout ways it would take him to reach it. He did not want Clara to come into possession of what he knew was not hers; he did not want her to be Don Casimiro's wife; he did not want her to be a nun either; and he did not want to create a scandal or embitter Don Valentín's life with a humiliating disillusionment. It was imperative, therefore, that he be the liberator, Clarita's rescuer.

A pesar de tener preocupado el ánimo con estas cosas, el comendador ejercía tanto dominio sobre sí que nada dejaba notar.

Paseaba con Lucía por las huertas o charlaba con ella y procuraba esquivar sus preguntas inquisitoriales.

Así transcurrieron ocho días. Durante ellos se informó el comendador, con el mayor secreto y diligencia, del valor exacto de todos los bienes de don Valentín. Pasaban de cuatro millones de reales.

Bastante se apesadumbró, no debemos ocultarlo, de que don Valentín hubiese llegado a ser tan rico. El comendador tenía poquísimo más capital, sumando el valor de algunas finquillas que había comprado cerca de Villabermeja, y lo que tenía en varias casas de banca en la Gran Bretaña y en Madrid. Su decisión, a pesar de la pesadumbre, fue firme, con todo.

El comendador sabía y estimaba cuánto vale el dinero. La vanidad de haberle adquirido diestra y honradamente le daba para él mayor hechizo. Pero ¿en qué mejor podía emplearse el caudal, la ganancia y el ahorro de toda una vida activa, el fruto del brío, del trabajo y del ingenio, que en salvar a un ser tan querido y que tan digno era de serlo?

Suponiéndose ya el comendador despojado de cuatro millones, se miraba reducido a la triste condición de un hidalgo labriego, que o tendría que salir otra vez a buscar fortuna, o tendría que acomodarse a vivir mal y humildemente en Villabermeja. Esto no le arredró.

Eliminadas, pues, varias soluciones, el problema quedó claro y sencillo. La única dificultad que había que vencer era la de pasar a poder de don Casimiro, de modo tan natural que apartase toda sospecha, una suma de cuatro millones, y hacer valer y constar, como era justo, este sacrificio cerca de doña Blanca, para que la terrible señora reconociese a su hija por libre de toda obligación y por apta para recibir, en su día, los bienes todos de don Valentín, como devolución, y no como herencia.

Despite being preoccupied with these reflections, the commander exercised so much self-control that he betrayed nothing.

He took walks in the gardens with Lucía or chatted with her and tried to dodge her inquisitorial questions.

Thus did eight days go by. During this time the commander made it his business to learn, with the utmost secrecy and diligence, the exact value of all of Don Valentín's possessions. It was in excess of four million *reales*.

It distressed him considerably, and we should not conceal it, that Don Valentín had become so well-to-do. The commander's own capital did not amount to much more, totaling the value of a few estates that he had purchased near Villabermeja, and what he had in several banks in Great Britain and in Madrid. However, his decision, notwithstanding the distress, was firm.

The commander knew and appreciated how much value money has. The pride in having acquired it skillfully and honestly lent it greater fascination for him. But in what better way could he use his fortune, the earnings and savings of his entire active life, the fruit of determination, of work, of ingenuity, than to save a being so dear to him, a being so worthy of his sacrifice?

Considering that he was already divested of four million *reales*, the commander saw himself reduced to the sad state of a country nobleman, who would either have to go off again to make his fortune, or would have to settle for living badly and humbly in Villabermeja. But this did not daunt him.

With several solutions now eliminated, the problem appeared clear and simple. The only difficulty that had to be overcome was that of putting in Don Casimiro's hands, in such a natural way that it would remove any and all suspicion, the sum of four million, and making the sacrifice known and understood by Doña Blanca, so that the terrible woman would deem their daughter free of all obligation and possessed of the right to receive in due course all of Don Valentín's assets as restitution and not as inheritance.

19

La familia de Solís continuaba incomunicada con sus vecinos. Sólo entraban en aquella casa don Casimiro y el fraile. Éste, a pesar de sus consejos, había sabido ingeniarse, volver a la gracia y recobrar la confianza de aquella adusta señora. No es tan llano desechar a un director espiritual, a quien se tiene por santo o poco menos, aunque este director nos contraríe, y sobre todo haga cosas opuestas a nuestro modo de pensar. La mayor falta del padre Jacinto, lo que apenas acertaba a explicarse doña Blanca, era que aquel virtuoso varón, aquel hijo de Santo Domingo de Guzmán, fuese tan íntimo amigo de un hombre a quien debía más bien llevar a la hoguera, si los tiempos no estuviesen tan pervertidos y la cristiandad tan relajada.

Doña Blanca no se calló sobre este punto, y varias veces manifestó al fraile su extrañeza; pero el fraile le contestaba:

–Hija mía, piensa lo que se te antoje. Yo no quiero calentarme la cabeza explicándotelo. Bástete saber que yo tengo a don Fadrique por muy amigo, aunque incrédulo, como él me tiene por muy amigo, aunque fraile. Cavilando en ello me asusto y prefiero no cavilar. No quiero dar por seguro que haya en las almas humanas algo que, a pesar de la radical oposición de creencias, sea lazo de unión amistosa y constante y fundamento de alta estimación mutua.

–Vaya si hace usted bien en no cavilar– contestaba doña Blanca –. No cavile usted, no venga a caer en herejía al cabo de sus años, fantaseando algo más esencial, más sublime que la creencia religiosa.

–No caeré en herejía– replicaba el fraile, que ya hemos dicho que era muy desvergonzado –; no caeré en herejía cuando tú no caíste. Nunca mi amistad será más inexplicable que lo fue tu amor.

Con esto doña Blanca exhalaba un suspiro, que tenía su poco de bufido, y se amansaba y se callaba.

Por lo demás, el padre Jacinto era leal y no abusó de su derecho de hablar en secreto con Clarita para excitarla en contra de la boda con don Casimiro.

Sólo una noticia se atrevió a dar a Clarita por instigación de don Fadrique: que don Carlos, amonestado por el comendador, se había vuelto a Sevilla con sus padres.

De esta suerte, Clarita hubo de tranquilizarse y no sobresaltarse de no

19

The Solís family continued to eschew contact with their neighbors. Only Don Casimiro and the friar enjoyed entrée into that house. The latter, despite his advice, had managed to ingratiate himself and regain the confidence of the austere Doña Blanca. It is not so simple a matter to dismiss a spiritual director whom we consider a saint or close to it, even if this director vexes us, and, above all, does things that are the opposite of our way of thinking. Father Jacinto's greatest fault, what Doña Blanca could scarcely comprehend, was that that virtuous man, that son of Saint Dominic, should be such intimate friends with a man whom he by rights ought to lead to the stake, if the times were not so corrupted and Christianity so relaxed.

Doña Blanca did not keep quiet on this point, and expressed her amazement to the friar a number of times, but the friar said to her: "Think whatever you like. I don't want to tire myself out explaining it to you. Suffice it to say that I regard Don Fadrique as a very good friend, even though he is an unbeliever, just as he regards me as a very good friend, even though I am a friar. If I dwell on it, I get scared, and so I prefer not to dwell on it. I do not want to take for granted that there is in human souls something that, despite the radical opposition of beliefs, may be a friendly, steadfast link and the foundation of high mutual esteem."

"Well, a good thing it is that you do not dwell on it," said Doña Blanca. "We wouldn't want you to fall into heresy at your age, fantasizing something more essential, more sublime than religious belief."

"I will not fall into heresy," responded the friar, who, as we have already said, was very saucy, "I will not fall into heresy when you haven't. My friendship will never be as unfathomable as your love affair was."

At this rejoinder Doña Blanca let out a sigh, which sounded a bit like a snort, and backed off, saying no more.

As to the rest, Father Jacinto was loyal and did not abuse his right to speak to Clarita in secrecy in order to turn her against marriage to Don Casimiro. At the instigation of Don Fadrique he undertook to pass on to Clarita only one piece of news: that Don Carlos, admonished by the commander, had returned to his parents' home in Seville.

As a result, Clarita calmed down and did not become alarmed at not

ver a don Carlos por la mañana en la iglesia. A quien vio varias veces casi en el mismo lugar en que don Carlos se colocaba, fue al comendador, cuya maldad su madre le había ponderado, y que ella se inclinaba irresistiblemente a creer bueno.

El comendador, como en desagravio de haber tenido olvidada tantos años aquella prenda de su amor, no se contentaba con disponerse a hacer por ella un gran sacrificio, sino que ansiaba verla y admirarla, aunque fuese a distancia.

Así iban lentamente los sucesos, cuando una mañana, en que doña Antonia había tenido una de sus jaquecas y no se hallaba con gana de salir, Lucía fue a paseo sola con el comendador. Ambos llegaron a la fuente o nacimiento del río que ya conocemos. Sentados a la sombra del sauce, oyendo el murmullo del agua, hablaron de las estrellas, de las flores, de mil diversas materias, hacia donde el tío procuraba llevar la atención de su sobrina para distraerla de su curiosidad sobre los asuntos de Clara.

Lucía, no llegando a distraerse lo bastante, dijo por último:

–Tío, usted va a hacer de mí una sabia. A veces me habla usted del sol y de lo grande que es y de cómo atrae a los planetas y cometas; y a veces me describe los abismos del cielo, y me señala las más hermosas estrellas, y me declara sus nombres y la inmensa distancia a que están de nosotros, y el tiempo que tardan los rayos alados de su luz en herir nuestras pupilas. Todo esto me deleita y pasma, haciéndome concebir más adecuado concepto del infinito poder de Dios. También me ha explicado usted los misterios extraños de las flores, y esto me ha interesado más, infundiéndome en el alma superior idea de la bondad y sabiduría del Altísimo. Pero, desechando el disimulo, recelo que usted no me instruye tanto sino para no responder a mis preguntas sobre sus proyectos de usted acerca de Clarita. Tal sospecha, lo confieso, me quita las ganas de oír las lecciones de usted, que de otro modo me entusiasmarían; tal sospecha disminuye el valor de dichas lecciones, que se me figuran interesadas y maliciosas: más que medio de enseñarme, me parecen medio de embaucarme.

–La malicia la pones tú, sobrina– respondió el comendador –. Yo procedo con la mayor sencillez. Cuanto hay que saber de Clarita lo sabes mejor que yo. ¿Qué puedo añadir a lo que tú sabes?

–Oiga usted, tío, aunque niña, no soy tan fácil de engañar. Aquí hay

seeing Don Carlos at church in the mornings. The one she did see several times almost in the same spot that Don Carlos used to occupy was the commander, whose wickedness her mother had impressed on her, and whom she was irresistibly inclined to believe good.

As if to make amends for having forgotten that fruit of his love during so many years, the commander did not content himself with preparing to make a great sacrifice for her; he also longed to see her and admire her, even though it was from a distance.

Thus were events slowly progressing when one morning Doña Antonia had another migraine and did not want to go out, so Lucía went by herself for a walk with the commander. They made their way to the spring or source of the river, with which we are familiar. Sitting in the shade of the willow, listening to the murmur of the water, they talked about the stars, about the flowers, about a thousand different subjects to which the uncle tried to steer his niece's attention in order to distract her curiosity away from Clara's affairs.

Not being sufficiently distracted, Lucía at length said:

"Uncle, you're going to make a learned woman of me. Sometimes you talk to me about the sun and how big it is and how it attracts the planets and comets; and other times you describe to me the depths of the heavens and point out to me the most beautiful stars, and you tell me their names and the immense distance that separates us from them, and how long a time the winged rays of their light take to reach our eyes. All this delights and amazes me, making me imagine a more adequate concept of the infinite power of God. You have also explained to me the strange mysteries of flowers, and this has interested me more, instilling in my soul a higher idea of the goodness and wisdom of the Almighty. But being completely candid, I suspect that you are instructing me so much only to keep from answering my questions about your plans concerning Clarita. This suspicion, I confess, takes away my desire to hear your lessons, which I expect are self-seeking and ill-intentioned, and rather than a means of instructing me, I think they are a means of leading me down the garden path."

"The ill intention is your perception, Lucía," responded the commander. "I'm proceeding in a most straightforward manner. Everything to be known about Clarita you know better than I do. What can I add to what you already know?"

"Listen, Uncle, although I'm very young, I am not gullible. There are

varios puntos oscuros, inexplicables, y yo no sosiego hasta que todo me lo explico.

–Pues ya estás aviada, hija mía, si no te sosiegas hasta que halles la explicación de todo. Condenada estás a desasosiego perpetuo.

–No confundamos las especies. Yo me aquieto sin explicación sobre muchos puntos en que usted, por desgracia, no se aquieta. No hablo de eso. Hablo de materias más llanas y más al alcance de mi inteligencia. En éstas requiero explicación, y sin explicación no hay reposo. ¿Qué diablo de palabra enrevesada fue aquella de que se valió usted el otro día para significar una suposición que se forja uno para explicar las cosas, y que se da por cierta, cuando las explica?

–Esa palabra es *hipótesis*.

–Pues bien; yo no hago más que forjar hipótesis a ver si me explico ciertas cosas. ¿Quiere usted que le exponga alguna de mis hipótesis?

–Exponla.

El comendador respondió aparentando serena indiferencia al dar aquel permiso; pero se puso colorado, y tuvo miedo de que Lucía, por arte mágica o poco menos, hubiese adivinado el lazo que unía a Clara con él.

Lucía, prevaliéndose del permiso y animada con lo poco de turbación que en su tío advirtió, expuso así una de sus hipótesis:

–Pues, señor, yo me cegué al principio por exceso de vanidad. Pensé que el cariño de tío que usted me tiene le llevaba, para complacerme, a mirar con interés a Clori y a Mirtilo, y a procurar el buen fin de sus amores. Ya he variado de opinión. Ya la hipótesis es otra. El interés de usted es demasiado para ser de reflejo. Noto también que es muy desigual: menos que mediano por Mirtilo; inmenso por Clori. ¡Ay, tío, tío! ¿Si querrá usted jugar una mala pasada al pobre zagal? Todo se sabe. Pues qué, ¿cree usted que no ha llegado a mi noticia que se ha hecho usted devoto (¡ojalá fuese de buena ley la devoción!) y que toditas las mañanas de madrugada va usted a la Iglesia Mayor a misa primera?

–Sobrina, no disparates– interrumpió el comendador.

–Yo no disparato. Hallo extraña, para explicada sólo por una simpatía cualquiera, esa devoción de usted, y recelo que la santita que se la infunde, ha cautivado a usted con más dulces cadenas que las de la piedad.

several obscure, inexplicable points here, and I won't rest until I resolve everything."

"Then you're in quite a fix, my dear, if you don't rest until you come up with the explanation of everything. You're doomed to perpetual unrest."

"Let's not confuse matters. I'm comfortable without an explanation of many points with which you, unfortunately, are not. I'm not speaking of that. I'm speaking of simpler concerns that are more within reach of my intelligence. I need an explanation of them, and without that explanation there is no rest for me. What devilishly complicated word was it that you used the other day to express a supposition that one thinks up to explain things and is assumed to be certain when it explains them?"

"That word is *hypothesis*."

"Well then, all I'm doing is setting forth a hypothesis to see whether I can explain things to myself. Do you want me to state one of my hypotheses?"

"Let's hear it."

The commander made a show of serene indifference when he answered in the affirmative, but he blushed, fearing that Lucía, through some magical art or other, had guessed or divined the tie that bound him to Clara.

Taking advantage of the permission and encouraged by the slight agitation that she noticed in her uncle, Lucía stated one of her hypotheses as follows:

"Well, sir, at first I was blinded by an excess of vanity. I thought that the affection you feel for me as my uncle led you, in order to please me, to take an interest in Chloris and Myrtilus, and to try to find a happy end for their love. I've changed my mind. I have another hypothesis now. Your interest is too great to be a reflection of mine. I see too that it is very uneven: less than middling in Myrtilus, immense in Chloris. Oh, Uncle, Uncle! Do you want to play a mean trick on the poor young shepherd? Everything is known. What did you expect? You don't think it hasn't come to my attention that you've become very devout (I wish the devotion was genuine!) and that every morning at dawn you go to church to attend the early mass?"

"Niece, don't spout nonsense."

"I'm not. It's just that this newfound devotion of yours is rather odd to be but a sympathy or solidarity of sorts, and I fear that the little saint who has inspired it has captivated you with sweeter chains than those of piety."

–Te repito que no disparates– volvió a decir el comendador poniéndose muy serio –. Confieso que es difícil de explicar el extraordinario cariño que Clarita me infunde. Aseguro, no obstante, por mi honor, que nada tiene de lo que tú imaginas. Si me quieres tú un poco, y si me respetas, te suplico, y si crees que puedo mandarte, te mando que apartes de ti ese pensamiento. Yo quiero a Clarita, aunque entre ella y yo no median los vínculos de la sangre, del mismo modo que te quiero a ti que eres mi sobrina: con amor casi paternal; con el amor que es propio de los viejos.

–¡Pero si usted no es viejo, tío!

–Pues aunque no lo sea. No amo a Clarita de otro modo. Y si esto sigue pareciéndote raro, no caviles ni busques más hipótesis para explicártelo satisfactoriamente.

–Está bien, tío. Suspenderé mis tareas de forjar hipótesis.

–Eso es lo más prudente.

–Ya que no valen las hipótesis, ¿vale hacer preguntas?

–Hazlas.

–¿Persiste usted en favorecer los amores de Mirtilo?

–Persisto y persistiré mientras Clara crea yo que le ama.

–¿Espera usted triunfar de la tenacidad de doña Blanca e impedir la boda con don Casimiro?

–Lo espero, aunque es difícil.

–¿Me atreveré a preguntar de qué medios va usted a valerse para vencer esa dificultad?

–Atrévete; pero yo me atreveré también a decirte que esos medios no tienes tú para qué saberlos. Confía en mí.

–Aunque usted, tío, está tan misterioso conmigo, que todo se lo calla, voy a portarme con generosidad: voy a revelar a usted mis secretos. Sé que don Carlos de Atienza le escribe a usted. También a mí me ha escrito. Pero usted no ha hecho lo que yo. Usted no ha puesto al pobre desterrado en comunicación con Clara: yo sí. Yo he escrito a Clara tres cartas nada menos, y a fuerza de súplicas he logrado que el padre Jacinto se las entregue. En mis cartas copio a Clara algunos parrafitos de los que me ha escrito don Carlos.

–Ese secreto le sabía en parte. El padre Jacinto me había dicho que había entregado tus cartas.

–Pues, ¿vaya que no sabe usted otra cosa?

–¿Qué?

–Que Clara me ha contestado. La contestación vino ayer por el aire, como la carta primera que juntos leímos.

"I repeat: don't spout nonsense," the commander said again, turning very serious. "I admit that it is difficult to explain the extraordinary affection that Clarita inspires in me. I assure you, though, on my honor, that there is nothing of what you imagine in it. If you love me a little, and if you respect me, I implore you; and if you think I can order you, I'm ordering you to push that thought out of your mind. I love Clarita, although we are not bonded by blood, the same way that I love you, my niece, with an almost paternal love, with the love of old men."

"But you're not old, Uncle!"

"Even if I'm not. I don't love Clarita any other way. And if this continues to seem strange to you, don't formulate or seek more hypotheses to explain yourself satisfactorily."

"All right, Uncle. I'll stop formulating hypotheses."

"That's the most prudent thing."

"Since hypotheses are of no use, is it worthwhile to ask questions?"

"Ask away."

"Do you persist in promoting Myrtilus's love?"

"I do, and I will as long as I believe that Clara loves him."

"Do you hope to triumph over Doña Blanca's tenacity and prevent the marriage to Don Casimiro?"

"I hope to, although it will be difficult."

"Shall I dare to ask what means you are going to use to overcome that difficulty?"

"Go ahead and ask, but I will dare for my part to tell you that you have no need to know them. Trust me."

"Although you, Uncle, are so mysterious with me that you keep everything to yourself, I am going to behave generously: I am going to reveal my secrets to you. I know that Don Carlos de Atienza writes to you. But you have not done what I have. You have not put the exile in contact with Clara. I have. I have written her three letters no less, and by dint of entreaties, I've persuaded Father Jacinto to hand them over to her. In my letters to Clara I copy some paragraphs from the ones that Don Carlos has written to me."

"I knew that secret in part. Father Jacinto had told me that he had handed over your letters."

"Well, I'll bet there's something you do not know."

"What?"

"That Clara has answered me. The answer came yesterday through the air, like the first letter that we read together."

–¿Tienes aquí la nueva carta?

–Sí, tío.

–¿Quieres leerla?

–No lo merece usted; pero yo soy tan buena que la leeré.

Lucía sacó un papel de su seno.

Antes de leer, dijo:

–En verdad, tío, esto me pone muy cuidadosa y sobresaltada. Clara, en los días que lleva de soledad, ha cambiado mucho. ¡Hay en su carta tan singular exaltación, tan profunda tristeza, tan amargos pensamientos!...

–Lee, lee– dijo el comendador con viva emoción. Lucía leyó como sigue:

«Amada Lucía: Mil gracias por todo cuanto estás haciendo por mí. Sería yo desleal si te ocultase nada de lo que siento. Ni al padre Jacinto me he confiado hasta ahora; pero a ti todo te lo confío. En mi ser pasa algo de extraño, que no acierto a entender. Quiero aún a don Carlos. Y, no obstante, conozco que no debo darle esperanzas; que no debo casarme con él nunca; que me toca obedecer a mi madre, la cual anhela mi boda con don Casimiro. Pero lo singular es que ha entrado en mi alma, en estos días, un sentimiento tan hondo de humildad, que hasta de don Casimiro me hallo indigna. A solas conmigo he penetrado en el fondo de mi conciencia y me he perdido allí en abismos tenebrosos. Cuando mi madre, que es buena y me ama, encuentra en mí no sé qué levadura, no sé qué germen de perversión, no sé qué mancha más negra del pecado original que en las demás criaturas, razón tendrá mi madre. Sí, Lucía: quizás en este pecho mío, en apariencia tranquilo, bajo la inocencia y superficial sencillez de mis pocos años, van adquiriendo ya ser y vida vehementes y malas pasiones, como nido de víboras bajo apiñadas rosas. Lo conozco; mi madre tiembla por mí; recela de mi porvenir y tiene razón. Yo me examino, me estudio y me asusto. Descubro en mí la propensión, difícil de resistir, a todo lo malo. Veo mi maldad nativa y mi inclinación al pecado por instinto. ¿Cómo comprender de otra suerte que yo, educada con tanto recogimiento y en tan santa ignorancia de las cosas del mundo, haya tenido la diabólica malicia de ponerme en relaciones

"Do you have the new letter with you?"

"Yes, Uncle."

"Will you read it?"

"You don't deserve to hear this letter, but I'm so good that I'll read it to you."

Lucía withdrew the paper from her bosom.

Before reading, she said:

"The truth be told, Uncle, this makes me very anxious and very concerned. In her days of solitude Clara has changed a lot. There's such a peculiar excitability in her letters, such profound sadness, such bitter thoughts … !"

"Read, read," said the commander with intense emotion. Lucía read as follows:

Dear Lucía:

A thousand thanks for all that you are doing for me. I would be disloyal if I held back from you anything of what I feel. Up till now I haven't even confided in Father Jacinto, but I'll confide everything to you. Something strange is happening to me, something I don't understand. I still love Don Carlos. And, nonetheless, I recognize that I should not give him hope, that I should never marry him, that I must obey my mother, who very much desires my marriage to Don Casimiro. But the odd thing is that these days such a deep feeling of humility has permeated my soul that I find myself unworthy even of Don Casimiro. Alone with my thoughts I have penetrated the depths of my conscience and lost myself in dark abysses. When my mother, who is good and loves me, finds in me I don't know what germ, I don't know what seed of perversion, I don't know what stain of the original sin that is blacker than in other creatures, my mother has to be right. Yes, Lucía, perhaps in this heart of mine, tranquil in appearance, beneath the innocence and superficial simplicity of my few years, vehement and evil passions are little by little acquiring life and existence, like a nest of vipers under clustered roses. I know it. My mother trembles for me; she fears for my future, and she's right. I discover in myself the propensity, difficult to resist, to everything bad. I see my innate wickedness and my inclination toward sin by instinct. How to comprehend otherwise that, raised in so much seclusion and in such holy ignorance of things of the world, I have had the diabolic

con don Carlos, de hacerle creer que le amaba, mirándole sólo (figúrate con qué perversidad le miraría), y de atraerle hasta aquí obligándole a que me siguiera, y todo con tan infernal disimulo que mi madre nada sabe? Todavía, si es posible, hay en mí algo peor. Lo noto, lo percibo y no sé, ni quiero, ni me atrevo a examinarlo. Lo que sí te declararé es que para mí el mundo ha de ser más peligroso que para otras mujeres, por naturaleza mejores. Lo que no hay en mí por naturaleza debo pedirlo por gracia al cielo. En él cifro mi esperanza. Procede, pues, que yo me aparte del mundo y busque el favor del cielo. Ya sabes tú cuánto he repugnado hasta aquí entrar en religión. No me juzgaba merecedora de ser esposa de Cristo. En esto no he variado, sino para juzgarme aún menos merecedora. En lo que sí he variado es en reconocer que, por mala que sea una persona, jamás debe desesperar de la bondad de Dios. Su Divina Majestad, si hago una vida santa, si me arrepiento, si me mortifico durante el noviciado, me dará fuerzas y merecimientos después para tomar el velo, sin que sea insolente audacia tomarle. Nada he dicho aún a nadie de esta reciente resolución; pero estoy decidida. Hablaré de esto al padre Jacinto para que él hable a mi madre, la convenza de que me conviene y quiero ser monja, y en vista de mi resolución desengañe a don Casimiro. Desengaña tú, desde luego, al infeliz don Carlos. No te niego que le he querido, que le quiero aún; pero no se lo digas. Dile que quiero a otro; que en mi corazón hay un inmenso vacío, donde reinan pavorosas tinieblas. No basta don Carlos a llenar ni a iluminar este vacío, y si Dios no le llena y le ilumina me moriré de miedo, y lo menos doloroso que ocurrirá será que le llene mi perturbada imaginación con espectros horribles que surgen de mi atribulada conciencia. Adiós.»

wickedness to strike up a relationship with Don Carlos, to make him believe that I loved him just by looking at him (imagine with what perversity I must have done it) and to attract him here, obliging him to follow me, and everything with such infernal craftiness that my mother knows nothing? If it is possible, there is something still worse in me. I notice it, I sense it and I don't know how, nor do I want nor do I dare to examine it. What I will declare to you is that for me the world must be more dangerous than for other women, who are by nature better. What there is not in me by nature I ought to seek through grace from heaven. On it do I pin my hopes. It follows, therefore, that I should withdraw from the world and solicit heaven's favor. You already know how much till now I have resisted entering religious life. I did not consider myself worthy of being Christ's bride. I have not changed my thinking on this, except to consider myself still less worthy. In what I have changed is in recognizing that, for as bad as a person may be, we should never despair of God's goodness. His Divine Majesty, if I live a holy life, if I repent, if I mortify myself during the novitiate, will give me strength and worthiness afterwards to take the veil, without it being insolent boldness to do so. I have not said anything to anyone yet of this recent resolution, but I've made up my mind. I will speak of this to Father Jacinto so that he can talk to my mother, convince her that it's the best thing for me and that I want to be a nun, and that in view of my decision to disabuse Don Casimiro. You disabuse, as soon as possible, poor Don Carlos. I don't deny to you that I loved him, that I still do love him, but don't tell him that. Tell him that I love another, that in my heart there is an immense void where dreadful darkness reigns. Don Carlos is not enough to fill or illuminate this void, and if God does not fill it and illuminate it, I'll die of fear, and the least distressing thing that will happen will be that my disturbed imagination will fill it with horrible specters that arise from my afflicted conscience.

Farewell.

20

La lectura de escrito tan melancólico aguó el contento del paseo del comendador y de su sobrina. Apenas se hablaron ya hasta volver a casa.

Aquella crisis repentina del alma de Clara puso a don Fadrique taciturno.

Las ideas que acudían a su mente no eran para reveladas a su sobrina.

Pensaba el comendador que el perpetuo roce del espíritu de doña Blanca con el de su hija, que la presión que ejercía sobre aquella joven de diez y seis años el severo y atrabiliario carácter de su madre, y que los terrores de que había cargado su conciencia tenían a la pobre Clara en un estado de ánimo no muy distante del delirio. La carta a Lucía era la señal alarmante que Clara daba de aquel estado.

El comendador, empero, aunque lleno de zozobra, decidió no intervenir aún en nada. La resolución de la crisis podía ser favorable si él no intervenía. Su intervención podía hacerla más peligrosa.

La sinceridad de Clara era evidente. De súbito, sin que el padre Jacinto, ni nadie, se lo inspirase, había cambiado de propósito y se hallaba resuelta a ser monja. Harto se comprende que para las creencias del comendador esta resolución era funesta: pero en virtud de esta resolución era casi seguro que don Casimiro sería despedido. Iba a eliminarse un obstáculo; iba a descartarse un adversario.

Don Fadrique determinó, pues, aguardar con calma, sin dejar de estar a la mira.

Al mismo padre Jacinto no le insinuó ningún aviso que pudiera servirle de regla de conducta. Se fió, por completo, de su buen natural, y le dejó seguir libremente sus propias inspiraciones.

La prudencia del comendador se vio coronada del éxito al cabo de pocos días.

Doña Blanca, persuadida de que la súbita vocación de su hija era sincera y profunda, tuvo con don Casimiro una conversación muy afectuosa y grave, y le dio sus pasaportes.

El padre Jacinto ponderó el fervor de Clara y animó a doña Blanca para que a la mayor brevedad la dejase entrar de novicia en un convento de carmelitas descalzas que en la ciudad había.

20

The reading of such a melancholy letter spoiled the pleasure of the commander and his niece's walk. They scarcely spoke to each other until they returned home.

That sudden crisis of Clara's soul made Don Fadrique taciturn.

The ideas that sprang to his mind were not ones that he could reveal to his niece.

The commander thought that the perpetual contact of Doña Blanca's spirit with that of her daughter, the pressure exercised by the severe and irascible character of the mother on that daughter of sixteen, and the terror that burdened her conscience, had poor Clara in a state of mind not too far removed from delirium. The letter to Lucía was the alarming sign of that state.

The commander, however, although filled with anxiety, decided not to intervene in anything yet. The resolution of the crisis could be favorable if he did not intervene. His intervention might make it more dangerous.

Clara's sincerity was obvious. All of a sudden, without being inspired by Father Jacinto or anyone else, she had changed her mind and was resolved to be a nun. It is abundantly clear that with respect to the commander's beliefs, this determination was disastrous, but by virtue of this determination it was almost certain that Don Casimiro would be dismissed. One obstacle was going to be removed; one adversary was going to be eliminated.

Don Fadrique decided, therefore, to bide his time calmly, always on the lookout.

Not even to Father Jacinto himself did he hint at or allude to anything that might guide his conduct. He trusted completely in his friend's sound judgment and left him to his own devices.

The commander's prudence was crowned with success a few days later.

Persuaded that her daughter's sudden vocation was sincere and profound, Doña Blanca had a very affectionate and serious tête-à-tête with Don Casimiro, calling off the projected marriage and giving him his walking papers.

Father Jacinto spoke warmly of Clara's fervor and encouraged Doña Blanca to allow her to enter – posthaste, as a novice – a convent of discalced Carmelites that was in the city.

Don Valentín se avino a todo sin chistar.

Clarita hubiera, pues, entrado en seguida en el convento, como lo deseaba y lo pedía, pero la crisis de su alma había influido poderosamente sobre su hermoso cuerpo. Sus ojeras eran más oscuras y extensas que de ordinario; había adelgazado mucho; la palidez de su rostro hubiera inspirado miedo, si su rostro no hubiera sido tan hermoso; su distracción y su embebecimiento parecían a veces más propios de un ser del otro mundo que de una criatura de éste; y en su andar vacilante y en el brillo momentáneo de sus ojos, seguido siempre del prolongado adormecimiento de tan divinas luces, había como un mal agüero, como un anuncio fatídico, que no pudo menos de perturbar la férrea conciencia de doña Blanca, de doblegar bastante su inflexibilidad, y de aterrarla por último.

Las causas del cambio de Clarita eran vagas y confusas, pero doña Blanca reconocía que de su modo de educar a Clara, de su involuntario y tenaz prurito de mortificarla y asustarla con los peligros del mundo y con su propia condición de pecadora, y de aquel duro yugo que desde la infancia había hecho pesar sobre la conciencia de su infeliz hija, provenía en gran parte la situación en que se hallaba. El motivo, o mejor dicho, la ocasión de exacerbarse el mal y de aparecer de repente con tan medrosos síntomas, era para todos un misterio. Esto no obstaba para que doña Blanca empezase a temer que pudiera caer sobre ella el crimen de infanticidio por esquivar el delito de hurto.

Doña Blanca procedió, pues, con inusitada blandura y exquisita prudencia, pero sin desmentir su carácter y sin faltar a su más importante propósito.

No contenta con estar persuadida de la firme resolución que tenía Clara de tomar el velo, hízola prometer que profesaría. Y esto de suerte que la promesa no pareció arrancada por instigación de doña Blanca, sino a su despecho. Así se aseguraba doña Blanca de que su hija, renunciando al mundo, renunciaría a los bienes de don Valentín y no podría transmitirlos a nadie.

Pero doña Blanca no quería matar a su hija. Atormentábase previamente con el remordimiento de que fuera al claustro desesperada y herida de muerte. Deseaba verla profesar, pero alegre, lozana, llena de vida: no apareciendo como una víctima, sino con el deleite, el gozo y la satisfacción de una esposa que vuela a los brazos de su gallardo y feliz prometido.

Don Valentín agreed to everything without saying a word.

As a result, Clarita would have entered the convent at once, as she desired and requested, but her soul crisis had had a powerful effect on her beautiful body. The rings under her eyes were darker and wider than usual; she had grown very thin; the pallor of her face would have caused alarm if her face had not been so beautiful; her distraction and self-absorption seemed at times more befitting of a being from the other world than of a creature from this one; and in her unsteady step and in the passing brilliance of her eyes, always followed by the prolonged drowsiness of such divine lights, there was a kind of ill omen, a kind of ominous sign, that could not help perturbing Doña Blanca's ironbound conscience, bending considerably her inflexibility, and in the end terrifying her.

The causes of the change in Clara were vague and confusing, but Doña Blanca recognized that the situation in which her disconsolate daughter found herself stemmed in large part from her method of raising Clara, from her involuntary and tenacious urge to mortify her and frighten her with the dangers of the world and with her own condition as a sinner, and from the onerous yoke that because of her had weighed on Clara's conscience since infancy. The reason, or rather, the occasion for exacerbating the ill and of it appearing out of the blue with such alarming symptoms, was a mystery to everyone. This did not prevent Doña Blanca from beginning to fear that she might commit the crime of filicide so as to avoid the crime of theft.

Doña Blanca proceeded, therefore, with unwonted kindness and exquisite prudence, but without gainsaying her character and without compromising her most important objective.

Not content with just being persuaded of Clara's firm decision to take the veil, she made her promise that she would profess. And this she managed in such a way that the promise did not seem exacted at Doña Blanca's instigation, but in spite of it. Thus did Doña Blanca assure herself that her daughter, by renouncing the world, would renounce Don Valentín's possessions and not be able to transfer them to anyone.

But Doña Blanca did not want to kill her daughter. She tormented herself in advance with remorse, knowing that Clara would be entering the convent in despair and mortally wounded. Yes, she wished to see her profess, but gladly and full of animation and life – not looking like a victim, but with the delight, joy, and satisfaction of a spouse who flies into the arms of her gallant and happy bridegroom.

A fin de lograr que las cosas fueran así, doña Blanca puso a un lado su constante severidad; empezó a tratar a Clara hasta con mimo, y, anhelante de que recobrase la alegría y la salud, rompió el entredicho, abrió las puertas de su casa para Lucía, y consintió en que Clara volviese a salir con ella de paseo, aun a pesar del comendador.

Doña Blanca, no obstante, antes de dar este permiso, preparó a su hija contra don Fadrique, pintándosele como un monstruo de impiedad y de infamia, y recomendándole mucho que hablase con él lo menos posible.

Doña Blanca, entre tanto, se propuso seguir encastillada en su caserón, sin ver a nadie más que al padre Jacinto, y a Lucía, si acaso.

21

El destino de don Casimiro es el más extraño y caprichoso entre los de cuantos personajes figuran en esta historia. En el tejido de su vida había puesto él un orden envidiable, y gastado poquísimo. Así es que, por más que don Casimiro distase mucho de ser un águila en nada, había atinado a darse tan buena traza, con economía y juicio, que era un señor acaudalado para lo que entonces se usaba en Villabermeja. Esto se lo debía a sí mismo, y de ello podía estar con razón y estaba orgulloso. Lo que debió a la casualidad, a un conjunto de hechos para él inexplicables, fue el momentáneo encumbramiento a novio de su linda y rica sobrina la señorita doña Clara.

Con cincuenta y seis años, no pocos padecimientos y la facha que ya hemos descrito, don Casimiro mismo, a pesar de su amor propio, que no era flojo, había hallado, allá en el centro de su conciencia, un sí es no es inverosímil que le quisiesen casar con aquel pimpollo. El amor propio, no obstante, es ingeniosísimo, estando casi siempre su ingenio en razón inversa del ingenio de las personas; por donde don Casimiro imaginó pronto que en su alma había de haber tan escondidos tesoros de bondad y de belleza, y que en sus modales y porte habían de trascender tal distinción hidalga y tal elegancia ingénita, que, descubierto todo por los ojos zahoríes de doña Blanca, bastó y sobró para que ella ansiase tener a don Casimiro por yerno. Don Casimiro, pues, desde que empezó a ser novio de Clara, se puso más orondo y satisfecho que antes.

So as to see things work out this way, Doña Blanca abandoned her accustomed severity. She began to treat Clara with indulgence even, and, eager for her to recover her gaiety and her health, lifted the prohibition that had closed the doors of her house to Lucía, and allowed Clara to resume their walks, despite the commander.

However, before granting this permission, Doña Blanca cautioned her daughter against Don Fadrique, painting him as a monster of ungodliness and iniquity, and strongly recommending that she speak to him as little as possible.

Doña Blanca, meanwhile, resolved to remain shut up in her big house, without seeing anyone except Father Jacinto, and perhaps Lucía.

21

The lot of Don Casimiro is the strangest and most capricious of all the people who figure in this story. In the web of his life he had established an enviable order and spent but a pittance. Thus it was that, however little accomplished he might have been in anything, through economy and prudence he had managed to conduct his affairs so adroitly that for Villabermeja at that time he was a wealthy man. This he owed to himself, and he rightly could be, and was, proud of it. What he owed to chance, to a set of circumstances for him inexplicable, was the short-lived elevation to fiancé of his pretty and rich niece, Señorita doña Clara.

With his fifty-six years of age, not a few ailments, and the appearance that we have already described, Don Casimiro himself, despite his self-esteem, which was not scant, had searched in the depths of his being and found it somewhat hard to believe that they would want to marry him to that budding beauty. However, self-esteem is highly ingenious, its ingeniousness almost always being in inverse ratio to the ingeniousness of the individual, whereby Don Casimiro soon imagined that in his soul there had to have been such hidden treasures of goodness and beauty, and that in his manners and demeanor there had to have been such noble distinction and such innate elegance that, all of it discerned by Doña Blanca's clairvoyant gaze, it sufficed – and more than sufficed – for her to long to have Don Casimiro for a son-in-law. So Don Casimiro, from the time that she chose him as Clara's intended, became more pompous and smug than before.

Terrible fue el desengaño cuando doña Blanca le despidió. El enojo interior de don Casimiro no fue menos terrible; pero él era encogido y muy torpe para expresarse; doña Blanca hablaba bien y con autoridad e imperio, y el señor don Casimiro se tragó su enojo, y recibió los pasaportes, hecho manso cordero.

Como sucede a todas las personas débiles y soberbias a la par, la ira de don Casimiro se fue aglomerando después y poco a poco en el corazón, cuando se detuvo a considerar el chasco que se le daba y el desaire grandísimo que se le hacía.

Cierto que el rival por quien Clara le dejaba era Dios mismo; pero don Casimiro no se aplacaba con esto.

–¿Si querrá ser monja– decía –, para no casarse conmigo? Valiera más haberlo pensado con tiempo y no ponerme en ridículo ahora. Sin duda que para mí es menos cruel que me deje por tan santo motivo que no que me deje para casarse con otro mortal. Yo no hubiera consentido esto último. Nos hubieran oído los sordos. Yo hubiera tenido un lance con mi rival. Pero ¿contra Dios qué he de hacer?

Don Casimiro se consolaba algo con la imposibilidad de tener un lance con Dios, y hasta con la obligación piadosa en que se veía de resignarse.

Su encono contra doña Blanca y contra Clarita no se mitigaba, a pesar de todo. No había quedado perro ni gato, en diez leguas a la redonda, a quien don Casimiro no hubiera dado parte de su ventura. Ahora, su caída y su desventura debían de ser e iban siendo no menos sonadas, y por desgracia harto más aplaudidas.

La vanidad del hidalgo bermejino recibía desaforados golpes. Pero ¿cómo vengarse?

–La venganza es el placer de los dioses– exclamaba a sus solas el dicho hidalgo –; pero decididamente yo no soy un dios. ¿Qué me conviene hacer? Es refrán frailuno, y muy discreto, que *la injuria que no ha de ser bien vengada ha de ser bien disimulada*. Disimulemos, pues. También hay otro refrán que reza: *cachaza y mala intención*. Sigamos lo que prescriben dichos refranes. Lo primero que me importa es dejar ver que no me afligen los desdenes de Clarita. Si ella no me quiere, otra que vale tanto como ella, más que ella, estoy seguro de que me querrá. Voy a volver a pretender a Nicolasa. No es rica, pero es mejor moza que Clarita.

His disillusionment was terrible when Doña Blanca dismissed him. His inner anger was no less terrible, but Don Casimiro was timid and inept at expressing himself; Doña Blanca spoke well, and with authority and arrogance, and Señor don Casimiro swallowed his anger and received his walking papers like a meek lamb.

As often happens with people who are weak and haughty at the same time, Don Casimiro's umbrage built up in his heart afterwards, and little by little, when he stopped to reflect on the letdown and the rebuff that he was being made to suffer.

It was true that the rival for whom Clara abandoned him was God himself, but Don Casimiro derived no solace on this account.

"Do you suppose she wants to be a nun," he wondered, "in order not to marry me? It would have been better if she had thought of that beforehand and not made me look the fool now. No doubt it's less cruel for her to abandon me for such a holy reason than to abandon me to marry another mortal. I would not have tolerated that; I would have raised the roof; I would have had a duel with my rival. But against God, what am I to do?"

Don Casimiro consoled himself somewhat with the impossibility of having a duel with God, and even with the pious obligation that he had to be resigned.

His ill feeling toward Doña Blanca and toward Clarita, though, did not lessen, in spite of everything. There was not a dog or a cat for thirty miles around to which Don Casimiro had not broadcast his good fortune. Now, his fall and his misfortune must be, and were going to be, no less sensational, and, unfortunately, quite a bit more applauded.

The vanity of the Villabermejan hidalgo received mighty blows. But how was he to avenge himself?

"Revenge is the pleasure of the gods," Don Casimiro exclaimed to himself, "and I am most decidedly not a god. What is the best thing for me to do? The friars have a saying, a very shrewd one, that goes, 'The affront that cannot be suitably avenged must be suitably disguised.' So let us disguise it. There is another saying that goes, 'Slowly, calmly, and with evil designs.' Let us follow what these sayings prescribe. The first matter of importance is to let it be seen that Clarita's disdain has not destroyed me. If she doesn't love me, I'm certain that another woman will, another woman who's as worthy as she is, who's more worthy. I'm going to court Nicolasa again. She's not rich, but she's more of a woman than Clarita."

Sin desistir, por consiguiente, de vengarse si se presentaba ocasión cómoda para ello, don Casimiro resolvió enamorar estrepitosamente a Nicolasa, esperando que así daría picón a la futura carmelita, o probaría al menos que tenía por amiga a una mujer de mucho mérito.

Nicolasa, en efecto, lo era. Hija del tío Gorico y de su primera mujer, alcanzaba fama en casi toda la provincia por su singular hermosura, discreción y rumbo. Caballeros, ricos hacendados y hasta usías o señores de título, menos comunes entonces que ahora, habían suspirado en balde por Nicolasa, la cual, con modesta dignidad, había respondido siempre en prosa aquello que dice en verso cierta dama de una antigua comedia nada menos que al rey:

> Para vuestra dama, mucho;
> para vuestra esposa, poco.

Nicolasa excitaba y provocaba con sus risas, con sus ojeadas lánguidas y con su libertad y desenvoltura. Los hombres se prendaban de ella, la perseguían y se llenaban de esperanzas; pero, no bien querían propasarse para que se lograsen, Nicolasa se revestía de gravedad y entono, propios de la mejor heroína de Calderón, hablaba de la inestimable joya de su castidad y limpísima honra, y ponía a raya todo atrevimiento, todo desmán y todo propósito amoroso algo positivo que no llevasen por delante al padre cura.

Nicolasa había heredado de su madre ciertas prendas que valen más que los bienes de fortuna, porque los conservan, si los hay, y suelen proporcionarlos, si no los hay. Tenía don de mando y don de gentes, extraordinaria energía de voluntad y perseverancia en sus planes. Se había propuesto o ser una señora principal o quedarse para vestir imágenes y, sirviéndole esto de pauta, ajustaba a ella todos los actos de su vida.

Aunque el tío Gorico había contraído segundas nupcias, y Nicolasa tuvo madrastra en vez de madre, casi desde la infancia, lejos de contribuir esto a que se criase con menos mimo, había ocasionado lo contrario. La madre de Nicolasa había sido tremenda, dominante, feroz: una doña Blanca a lo rústico; mientras que Juana, la segunda mujer del tío Gorico, era la propia dulzura, sometida siempre a su marido, quien a su vez no hacía más que lo que a Nicolasa se le ocurría. Nicolasa lo podía y lo mandaba todo en casa de su padre, menos impedir que el tío Gorico dejase de beber bebida blanca.

Consequently, without desisting in his wish to avenge himself if a convenient opportunity arose, Don Casimiro resolved to woo Nicolasa ostentatiously, hoping in this way to nettle the future little Carmelite, or at the very least to prove that he had a woman of much merit for a ladylove.

Nicolasa was, in fact, such a woman. The daughter of Tío Gorico and his first wife, she had gained renown in practically the entire province for her singular beauty, discretion, and allure. Gentlemen, rich landowners, and even nobles and men of title, less common then than now, had sighed in vain for Nicolasa, who, with modest dignity, had always responded in prose what a certain lady in an old play says in verse to the king no less:

> To be your mistress, I'm too high;
> To be your wife, I'm too low.[85]

Nicolasa excited and provoked men with her laughter, with her languid glances, and with her freedom and brazenness. They would fall for her, chase after her, and get their hopes up, but as soon as they wanted to take liberties in order to fulfill those hopes, Nicolasa assumed an air of gravity and haughtiness, worthy of the best of Calderón's heroines, and spoke of the invaluable gem of her chastity and immaculate honor, keeping at bay every instance of boldness, every act of excess, and every somewhat positive amorous intention that did not lead to a priest at the altar.

Nicolasa had inherited from her mother certain talents that are worth more than material riches, because they preserve these very riches when they do exist, and they are usually instrumental in acquiring them when they do not exist. She had a knack for giving orders, and she also had a way with people, extraordinary backbone, and perseverance in her plans. She had determined to be either a woman of standing or an old maid, and, with this as her guideline, took every step in accordance with it.

Although Tío Gorico had married a second time and Nicolasa had a stepmother instead of a biological mother almost from infancy, far from giving rise to a less pampered upbringing, this had brought about just the opposite. Nicolasa's mother had been a fearsome, domineering, fierce woman, a rustic Doña Blanca; Juana, on the other hand, Tío Gorico's second wife, was gentleness personified, always submissive to her husband, who for his part did only what Nicolasa wanted him to do. Nicolasa, in short, dominated and directed everything in her father's house; she failed only in preventing Tío Gorico from doing without his spirits.

Los preliminares amorosos de Nicolasa, que estaba entre los veinte
y los treinta años de su edad, habían sido ya innumerables. Todos sus
amores habían muerto al nacer. A los pretendientes encopetados los había
Nicolasa despedido, apelando al cura. A los pretendientes de su clase,
los había desdeñado, cuando ya llegaban a lo serio y hablaban del cura
ellos mismos.

Nicolasa, no obstante, como todas las mujeres frías, pensadoras y
traviesas, había sabido retener en sus redes, en este crepúsculo de amor,
que califican de platónico, a varios suspiradores perpetuos, de los que
llaman en Italia *patitos*. Uno, sobre todo, pudiera servir de ejemplo
portentoso por su pertinacia, resignación y fervor en las incesantes
adoraciones. Tal era el hijo del maestro herrador, Tomasuelo.

Desde los diez y siete hasta los veinticinco años que ya tenía, estaba
como en cautiverio agridulce. Jamás Nicolasa le dijo que le amaba de
amor, y jamás le quitó la esperanza de que tal vez un día podría amarle.
En cambio, le declaraba de continuo que le amaba más de amistad que a
ningún otro ser humano; y cuando le declaraba esto, se le veía al chico
hasta la última muela, sentía una beatitud soberana, y daba por bien
empleados sus, para otras cosas, inútiles y perennes suspiros.

Y no se crea que Tomasuelo era canijo, ruin y tonto. Tomasuelo era
listo, despejado y fuerte: el mozo más guapo del lugar; pero Nicolasa le
había hechizado. Con un rayo de luz de sus ojos podía darle una dosis
de aparente bienaventuranza que le durase una semana. Con una palabra
sola podía hacerle llorar como si fuese un niño de cuatro años.

Las cadenas en que Tomasuelo gemía y gozaba a la vez de verse
cautivo, estaban suavizadas para el mozo, y en cierto modo justificadas
para el público, con notable habilidad y profundo instinto. Tomasuelo
podía entrar cuando se le antojaba en casa del tío Gorico, ver a Nicolasa,
requebrarla, mirarla con amor, acompañarla cuando salía; en suma,
servirla y cuidarla, sin que nadie fuese osado a censurar lo más mínimo.
Aunque entre Nicolasa y el hijo del herrador no había el más remoto
grado de parentesco, Nicolasa había preconizado a Tomasuelo por su
hermano. Dios naturalmente no le había dado objeto en quien poner
amor fraternal; pero ella, que sentía con viveza y hondura este amor, se
proporcionó a Tomasuelo para consagrársele. Con frases sencillas y con
ánimo imperturbable, Nicolasa explicaba de esta manera sus extrañas

Nicolasa, who was in her mid twenties, had already had countless amorous adventures. All her love affairs, though, had died at their inception. She had dismissed the wellborn suitors by resorting to mention of the priest; she had then scorned the suitors of her own class when they got serious and themselves spoke of the priest.

Nonetheless, Nicolasa, like all cold, shrewd, and unpredictable women, had known how to retain in her snares, in this twilight of love labeled platonic, several perpetual "sighers" of the sort that are called *patitos* in Italy. One in particular could serve as an amazing example on account of the persistence, resignation, and fervor of his incessant adoration: Tomasuelo, the son of the master blacksmith.

From the age of seventeen to the age of twenty-five, his present age, he was in a kind of bittersweet captivity. Nicolasa never told him that she *actually* loved him, but neither did she ever take away from him the hope that she *might* love him one day. On the other hand, she continually said to him that as a friend she loved him more than any other human being; and whenever she did say this, the youth's grin spread so wide that even his molars could be seen, and he felt overcome with a supreme happiness and considered his otherwise fruitless and constant sighs put to good use.

And let it not be thought that Tomasuelo was sickly, despicable, and foolish. Tomasuelo was clever, handy, and strong, the handsomest youth in the town, but Nicolasa had bewitched him. With a ray of light from her eyes she could give him a dose of seeming bliss that would last him a week. With a single word she could make him cry as if he were a four-year-old child.

The chains in which Tomasuelo groaned and delighted simultaneously at being captive were softened for him, and in a certain way justified for the public, with remarkable ability and profound instinct. Tomasuelo could enter Tío Gorico's house whenever he had a mind to, see Nicolasa, flirt with her, gaze lovingly at her, accompany her when she went out, in short, wait on her and look out for her without anyone daring to be the least bit critical. Although there was not the remotest degree of kinship between Nicolasa and the blacksmith's son, Nicolasa had publicly proclaimed Tomasuelo her brother. God naturally had not given her someone to be the object of her sisterly love, but she, who felt this love intensely and deeply, latched onto Tomasuelo to devote it to him.[86] With simple phrases and an unflappable spirit, Nicolasa would explain in this

relaciones con Tomasuelo; y como Tomasuelo hacía gala de su adoración espiritual y se lamentaba resignado de no ser querido de otra suerte, todos, en el lugar, lejos de censurar, se maravillaban de aquel purísimo y angélico lazo que estrechaba así dos almas.

Cuanto pretendiente se acercaba a Nicolasa era respetado por Tomasuelo, quien no le ponía el menor estorbo, durante los preliminares y coqueteos; pero si más tarde se extralimitaba y dejaba ver que venía con mal fin, ya podía temer el enojo y las pesadas manos de aquel hermano adoptivo, celoso de la honra de su familia. Asimismo Tomasuelo se ponía zahareño y poco agradable en su trato con todo aquel rival que por cualquier causa era despedido definitivamente y seguía importunando.

Don Casimiro había estado, antes del noviazgo con Clara, en un largo período de coqueteo con Nicolasa, la cual, con exquisita circunspección, había sabido ir templando y moderando la máquina de los afectos, a fin de no precipitar al hidalgo en declaraciones y demostraciones tales que no tuviesen más salida que la de ponerle en la disyuntiva de prometer boda o de abandonar la empresa. Gracias a esta conducta, que pasa de hábil y raya en primorosa, don Casimiro no había sido despedido; sus amores con Nicolasa habían sido como aurora, como amanecer poético de un día, que no llegó por haberse interpuesto el compromiso con Clarita. Roto ya este compromiso, don Casimiro pudo volver, previo el perdón de su inconsecuencia, pedido con humildad y concedido magnánimamente, al mismo punto en que lo había dejado: al amanecer; a la aurora.

Las cosas estaban dispuestas con tal arte, que en lugar de escamarse un pretendiente con Tomasuelo, lo primero que tenía que hacer era como impetrar el beneplácito de aquel espiritual hermano, tan celoso, vigilante e interesado en el bien de su hermanita. Don Casimiro obtuvo la confianza y venia de Tomasuelo, y lo consideró buena señal.

Abandonada la ciudad, y vuelto don Casimiro a sus reales de Villabermeja, se puso a galantear a Nicolasa con la imprudencia y el ímpetu del despechado. Ella era harto discreta para no conocer que entonces o nunca: que la fortuna le presentaba el copete y que importaba asirle. Don Casimiro buscaba en Nicolasa refugio y compensación contra el desdén de Clarita. Don Casimiro estaba en su poder.

manner her strange relationship with Tomasuelo; and since Tomasuelo made a show of his spiritual adoration and resignedly lamented not being loved in another way, everybody in the town, far from criticizing it, marveled at that pure and angelic bond that joined two souls in such a fashion.

Every suitor who approached Nicolasa was respected by Tomasuelo, who did not place the slightest obstacle in his path during the preliminaries and flirtations, but if later on he overstepped himself and revealed that he had come with bad intentions, he could count on fearing the anger and heavy hands of that adopted brother who was jealous of his family's honor. Tomasuelo likewise became testy and not very pleasant in his treatment of every rival who for whatever reason was dismissed for good and still continued to be a pest.

Before his engagement to Clara, Don Casimiro had been occupied in a long period of flirtation with Nicolasa, who, with exquisite circumspection, had managed to temper and moderate the machine of effects so as not to hurry the hidalgo into declarations and demonstrations of a kind that would present no other alternative but to put him in the dilemma of proposing marriage or abandoning the undertaking. Thanks to this conduct, which goes beyond shrewd and borders on consummate, Don Casimiro had not been dismissed; his love affair with Nicolasa had been like aurora, like the poetic dawn of a day, which never arrived because the engagement to Clarita intervened. With this engagement broken now, Don Casimiro could come back, having first obtained forgiveness for his fickleness – which he humbly implored and which was magnanimously granted – and be at the same point where he had left his pursuit: at the dawn, at the aurora.

Things were arranged so artfully that, instead of becoming leery of Tomasuelo, the first step a suitor had to take was, so to speak, to obtain the approval of that spiritual brother who was so jealous, so vigilant, and so interested in his sister's well-being. Don Casimiro won Tomasuelo's trust and permission, which he considered a good omen.

Having left the city and returned to his residence in Villabermeja, Don Casimiro set out to woo Nicolasa with the imprudence and impetuosity of a peeved, indignant man. She was too sensible not to realize that it was then or never – that fortune was offering her the chance and that it was important for her to seize it. Don Casimiro sought in Nicolasa refuge and compensation for Clarita's disdain. Don Casimiro was in her power.

Nicolasa provocó la declaración seria y definitiva. Hecha ésta, planteó los dos términos del fatal dilema: o promesa formal de casamiento, o despedida y nuevas calabazas ruidosas. Don Casimiro no pudo resistir y prometió casarse.

Espantoso día de prueba fue aquel en que supo este triunfo el platónico Tomasuelo. Hasta entonces no había tenido rival que fuese más dichoso que él. Ya le tenía. La amargura de los celos le acibaró el corazón; las lágrimas brotaron en abundancia de sus ojos.

Cuando vio a solas a Nicolasa, con los ojos encarnados de llorar y con voz trémula, le dijo:

–¿Conque cedes al amor de don Casimiro? ¿Conque vas a casarte? ¿Conque me matas?

–Calla, tontito mío– contestó ella –. ¿A qué vienen esas quejas? ¿Te he engañado yo jamás?

–No; no me has engañado.

–¿Querías que dejase pasar tan buena proporción de ser señora principal y millonaria? ¿Tan mal me quieres, egoísta?

–No porque te quiero mal, sino porque te quiero a manta, lo siento y lo lloro.

Y Tomasuelo lloraba en efecto.

–Anda, no llores, majadero. ¡Si vieses qué feo te pones! ¿Quién ha visto llorar a un hombrón como un castillo?

–Pero ¡si no puedo remediarlo!

–Sí puedes; haz un esfuerzo, ten valor y sosiégate. Ten en cuenta que, de aquí en adelante, no sólo hallarás en mí a una hermana, sino a una madrina y a una protectora muy pudiente.

–Y a mí ¿qué se me da todo eso? Nada. Lo que yo codiciaba era tu cariño.

–¿Y no lo tienes como antes, ingrato? Pues qué, ¿los buenos hermanitos dejan de amarse aunque se case uno de ellos?

–No seas tramoyona, no me aturrulles. Ya sabes tú que la ley que yo te tengo no puede sufrir...

–Vamos, vamos; déjate de niñerías. ¿Quién crees tú que ocupa y llena el lugar más bonito, principal y escondido de mi corazón? Tú. Mi alma es tuya. Te la di toda con el amor que en ella se cría; con afecto de hermana. ¿Qué sombra puede hacerte que sea yo la mujer legítima

Nicolasa contrived to gain a serious, definitive declaration. With Don Casimiro having made it, she posed the two choices of the fatal dilemma: either a formal promise of marriage or a dismissal and another resounding snub. The man could not resist and promised to marry her.

It was a frightful day of trial when the platonic Tomasuelo learned of this triumph. Until then he had not had a rival who enjoyed more favor than he. Now he did. The sour taste of jealousy embittered his heart; copious tears welled up in his eyes.

When he saw Nicolasa alone, he said to her in a faltering voice, his eyes red from crying:

"So you're giving in to Don Casimiro's love? So you're going to get married? So you're going to kill me?"

"Quiet, you foolish thing!" she replied. "Why these complaints? Have I ever played you false?"

"No, you haven't."

"Did you want me to pass up such a good chance to be a lady of standing? A millionaire? That's how little you love me, you selfish creature?"

"Not because I love you a little, but because I love you a lot, that's why. I'm sorry and that's why I'm crying."

And Tomasuelo was in fact crying.

"Come on now, don't be an idiot and stop crying. If you saw how ugly you look! Who has ever seen a man as big as a castle crying?"

"But I can't help it!"

"Yes, you can. Make an effort, be brave, and calm down. Bear in mind that from now on you'll not only have a sister in me, but a sponsor and very powerful protector as well."

"And what do I care about all that? Not a thing. What I wished for was your affection."

"And don't you have it as you did before, you ingrate? What did you expect? Do good brothers and sisters stop loving one another if one of them happens to marry?"

"Don't get cute with words, don't get me flustered. You know that what I feel for you can't tolerate – "

"All right, all right, no more of this childishness. Who do you think occupies and fills the prettiest, the foremost and innermost corner of my heart? You. My soul is yours. I gave it to you with all the love that grows in it, with the affection of a sister. How can it be a millstone around your

de don Casimiro? ¿Por eso hemos de dejar de querernos como hasta
aquí, más que hasta aquí? Nos querremos cuanto tú quieras y cuanto sea
posible quererse, sin ofender a Dios. ¿Supongo que tú no querrás ofender
a Dios? Contesta.

–No, mujer; ¿cómo he de querer yo ofender a Dios? Pues qué, ¿no soy
buen cristiano?

–Lo eres. Es una de las partes que más aprecio en ti. Por eso confío en
que pienses que voy a ser esposa de otro y no desees nada. Sólo el deseo
es ya pecado. Acuérdate de los mandamientos.

–Oye, ¿y está en mi poder no desear?

–Sí. Cállate; no digas nada a nadie, ni a ti mismo, cuando desees, y el
silencio matará el deseo.

Tomasuelo lloró más fuerte que nunca. Las lágrimas caían a modo de
lluvia, acompañadas por tempestad de sollozos.

–¡Por vida de los hombres endebles!– exclamó Nicolasa –. ¿Qué
locura es ésta? Cálmate por Dios y ten pecho ancho.

Nicolasa, con suma blandura, enjugó las lágrimas del mozo con el
propio pañuelo de ella; luego le dio tres o cuatro palmaditas en el grueso
y robusto cogote; luego le hizo unas cuantas muecas como remedando
la desconsolada cara que ponía; y, por último, le pegó un afectuoso y
archifamiliar tirón de las narices.

Tomasuelo no supo resistir a tanto favor y regalo. Como rayos de
sol entre nubes, la alegría y la satisfacción aparecieron en sus ojos a
través de las lágrimas. La boca de Tomasuelo se abrió, enseñando la
blanca, completa y sana dentadura. No pudo sonreír, porque se quedó
boquiabierto y como traspuesto.

Nicolasa entonces repitió los cogotazos; añadió al tirón de las narices
unos cuantos tirones de las orejas, y Tomasuelo pensó que se le llevaban
al paraíso y que era el más feliz de los mortales.

En esta situación de ánimo convino en que Nicolasa debía casarse
con don Casimiro; en que él debía seguir siendo su hermano, sin pensar,
o sin decir al menos que pensaba en otra cosa; y concibió con claridad,
más que por el discurso y las razones, por los blandos cogotazos y por
los tirones de orejas, toda la suavidad, hechizo, consistencia y deleite del
amor espiritual que a Nicolasa le ligaba.

neck for me to be Don Casimiro's lawful wife? For that reason we're
going to stop loving each other as we have till now, more than till now?
We'll love each other as much as you want and as much as it's possible
to love each other, without offending God. I suppose you won't want to
offend God? Answer."

"No, woman. Why would I want to offend God? What? Am I not a
good Christian?"

"You are. It's one of the things I prize most in you. I trust therefore
that you'll understand that I am going to be the wife of another and
that you won't covet anything. Just the desire is a sin. Remember the
commandments."

"Listen. You think it's in my power not to desire?"

"Yes. Be quiet and don't say anything to anyone, not even to yourself,
whenever you desire, and silence will kill the desire."

"It'll kill me first."

Tomasuelo cried with more abandon than ever. Tears fell like raindrops,
accompanied by a tempest of sighs.

"My word! Weak men!" exclaimed Nicolasa. "What madness is this?
Calm down, for heaven's sake, and show some mettle."

With the utmost gentleness, Nicolasa wiped the youth's tears with her
own handkerchief; then she gave him three or four light taps on the back
of his thick, robust neck; then she made a few faces at him, as though
mimicking his disconsolate expression; and finally she gave his nose an
affectionate, fondly familiar pull.

Tomasuelo could not resist so much kindness and coddling. Like
sunbeams slicing through clouds, joy and satisfaction appeared in his
eyes despite the tears. His lips spread open, revealing a complete set of
healthy white teeth; he could not smile because he stood there gaping at
her, as though spellbound.

Nicolasa then repeated the pats on the neck; for good measure she
pulled his ears in addition to his nose, and Tomasuelo thought he was
being transported to paradise and that he was the happiest of mortals.

In that frame of mind he agreed that Nicolasa ought to marry Don
Casimiro and that he ought to continue being her brother, without
thinking, or at least without saying that he was thinking, of any other role.
He understood clearly, not so much because of her words and reasons,
but because of the gentle pats on his neck and the tugs at his ears, and all
the sweetness, charm, consistency, and delight of the spiritual love that
bound him to Nicolasa.

Así venció Nicolasa los obstáculos todos y aseguró su proyectada boda con don Casimiro.

La fama difundió al punto la noticia por toda Villabermeja; salvó luego su término y la llevó a la ciudad, y a los oídos del comendador, de su familia y de los señores de Solís.

El comendador había sido visitado por don Casimiro y le había pagado la visita. No se habían hallado en casa y no se habían visto. La frialdad de sus relaciones no hacía necesario más frecuente trato.

No bien supo el comendador el resuelto proyecto de boda entre don Casimiro y Nicolasa, fue a Villabermeja, visitó a la chacha Ramoncica y tuvo una larga conferencia con ella, de cuyo objeto se enterará más tarde el curioso lector. Después de esto se volvió a la ciudad don Fadrique.

22

Clara había vuelto a salir de paseo con Lucía y acompañada del comendador y de doña Antonia; pero Clara estaba cambiada.

Su palidez y su debilidad eran para inspirar serios temores. Su distracción continua asustaba también al comendador. Cuando éste le dirigía la palabra, Clara se estremecía como si la sacasen de un sueño, como si cortasen el vuelo remoto de su espíritu y le hiciesen caer de pronto del cielo a la tierra, a modo de pajarillo herido por el plomo allá en lo sumo del aire.

A pesar de la benignidad y dulce condición de Clara, don Fadrique advertía con pena que aquella linda criatura esquivaba su conversación; casi no le respondía sino con monosílabos, y hasta procuraba que él no le hablase.

Con Lucía era Clara más expansiva, y Lucía seguía siéndolo siempre con el comendador. Por medio, pues, de Lucía penetraba aún el comendador en el espíritu de aquel ser querido y comunicaba algo con él.

Las nuevas que Lucía le daba eran en sustancia siempre las mismas, si bien más inquietantes cada vez.

–No lo comprendo, tío– decía Lucía –; pero a veces me doy a cavilar que a Clara le han dado un bebedizo. ¡Tiene unos terrores tan inmotivados! ¡Siente unos remordimientos tan fuertes de razón!... No sé qué sea ello.

Thus did Nicolasa overcome all the obstacles and assure her projected marriage to Don Casimiro.

Word of mouth spread the news at once throughout Villabermeja; it then traveled beyond the town limits and reached the city and the ears of the commander, his family, and the Solís household.

The commander had been visited by Don Casimiro and had returned the visit. They had not found each other at home and had not seen each other. The coolness of their relations did not call for more frequent contact.

As soon as the commander learned of the upcoming marriage between Don Casimiro and Nicolasa, he went to Villabermeja, visited Chacha Ramoncica, and had a long talk with her, the subject of which will be made known to the curious reader at a later point. After this, Don Fadrique returned to the city.

22

Clara had begun to go for walks again with Lucía, and accompanied by the commander and Doña Antonia, but she had changed.

Her pallor and her weakness were cause for serious concern. Her continual distraction also worried the commander. Whenever he spoke to her, Clara would shudder as if she were being awakened from a dream, as if the soaring flight of her spirit were being curtailed and she were being made to fall precipitately from sky to earth, like a bird wounded by lead in the ether.

Despite Clara's kindliness and sweet disposition, Don Fadrique noted with sorrow that that lovely creature shunned his conversation; more often than not she uttered monosyllabic replies, and she even tried to keep him from talking to her.

With Lucía Clara was more expansive, as Lucía always was with the commander. So through Lucía the commander still penetrated the spirit of that beloved being and communicated somewhat with it.

The news that Lucía brought was always the same in substance, although more disturbing each time.

"I don't understand it, Uncle," Lucía said, "but at times I'm given to wondering whether Clara's been administered a potion. She has such groundless fears! She feels such irrational pangs of remorse! I don't

Doña Blanca le ha puesto tan feroces escrúpulos en el alma, le ha hecho recelar tanto de su apasionada natural condición... que la infeliz se cree un monstruo y es un ángel. Tal vez imagina que la persiguen las furias del infierno, los enemigos del alma, una legión entera de diablos, y entonces no se considera en salvo sino acogiéndose al pie del altar. Es menester que avisemos a don Carlos que venga pronto, a ver si liberta a Clara de este género de locura.

El comendador y Lucía escribieron con la misma fecha a don Carlos de Atienza, participándole la novedad de la despedida de don Casimiro, de la resolución de Clara de retirarse a un convento y del estado poco satisfactorio de su salud. Don Carlos partió desatentado de Sevilla, y estuvo en la ciudad a poco.

Con el mismo recato y disimulo de siempre don Carlos volvió a ver a Clara en los paseos que ésta daba con Lucía; pero la delicada salud de Clara le llenó de desconsuelo. Y más aún, si cabe, le atormentó y afligió el ver a Clara esquiva, tímida como nunca, apartándose de él y no queriendo apenas hablarle, aunque mirándole a veces con involuntarias amorosas miradas, que se conocía que ella dejaba escapar a su despecho, y con las cuales, más que amor, reclamaba piedad, conmiseración y hasta perdón por su inconsecuencia de dejarle, de haber alentado sus esperanzas y de matarlas ahora entrando en el claustro.

La desesperación de don Carlos de Atienza llegó a su colmo. Con no poca amargura echaba la culpa de todo al comendador.

–Para esto– decía –, me obligó usted a que me ausentase. En esto han parado las promesas de arreglarlo todo en menos de un mes. En que Clara se esté muriendo, y en que además haya dejado de amarme y quiera ser monja; en que acabe por tomar el velo... y luego la mortaja. Pero yo me moriré también. Yo no quiero sobrevivir. Me mataré si no me muero.

El comendador no sabía qué responder a tales quejas. Procuraba consolar a don Carlos, que le juzgaba indiferente y extraño; que ignoraba que él tenía mayor necesidad de consuelo.

Iba don Fadrique a buscarle en el padre Jacinto. Iba asimismo a buscar en él alguna luz sobre aquel misterio; pero ¡caso extraño!, el padre Jacinto, todo franqueza y jovialidad antes, se había vuelto muy grave, muy misterioso y muy callado.

know what it can be. Doña Blanca has planted such fierce scruples in her soul, has made her distrust her natural passionate temperament to such an extent that the poor thing believes herself a monster when she's an angel. Maybe she imagines that she's being pursued by the furies of hell, an entire legion of devils, and doesn't consider herself safe except by seeking refuge at the foot of the altar. We must warn Don Carlos and tell him to come soon to see whether he can deliver Clara from this kind of madness."

The commander and Lucía wrote on the same day to Don Carlos de Atienza, informing him of the recent news of Don Casimiro's dismissal, of Clara's decision to retire to a convent, and of the not very satisfactory state of her health. Don Carlos departed from Seville in great haste and shortly thereafter arrived in the city.

With the same caution and pretense as always, Don Carlos started seeing Clara again on her walks with Lucía, but Clara's delicate health filled him with distress. And still more, if possible, did it torment and afflict him to see Clara aloof as never before, to see her keeping her distance from him and scarcely wanting to talk to him, although looking at him on occasion with tender glances that were involuntary, a reflex act in spite of herself, and with which more than love she sought pity, commiseration, and even forgiveness for her fickleness in abandoning him, for having raised his hopes and then having shattered them by entering the cloister.

Don Carlos de Atienza's despair reached its highest point. With more than a little bitterness he blamed the commander for everything.

"For this," he said, "you made me go away. The end result of your promises to settle everything inside of a month has taken this turn: Clara is dying on me. Besides that, she has stopped loving me and wants to be a nun, and will end up taking the veil ... and then the shroud. But I'll die too. I don't want to outlive her. I'll kill myself if I don't die."

The commander did not know how to respond to such complaints. He tried to console Don Carlos, who considered him indifferent and strange, who was unaware that the commander himself had a greater need of consolation.

Don Fadrique went to seek it in Father Jacinto. He likewise went to see if the priest could shed some light on that mystery, but – the strangest thing! – Father Jacinto, all frankness and joviality before, had become very grave, very mysterious, and very reticent.

Don Fadrique entrevia, no obstante, que el padre Jacinto aprobaba la resolución de Clara de ser monja. Esto le ponía fuera de sí, y a veces estaba a punto de romper con el padre Jacinto y de mirarle como a amigo desleal o como a fanático sin entrañas. Con todo, en medio de sus tribulaciones el comendador se reportaba y no perdía la calma. Había tomado sus medidas. Su conducta estaba prescrita y determinada con firmeza, y aguardaba sereno el resultado.

Este no tardó mucho en venir.

Era muy de mañana cuando trajo un criado desde Villabermeja una carta para don Fadrique. Don Fadrique la leyó rápidamente, estando en la cama aún. Se levantó a escape, se vistió y se fue al convento de Santo Domingo en busca de su maestro.

El padre acababa de levantarse y recibió a don Fadrique en su celda. Sentados ambos, como en la otra celda de Villabermeja, hablaron de este modo.

23

Padre Jacinto– dijo el comendador con aire de jubiloso triunfo –, Clara es libre ya. No es menester que se case con don Casimiro ni que sea monja.

–¿Cómo es eso, hijo mío?

–He dado por ella una suma igual a todo el caudal de don Valentín.

–¿A quién?

–A don Casimiro.

–¿Y con qué razón? ¿Con qué pretexto ha podido aceptarla?

–La ha aceptado con una razón que promete callar; por un motivo secreto.

–¡Válgame Dios, hijo mío! ¡Qué delirio! ¡Qué sacrificio inútil! Y dime... ese motivo secreto... ¡Confiar así a don Casimiro la honra de una familia ilustre!...

–Yo no le he confiado nada.

–¿Pues de qué medio te has valido?

–De una mentira; pero mentira indispensable y con la cual nadie pierde.

–¿Puedo saber esa mentira?

Don Fadrique suspected, however, that Father Jacinto approved of Clara's decision to become a nun. This drove him crazy, and at times he was on the verge of falling out with Father Jacinto and regarding him as a disloyal friend or as a heartless fanatic.

Nonetheless, in the midst of his tribulations, the commander controlled himself and did not lose his calm. He had taken his measures. His conduct was preordained and firmly determined, and he serenely awaited the result.

It was not long in coming.

Very early one morning a servant brought a letter for Don Fadrique from Villabermeja. As he was still in bed, he read it quickly. Don Fadrique then rose in a great hurry, dressed, and left for the Santo Domingo monastery to find his master.

The priest had just got up and received Don Fadrique in his cell. When they both had taken a seat, as they had in the other cell in Villabermeja, they spoke as follows:

23

"Father Jacinto," said the commander with an air of jubilant triumph, "Clara is free now. It's not necessary for her to marry Don Casimiro or to be a nun."

"How's that, my son?"

"I have given for her a sum of money equal to all of Don Valentín's assets."

"To whom?"

"To Don Casimiro."

"And for what reason? Under what pretext has he been able to accept it?"

"He has accepted it for a reason that he promises to keep to himself, for a secret reason."

"Good Lord! What insanity! What a useless sacrifice! And tell me ... this secret reason ... Entrust to Don Casimiro like that the honor of an illustrious family!"

"I've entrusted nothing to him."

"Then, what means did you use?"

"A lie, but an indispensable lie, and one whereby nobody loses."

"Can I know what this lie is?"

–Todo lo va usted a saber.

El padre prestó la mayor atención. Don Fadrique prosiguió diciendo:

–De sobra sabe usted que Paca, la primera mujer del tío Gorico, fue una mala pécora.

–Es evidente. Dios la haya perdonado.

–La buena reputación de Paca no tiene nada que perder.

–Absolutamente nada.

–Pues bien. Hay la feliz coincidencia de que Nicolasa nació pocos meses después de mi ida de Villabermeja, cuando estuve allí de vuelta de La Habana.

–¿Y qué?

–He hecho creer primero a la chacha Ramoncica, con el mayor sigilo, que Nicolasa es hija mía. Le he dicho que un deber imperioso de conciencia me obliga a dotarla, ahora que ella se va a casar. La chacha entiende poco de números. Se ha espantado, no obstante, de la enorme cantidad que yo quería dar por dote; pero la he echado de espléndido y me he supuesto más rico de lo que soy. A las observaciones que la chacha me ha hecho, he respondido que mi resolución era irrevocable. He persuadido, por último, a la chacha de que no conviene que Nicolasa sepa los lazos que a ella me unen, y que es más delicado y honesto que lo sepa sólo el sujeto que va a ser su marido. He logrado, pues, que la chacha se encargue de persuadir a don Casimiro a que tome lo que libre, aunque misteriosamente, quiero dar y doy a su futura. No creo que la chacha haya tenido que hacer grandes gastos de elocuencia para convencer a don Casimiro de que debe aceptar. Don Casimiro me ha escrito esta carta, donde me dice que acepta, me colma de elogios por mi generosidad, y me promete callar el motivo de la donación que le hago, y la misma donación, hasta donde sea posible.

El padre Jacinto leyó la carta que le entregó don Fadrique. Luego sacó éste del bolsillo un paquete de papeles. Le puso sobre la mesa, y dijo:

–Aquí están los papeles todos que se requieren para formalizar la donación, la cual deseo que se lleve a feliz término por medio de usted. Éste es el poder más amplio, otorgado ante un escribano de esta ciudad, para que usted disponga, venda, enajene y haga lo que convenga con todo cuanto me pertenece. Estas son las cartas a los banqueros que tienen fondos míos, poniéndolos todos a la orden de usted. Ésta, por último, es la lista, inventario, cuenta o como quiera llamarse, de lo que en poder

"You're going to know everything."

The priest gave him his fullest attention. Don Fadrique continued:

"You're well aware that Paca, Tío Gorico's first wife, was a real jezebel."

"For certain. May God have forgiven her."

"Paca's good reputation has nothing to lose."

"Absolutely nothing."

"All right, then. By a happy coincidence Nicolasa was born a few months after my departure from Villabermeja, when I was there following my return from Havana."

"So?"

"So, first I've made Chacha Ramoncica believe, with the utmost secrecy, that Nicolasa is my daughter. I told her that an overriding duty of conscience compels me to give her a dowry now that she's going to marry. Chacha understands very little about numbers. She was astounded, though, by the enormous sum that I wanted to give, but I put on airs of magnificence and made myself look richer than I am. When she raised objections I said that my decision was irrevocable. Lastly, I persuaded Chacha that it's not good for Nicolasa to know of the 'tie' between us, and that it is more tactful and proper that it be known only by the man who is going to be her husband. I managed, therefore, to get Chacha to persuade Don Casimiro to accept what I freely, although mysteriously, want to give and do give to his fiancée. I don't believe that Chacha had to be especially eloquent in order to convince Don Casimiro that he should accept. Don Casimiro has written me this letter, in which he says that he does accept, heaps praises on me for my generosity, and promises to keep secret the reason for the gift I'm giving him, and the gift itself, to the extent possible."

Father Jacinto read the letter that Don Fadrique handed him. The latter then withdrew from his pocket a sheaf of papers. He set it on the table and said:

"Here are all the documents that are required to formalize the gift, which I would like to be brought to a happy end through your good offices. This is full authority, granted by me before a notary of this city, for you to allocate, sell, transfer, and do whatever may be necessary with all that belongs to me. These are the letters to the bankers who hold funds of mine, authorizing you access to them. This paper, lastly, is the list, inventory, accounting, or whatever it is called, of the amount of the

de dichos banqueros tengo hasta ahora; y esta otra es la cuenta de lo que valen los bienes de don Valentín, justipreciados por peritos. Escasamente llegará lo mío a cubrir el importe de lo que disfruta dicho señor; pero usted sabe que poseo algunas finquillas, y, si fuere menester, supliré la falta. Querido maestro, usted va a ser ejecutor fiel y pronto de mi decidida voluntad, de la cual pretendo que dé usted noticia y testimonio a doña Blanca, exigiéndole en cambio de mi parte la libertad de mi hija. Y digo exigiéndole la libertad de mi hija, porque si no le da libertad, si no procura quitarle de la cabeza tanto insano delirio, si no determina curarla de la mortal enfermedad de alma y de cuerpo, que su orgullo, su fanatismo y sus remordimientos, mil veces más odiosos que el pecado, han hecho nacer, yo me he de vengar, dando el más insolente escándalo que se ha dado jamás en el mundo. Espero que aceptará usted gustoso mi encargo.

–Le acepto– respondió el padre –; mas no sin condiciones. Yo no he de ser instrumento de tu ruina, si tu ruina es inútil.

–¿Y por qué inútil?

–Porque Clara, a mi ver, no desistirá ya de tomar el velo.

–¿Cómo que no desistirá? Sobre Clara pesa el yugo férreo de su madre. Quitémosle ese yugo, y Clara volverá a vivir, y volverá a amar a su gallardo estudiante, y se casará con él, y será dichosa.

–Lo dudo.

–Yo no lo dudo. Lo que no me explico es cómo se ha vuelto usted tan tétrico.

–Me parece que es ya tarde,– dijo el padre Jacinto, suspirando.

–Voto al mismo Satanás– replicó don Fadrique –: no es tarde aún, si la dicha es buena. Vaya usted hoy mismo a ver a doña Blanca. Infórmela de todo. Convénzala de que es libre Clara; de que los bienes que de don Valentín ha de heredar están ya pagados. Sepa doña Blanca que yo rescato misteriosamente a nuestra hija. Sepa también que si no admite ella el rescate, romperé todo freno; lo diré todo; seré capaz de una villanía; la deshonraré en público; leeré a don Valentín cartas que aún de ella conservo; haré doscientas mil barbaridades.

–Vamos, hombre, modérate. En seguida iré a hablar con doña Blanca. Ella es madrugadora. Estará ya de punta y me recibirá. Aguárdame en tu casa, y allá acudiré a referirte mi entrevista.

monies I currently have in the hands of said bankers, and this other one is the accounting of the worth of Don Valentín's assets, appraised by experts. My holdings will just barely cover the total of his net worth, but you know that I possess a few small country estates, and should it become necessary, I'll have the means to make up the shortfall. Dear master, you are going to be the prompt, faithful executor of my resolute will, of which I ask that you give notice and testimony to Doña Blanca, requiring of her in exchange for my acts the freedom of my daughter. And I say requiring of her the freedom of my daughter, because if she does not give her her freedom, if she does not try to rid her head of so many insane manias, if she does not decide to cure her of the mortal illness of body and soul that her pride, her fanaticism and her remorse – a thousand times more odious than her sin – have brought about, I will avenge myself by causing the most barefaced scandal the world has ever known. I hope that you will readily agree to my request."

"I will," said the priest, "but not without conditions. I am not going to be the instrument of your ruin, if your ruin is in vain."

"And why in vain?"

"Because in my view, at this point Clara will not desist from taking the veil."

"What do you mean she won't desist? The iron yoke of her mother weighs on Clara. Let's remove that yoke, and Clara will live again, she'll love her dashing student again, and she'll marry him and be happy."

"I doubt it."

"I don't. What puzzles me is how you have become so pessimistic."

"I think it's already too late," said Father Jacinto, sighing.

"The devil you say!" exclaimed Don Fadrique. "It's not too late yet if fortune smiles. Go this very day to see Doña Blanca. Tell her everything. Convince her that Clara is free, that the assets she is to inherit from Don Valentín are now paid for. Let Doña Blanca know that I am secretly ransoming our daughter. Let her also know that if she does not recognize the ransom I won't treat her with kid gloves. I'll spill everything; I'll be capable of doing something despicable; I'll dishonor her publicly; I'll read to Don Valentín letters of hers that I still have; I'll do no end of barbarous things."

"All right now. Come on, calm down. I'll go and talk to Doña Blanca at once. She's an early riser, so she'll be up already and will receive me. Wait for me at your house and I'll go there to tell you about my meeting."

–En casa aguardaré a usted. Apresúrese, padre, porque estoy devorado por la impaciencia.

Dicho esto, el fraile y don Fadrique se levantaron y salieron juntos de la celda a la calle, por la cual caminaron en silencio, hasta que el uno entró en casa de su hermano y el otro en casa de doña Blanca Roldán.

Dando paseos por su estancia, despidiendo desabridamente a la curiosa Lucía, que asomó la rubia cabeza a la puerta, y preguntó, como de costumbre, qué había de nuevo, y lleno todo de agitación, esperó don Fadrique más de hora y media.

El fraile llegó al cabo; pero, antes de que abriese los labios, columbró don Fadrique, en lo melancólico que venía, que era portador de malas nuevas.

No bien entrado el fraile, cerró la puerta con llave el comendador, para que nadie viniese a interrumpirlos, y en voz baja dijo, mientras él y su maestro tomaban asiento:

–Cuente usted lo que ha pasado. No me oculte nada.

–Hablaré en resumen porque ha sido larga la discusión. Doña Blanca ha celebrado tu generosidad. Dice que no atina a comprender cómo un impío es capaz de acción tan noble. Supone que es obra del orgullo; pero al fin la celebra. Mas no por esto te excita a que consumes el sacrificio. Afirma que será inútil, y te ruega que no le hagas. Doña Blanca considera que su hija tiene hoy una verdadera vocación; que Dios la llama a ser su esposa; que Dios la quiere apartar de los peligros del mundo; que Dios quiere salvarla, y que ella no puede, sin gravísima culpa, retraer ahora a su hija de tan santos propósitos.

–¡Hipocresía! ¡Refinamiento de maldad!– interrumpió don Fadrique –. ¿Y usted no la ha amenazado con mi venganza? ¿No le ha dicho usted que estoy determinado a todo: que le arrancaré la máscara; que se acordará de mí; que la burla que de mí hace no quedará sin afrentoso castigo?

–Se lo he dicho todo; pero doña Blanca ha contestado que, si bien te cree un hombre sin religión, todavía te tiene por caballero, y que no teme de ti esas villanas e infames acciones con que en tu rabia la amenazas. Añade, no obstante, que, aun cuando se engañase, aun cuando tú te olvidases de la honra y te vengases así, lo sufriría todo antes de disuadir a su hija contra lo que la conciencia le dicta.

"Agreed. Hurry, Father, because I am consumed with impatience."

Having concluded their talk, the friar and the commander got up from their seats and left the cell together. They walked along the street in silence until the one entered his brother's house and the other that of Doña Blanca Roldán.

Pacing back and forth in his room, brusquely dismissing the curious Lucía, who poked her blond head around the door and asked, as usual, what was new, a wholly agitated Don Fadrique waited for more than an hour and a half.

The friar finally arrived, but before he opened his mouth Don Fadrique surmised from his gloomy expression that he was the bearer of bad tidings.

No sooner did the friar enter the room than the commander locked the door, so that no one would interrupt them. Then, while he and his master were taking a seat, he said in a low voice:

"Tell me what happened. Don't hold anything back."

"I'll sum up the conversation because it was a long one. Doña Blanca praised your generosity. She says she can't understand how an infidel could be capable of such a noble act. She assumes that it was the work of pride, but still praises it. But not for that reason does she urge you to carry out the sacrifice. She says that it would be futile and begs you not to do it. Doña Blanca considers that her daughter now has a true vocation; that God calls her to be his spouse; that God wishes to remove her from the dangers of the world; that God wishes to save her, and that she cannot, without committing the gravest sin, dissuade her daughter now from such a holy intention."

"Hypocrisy! Refinement of evil!" interrupted Don Fadrique. "And you didn't threaten her with my revenge? You didn't tell her that I am determined to do whatever is necessary? That I'll tear the mask off of her? That I'll show her? That her mockery of me will not go without humiliating punishment?"

"I told her everything, but Doña Blanca replied that although she believes you to be a man without religion, she still believes you are a gentleman, and that she does not fear those villainous and infamous acts with which you threaten her in your rage. She adds, nonetheless, that even if she were mistaken, even if you were to forget about honor and took revenge in such a manner, she would suffer it all before dissuading her daughter from the dictates of her conscience."

–Esa mujer está loca, padre Jacinto. Esa mujer está loca, y creo que su locura es contagiosa; que a Clara y a usted los tiene ya enloquecidos, y que falta poco para que yo también lo esté. Pero, lo juro por mi honor, por Dios, por lo más sagrado: mi locura será de muy diversa índole. Soñará con mi locura. Pues qué, ¿imagina que soy yo un segundo don Valentín? ¿Piensa que me someteré a sus monstruosos caprichos? ¿Entiende que soy necio y que voy a creer lo que a ella se le antoje hacerme creer? Clara tiene trastornada la cabeza, y por eso quiere ser monja de repente. ¿Qué vocación ha de tener, cuando me consta que estaba, que está aún, enamorada de ese muchacho rondeño, con quien podría ser felicísima? Aquí hay algún misterio abominable. Algo se ha hecho para infundir el delirio en Clara y perturbar su natural despejo. Yo ni puedo, ni quiero, ni debo consentir extravagancias tan criminales. ¿No comprende esa mujer de Satanás que la educación que ha dado a su hija, que esos terrores que le ha infundido son como un veneno? ¿Quiere saciar el odio que me tiene asesinando a su hija, porque también es mi hija?

–Comendador, ten sangre fría; mira que te engañas. Mira que Clara no siente hoy la vocación religiosa por causa de su madre.

–Me importa poco que sea hoy o ayer cuando su madre le ha dado la ponzoña. El corazón me dice que las rarezas, que los extravíos de Clara provienen del tormento espiritual que le está dando su madre desde que la niña tiene uso de razón. Esto es menester que acabe. Si Clara, cuando esté en completa tranquilidad y serenidad de espíritu, sanos su cuerpo y su alma, persiste en ser monja, que lo sea: yo no me opondré. Mi sacrificio habrá sido inútil. No exhalaré una queja. Que disfrute de todos mis bienes don Casimiro. Pero mientras Clara esté enferma, casi fuera de sí, con una especie de fiebre continua, no he de sufrir que se tome ese estado febril por éxtasis místico, y esos ataques nerviosos por llamamientos del cielo. Es mi hija, voto a quince mil demonios, y no quiero que me la maten. Ahora mismo voy a ver a doña Blanca. Romperé la consigna para entrar. Romperé la cabeza a quien quiera oponerse a mi entrada. Si no la veo y la hablo, estallo como una bomba. No me detenga usted, padre Jacinto. Déjeme usted salir.

El comendador había abierto la puerta, se había puesto el sombrero, y forcejeaba por salir con el padre Jacinto, que procuraba detenerle.

"That woman is mad, Father Jacinto. That woman is mad, and I believe that her madness is contagious, and that she has driven Clara and you mad, with me well on the way. But I swear by my honor, by God, by what is most sacred: my madness will be of a very different kind. She'll dream about my madness. What does she think? That I'm a second Don Valentín? Does she expect that I'll submit to her monstrous whims? Has she got it in her head that I'm a fool and that I'm going to believe whatever she has a mind to make me believe? Clara's become unhinged and for that reason wishes to be a nun all of a sudden. What vocation can she have, when I know for sure that she was, that she still is, in love with that youth from Ronda, with whom she could be happy beyond words? There's some abominable mystery here. Something has been done to instill this mania in Clara and to upset her natural clear-sightedness. I neither can, nor want, nor ought to consent to such criminal extravagances. Doesn't that satanic woman understand that the education she has given her daughter, that those terrors she has instilled in her, are like a poison? Does she want to sate the hatred she has for me by murdering her daughter, because she is my daughter too?"

"Commander, sang-froid is called for. You're wrong. Clara does not feel a religious vocation today on account of her mother."

"It's of little import to me whether it be today or yesterday that her mother gave her the poison. My heart tells me that Clara's oddities, that Clara's aberrations, stem from the spiritual torment inflicted on her ever since the girl has had the power of reasoning. This must come to a stop. If Clara, when she is completely at peace and serene of spirit, sound of body and mind, persists in becoming a nun, so be it; I won't oppose her decision. My sacrifice will have been in vain. I'll not utter a complaint. Let Don Casimiro enjoy all my assets. But while Clara is ill, nearly deranged, with a kind of never-ending fever, I will not put up with this feverish state being taken for mystic ecstasies, and those nervous attacks for calls from heaven. She is my daughter – confound it! – and I don't want her to be killed. I'm going to go see Doña Blanca right now. I'll defy her orders to gain entry. I'll beat down anyone who tries to prevent me. If I don't see her and talk to her, I will explode like a bomb. Don't stop me, Father Jacinto. Let me go."

The commander had opened the door, had put his hat on, and, in order to make his exit, was struggling with Father Jacinto, who was trying to restrain him.

–Quien está desatinado eres tú– decía el padre –. ¿A dónde vas? ¿No calculas el escándalo de lo que te propones hacer?

–Déjeme usted, padre. Yo no calculo nada.

–Esto es una perdición. Dios te ha dejado de su mano. Oye cuatro palabras con reposo y haz luego lo que quieras. Carezco de fuerzas para detenerte.

El padre Jacinto cedió en su resistencia y el comendador se paró a escucharle.

–Quieres ver a doña Blanca, y la verás, pero con menos peligro de lances y de escándalo. Pasado mañana va don Valentín a la casería con el aperador, a vender unas tinajas de vino. Entonces podrás ver y hablar a doña Blanca. Para evitar mayores males, te llevaré yo mismo. Yo entretendré a Clara a fin de que hables a solas con doña Blanca y le digas cuanto tienes que decirle. Ya ves a lo que me allano. Ya ves a lo que me comprometo. Vas a sorprender desagradablemente a doña Blanca con tu inesperada visita. Vuestra conversación va a tener algo de un duelo a muerte; mas prefiero intervenir en él, ser cómplice en el delito de vuestro espantoso diálogo, a que sucedan cosas peores. Por las ánimas benditas, comendador: aguarda hasta pasado mañana. Vendrás conmigo. Verás a doña Blanca. Por la amistad que me tienes, por la pasión y muerte de Cristo te suplico que te calmes para entonces, y trates de que sea lo menos cruel posible la entrevista que te voy a procurar.

El comendador cedió a todo y agradeció al padre Jacinto los consejos que le daba y la protección que le ofrecía.

24

Con febril impaciencia aguardó don Fadrique el plazo que el padre le había pedido.

No hay plazo que no se cumpla, y dicho plazo se cumplió al cabo. Cumpliéronse también los pronósticos del padre. Don Valentín salió aquel día muy de mañana con el aperador para ir a la casería, de donde no pensaba volver hasta la noche.

El comendador, que lo espiaba todo, se preparó para la entrevista prometida. El padre Jacinto no se hizo aguardar mucho tiempo y vino a buscarle.

"The one who's acting like a madcap is you," said the priest. "Where are you going? Have you no idea of the scandal you're contemplating?"

"Let me go, Father. I don't care."

"This is a calamity. God has abandoned you. Hear me out calmly and then do whatever you wish. I lack the strength to restrain you."

Father Jacinto ended his resistance and the commander stopped to listen to him.

"You want to see Doña Blanca, and you will, but with less risk of a row and a scandal. The day after tomorrow Don Valentín is going to the country estate with the overseer to sell some jars of wine. Then you'll be able to see and talk to Doña Blanca. In order to avoid greater evils, I'll take you myself. I'll entertain Clara so that you can speak alone to Doña Blanca and say everything that you have to say to her. You see what I'm stooping to. You see what I'm getting involved in. You're going to surprise Doña Blanca, and unpleasantly, with your unexpected visit. Your conversation will be something like a duel to the death, but I prefer to intervene in it, to be an accomplice in the crime of your terrible exchange, rather than see worse things happen. By the souls in purgatory, Commander, wait until the day after tomorrow. You'll come with me. You'll see Doña Blanca. In the name of our friendship, in the name of the passion and death of Christ, I beg you to remain calm until then, and to try to make as little cruel as possible the meeting I'm going to arrange for you."

The commander yielded to everything and thanked Father Jacinto for the counsel that he gave him and for the protection that he offered him.

24

With feverish impatience, Don Fadrique waited for the time limit that the priest had set for him.

There is none that is not fulfilled, and that one finally was. Also fulfilled were the priest's predictions. That day Don Valentín left very early in the morning with the overseer to go to the country estate, from which he did not intend to return until evening.

The commander, who was keeping watch on everything, made ready for the promised meeting. Father Jacinto did not tarry and soon came for him.

Reconociendo que lo menos peligroso, lo menos ocasionado a males, era que se viesen ambos cómplices, por si lograban entenderse y convenir en algo acerca de la hermosa Clarita, no quiso el padre hablar con doña Blanca y proponerle una conferencia con el comendador. Tenía por seguro que se negaría, y que, ya sobre aviso, le haría más difícil, casi imposible, el hacer entrar al comendador hasta donde ella estuviese. Así, pues, se resolvió por la sorpresa. Sabía las costumbres de la casa, sabía las horas de todo, y todo lo dispuso con sencillez y habilidad.

Antes de las diez de la mañana, una hora después del almuerzo, Clara se retiraba a su cuarto, y doña Blanca se quedaba sola en la sala donde estaba de diario.

El padre se puso en marcha en punto de las diez llevando al comendador en pos de sí. Entraron en el zaguán, y el padre dio dos aldabonazos.

La voz de una criada gritó desde arriba:

–¿Quién es?

–Ave María Purísima. Gente de paz– contestó el padre.

La moza, que reconoció la voz, tiró del cordel desde un balcón del piso principal, que daba al patio. Con este cordel se abría la puerta sin bajar la escalera.

La puerta se abrió, y entraron el comendador y el fraile, sin que los viese nadie, ni la misma criada que les había abierto, pues entre el patio, a donde daba el balcón en que se hallaba la criada, y la puerta de la calle, había otro zaguán, del cual arrancaba la escalera principal o de los señores.

No bien entró el padre Jacinto con su compañero, cerró de nuevo la puerta y dijo en voz alta:

–Dios te guarde, muchacha.

–Dios guarde a su merced– contestó ella.

Entonces el comendador y su guía subieron rápidamente la escalera. Ya en la antesala, donde tampoco había un alma, dijo el fraile a don Fadrique señalándole una puerta:

–Allí está doña Blanca. Entra... háblale: pero ten juicio.

Don Fadrique, con ánimo decidido, con verdadero denuedo, se dirigió a la puerta señalada, entró, y la volvió a cerrar.

No bien desapareció don Fadrique, llegó la criada.

Recognizing that the least dangerous approach, the least likely to trigger dire consequences was to have both parties come face to face to see whether they could understand each other and reach an agreement concerning the beautiful Clarita, the priest did not want to talk to Doña Blanca himself and propose to her that she meet with the commander. He was certain that she would refuse, and that, forewarned now, she would make it more difficult, well-nigh impossible for him to bring the commander to where she was. So for that reason he decided on a surprise. He knew the routine of the house, knew the hours when things were done, and arranged everything simply and cleverly.

Before ten o'clock in the morning, an hour after breakfast, Clara withdrew to her room and Doña Blanca remained alone in the drawing room, where she was to be found everyday.

The priest started out at ten o'clock on the dot, taking the commander with him. They entered the vestibule and the priest knocked twice on the door.

A servant girl called out from above:

"Who is it?"

"God bless this house.[87] Peace-loving people," answered the priest.

The girl, who recognized the voice, pulled a cord from a main-floor balcony that gave onto the patio. With this cord the door could be opened without going down the stairway to do it.

The door opened and the commander and the friar entered without being seen by anyone, not even by the servant girl who had opened it for them, because between the patio, onto which gave the balcony where she stood, and the street door, there was another vestibule from which rose the main or family stairway.

As soon as Father Jacinto entered with his companion, he closed the door again and said out loud:

"God be with you, girl."

"God be with your Reverence," replied the girl.

Then the commander and his guide swiftly climbed the stairs. In the anteroom, where nary a soul was to be found either, the friar said to Don Fadrique, pointing to a door:

"Doña Blanca is in there. Go in and talk to her, but use your head."

With a resolute will, with true boldness, Don Fadrique walked over to the indicated door, stepped inside, and closed it behind him.

No sooner did Don Fadrique disappear than the servant girl showed up.

–¡Hola!– dijo el padre Jacinto –¿está doña Blanca sola?

–Sí, padre. ¿No entra su merced a verla?

–No; más tarde. Déjala tranquila. No entres ahora, que estará ocupada en sus negocios. No la distraigamos. ¿Está Clarita en su cuarto?

–Sí, padre.

–Ea, vete a tus quehaceres, que yo voy a ver a Clarita.

Y, en efecto, el padre Jacinto y la criada se fueron por su lado cada uno.

Entre tanto, don Fadrique se hallaba ya en presencia de doña Blanca, sorprendida, pasmada, enojada de tan imprevisto atrevimiento. Sentada en un sillón de brazos, había levantado la cabeza al sonar el pestillo y la puerta que se abría, había visto que la volvía a cerrar quien había entrado, había reconocido al punto al comendador, y aún casi inmóvil, silenciosa, le miraba de hito en hito, sospechaba si estaría soñando, y apenas si se atrevía a dar crédito a sus ojos.

El comendador se adelantó lentamente dos o tres pasos.

No saludó de palabra; no pronunció una sola; no hallaba, sin duda, fórmula de saludo que no disonase en aquella ocasión; pero con el gesto, con el ademán, con la expresión de toda su fisonomía, mostraba que era un caballero respetuoso que pedía humildemente perdón de la astucia y de la audacia que se había visto obligado a emplear para llegar hasta allí. En su rostro se leían las disculpas que de palabra no daba. Si atropellaba respetos, lo hacía con razón suficiente. A par de estas cosas, se leía asimismo en el ¿rostro varonil del comendador la firme resolución de no salir de allí hasta que no se le oyese.

Doña Blanca se hizo al punto cargo de todo esto. Conocía tan bien a aquel hombre, que no necesitaba a veces oírle hablar para penetrar sus intenciones y sus sentimientos. Doña Blanca comprendió que lo menos malo era oírle; que no podía echarle sin exponerse a dar el mayor de los escándalos. No quiso, sin embargo, aparecer desde luego resignada. Se alzó de su asiento, y antes de que el comendador hablase, le dijo:

–Váyase usted, don Fadrique, váyase usted. ¿Qué palabras, qué explicaciones pueden mediar entre nosotros que no produzcan una tempestad, sobre todo si nos hablamos sin testigos? ¿Para qué me busca usted? ¿Para qué me provoca? No podemos hablarnos; apenas si podemos mirarnos sin herirnos de muerte. ¿Es usted tan cruel, que desea matarme?

–Señora– contestó el comendador –: si no creyese que cumplo un

"Hello," said Father Jacinto. "Is Doña Blanca alone?"

"Yes, Father. Isn't your Reverence going in to see her?"

"No. Later on. Ler her be. Don't go in now, as she's probably occupied with business matters. Let's not distract her. Is Clarita in her room?"

"Yes, Father."

"All right, then, go about your chores, because I'm off to see Clarita." And Father Jacinto and the servant girl then went their separate ways.

Meanwhile, Don Fadrique found himself in the presence of Doña Blanca, who was surprised, astonished, and furious at such unexpected audacity. Sitting in an armchair, she had raised her head at the sound of the latch and the door being opened, had seen that whoever had come in was closing it, had recognized the commander at once, and still almost motionless and silent, was staring at him, wondering whether she was dreaming, and scarcely dared to believe her eyes.

Moving slowly, the commander took two or three steps forward.

He spoke not a single word of greeting, as he no doubt failed to hit upon one that would not be out of keeping with the occasion, but with his expression, his attitude, and all his features he proclaimed that he was a respectful gentleman humbly asking forgiveness for the ruse and the audacity that he had been compelled to use in order to enter her drawing room. On his face you could see the apologies that he did not make verbally. If he trampled sensibilities, he had his reasons. Along with these things, you could likewise read on the commander's manly face the firm resolve not to leave there until he was heard.

Doña Blanca realized all this instantly. She knew that man so well that at times she did not need to hear him speak in order to see through his intentions and his feelings. Doña Blanca understood that the least disastrous response was to listen to him, that she could not have him thrown out without exposing herself to the mother of all scandals. She refused, though, to appear immediately resigned. She rose from her seat, and before the commander could speak, said to him:

"Go away, Don Fadrique, go away. What words, what explanations can be spoken between us that won't kick up a storm, especially if we speak to each other without witnesses? Why do you seek me out? Why do you provoke me? We can't talk to each other; we can scarcely look at each other without inflicting mortal wounds. Are you so cruel that you wish to kill me?"

"Señora," replied the commander, "if I didn't believe that I was

deber imperioso viniendo hasta aquí, no hubiera venido. Cuando penetro furtivamente en esta sala es porque tengo razones suficientes para ello.

—¿Qué razones alega usted para turbar mi reposo?

—El interés que me inspira un ser a quien me une un estrechísimo lazo.

—Muy disimulado, muy oculto ha tenido usted ese interés durante diez y seis años. No se ha acordado usted de ese ser hasta que por casualidad ha tropezado con él en su camino. Ha sido menester que salga usted de paseo con una sobrina suya, y que esta sobrina tenga una amiga, y que esta amiga vaya con ella, para que el amor paternal, que vivía latente y ni siquiera sospechado allá en las profundidades de su magnánimo corazón, se revele de pronto y dé gallarda y briosa muestra de sí. Si el acaso no nos hubiese traído a vivir en la misma población, o si Clara no hubiese sido amiga de Lucía, aunque en la misma población viviésemos, su interés de usted, su amor paternal, sus deberes imperiosos, confiéselo usted, dormirían tranquilos en el fondo de esa envidiable y harto cómoda conciencia.

—Justo es que me moteje usted. No debo defenderme. Confieso mi culpa. Voy, con todo, a tratar de explicarla y de atenuarla. Yo no podía sospechar que al lado de usted, bajo el amparo de una madre cariñosa, corriese mi hija ningún peligro, hallase motivo para ser desventurada.

—Su desventura no proviene de mí solamente. Su desventura proviene del pecado en que fue concebida, y del cual ni usted ni yo, que somos los pecadores, podemos salvarla ni redimirla.

—Ella no es responsable: nadie es responsable de faltas que no comete. Esa transmisión es un absurdo. Es una blasfemia contra la soberana justicia y la bondad del Eterno.

—No llevemos la conversación por ese camino, señor don Fadrique. Si a usted le parece blasfemia lo que yo creo, impiedad y blasfemia me parece a mí cuanto usted dice y piensa. ¿A qué, pues, hablar conmigo de Dios? Deje usted a Dios tranquilo, si por dicha cree en Él, allá a su modo. La desventura de mi hija, llámela usted falta, llámela como guste, procede de su nacimiento. Pues qué, ¿no ha reconocido usted mismo esa desventura, al querer librar de ella a mi hija haciendo un gran sacrificio, que yo le agradezco, pero que juzgo ya inútil?

fulfilling an imperative duty by coming here, I would not have come. When I enter this room in a furtive manner it's because I have powerful reasons to do so."

"What reasons do you cite for coming to disturb my peace?"

"The interest inspired in me by a being to whom I am bound by a very close tie."

"Well, you have kept that interest under wraps and hidden for sixteen years. You didn't remember that being until you ran into her by chance on your journey through life. It was necessary for you to go for a walk with a niece of yours, and for this niece to have a friend, and for this friend to go with her, for your paternal love, which existed in a latent state, not even suspected in the depths of your magnanimous heart, to reveal itself promptly and to give a splendid and spirited account of itself. If chance had not brought us to live in the same city, or if Clara had not been Lucía's friend, even though we lived in the same place, your interest, your paternal love, your imperative duty – confess it – would be peacefully asleep in the depths of that enviable and most comfortable conscience."

"It's only right that you should censure me. I ought not to defend myself. I confess my guilt. However, I am going to try to explain it and to attenuate it. I couldn't suspect that at your side, under the protection of an affectionate mother, my daughter would be in any danger, would have any reason to be unhappy."

"Her unhappiness does not stem from me only. Her unhappiness stems from the sin in which she was conceived, and from which neither you nor I, who are the sinners, can save her or redeem her."

"She is not responsible. Nobody is responsible for misdeeds they don't commit. That transmission is an absurdity. It's a blasphemy against the sovereign justice and goodness of the Eternal Father."

"Let's not steer the conversation in that direction, Señor don Fadrique. If what I believe seems like blasphemy to you, everything that you say and think seems like ungodliness and blasphemy to me. To what end, then, do you speak to me of God? Leave God alone, if by chance you believe in him, in your way. My daughter's unhappiness – call it fatal, call it what you will – springs from her birth. What did you expect? Haven't you yourself acknowledged that unhappiness when you wished to rescue my daughter from it by making a great sacrifice, for which I thank you, but which I regard as useless now?"

–Alguna verdad hay en lo que usted dice. Yo reconozco que Clara, sin culpa, estaba condenada por la suerte o a sacrificarse o a ser una usurpadora indigna.

–Estamos de acuerdo, salvo que donde usted dice por la suerte, digo yo el pecado, y no por el pecado de ella, sino por el pecado de otros. Esto es inicuo para usted, que no acata los inescrutables designios de la Providencia. Esto es sólo misterioso para mí. Por eso es mejor no tocar tales cuestiones. Hablemos de aquello en que convenimos. Convenimos en que Clara estaba, sin culpa suya, condenada a una pena.

–Convenimos; pero convenga usted también en que yo la he libertado.

–Si la ha liberado usted, habrá sido por una serie de casos fortuitos: porque vio usted a Clara y la reconoció; porque Clara es bonita, ya que, si hubiera sido fea, no se hubiera usted entusiasmado tanto, ni la vanidad de padre hubiera provocado con ímpetu el amor de padre, y porque, en suma, tiene usted bastante dinero que dar, y halla usted un hidalgo con bastante poca vergüenza para tomarle sin motivo justificado.

–A mi vez suplico yo también a usted que no entremos en cuestiones inútiles. Yo no he venido aquí a discretear ni a filosofar.

–Yo no discreteo ni filosofo. Digo lo que es cierto. El pecado no fue un acaso; no fue algo independiente de nuestro libre albedrío. El que usted haya encontrado a Clara; el que ella sea bonita, por donde juzga usted que no debe casarse con don Casimiro ni ser monja, y el que tenga usted más de cuatro millones, no son cosas que de su voluntad de usted han dependido. Para usted son casuales, aunque por Dios estuviesen previstas y preparadas, como lo está cuanto ocurre en el universo.

–Vamos, señora, no apure usted mi paciencia. Tan casual será todo eso, como el haber yo encontrado a usted en Lima, el que fuese usted bonita y el que yo no fuese un monstruo de feo. Lo que no fue casual, sino voluntario, fue la caída; pero tampoco es casual, sino voluntario, el rescate. Será casual, no dependerá de mi voluntad el tener cuatro millones; pero es voluntario, es mi voluntad misma el darlos. Clara, no por casualidad, sino por un acto libre, está ya rescatada del cautiverio, al cual, según usted juzga, y no sin razón, se hallaba sometida por otro acto, que no supongo que considere usted más voluntario, más reflexionado, más meditado y más deliberado con perfecta claridad en la conciencia.

"There is some truth in what you say. I recognize that Clara, who is blameless, was condemned by fate either to sacrifice herself or to be a contemptible usurper."

"We are in agreement, except that when you say because of fate, I say because of sin, and not because of her sin, but because of the sin of others. This for you is iniquitous, as you do not heed the inscrutable designs of Providence. It is only mysterious to me. Therefore it is better not to touch upon such questions. Let us talk about the points on which we do agree. We agree that Clara, through no fault of her own, was condemned to grief."

"We are in agreement, but accept too that I have freed her."

"If you have freed her, it must have been on account of a series of fortuitous circumstances: because you saw Clara and you recognized her; because Clara is pretty, since if she had been ugly you would not have been so enthusiastic, nor would a father's vanity have stirred a father's love with such impetus; and because, in short, you have enough money to give away and you have found a nobleman with so little shame that he accepts it without justifiable cause."

"Now it's my turn to implore you not to enter into futile questions. I haven't come here to be clever or to philosophize."

"I am neither being clever nor philosophizing. I am saying what is true. The sin was not by chance; it was not something independent of our free will. The fact that you have met up with Clara; the fact that she is pretty, which prompts you to believe that she should not marry Don Casimiro nor be a nun; and the fact that you have more than four million in assets, are not things that have depended on your will. For you they are accidental, even though they were foreseen and predisposed by God, as is everything that happens in the universe."

"Come now, Señora, do not try my patience. All that is as accidental as the fact that I met you in Lima, that you were pretty, and that I was not a monster of ugliness. What was not accidental, but willful, was the fall, but neither is the rescue or ransom accidental, but willful. It might be accidental, might not depend on my will to have the four million, but it is willful, it is my will to give them away. Not by chance, but by a free act, Clara is now rescued from the captivity to which, as you believe and not without reason, she was subjected by another act, an act that I do not suppose you consider more willful, more pondered, more thought over, and more carefully weighed in your conscience with perfect clarity."

Hasta este punto el diálogo había sido de pie. Doña Blanca ni se sentaba ni ofrecía asiento al comendador. Este, después de un momento de pausa, porque doña Blanca no respondió al punto a su último razonamiento, dijo con serenidad:

–Mire usted, señora: yo no quiero que disertemos ni que divaguemos. Tengo, no obstante, mucho que hablar; y para que la conferencia sea breve, importa proceder sin desorden. El desorden no se evita sino con la comodidad y el reposo. ¿No le parece a usted, pues, que sería bueno que nos sentásemos?

Doña Blanca siguió silenciosa, lanzó una mirada al comendador, entre iracunda y despreciativa, y se dejó caer de nuevo en el sillón, como aplanada. Entonces se sentó el comendador en una silla, y prosiguió hablando.

–Mi resolución– dijo –, es irrevocable. Sea por lo que sea; por un capricho, porque Clara es bonita, porque he tropezado con ella casualmente en mi camino, por lo que a usted se le antoje, yo la he rescatado. Todo lo que herede ella por muerte de su marido de usted, lo gozará ya, con años de anticipación, el que debiera heredarle, si Clara no viviese. Viva, pues, Clara. Vengo a pedir a usted su vida.

–A lo que viene usted es a insultarme. ¿Mato yo acaso a Clara?

–Lejos de mí el propósito de insultar a usted. Sin querer, podría acaso matar a Clara, y esto es lo que vengo a evitar. Para ello estoy resuelto a apelar a todos los medios.

–¿Me amenaza usted?

–No amenazo. Declaro mi pensamiento sin rebozo.

–¿Y qué me toca hacer, según usted, para evitar que Clara muera?

–Disuadirla de que sea monja.

–Eso es imposible. Yo no creo que entrar monja sea morir, sino seguir la mejor vida.

–Ya he dicho que no discuto, ni trato de teologías con usted. Concedo, pues, que la vida del claustro es la mejor vida: pero es cuando hay vocación para seguirla; cuando no se va al claustro desesperada, casi loca, llena de desatinados terrores.

–Vuelvo a repetir a usted que me deje, señor don Fadrique. ¿Para qué hablar? Nos atormentamos y no nos entendemos. Usted llama terrores desatinados al santo temor de Dios, desesperación al menosprecio del mundo, y locura a la humildad cristiana y al recelo de caer en tentación

Till this point the conversation had continued with them on their feet. Doña Blanca had neither sat back down nor offered the commander a seat. After a moment's pause, because Doña Blanca did not respond immediately to his last line of reasoning, he said calmly:

"Look, Señora, I do not wish for us to engage in a lengthy discussion nor to digress. However, I do have much to say, and in order for our meeting to be brief, it is important to proceed without confusion. And confusion is best avoided with comfort and quiet. Do you not think, therefore, that it would be better were we to sit down?"

Still silent, Doña Blanca shot a half-irate, half-contemptuous glance at the commander and dropped back into her armchair, as though torpid. Then the commander took a seat and continued speaking.

"My decision," he said, "is irrevocable. For whatever reason: because of a whim, because Clara is pretty, because I have accidentally run into her in my journey, for whatever reason you fancy, I have rescued her. All that she will inherit by the death of your husband will now be enjoyed, years ahead of time, by the man who should have been his heir if Clara were not alive. So let Clara live. I have come to ask you for her life."

"What you have come to do is insult me. Am I by chance killing Clara?"

"I have no intention whatsoever of insulting you. Without meaning to, you might perhaps kill Clara, and this is what I have come to prevent. I am determined to resort to every means necessary."

"Are you threatening me?"

"I am not threatening. I am openly stating my resolve."

"And what am I to do, in your opinion, to prevent Clara from dying?"

"Discourage her from being a nun."

"That's impossible. I do not believe that to become a nun is to die, but to lead a better life."

"I've already said that I won't debate or discuss theology with you. I concede, though, that the life of the cloister is the better life, but that's when there is a vocation to take it up, when one doesn't enter the cloister in despair, practically mad, overcome with senseless terror."

"I repeat, and again ask you to leave me, Señor don Fadrique. Why talk? We'll only torment each other and not reach an understanding. You call senseless terror the holy fear of God; despair, disdain for the world; and madness, Christian humility and the fear of falling into temptation

y de faltar a los deberes. Usted considera muerte la vida que en este mundo se asemeja más al vivir de los ángeles. ¿Cómo, pues, hemos de entendernos? Usted me honra más de lo que merezco, pensando que me acusa, al suponer que yo he inspirado a mi hija tales ideas y tales sentimientos.

–Por amor del cielo, mi señora doña Blanca; yo no sé por quién conjurar a usted, en nombre de quién suplicarle, que no involucre las cosas, que no me oiga con prevención, que atienda al bien de su hija, y que no dude de que yo vengo aquí, la molesto con mi presencia y la mortifico con mis palabras, sin prevención también, y sólo por el deseo de ese bien impulsado. ¿Cómo he de condenar yo el santo temor de Dios, el menosprecio del mundo, si es razonable, y la humildad cristiana, que nos lleva a desconfiar de nuestra flaca y pecadora naturaleza? Lo que yo condeno es el delirio. Concedería que Clara tomase el velo, aun cuando no le tomase después de pensarlo reflexivamente; aun cuando le tomase por un rapto fervoroso de devoción; pero lo que no concedo, lo que no consiento es que le tome en un arrebato de desesperación. Sería un suicidio abominable y sacrílego.

–¿Y de dónde infiere usted que Clara está desesperada? ¿Quién se lo ha dicho a usted? ¿Qué motivos tiene ella para desesperarse?

–Nadie me lo ha dicho. Basta mirar a Clara para conocerlo. Usted misma lo conoce. No disimule usted que lo conoce. Si no temiese usted hasta por su vida corporal, ¿no hubiera ya dejado que entrase en el convento? Al darle ahora la libertad que le da, ¿no lo hace usted excitada por el deseo de que su salud mejore? En cuanto a los motivos de su desesperación, concretamente yo los ignoro; pero los percibo de cierta manera confusa. Usted la ha hecho dudar de sí más de lo que debiera: sin prever un resultado tan funesto, ha infundido usted en su espíritu que está predestinada a pecar si no busca asilo al pie de los altares. En suma, usted la ha envenenado con tal desconfianza, que ella, al sentir los latidos de su corazón juvenil y la lozanía de la vida en su verde primavera, al ver el fuego, si puro, ardiente de sus ojos, al oír la voz de la naturaleza que la incita a que ame, al soñar acaso con lícitas venturas, logradas en este mundo al lado de un ser de su misma humana condición, se ha figurado que era presa de impuras pasiones, se ha creído perseguida por los monstruos del infierno, y para no ser ella un monstruo, ha querido refugiarse en el santuario.

and failing to fulfill your duties. You see as death the life in this world that most resembles the life of the angels. How, then, are we to come to an understanding? You honor me more than I deserve, thinking that you accuse me by assuming that I have inspired such ideas and such feelings in my daughter."

"For the love of heaven, Señora doña Blanca, I don't know in whose name to beseech you, in whose name to entreat you not to turn things upside down, to hear without prejudice, to look to the well-being of your daughter, and not doubt that I have come here, that I trouble you with my presence and mortify you with my words, also without prejudice, motivated by a desire for that well-being. How am I going to condemn the holy fear of God, disdain for the world, if it is reasonable, and Christian humility, which leads us to beware of our weak and sinful nature? What I condemn is delirium, madness. I would agree to Clara's taking the veil even if she did not then take it after careful thought, even if she took it because of a fervent rapture of devotion, but what I will not agree to, what I will not consent to, is that she take it in a fit of despair. It would be an abominable, sacrilegious suicide."

"And from what do you infer that Clara is in despair? Who told you that? What reasons does she have to despair?

"Nobody has told me. It's enough to look at Clara to know. You yourself know it. Do not pretend that you don't. If you did not even fear for her physical welfare, wouldn't you have already allowed her to enter the convent? On giving her the freedom that you now give her, do you not do so moved by a desire to see an improvement in her health? As to the reasons for her despair, I have no concrete knowledge of them, but I do have a vague perception of what they are. You have made her doubt herself more than you should have; without foreseeing such a disastrous result, you have instilled into her spirit the notion that she is predestined to sin if she does not seek refuge at the foot of the altar. In short, you have poisoned her with such distrust that, feeling the pulsations of her youthful heart and the exuberance of life in its early springtime, seeing the pure and glowing fire of her eyes, hearing the voice of nature that urges her to love, dreaming perhaps of licit happiness found in this world at the side of a being of her same human condition, she has imagined that she was the prey of impure passions, she has believed that she was pursued by monsters from hell, and in order for her not to be a monster herself, she has wished to take refuge in the sanctuary."

–Demos que todo eso sea exacto– replicó imperturbable doña Blanca –. Demos que los hechos son los mismos para usted y para mí. La diferencia subsistirá siempre en la manera de apreciarlos. Si Clara se va al claustro, no ya por puro amor de Dios, sino por temor de ofenderle, por considerarse sobrado frágil para resistir las tempestades del mundo y por miedo de sí misma y del infierno, Clara, a mi ver, no desatina: Clara procede con recto juicio y consumada prudencia. Los motivos de su vocación para la vida religiosa, si no son los más elevados, son buenos. Lejos de mí el tratar de disuadirla, aunque pudiese. A fin de que goce Clara una efímera e incierta dicha en la tierra, no he de oponerme yo a que tome el camino que más derechamente pueda llevarla al cielo. No por dar gusto a usted he de aconsejar yo a Clara, cuando la nave de su vida va a entrar ya en el puerto segurísimo y abrigado, que vuelva la proa y que se engolfe en el piélago borrascoso, donde puede zozobrar y hundirse con eterno hundimiento.

–Sí– interrumpió el comendador, harto ya –, lo mejor es que se muera para que se salve.

–¿Y cómo negarlo?– respondió fuera de sí doña Blanca –. Más vale morir que pecar. Si ha de vivir para ser pecadora, para su eterna condenación, para su vergüenza y su oprobio, que muera. ¡Llévatela, Dios mío! Así me hubiera muerto yo. ¡Cuánto más me valiera no haber nacido!

–Los mismos furores de siempre. Está usted como atormentada de un espíritu maligno. Yo me lo sabía. Yo tengo la culpa de todo. Yo hubiera debido robar a mi hija de la casa de usted, y criarla conmigo, y hacerla dichosa, y darle mi nombre.

–Bendito sea Dios porque no ha sido así. ¡Criada mi hija por un impío! ¿Qué hubiera sido de ella? ¡Debe de ser repugnante una mujer sin religión!

–No sé lo que será una mujer sin religión, ni hubiera sido mi propósito que mi hija no la tuviera. Lo que sé es que una mujer exaltada por el fanatismo religioso puede hacerse insufrible.

–¡Qué feliz sería yo si tal hubiera aparecido a los ojos de usted desde el principio! ¡Cuántos males se hubieran evitado! Pero usted pensaba entonces de otra manera, y me persiguió con constancia, me pretendió con terquedad, y no hubo medio de seducción, ni mentira, ni engaño, ni blandura de regaladas palabras, ni encarecimiento de amante que muere

"Let's concede that all of what you say is true," Doña Blanca replied impassively. "Let's concede that the facts are the same for you and for me. The difference in the way we construe them will always exist. If Clara goes into the cloister, no longer for pure love of God, but for fear of offending him, for considering herself too fragile to resist the storms of the world, and for fear of herself and hell, Clara, in my opinion, does not act foolishly; Clara comports herself with sound judgment and consummate prudence. The reasons behind her vocation to the religious life, if not the most lofty ones, are good ones. Far be it from me to try to dissuade her, even if I could. So that Clara might enjoy a short-lived and uncertain happiness on earth, I shall not oppose her taking the path that can most directly lead her to heaven. Not in order to oblige you will I advise Clara, when the ship of her life is about to enter a safe and sheltered harbor, to set a new course and sail into the plangent waves of a stormy sea, where it might capsize and sink to be eternally sunk."

"Yes," interrupted the commander, at his wit's end now, "the best thing is for her to die in order to be saved."

"And how to deny that?" responded Doña Blanca, beside herself with indignation. "It's better to die than to sin. If she's to live in order to be a sinner – to her eternal condemnation, to her shame, and to her ignominy – let her die. Take her unto you, dear God! Would that I had died thus! How much better it would have been had I not been born!"

"The same frenzies, the same furors as always. You seem to be tormented by an evil spirit. I knew it. I'm to blame for everything. I should have abducted my daughter from your house, raised her with me, and made her happy, and given her my name."

"Thanks be to God that you didn't. My daughter raised by an infidel! What would have become of her? A woman without religion must be repugnant!"

"I don't know what a woman without religion might be like, nor would it have been my intent to deprive my daughter of religion. What I do know is that a woman carried away by religious fanaticism can make herself insufferable."

"How happy I would be had I appeared that way in your eyes from the very beginning! How many evils would have been avoided! But back then you thought differently and pursued me tenaciously. In a dogged way you sought me out, and there was no means of seduction, no lie, no deception, no tender, sweet-sounding words, no terms of endearment

de amor, ni promesa de darme toda el alma, que usted no emplease para vencer mi honrado desvío. Llegó usted a alucinarme hasta el extremo de anhelar yo perderme para salvar a usted, ¡Aquél sí que fue delirio! ¿Pues no llegué a soñar con que, cayendo yo, iba a ganar su alma de usted y a sacarla de la impiedad en que estaba sumida? ¿Pues no me desvanecí hasta el punto de creer que, incurriendo con usted en el pecado, había de levantarle y traerle luego conmigo en la purificación y en la penitencia? ¿De qué artificios no se vale el demonio para envolvernos en sus redes? Yo estaba ciega. Creí ver en usted un hombre extraviado que me enamoraba, que estaba prendado de mí, a quien por amor mío iba yo a cautivar el alma, haciéndola capaz de más altos amores. No advertí que ni siquiera era usted capaz del bajo y criminal amor de la tierra. Usted buscaba sólo la satisfacción de un capricho, un goce fácil, un triunfo de amor propio. Usted creyó que, una vez vencido mi desvío, que después de un instante de pasión y de abandono, todo sería paz: todo lo olvidaría yo por usted, para que usted me hallase siempre sumisa, alegre, con la risa en los labios. Usted imaginó que yo iba a matar en mi alma todo remordimiento, toda vergüenza, toda idea del deber a que había faltado, todo temor de Dios, todo respeto a mi honra, todo sentimiento amargo de su pérdida, todo miedo a las penas del infierno, todo aguijón en la conciencia. Se equivocó usted, y por eso le parecí insufrible. Era usted dueño de mi alma; pero, así como en tierra de valientes y generosos, que jamás olvidan lo que deben a su patria, sólo posee el feroz conquistador la tierra que pisa, así usted no me poseía sino cuando hasta de mí misma me olvidaba. Cuando no, me alzaba yo contra usted, trataba de limpiar mi culpa con la penitencia, y luchaba siempre por libertarme. ¿Cuánto, no obstante, hubiera debido enorgullecer a usted cada una de sus victorias, aun siendo impío, si hubiera usted acertado a comprender la grandeza sublime y tempestuosa de las grandes pasiones? Horribles eran aquellas frecuentes luchas, pero usted, cuando triunfaba, triunfaba, no sólo de mí, sino de los ángeles que me asistían, de mi fe profunda, del cielo a quien yo invocaba, del principio del honor arraigado en mi alma, y de mi conciencia acusadora y severa contra mí misma. Usted, que sólo buscaba alegría y deleite, se fatigó de luchar. Así me liberté del cautiverio infame. Alabado sea Dios, que lo dispuso. Alabado sea Dios, que ha castigado después tan justamente mi culpa; pero, se lo confieso a usted, el castigo

from a lovesick paramour, no promise to give me your entire soul, of which you did not avail yourself in order to overcome my chaste indifference. You managed to delude me to such an extreme that I longed to lose myself so as to save you. That was indeed madness! Did I not even dream that by falling I was going to win over your soul and draw it out of the ungodliness in which it was engulfed? Did I not beguile myself to the point of believing that, by committing a sin with you, I would be able to raise you up and then bring you with me to purification and penance? What stratagems does the devil not set in motion in order to ensnare us in his nets? I was blind. I thought I saw in you a man gone astray who was wooing me, who was enchanted with me, a man whose soul I was going to captivate because of his love for me, making it capable of a higher love. I didn't take heed that you were not even capable of the low and criminal earthly love. You were only looking for the satisfaction of a whim, an easy pleasure, a triumph of *amour-propre*. You believed that once my indifference was overcome, that after an instant of passion and abandon, everything would be peace: I would forget everything for you so that you would find me always submissive, cheerful, with a smile on my lips. You imagined that I was going to kill in my soul all remorse, all shame, all idea of the duty that I had betrayed, all fear of God, all respect for my honor, all bitter feeling over its loss, all dread of the pains of hell, all pangs of conscience. You were mistaken, and for that reason you thought me insufferable. You were the master of my soul, but just as in a land of brave and noble men, who never forget what they owe their native country, the fierce conqueror possesses only the ground he treads, so did you possess me only when I forgot even myself. When such was not the case, I rose up against you, I tried to erase my sin with penance, and I struggled endlessly to free myself. In spite of all that, how much would each of your victories have filled you with pride, even being impious, if only you had been able to understand the sublime and tempestuous grandeur of the great passions? Those frequent struggles were horrible, but you, when you triumphed, triumphed not only over me, but over the angels who aided me, over my profound faith, over the heaven that I invoked, over the principle of honor rooted in my soul, and over my conscience, which was severe in reproaching me. You, who only sought joy and pleasure, wearied of struggling. Thus did I free myself from the infamous captivity. Praised be God, who brought it about. Praised be God, who afterwards so justly punished my sin. But, I

que más me ha dolido siempre, el que más me duele todavía, es el tener
que despreciar al hombre que he amado. Ya lo sabe usted. Usted me
halla insufrible: yo le hallo a usted despreciable. Váyase de aquí. Salga
de aquí, o haré que le echen. ¿Quiere usted delatarme? ¿Quiere usted
declararme culpada? Hágalo. No temo ya desventura ni humillación por
grande que sea. Sépalo usted de una vez para siempre: me alegro de que
Clara entre en un convento. No seré tan vil, que por miedo de usted falte
a mi deber inculcándole lo contrario. Ahora, márchese; salga de mi casa;
déjeme tranquila.

Doña Blanca, puesta de pie otra vez, con ademán imperioso, señalando
la puerta con la mano, expulsaba al comendador. ¿Qué debía de hacer,
qué había de contestar éste? Doña Blanca pareció frenética a los ojos
del comendador, lleno de piedad y casi de susto. Temió ser cruel y mal
caballero si respondía. Guardó silencio. Vio el asunto perdido, al menos
por aquel lado, y no quiso prolongar más el doble martirio.

Don Fadrique inclinó la cabeza y salió de la sala harto apesadumbrado.
Apenas se vio en la antesala, bajó la escalera, abrió la puerta del zaguán,
y se lanzó a la calle, respirando con delicia el ambiente, como quien
se está ahogando y logra sacar la cabeza del agua en que se hallaba
sumergida.

25

A pesar de su optimista y regocijada filosofía; a pesar de su propensión
natural a reír y a ver las cosas por el lado cómico, don Fadrique estuvo
todo aquel día meditabundo, callado, con una seriedad melancólica harto
extraña en él.

A la hora de comer apenas si probó bocado; apenas si habló con su
hermano, con su cuñada y con su sobrina, los cuales, cada uno por su
estilo, le agasajaban mucho.

Don José era un señor excelente, que no hacía más que cuidar de su
hacienda, jugar a la malilla en la reunión de la botica, y dar gusto a doña
Antonia.

Esta señora tenía una pasta de las mejores: cuidaba de la casa con
esmero, cosía y bordaba. Era buena cristiana; iba a misa todos los

will confess to you, the punishment that has always pained me most, the one that still pains me, is having to despise the man I once loved. Now you know. You find me insufferable; I find you despicable. Leave this house. Go away from here or I'll have you thrown out. Do you want to betray me? Do you want to declare me the guilty party? Go ahead. I no longer fear the misfortune or humiliation, however great either one may be. Know once and for all: I rejoice that Clara is entering a convent. I will not be so base that, for fear of you, I fail in my duty by prevailing upon her to do the contrary. Now go away. Get out of my house. Leave me alone."

On her feet once again, imperiously pointing to the door with her hand, Doña Blanca dismissed the commander. What was he to do? What could he say? Doña Blanca seemed frenzied in the eyes of the commander, who was himself overcome with pity and almost with shock. He feared being a cruel and unworthy gentleman were he to respond. He kept silent. He saw his mission as a lost cause, at least with respect to her, and had no wish to prolong the mutual torment.

Don Fadrique inclined his head and left the room greatly distressed. As soon as he found himself in the antechamber, he descended the staircase, opened the vestibule door, and rushed into the street, avidly breathing in air, like someone who is drowning and manages to raise his head above the surface of the water.

25

Despite his optimistic and sunny philosophy, despite his natural propensity to laugh and to see the comic side of things, that whole day Don Fadrique was pensive, quiet, imbued with a melancholy seriousness that was uncommonly strange in him.

At the midday meal he scarcely touched his food, and he scarcely spoke to his brother, to his sister-in-law, and to his niece, all of whom, each in his or her own way, showered him with attention.

Don José was an excellent man, who did no more than look after his properties, play *malilla* at the pharmacy gathering, and please Doña Antonia.

This lady, possessed of a most benign temperament and disposition, tended her home with great care, and sewed and embroidered. She was a

días y rezaba el rosario con los criados todas las noches; pero, en todo ello había algo de maquinal, de fórmula, costumbre o rutina, sin que doña Antonia se metiese en honduras religiosas. Sólo salía algo de sus casillas y mostraba cierto entusiasmo apasionado en favor de la Virgen de Araceli de Lucena (doña Antonia era lucentina), prefiriéndola a las demás Vírgenes y hallándola más milagrosa.

En cuanto a director espiritual, doña Antonia tenía a un capuchino fervoroso y elocuente, cuya fama eclipsaba entonces la del padre Jacinto, el cual, como más tibio en el predicar y en el reprender, no hacía tantas conversiones ni traía al redil tantas ovejas descarriadas como su cofrade barbudo.

Lucía tenía por confesor al padre Jacinto; y se llevaba tan bien con su madre, que las únicas discusiones que había entre ellas eran sobre los méritos de sus respectivos confesores. Por lo demás, como doña Antonia no tenía voluntad ni opinión, y de todo se le importaba lo mismo, francamente no era gran prueba de sumisión y deferencia en Lucía el no discutir nunca con su madre, salvo sobre el capuchino, y alguna que otra vez, aunque raras, acerca de la Virgen de Araceli. Lucía no era muy devota, y careciendo de otra Virgen predilecta, concedía pronto a su madre la superior excelencia de la suya.

La única causa de disidencia era, pues, el padre Jacinto, en quien Lucía hallaba superior entendimiento e ilustración; mas al cabo, como buena hija que era, y a fin de contentar a su madre, declaraba que el capuchino había reunido a un sinnúmero de malos casados, que andaban campando por sus respetos y viviendo aparte engolfados en mil marimorenas, y había logrado que no pocos pecadores y pecadoras dejasen las malas compañías y peores tratos, e hiciesen vida ejemplar y penitente: de todo lo cual podía jactarse muchísimo menos el padre Jacinto. De donde infería Lucía que el capuchino era mejor director espiritual de los extraviados, y el padre Jacinto mejor director de los que estaban en el buen sendero o dentro del aprisco. El uno valía para vencer y reducir a la obediencia a los rebeldes; el otro para gobernar sabia y blandamente a los sumisos.

Con esto se aquietaba doña Antonia y vivía en santa y dulce paz con su hija, a quien había enseñado todas sus habilidades caseras, reconociendo la maestra, sin envidia y con júbilo, que casi siempre se le aventajaba

good Christian, went to mass daily, and said the rosary with the servants every night, but in all her rituals there was something mechanical, something that smacked of formula, habit or routine, as Doña Antonia did not delve into religious profundities. She only came out of her routine and showed a certain passionate enthusiasm on behalf of the Virgin of Araceli, in Lucena[88] (Doña Antonia hailed from Lucena), preferring her to the other Virgins and regarding her as more apt to work miracles.

Doña Antonia had as her spiritual director an eloquent and fervent Capuchin whose fame at that time eclipsed that of Father Jacinto, who, being more lukewarm in his homilies and his reprimands, did not make as many conversions nor bring as many stray sheep back to the fold as his bearded brother cleric.

Lucía had Father Jacinto as her confessor, and she got along so well with her mother that their only disagreements turned on the merits of their respective confessors. As to the rest, since Doña Antonia had neither a will of her own nor opinions of her own, and took things pretty much as they came, in all honesty it was no great proof of submissiveness and deference in Lucía never to argue with her mother, except about the Virgin of Araceli. Lucía was not very devout, and, not having some other favorite Virgin, readily conceded to her mother the spiritual excellence of hers.

The only source of disagreement, then, was Father Jacinto, in whom Lucía saw superior intelligence and erudition, but in the end, like the good daughter that she was, and so as to make her mother happy, she granted that the Capuchin had brought back together untold married couples who had gone their separate ways and who were doing as they pleased, living apart but forever quarreling, and had induced not a few sinners – men and women – to shun bad company and to put an end to worse behavior, and to lead a penitent, exemplary life. Father Jacinto could boast much, much less about such endeavors, from which Lucía inferred that the Capuchin was a better spiritual director for those who had gone astray, and Father Jacinto a better director for those who were on the right path or inside the fold. The one served to overcome and reduce rebels to obedience; the other to guide the submissive wisely and gently.

With this accord Doña Antonia calmed down and lived in holy and sweet peace with her daughter, to whom she had taught all her domestic skills, acknowledging – not with envy, but with great joy – that the

ya la discípula. Lucía bordaba con todo primor, en blanco, en seda y en oro; hacía calados, pespuntes y vainicas como pocas; y en guisos y dulces nadie se le ponía delante que no saliera con la ceniza en la frente. Sólo resplandecía aún la superioridad de doña Antonia en las faenas de la matanza. Era un prodigio de tino en el condimentar y sazonar la masa de los chorizos, morcillas, longanizas y salchichas; en adobar el lomo para conservarle frito todo el año, y en dar su respectivo saborete, con la adecuada especiería, a las asaduras, que ya compuestas llevan siempre el nombre de pajarillas, sin duda porque alegran las pajarillas de quien las come, y a los riñones, mollejas, hígado y bazo, que se preparan de diverso modo, con clavo, pimienta y otras especias más finas, excluyendo el comino, el pimentón y el orégano.

El lector no ha de extrañar que entremos en estos pormenores. Convenía decirlos, y distraídos con la acción principal no los habíamos dicho.

El niño mayorazgo, hijo de don José y de doña Antonia, había ido, hacía poco, al Colegio de Guardias Marinas de la Isla, con buenas cartas de recomendación de su señor tío.

Doña Antonia andaba siempre con las llaves de una parte a otra; ya en la repostería; ya en la despensa; ya en la bodega del aceite, ya en la del vino, ya en la del vinagre.

La casa tenía todo esto, como casa de labrador, a par que de señores; pues don José, al trasladarse a la ciudad, había traído a ella muchos de sus frutos para venderlos con más estimación y darles más fácil salida.

Don José, cuando no hacía cuentas con el aperador, o bien oía a los caseros, que venían a verle y a informarle de todo desde las caserías, o se largaba a la botica, donde había tertulia perpetua y juego por mañana, tarde y noche.

Resultaba, pues, que el comendador, salvo a las horas de las tres comidas, y un rato de noche, cuando había tertulia, a la cual no faltaba jamás don Carlos de Atienza, se hallaba en una grata y apacible soledad, no interrumpida sino por la rubia sobrina, la cual le buscaba siempre, preguntándole qué había de nuevo respecto a Clara.

Don José y doña Antonia, que estaban en Babia, nada sabían de los

pupil almost always surpassed the teacher now. Lucía embroidered exquisitely in white, in silk, and in gold; she did openwork, backstitches, and hemstitches that few women could match; and in cooked dishes and sweetmeats nobody held a candle to her. Doña Antonia's superiority still shone only in the several steps of a hog or pig slaughter. She was a prodigy with a sure touch in seasoning and spicing the bulk of the diverse smoked and blood sausages; in pickling the loin to preserve it the whole year; in giving their respective taste, with the right spices, to the chitterlings, which, once prepared, are always called "innards," no doubt because they gladden the innards of the people who eat them; and in flavoring kidneys, gizzards, livers, and spleens that are garnished in sundry ways with clove, pepper, and other finer spices, except cumin, paprika, and oregano.[89]

The reader should not be surprised that we are going into these details. It was as well to cite them, but, distracted by the main story line, we had not gotten around to them.

Don José and Doña Antonia's son, their heir by primogeniture, had gone away a short time ago to the Naval Academy, the same one attended by his uncle, who had provided him with very good letters of recommendation.

Doña Antonia was always on the go from one place to another with her keys: from the pantry to the larder to the cellars for olive oil, wine, and vinegar. The house accommodated them all, being a combination of sorts, a tenant and master's dwelling both, because when Don José moved to the city he brought to it many of his agricultural products in order to sell them for a better price at a better outlet.

When he was not going over accounts with his foreman, Don José would either discuss work with his tenants (who came to the city from the farms to inform him of everything) or go off to the pharmacy, where there was a perpetual *tertulia* and card games morning, afternoon, and night.

It turned out, therefore, that except at the three mealtimes, and a short while in the evening, when there was a family *tertulia*, which Don Carlos de Atienza never failed to attend, the commander found himself in pleasant and peaceful solitude, broken only by his fair-haired niece, who continually sought him out, asking whether there was anything new with regard to Clara.

Don José and Doña Antonia, who had their heads in the clouds,

disgustos y cuidados del comendador. Lucía los sabía a medias, distando infinito de presumir, a pesar de sus hipótesis, que Clara estaba ligada a su tío con vínculo tan natural.

Los criados de la casa y el público todo seguían desorientados en punto a don Carlos de Atienza. Viéndole joven, elegante y lindo, que venía con frecuencia a la casa, y que cuchicheaba siempre con Lucía, supusieron con visos de fundamento que era su novio; y ya en la casa le apellidaban el novio de la señorita.

Tal era la situación de cada uno de los personajes secundarios de esta historia cuando el comendador, después de su entrevista con doña Blanca, se hallaba tan desazonado.

Durante la comida le colmaron de cuidados, creyéndole indispuesto. Doña Antonia supuso que tendría jaqueca y le excitó a que se fuese a reposar. Don José, después de decirle lo mismo, se largó a la botica. Lucía, con más vivo interés, trató de informarse mil veces de la causa del disgusto de su tío, pero no consiguió nada.

El comendador, a sus solas, no hacía más que pensar sobre su diálogo con doña Blanca y concebir los más encontrados pensamientos, aunque siempre poco gratos.

Ya se le figuraba que dicha señora tenía un orgullo satánico, un genio infernal, y entonces se culpaba a sí mismo de no haberle robado a la hija; de haberla dejado en su poder para que la enloqueciera y la hiciera desgraciada. Ya imaginaba, por el contrario, que, desde su punto de vista, doña Blanca tenía razón en todo.

El comendador entonces calificaba su persecución en pos de doña Blanca, y su victoria ulterior (que en otro tiempo había mirado como una ligereza perdonable, como una bizarría de mocedad) de conducta inicua y malvada a todas luces, aun juzgada por su criterio moral, lleno de laxitud en ciertas materias.

–Por cierto que no merezco perdón– se decía don Fadrique –. La maldita vanidad me hizo ser un infame ¡Había tantas mujeres guapas cuando yo era mozo, a quienes cuesta tan poco otro tropiezo, una caída más o menos! ¿Por qué, pues, no siendo arrastrado por una pasión vehemente, que ni siquiera tengo esta excusa, ir a turbar la paz del alma de aquella austera señora? Tiene razón sobrada. Soy digno de que me

knew nothing about the commander's vexations and concerns. Lucía knew of them by halves, but she was a very long ways from imagining, notwithstanding her hypotheses, that Clara was bound to her uncle by such a blood tie.

The servants of the house and the public at large continued to be thrown off the track with respect to Don Carlos de Atienza. Seeing that he was young, elegant, and handsome, that he frequented the house, and that he was always whispering with Lucía, they supposed, based on appearances, that he was her suitor, and in the house they referred to him as the "*señorita*'s fiancé."

Such was the situation of each of the secondary characters of this story when the commander, subsequent to his meeting with Doña Blanca, found himself so anxious.

During the meal they lavished attention on him, expressing concern because they thought him indisposed. Doña Antonia imagined that he had a migraine and urged him to go and rest. Don José, after saying the same thing, retreated to the pharmacy. Lucía, with keener interest, tried repeatedly to ascertain the cause of her uncle's uneasiness.

When he was by himself, the commander could think of naught but his conversation with Doña Blanca and entertained the most conflicting thoughts, although not always the most pleasant kind.

First he fancied that the woman had a satanic pride, an infernal temper, and then he blamed himself for not having abducted his daughter, for having left her in her mother's clutches so that she could drive her mad and make her miserable. On the heels of these musings he imagined just the opposite, that, from her point of view, Doña Blanca was right about everything.

The commander then characterized his pursuit of Doña Blanca and his eventual triumph (which in another time he had regarded as an excusable frivolity, as a gallantry of his youth) as wicked, iniquitous conduct by any standard, even judged by his moral yardstick, lax in the extreme in certain matters.

I certainly don't deserve to be forgiven, Don Fadrique thought to himself. *My damned vanity made me into a villain. There were so many good-looking women when I was young ... and what was a moral lapse or two, one slip more or less? So why, not having been carried away by a fervent passion then, for I do not even have that excuse, should I now go and disturb the peace of mind of that austere lady? She's clearly*

aborrezca o me desprecie. Lo único que mitiga un tanto la enormidad de mi delito es la mala opinión que tenía yo entonces de casi todas las mujeres. No me cabía en la cabeza que ninguna pudiera (después sobre todo) tomar tan por lo serio los remordimientos, la culpa... En fin, yo no preví lo que pasó después. Si lo hubiera previsto... me hubiera guardado bien de pretender a doña Blanca. Aunque no hubiera habido otra mujer en la tierra... su corazón hubiera quedado entero para don Valentín, sin que yo se le robara. Pero nada... ¡esta pícara costumbre de reír de todo... de no ver sino el lado malo! Me gustó... me enamoró... eso sí... yo estaba enamorado... y como creí que la gazmoñería era sal y pimienta que haría más picante y sabroso el logro de mi deseo, y que luego se disiparía, insistí, porfié, hice diabluras... sí... hice diabluras: creé dentro de su conciencia un infierno espantoso; por un liviano y furtivo deleite dejé en su espíritu un torcedor, una horrible máquina de tormento, que sin cesar le destroza el pecho diez y siete años hace. ¡Como tengo este carácter tan jocoso!... Las cañas se volvieron lanzas. La burla fue pesada. Pero ¡Dios mío... si yo no podía sospecharlo! Aunque me lo hubieran asegurado mil y mil personas, no lo hubiera creído. Lo repito, no cabía en mi cabeza. Yo no comprendía arrepentimiento tan feroz y tan persistente, simultáneo casi con el pecado. Yo no había medido toda la violencia de una pasión, que, a pesar del grito airado y fiero de la conciencia, que a despecho del sangriento azote con que el espíritu la castiga, rompe todo freno y sale vencedora. Cuando exclamaba ella casi rendida ya a mi voluntad, cayendo entre mis brazos, doblándose quebrantada al toque de mis labios, recibiendo mis besos y mis caricias, cediendo a un impulso irresistible y no obstante luchando. «¡Dios mío, mátame antes que caiga de tu gracia! ¡Prefiero morir a pecar!»; cuando decía esto, que hoy ha repetido a propósito de su hija, no me inspiraba compasión, no me apartaba de mi mal propósito; antes bien era espuela con que aguijoneaba mi desbocado apetito. ¡Cuán hermosa me parecía entonces, al pronunciar, con voz entrecortada por los sollozos, aquellas palabras, a las cuales yo no prestaba sino un vago sentido poético, y en cuya verdad profunda yo no creía! Hasta la dulzura de su misma religión se maleaba y viciaba en mi mente, interpretada por mi concupiscencia, y quitaba a mis ojos todo valor a aquella desolación suya, a aquella angustia con que miraba y repugnaba la caída, sin hallar fuerzas para evitarla. Yo me

in the right. I'm worthy of being loathed or despised by her. The only thing that mitigates somewhat the enormity of my offense is the low opinion that I held back then of almost all women. It never occurred to me that any of them (especially afterwards) could take remorse and sin so seriously. At all events, I did not foresee what happened afterwards. If I had foreseen it, I would have refrained from wooing Doña Blanca. Even if there had not been another woman on earth ... her heart would have remained whole for Don Valentín, without my stealing it from him. But no ... This nasty habit of mine of laughing at everything, of seeing only the bad side. I liked her, I fell in love with her ... yes, I was in love with her, and since I believed that her prudishness was salt and pepper that would make the attainment of my desire spicier and tastier and would then dissipate, I insisted, I persisted, I did a diabolic thing, yes, a diabolic thing: I created a dreadful hell inside her conscience, and for a shallow and short-lived pleasure I left a spiritual thorn in her side, a horrible instrument of torment that has been tearing incessantly at her heart for seventeen years. It's this jocular character of mine! What began as a joke ended in tragedy. The jest was heavy-handed. But, good Lord, how could I have suspected it? Even if thousands of people had assured me of the truth of the matter, I wouldn't have believed it. I repeat, it never occurred to me. I didn't understand such fierce and persistent repentance, almost simultaneous with the sin. I had not measured all the vehemence of a passion that, despite the wild, angry cry of conscience, despite the bloody scourge with which the spirit mortifies it, breaks free of restraint and emerges victorious. When she exclaimed – having nearly submitted to my will, falling into my arms, yielding helplessly at the touch of my lips, receiving my kisses and my caresses, giving in to an irresistible impulse, and nonetheless struggling – 'Dear God, kill me before I fall from your grace! I prefer to die rather than sin!', when she said this, which she repeated today apropos of her daughter, she didn't arouse compassion in me, didn't dissuade me from my evil designs. On the contrary, the words acted as a spur and whetted my appetite. How beautiful she seemed to me then, when, in a voice choked with sobs, she spoke those words to which I lent only a vague poetic meaning and in whose profound truth I did not believe. Even the gentleness of her religion was corrupted and tainted in my mind, interpreted as it was by my lustfulness, and lost in my eyes all the value of that desolation of hers, of that anguish with which she regarded and loathed the fall, without

atrevía a decir que no era tan gran mal el que tenía tan fácil remedio. Yo me convertía en redentor del alma que cautivaba y en salvador del alma que perdía, parodiando la sentencia divina y diciendo en mi interior: «Levántate: estás perdonada, por lo mucho que has amado». ¡Ah, cielos! ¿Por qué ocultármelo? Procedí con villanía. Era yo tan bajo y tan vil, que no comprendí nunca el vigor, la energía de la pasión que sin merecerlo había excitado. Era yo como salvaje, que sin conocer un arma, la dispara y hiere de muerte. La grandeza y la omnipotencia del amor me eran tan desconocidas como la persistencia y el indómito poderío de una conciencia recta, que acepta el deber y le cumple, o jamás se perdona si no le cumple. ¿Será que soy un miserable? ¿Tendrán razón los frailes y los clérigos al sostener que no hay verdadera virtud sin religión verdadera?

De esta suerte se atormentaba don Fadrique en afanoso soliloquio, en que volvía cien y cien veces a repetirse lo mismo.

El que no viniese el padre Jacinto a hablar con él inspiraba al comendador la mayor inquietud. Varias veces se asomó al balcón de su cuarto, que daba a la calle, a ver si le veía salir de casa de doña Blanca. Varias veces salió a la calle y fue hasta el convento de Santo Domingo, aunque estaba lejos, a preguntar si el padre Jacinto había vuelto. El padre Jacinto no parecía en parte alguna.

A la caída de la tarde, estando don Fadrique en su estancia, oyó pisadas de caballos que paraban cerca. Salió al balcón y vio apearse a don Valentín, que volvía de la casería.

Llegó la noche y no parecía el padre Jacinto.

Don Fadrique echaba a volar su imaginación con vuelo siniestro. Hacía las suposiciones más extrañas y dolorosas –¿Qué habrá sucedido?– se preguntaba.

A las ocho de la noche, por último, el comendador vio aparecer al padre Jacinto bajo el dintel de la puerta de su cuarto.

Al verle, le dio un vuelco el corazón. El padre traía la cara más grave y melancólica que había tenido en su vida.

–¿Qué es esto? ¿Qué pasa?– dijo el comendador –. ¿Dónde ha estado usted hasta ahora?

–¿Dónde he de haber estado? En casa de doña Blanca, donde hice

finding the strength to avoid it. I dared to conclude that it was not such a great evil when it had such an easy remedy. I transformed myself into the redeemer of the soul that I held captive and into the savior of the soul that I plunged into ruin, parodying the divine words and saying in my heart: 'Rise: You are forgiven because of how much you have loved.' Ah, heavens! Why should I hide it from myself? I behaved abominably. I was so base and so despicable that I never understood the vitality, the energy of the passion that, undeserving, I had excited. I was like the savage who, not familiar with a firearm, shoots it and wounds someone mortally. The greatness and omnipotence of love were as unknown to me as the persistence and indomitable power of a righteous conscience, which accepts duty and fulfills it, or never forgives itself if it does not. Can it be that I am a wretch of a human being? Can the friars and priests be right when they maintain that there is no true virtue without true religion?

Thus did Don Fadrique torment himself in an agonizing soliloquy, one in which he repeated the same things hundreds of times.

The fact that Father Jacinto did not come to talk with him unsettled the commander considerably. Several times he peered out from the balcony of his room, which overlooked the street, to see if he was exiting Doña Blanca's house. Several times he went outside and betook himself to the Santo Domingo monastery, even though it was a long way off, to ask whether Father Jacinto had returned. Father Jacinto was nowhere to be seen.

At the close of the day, when Don Fadrique was in his room, he heard horses' hooves coming to a halt nearby. He stepped over to the balcony and caught sight of Don Valentín dismounting upon his return from the country.

Night fell and Father Jacinto did not turn up.

Don Fadrique's imagination took wing on a sinister flight. He dreamed up the strangest and most distressing scenarios. *What can have happened?* he wondered.

Finally, at eight o'clock, the commander saw Father Jacinto appear at the doorway of his room and his heart jumped, because the priest's face bore the gravest and gloomiest expression he had ever exhibited in his life.

"What's this? What's going on?" asked the commander. "Where have you been until now?"

"Where was I going to be? At Doña Blanca's house, where I was

mal y remal en introducirte traidoramente. ¡Buena la has hecho! ¿Qué demonios te aconsejaron cuando hablabas? ¿Qué dijiste a la infeliz? ¡Vaya un berrinche que ha tomado! Está mala. ¡Dios quiera que no se ponga peor!

El comendador se mostró consternado; se quedó mudo. El fraile añadió:

–Clarita es una santa. Allá la dejo cuidando a su madre. No sé para qué todas estas desazones. La chica está resuelta, firmemente resuelta. Todo es inútil. Bien hubiera podido evitarse tu endemoniada conversación con la madre. Tiempo es de evitar aún que te arruines a tontas y a locas.

El comendador, recobrando el habla, respondió:

–Lo hecho, hecho está. Yo no gusto de arrepentirme. Yo no deshago mis promesas. Yo no me vuelvo atrás nunca. Lo que prometí a don Casimiro y él ha aceptado tiene que cumplirse. Pero ¿qué enfermedad es ésa de doña Blanca? ¿Sigue Clara poseída de su lúgubre locura? Voto a todos los demonios y condenados que hay en el infierno, que jamás hubiera yo podido soñar que iba a ser víctima de tan enrevesados sentimentalismos.

El comendador se paseaba a largos pasos por la estancia. El padre le miraba con pena y algo aturdido.

En esto, Lucía, que había visto entrar al padre, asomó la rubia y linda cabeza a la puerta, que había quedado entornada, y dijo con dulce ansiedad.

–Tío, ¿qué hay de nuevo?

–Nada, niña. Por Dios, déjanos en paz ahora, que vamos a tratar de asuntos muy graves.

Lucía se retiró, lastimada de inspirar tan poca confianza.

26

Cuando el padre y el comendador se quedaron solos de nuevo, cerró éste la puerta e interrogó al padre en voz baja sobre lo que había oído a doña Blanca, sobre lo que había hablado con Clarita: pero nada sacó en limpio.

El padre Jacinto parecía otro del que antes era. Mostrábase preocupado; buscaba evasivas para no contestar a derechas; sus misterios y reticencias daban a su interlocutor una confusa alarma.

wrong, very wrong to take you like a traitor. A fine mess you've made of things! What demons advised you when you were talking to her? What did you say to the poor woman? She's flown into a rage. She's ill. Let's hope she doesn't get worse."

The commander, dismayed, said not a word. The friar added:

"Clarita is a saint. I've left her there taking care of her mother. I don't know what you expect to accomplish with all these aggravations. The girl is determined, firmly determined. Your diabolic conversation with the mother could easily have been avoided. There's still time for you to avoid self-destruction without rhyme or reason."

The commander, recovering his speech, responded:

"What's done is done. I don't like to repent. I don't break my promises. I don't ever look back. What I promised to Don Casimiro and he has accepted, must be carried out. But, what is this illness of Doña Blanca's? Is Clara still possessed of her gloomy derangement? I swear by all the devils and damned souls in hell that never would I have been able to dream that she was going to be the victim of such complicated sentimentalism."

The commander was pacing to and fro in the room with long strides while the priest, somewhat dazed, eyed him with sorrow.

At this juncture, Lucía, who had seen the priest enter, poked her pretty blond head around the door, which had remained ajar, and asked, gently solicitous:

"Is there any news, Uncle?"

"No, girl. And for heaven's sake, leave us alone now that we are going to discuss very grave matters."

Lucía withdrew, hurt on seeing that she inspired so little trust.

26

When the priest and the commander were alone again, the latter closed the door and asked the priest in a low voice what he had heard from Doña Blanca, what he had said to Clarita, but he learned nothing concrete.

Father Jacinto seemed different from before. He was preoccupied; he answered evasively so as not to answer directly; and his air of mystery and reticence set off a confused alarm in his interlocutor.

Al fin tuvo don Fadrique que dejar partir al fraile, sin averiguar nada más de lo que ya sabía.

Aquella noche no salió de su cuarto; no quiso ver a nadie: pretextó hallarse indispuesto, para encerrarse y aislarse.

Se pasaron horas y horas, y aunque se tendió en la cama, no pudo dormir. Mil tristes ideas le atormentaban y desvelaban.

Rendido de la fatiga se entregó al sueño por un momento, pero tuvo visiones aterradoras.

Soñó que había asesinado a doña Blanca, y soñó que había asesinado a su hija. Ambas le perdonaban con dulzura después de muertas; pero este perdón tan dulce le hacía más daño que las punzantes palabras que aquel día había escuchado de boca de su antigua querida. Ésta y Clara se ofrecían a su imaginación con la palidez de la muerte, con los ojos fijos y vidriosos, pero como triunfantes y serenas, subiendo lentamente por el aire, hacia la región del cielo, y entonando un antiguo himno religioso, que siempre había atacado los nervios y contrariado los sentimientos harto gentílicos del comendador por su fúnebre ternura; por su identificación del amor y de la muerte, y por su misantrópica exaltación del ser del espíritu por cima de todo deleite, contento, esperanza, consolación o bien posible en la tierra.

Las mujeres, que iban subiendo al cielo, cantaban; y don Fadrique oía, a través del ambiente tranquilo, los últimos versos del himno, que decían:

Mors piavit, mors sanavit
Insanatum animum.

Con estos dos versos en la mente se despertó don Fadrique.

Apenas se hubo vestido, oyó que daban golpecitos a la puerta.

–¿Quién es?– preguntó.

–Soy yo, tío– dijo la dulce voz de Lucía –. Tengo que hablar con usted. ¿Puedo entrar?

–Entra– contestó el comendador con bastante zozobra de que Lucía trajese malas noticias.

La cara de Lucía estaba demudada. Los ojos algo encarnados, como si hubiesen vertido lágrimas.

–¿Qué hay?– dijo don Fadrique.

–Que doña Blanca está muy mala. Clara me escribe diciéndomelo, y me ruega que haga la caridad de ir a acompañarla.

In the end, Don Fadrique had to allow the friar to take his leave, and he had not learned any more than what he already knew.

That night he did not set foot out of his room. He refused to see anyone, claiming that he was indisposed so as to be able to shut himself up and be alone.

Hour after hour went by, and although he stretched out on the bed he could not sleep. A thousand ideas tormented him and kept him awake.

Overcome with fatigue, he dropped off for a moment but had terrifying visions.

He dreamed that he had murdered Doña Blanca, and he dreamed that he had murdered his daughter. Both gently forgave him after they were dead, but this gentle forgiveness hurt him more than the caustic words he had heard that day on the lips of his former lover. She and Clara appeared in his imagination with the pallor of death, with their eyes fixed and glassy, but as though triumphant and serene, slowly ascending through the air towards the ether, and intoning an ancient religious hymn that had always chafed the nerves and upset the heathenish sentiments of the commander owing to its mournful tenderness, its identification of love and death, and its misanthropic exaltation of the existence of the spirit above every delight, contentment, hope, consolation, or good possible on earth.

The women were singing as they rose up to heaven, and Don Fadrique heard, through the peaceful atmosphere, the last lines of the hymn that said:

> *Mors piavit, mors sanavit*
> *insanatum animum.*[90]

With these two lines in his head Don Fadrique awoke.

No sooner had he dressed than he heard someone knocking lightly at the door.

"Who is it?" he asked.

"It's me," said Lucía's sweet voice. "I have to talk to you. May I come in?"

"Yes, come in," replied the commander, rather jittery for fear that Lucía might be bringing bad news.

Lucía's face was wan, her eyes a touch red, as if she had shed tears.

"What's wrong?" asked Don Fadrique.

"Doña Blanca is in a very bad way. Clara has written to tell me and to ask me to please go and keep her company."

–¿Y se sabe qué tiene doña Blanca?

–Yo, tío, no lo sé. El mal ha venido de súbito. La criada, que me trajo la carta de Clarita, dijo que su ama cayó enferma como herida por un rayo; que, eso es verdad, la señora estaba delicada, pero que al fin lo pasaba regular, como casi todos, cuando de repente, cual si hubiera tenido alguna aparición de los malos y hubiera peleado con ellos, cayó en tal postración, que ha sido menester ponerla en la cama, donde está aún con calentura.

Don Fadrique sintió un frío repentino, que discurría por todo su cuerpo y que hasta los huesos le penetraba. Imaginó que se le erizaban los cabellos. Se inmutó; pero con habla interior dijo para sí:

–En efecto, ¿habré sido tan brutal que la haya asesinado?

Notando después que Lucía no tenía más que decir y aguardaba respuesta, el comendador hizo un esfuerzo para aparentar serenidad, y dijo a su sobrina:

–Ve, hija mía; ve a cumplir con ese deber de caridad y de amistad para con Clarita. Procura consolarla, ¡Ojalá que el padecimiento de doña Blanca no tenga peores consecuencias!

–Voy volando,– replicó Lucía.

Y sin aguardar más, con la venia de su madre que ya tenía, bajó la escalera y se fue a la casa inmediata.

27

La sobrina del comendador tenía tan alegre carácter como su tío. Era, por naturaleza, tan optimista como él. Casi todo lo veía de color de rosa; pero, compasiva y buena, tomaba pesar por los males y disgustos de los otros, si bien procurando más consolarlos o remediarlos que compartirlos.

Con esta disposición de ánimo entró Lucía a ver a Clara. Apenas se vieron, se abrazaron estrechamente.

Clara, al contrario que Lucía, era melancólica, vehemente y apasionada, como su madre. Sobre esta condición del carácter, que era ingénita en ella, la educación severísima de doña Blanca, su continuo hablar de

"And what's the matter with Doña Blanca? Do they know?"

"I have no idea, Uncle. The affliction came on all of a sudden. The maid who brought me Clarita's letter said that her mistress fell ill as though she were struck by a thunderbolt, and that, to be sure, Doña Blanca's health was delicate, but that she was doing moderately well, like just about everyone else, when all at once, as if she had been visited by an apparition of demons and had done battle with them, she collapsed into such prostration that it became necessary to put her to bed, where she still is with a fever."

Don Fadrique felt a sudden chill course through his body, even penetrating his bones. He imagined that his hair was standing on end. His face fell and he thought to himself: *Can I really have been so brutal that I killed her?*

Realizing then that Lucía had no more to say and that she was waiting for a response, the commander made an effort to affect calmness and said to his niece:

"Go on. Go and fulfill that duty of charity and be a friend to Clara. Try to console her. I hope Doña Blanca's affliction will not bring worse consequences."

"I'll go as quickly as I can," said Lucía.

And without further delay, with her mother's permission, which she had already obtained, she descended the stairs and went over to the adjoining house.

27

The commander's niece had the same cheerful disposition as her uncle. She was by nature as optimistic as he. She saw almost everything through rose-colored lenses, but compassionate and good, she sorrowed over the ills and misfortunes of others, although trying more to console them than to share them.

In this frame of mind Lucía went inside to accompany Clara. As soon as they saw each other they embraced warmly.

Clara, unlike Lucía, was melancholy, vehement, and passionate, like her mother. Over and above these character traits, which were inborn in her, Doña Blanca's exceptionally strict upbringing, her constant talk

nuestra perversidad nativa, su concepto del mundo y del vivir como valle
de lágrimas y tiempo de prueba, y su terror de la eterna condenación y
de lo fácil que es caer en el pecado, habían difundido por toda el alma
de Clara una sombra de amarga tristeza y de medrosa desconfianza. Por
dicha, Clara carecía de aquel orgullo, de aquel imperio de su madre, y el
lado oscuro y tenebroso de su espíritu estaba suavemente iluminado por
un rayo celeste de humildad, resignación y mansedumbre.

Clara era mil veces más amante que su madre, y se abandonaba a la
dulzura de amar, si bien con recelo siempre de pecar amando.

Ambas amigas se hallaban en un cuarto contiguo a la alcoba de doña
Blanca.

El cuitado de don Valentín no sabía qué hacer: andaba inquieto; bullía
de un lado a otro, sin atreverse a entrar en la alcoba de su mujer para
que no le despidiese a gritos, porque venía a turbar su reposo, y sin
atreverse tampoco a no estar allí cerca para que su mujer no le acusase
de indiferente, egoísta y desalmado, que no miraba con interés sus males
y ni siquiera preguntaba por su salud. En esta perplejidad, don Valentín
entraba y salía, asomaba de vez en cuando la nariz a la alcoba, a ver si le
veía doña Blanca y le decía que entrase; y, sin decidirse a entrar, mientras
no alcanzaba la venia, preguntaba a Clara por su madre, ni en voz muy
alta para que doña Blanca se incomodase, ni en voz muy baja para que
fuera posible que doña Blanca le oyese y comprendiese que su marido
cuidaba de ella y no era un hombre sin entrañas.

Este procedimiento prudentísimo no le valió sin embargo. Ya una vez,
como repitiese con harta frecuencia lo de asomar la nariz a la puerta de
la alcoba, doña Blanca había dicho:

–¿Qué haces ahí? ¿Vienes a molestarme? Pareces un buho que me
espanta con sus ojos. Déjame en paz, por Dios.

Poco después se descuidó algo don Valentín, alzó la voz demasiado al
preguntar a Clara por su madre, y ésta exclamó desde la alcoba:

–¡Qué pesadilla de hombre! Se ha propuesto no dejarme descansar. ¡Si
parece que está hueco! Valentín, habla bajo y no me mates.

Don Valentín salió entonces zapeado de la estancia en que se hallaban
Clara y Lucía, y las dejó solas.

about our innate perversity, her conception of the world and of life as a vale of tears and a time of trial, and her terror of eternal condemnation, and how easy it is to fall into sin, had spread throughout Clara's soul a shadow of bitter sadness and fainthearted distrust. Missing in Clara, fortunately, was that pride, that imperiousness of her mother's, and the dark, gloomy side of her spirit was softly illuminated by a celestial ray of humility, resignation, and meekness.

Clara was a thousand times more loving than her mother and abandoned herself to the sweetness of loving, although with the fear that she always committed a sin by loving.

Both friends were in a room contiguous to Doña Blanca's bedroom.

A worried Don Valentín did not know what to do: he paced anxiously; he moved from one spot to another without daring to enter his wife's bedroom so that she would not dismiss him at the top of her voice, saying that he came to disturb her peace; and he dared not to remain close by so that his wife would not accuse him of being indifferent, selfish, and heartless, a husband who did not take an interest in her afflictions and did not even inquire about her health. In this limbo of perplexity Don Valentín came and went, from time to time poking his head around the bedroom door to see if Doña Blanca caught a glimpse of him and told him to come in, and, undecided whether to enter without her permission, he would ask Clara how her mother was, not so loudly that Doña Blanca would be vexed, nor so softly that she might possibly not hear him and think that her husband was not concerned about her and that he was a heartless man.

This most prudent of approaches availed him nothing, however. On one occasion, when he peeked around the bedroom door once too often, Doña Blanca had said:

"What are you doing there? Coming to annoy me? You look like a horned owl scaring me with its eyes. Leave me in peace, for heaven's sake."

Shortly afterwards Don Valentín committed a peccadillo by raising his voice too much to ask Clara about her mother, and the latter exclaimed from her bed:

"What a nightmare of a man! He's determined not to let me rest. Why, he must be scatterbrained! Valentín, do speak softly and don't kill me."

Thus shooed away, Don Valentín withdrew from the room that Clara and Lucía were in and left the two girls alone.

Aunque doña Blanca era buena cristiana, estos raptos de mal humor contra su marido se comprenden y explican como en cierto modo independientes de su voluntad. Doña Blanca no había encontrado en él ni un átomo de la poesía, ni una chispa de las sublimidades que había soñado hallar, en su inexperiencia, en el hombre a quien dio su mano, siendo aún muy niña. Luego, hacía diez y siete años, no veía ella en don Valentín sino un hombre cuya serenidad era el perpetuo sarcasmo de las borrascas de su corazón; cuya unión con ella había hecho que lo que pudo ser un bien lícito, una felicidad santificada, fuese un pecado abominable; y cuya salud corporal parecía una burla de los achaques y padecimientos que a ella le atormentaban. Hasta la paciencia con que don Valentín la sufría era odiosa a doña Blanca, cual si implicase bajeza, gana de no incomodarse por no molestarse, desdén o menosprecio.

En balde procuraba doña Blanca formar mejor opinión de su marido, a fin de respetarle, como reflexivamente conocía que era su deber: doña Blanca no lo lograba. Las mejores prendas del alma de don Valentín, con intervención quizás de algún demonio astuto, se trocaban, en el alma de doña Blanca, en defectos ridículos. En balde le pedía a Dios doña Blanca que le concediese, ya que no amar, estimar a su marido. Dios no la oía.

Zapeado, pues, don Valentín, doña Blanca quedó sola en la alcoba, abismada, sin duda, en sus hondos y amargos pensamientos, y Clara y Lucía, casi al oído la una de la otra, hablaron así:

–¿Qué ha dicho el médico, Clara? ¿Qué tiene tu madre?– preguntó Lucía.

–El médico hasta ahora– respondió Clara –, no ha dicho más que lo que cualquiera de nosotros ve y comprende: que mi madre tiene calentura; pero la calentura es sólo síntoma de un mal que el médico desconoce aún. Anoche la calentura fue muy fuerte y nos asustamos mucho. Hoy de mañana ha cedido.

–Vamos, Clarita, ya veo que exageraste en tu carta y me alarmaste sin motivo. Tu madre se curará pronto. Apuesto que la causa de toda su indisposición ha sido alguna rabieta que ha tenido con don Valentín.

–Pues te equivocas. Mi madre no ha tenido la menor rabieta con nadie en todo el día de ayer. Papá estuvo en el campo.

–Entonces se concibe que no rabiase con él. ¿Y contigo no rabió?

Although Doña Blanca was a good Christian, these fits of ill temper can be understood and explained as being in a certain way independent of her will. Doña Blanca had found in him not a trace of poetry, not a spark of the sublime qualities that as a very young and inexperienced girl she had dreamed of finding in the man to whom she gave her hand. Then, for seventeen years she saw in Don Valentín only a man whose serenity was the perpetual sarcasm of the tempests of her heart, whose union with her had made what could have been a lawful good, a sanctified happiness, become an abominable sin, and whose physical health seemed like a mockery of the ailments and sufferings that tormented her. Even the patience with which Don Valentín suffered her was anathema to Doña Blanca, as if it implied baseness, a wish not to take the trouble to be inconvenienced, scorn or contempt.

In vain did Doña Blanca endeavor to form a better opinion of her husband, in order to respect him, as she knew from reflection was her duty, but she failed. The best qualities of Don Valentín's soul were changed in Doña Blanca's soul, with the intervention perhaps of some astute devil, into ridiculous defects. In vain did Doña Blanca petition God to grant that she might esteem her husband, if not love him. God turned a deaf ear to her.

With Don Valentín having been shooed away, Doña Blanca remained alone in the bedroom, plunged, no doubt, into her deep and bitter thoughts, while Clara and Lucía, practically whispering in each other's ears, spoke as follows:

"What did the doctor say, Clara? What's the matter with your mother?" asked Lucía.

"Up till now," replied Clara, "the doctor has said only what any of us can see and understand, that my mother has a fever, but that the fever is only a symptom of an ailment that the doctor has yet to identify. Last night the fever ran very high, which scared us a great deal. This morning it came down."

"So, Clarita, I see now that you exaggerated in your letter and alarmed me unnecessarily. Your mother will get well soon. I'll bet that the cause of her indisposition was a tantrum that she took out on Don Valentín."

"Well, you're mistaken. My mother did not have the least flareup with anyone yesterday. Papá was in the country."

"Then, needless to say, she did not get furious with him. Did she with you?"

–Hace días que mi madre está dulcísima conmigo. Te repito que ayer no se sofocó mamá con nadie; no riñó a ninguna criada; estuvo apacible y silenciosa.

Clara, si bien era una criatura de singular despejo, se forjaba la extraña ilusión de que una buena madre de familia tenía forzosamente que rabiar, y así no decía nada de lo dicho para censurar a su madre, sino candorosamente.

Lucía no insistió en buscar el origen del mal de doña Blanca; se inclinó a creer que este mal era pequeño, a fin de no tener que afligirse; y volviendo la conversación hacia otros puntos, preguntó a su amiga:

–Clara, ¿sigues firme en tu resolución de tomar el velo?

–Estoy más resuelta que nunca. Una voz misteriosa me grita en el fondo del alma que debo huir del mundo; que el mundo está sembrado de peligros para mí.

–Confieso que no te entiendo. ¿Qué peligros tendrá el mundo para ti, que para los demás no tenga?

–¡Ay, querida Lucía: el desorden de mi espíritu, los extraños impulsos de mi corazón, la violencia de mis afectos!

–Pero, muchacha, ¿qué violencia, ni qué desorden es ése? Yo no hallo desordenado ni violento el que ames a don Carlos, que es muy guapo y joven, y el que no gustes de don Casimiro, que es viejo y feo. Esto me parece naturalísimo.

–Será natural, porque la naturaleza es el pecado.

–¿Dónde está el pecado?

–En desobedecer a mi madre, en engañarla, en haber atraído a don Carlos con miradas amorosas y profanas, en complacerme en que guste de mí y en que me persiga, en desear que siga queriéndome hasta en este instante, cuando ya estoy decidida a no ser suya. En suma, Lucía, mi alma es un tejido de marañas y de enredos que el mismo diablo trama y revuelve. Además, yo he prometido a mi madre que seré monja, y para que lo sea, ha despedido ella a don Casimiro. ¿Cómo faltar ahora a mi promesa, burlarme de mi madre y hasta de Cristo, a quien he dado palabra de esposa? ¿Qué infamia me propones?

–Es verdad, hija mía: el caso es apurado; pero ¿quién te mandó que dijeses que querías ser monja y que lo prometieses? ¿Por qué no declaraste con valor a tu madre que no querías a don Casimiro y que no querías ser monja tampoco?

"For days now my mother has been very sweet to me. I repeat: yesterday Mamá did not get upset with anyone; she did not scold any maid; she was calm and quiet."

Although she was a person of exceptional clear-sightedness, Clara hatched the strange notion that a good materfamilias had perforce to flare up, so that nothing of what she said was intended to find fault with her mother, except perhaps naively.

Lucía did not insist on discovering the source of Doña Blanca's affliction; she tended to believe that this affliction was minor, in order for her not to have to be distressed, and, steering the conversation into other concerns, asked her friend:

"Are you still firmly resolved to take the veil, Clara?"

"I am more resolved than ever. A mysterious voice cries out to me in the depths of my soul that I should flee from the world, that the world is strewn with dangers for me."

"I own that I don't understand you. What dangers can the world have for you that it doesn't have for the rest of us?"

"Oh, my dear Lucía. The disorder of my spirit, the strange impulses of my heart, the violence of my affections!"

"But, girl, what violence, what disorder? I find it neither disordered nor violent that you love Don Carlos, who is very handsome and young, and that you do not like Don Casimiro, who is old and ugly. This seems eminently natural to me."

"It may be natural, because nature is the sin."

"Where is the sin?"

"In disobeying my mother, in deceiving her, in having attracted Don Carlos with loving and immodest glances, in being pleased that he likes me and courts me, in wishing that he'll continue loving me even to this very moment, when I have already decided not to be his. In short, Lucía, my soul is a web of lies and intrigues, which the devil himself plots and stirs up. Besides, I have promised my mother that I'll be a nun, and for me to be one, she has dismissed Don Casimiro. How can I go back on my word now, make a fool of my mother and even of Christ, whose bride I said I would be? What sort of infamy are you suggesting to me?"

"It's a dilemma to be sure, but who told you to go and say that you wanted to be a nun and to promise to be one? Why didn't you straight out tell your mother that you didn't love Don Casimiro and that you didn't want to be a nun either?"

–Bien sabe Dios– respondió Clara –, que deseo desahogarme contigo, depositar en tu amistoso corazón el secreto de mi infortunio, confiártelo todo; pero yo misma no me comprendo sino de un modo imperfecto; y lo que de mí misma comprendo está tan enmarañado, que no encuentro palabras para explicártelo. Siento la razón y causa de todas mis acciones, y no las percibo bien para exponerlas. Quiero, no obstante, sincerarme y tratar de probarte que no es absurda mi conducta. Voy a ver si lo consigo. Yo he amado, yo amo aún a don Carlos de Atienza. Yo detesto a don Casimiro. Esto es verdad; pero mi amor por don Carlos y mi odio a don Casimiro no han tenido jamás la suficiente energía para hacerme arrostrar la cólera de mi madre, declarándole que amaba al uno y odiaba al otro. Así, pues, te aseguro que durante meses he estado resignada a sofocar en mi alma el naciente amor a don Carlos y a casarme con don Casimiro para ser una hija obediente. Hubiera yo preferido a todo ser esposa de Cristo; pero me consideraba indigna. Para ser mujer de don Casimiro me sentía con fuerzas. Yo esperaba vencer mi fatal inclinación a don Carlos, y, logrado esto, ser modelo de casadas, cuidar al achacoso don Casimiro, y hasta quererle, imponiéndome como deber el cariño. Hallándome de esta suerte, nuevos y extraños sentimientos han combatido mi alma y han hecho que mi espíritu dude más de sí. Me he llenado de terror. En mi humildad, no me he creído digna ni de ser mujer de don Casimiro. Me he espantado de mi flaqueza, de la perversidad de mis inclinaciones, y entonces he pensado en refugiarme en el claustro. Juzgándome menos digna que antes de ser esposa de Cristo, he pensado en la infinita bondad de aquel Soberano Señor, padre de las misericordias, y he comprendido que, aun siendo yo indigna de todo, podía acudir a Él y refugiarme en su seno, segura de que no me rechazaría, de que me acogería amoroso, purificándome y santificándome con su gracia.

–Tú me hablas de nuevos y extraños sentimientos, pero sin decir cuáles son– dijo Lucía –. Aquí hay un misterio que no me dejas penetrar.

–¡Ay!– exclamó Clara –, apenas si yo le penetro. ¿Cómo declarártele? Mira, Lucía, yo conozco que amo siempre a don Carlos. Si me finjo en completa libertad de elegir mi vida, me parece que mi elección será ser mujer de don Carlos. Su talento, su bondad, su delicada ternura, me

"God only knows," responded Clara, "that I wish to unburden myself to you, to entrust to your friendly heart the secret of my misfortunes, to confide everything to you, but I myself do not understand who or what I am, except in an imperfect way, and what I do understand about myself is so tangled that I cannot come up with the right words to explain it to you. I feel the reason and cause of all my actions, but I do not comprehend them well enough to interpret them. I want, nonetheless, to open my heart to yours and to try to prove that my behavior is not absurd. I'm going to see if I can.

"I loved, still do love Don Carlos de Atienza. I detest Don Casimiro. This is true, but my love for Don Carlos and my dislike for Don Casimiro have never made me courageous enough to defy my mother's anger, telling her that I loved the one and detested the other. So I assure you that for months I have been resigned to smothering in my soul the budding love for Don Carlos and marrying Don Casimiro in order to be an obedient daughter. I would have preferred being Christ's bride to everything else, but I considered myself unworthy. To be Don Casimiro's wife I felt I had the strength. I hoped to overcome my fatal inclination toward Don Carlos, and, once having managed to do so, to be a model married woman, to look after the sickly Don Casimiro, and even to love him, imposing affection on myself as a duty. In such a state as this, new and strange feelings have assailed my soul and have made my spirit doubt itself more. I've been filled with terror. In my humbleness I didn't think myself worthy even of being Don Casimiro's wife. I've been frightened by my weakness, by the perversity of my inclinations, which made me think of taking refuge in the cloister. Judging myself less worthy than before of being Christ's bride, I thought of the infinite goodness of that Sovereign Lord, father of compassion, and I realized that, even with me being unworthy of everything, I could still go to him and take refuge in his bosom, certain that he wouldn't reject me, that he would receive me lovingly, purifying me and sanctifying me with his grace."

"You're speaking to me of new and strange feelings, but without saying what they are," said Lucía. "There's a mystery here that you're not letting me penetrate."

"Oh, I can scarcely penetrate it myself!" exclaimed Clara. "So how am I going to explain it to you? Look, Lucía, I recognize that I still love Don Carlos. Were I to pretend to be completely free to choose my life, I think my choice would be as Don Carlos's wife. His talent, his kindness,

hacen presentir que sería yo dichosa viviendo a su lado. Te lo confesaré. A pesar del horror que mi madre ha sabido inspirarme a la complacencia de los sentidos, la imagen material de don Carlos, su porte, la gallardía de su cuerpo, la elegancia y pulcritud de su vestido, el fuego de sus ojos y la viva animación de su semblante y la frescura de su boca, me atormentan y me hieren y me distraen de mis piadosas meditaciones.

—Te lo repito, Clarita; en nada de eso veo yo la obra del diablo; en nada descubro influencias sobrenaturales; todo es naturalísimo. Y si, como tú afirmas, la naturaleza es pecado, bien es menester, o que Dios nos dé medios sobrenaturales para vencerla, o que nos perdone con muchísima generosidad cuando ella nos venza. ¿Dónde están esos sentimientos singulares que te perturban?

—Lucía, tú hablas con suma ligereza. Tus razones tienen no sé qué fondo de impiedad. Me da miedo. Mi madre no se engañaba. El trato, la conversación con tu tío debe de ser muy peligrosa.

—No disparates, Clara. A mi tío no se le ha ocurrido jamás darme lecciones de impiedad. Si lo que yo sostengo es poco piadoso, la culpa es completamente mía. Seré yo la que está endiablada. Pero dejemos a un lado estas cuestiones; vamos a lo que importa. Dime qué raros sentimientos te asaltan el alma, inspirándote esa humildad, esa desconfianza profunda, que te induce a tomar el velo.

—No acierto a decírtelo. Me falta valor.

—Ea... ánimo... di lo que es.

—Mi madre no ha hecho más que hablarme de tu tío desde que apareció en esta ciudad... desde que yo le vi y paseé con él una tarde. Me le ha pintado como pudiera haberme pintado a Luzbel, rodeado aún de hermosos fulgores de su primitiva naturaleza angélica, valeroso, audaz, inteligente como pocos seres humanos. Me ha hecho creer que ejerce tal imperio sobre las almas, que las atrae y las cautiva y las pierde si gusta. En su mirada hay una luz siniestra que ciega o extravía. En su palabra, una música seductora que embelesa los entendimientos y ensordece la voz del deber en la conciencia. Según mi madre, tu tío es la maldad personificada, el dechado de la irreligión, un rebelde contra Dios, de quien conviene apartarse para no contaminarse. En resolución, cuanto mi madre ha dicho de tu tío debiera infundirme hacia él un odio, una aversión grandísima. Sé por mi madre que el comendador es un réprobo.

his refined tenderness, lead me to believe that I would be happy living at his side. I'll reveal all of it to you. Despite the horror that my mother has instilled in me of the indulgence of the senses, the physical image of Don Carlos, his demeanor, the gracefulness of his figure, the elegance and smartness of his dress, the fire of his eyes, and the liveliness of his face and the freshness of his mouth torment me and hound me and distract me from my devout meditations."

"I'll say it again, Clarita: in none of this do I see the hand of the devil; in none of this do I detect supernatural influences; it's all as natural as can be. And if, as you maintain, nature is the sin, then either God must provide us with supernatural means to overcome nature, or very generously forgive us when it overcomes us. Where are those peculiar feelings that disturb you?"

"You're speaking frivolously, Lucía. Your reasons smack of a certain impiety. It scares me. My mother was not mistaken. Your uncle's company and conversation must be very dangerous."

"Don't spout nonsense, Clara. It has never occurred to my uncle to give me lessons in impiety. If what I maintain is not very pious, the fault is mine, and mine alone. I am probably the bedeviled one. But let's set these matters aside and move on to what's important. Tell me what strange feelings afflict your soul, inspiring you with that humility, that profound distrust that induces you to take the veil."

"I don't know how to tell you. I lack the courage."

"Come on, take heart. Tell me what it is."

"My mother has done nothing but talk to me about your uncle since he arrived here in this city, since I saw him and took a walk with him that first afternoon. She has portrayed him to me as she could have portrayed Lucifer, still surrounded by the beautiful splendors of his original angelic nature, brave and bold and intelligent as few human beings are. She has made me believe that he holds such sway over souls that he attracts them and captivates them and ruins them if he pleases. In his expression there is a sinister light that blinds or leads one astray. In his speech there is a seductive music that entrances the intellect and deafens the voice of duty in one's conscience. According to my mother, your uncle is evil personified, the epitome of the irreligious man, a rebel against God, whom it behooves one to avoid so as not to be contaminated. In short, everything that my mother has said about your uncle ought to instill in me a dislike for him, a strong aversion. I know from my mother that the

No hay esperanza de que se salve. Está condenado. Es como Luzbel. Y, sin embargo, lejos de producir en mí los discursos de mi madre el horror hacia el comendador que ella deseaba, tal es mi perversidad, tan pecaminoso es mi espíritu de contradicción, que han avivado más mis simpatías hacia tu tío. Yo no debiera decírtelo; yo no sé cómo tengo la desvergüenza de decírtelo. Apenas si a mi confesor le he dejado entrever algo de lo que siento en el negro abismo de mi corazón. Pero, si no te lo digo... ¿con quién me desahogo?... Lucía, tú eres mi mejor amiga... Yo quiero al comendador de un modo inexplicable. Me siento arrastrada hacia él. Creo en todas sus maldades porque mi madre me las ha dicho; y creo que Dios, a quien el comendador es simpático, se las va a perdonar, como yo se las perdono. ¿No es una monstruosidad, no es una aberración este cariño hacia una persona casi desconocida? Yo me condenaba antes por mi inclinación a don Carlos, a despecho, a escondidas de mi madre. Ahora me sucede casi lo mismo que a ti; mi inclinación a don Carlos me parece natural. Lo diabólico, lo abominable es mi inclinación a tu tío. Es un sentimiento tan distinto, que no destruye ni aminora mi afecto a don Carlos. Esto mismo prueba mi desordenada índole, mi pecadora y perturbada manera de ser. No sé con qué pretexto, bajo qué título, con qué nombre cariñoso he de acercarme a él, hablarle, llegar a su intimidad, y lo deseo. Cuantas cualidades detestables mi madre le atribuye, se me antoja que no lo son en él, porque es un ser de superior natural jerarquía y está exento de la ley común para los demás mortales.

Con la mirada fija, con el semblante, no risueño como le tenía de costumbre, sino triste y grave, y sin acertar a contestar palabra, oyó Lucía la inesperada confesión de Clara.

Después de unos instantes de silencio Clara prosiguió:

–Nada me respondes; nada observas; te callas; reconoces que soy un monstruo. Será amor de otro género, será un sentimiento indefinido, que carece de nombre en la clase e historia de las pasiones; pero yo quiero a tu tío y le quiero por esa misma pintura con que mi madre ha procurado que yo le aborrezca.

A este punto llegaba Clara, cuando vino a interrumpirla la voz de doña Blanca, que decía:

–¡Hija, hija!

Lucía y Clara se estremecieron. Aunque era imposible que doña

commander is a reprobate. There is no hope that he'll be saved. He's condemned. He's like Lucifer. And, nevertheless, her diatribes, far from producing in me the horror of the commander that my mother desired, have heightened my sympathies for your uncle, such is my perversity, so sinful is my spirit of contradiction. I shouldn't be telling you this; I don't know how I can be so shameless as to tell you. I've only barely let my confessor glimpse something of what I feel in the black abyss of my heart. But if I don't tell you, to whom do I unbosom myself? Lucía, you're my best friend. I love the commander in an unexplainable way. I feel myself drawn to him. I believe in all his wicked ways because my mother has spelled them out to me, and I believe that God, to whom the commander is a sympathetic figure, will forgive them, as I forgive them. Is it not a shocking thing, is it not an aberration to have this kind of affection for a person who is practically a stranger? I reproached myself earlier on account of my favorable disposition toward Don Carlos, in defiance of, behind my mother's back. Now, though, I have almost the same reaction as you – I mean that my inclination toward Don Carlos seems natural to me too. The diabolic thing, the abominable thing, is my inclination toward your uncle. It's such a different feeling that it neither destroys nor lessens my affection for Don Carlos. This demonstrates my confused nature, my sinful and unbalanced behavior. I do not know with what pretext, with what right, with what affectionate name or connection I can go to him, talk to him, get close to him, and I want to. No matter how many detestable qualities my mother attributes to him, I feel that they are not in his makeup, because he is a being of a higher natural order and is exempt from the common law that exists for the rest of mortals."

With a fixed stare and an expression devoid of her customary smile, Lucía, sad and grave and at a loss to respond, listened to Clara's unexpected confession.

After a few moments of silence Clara continued:

"You have nothing to say, nothing to observe, you're quiet; you recognize that I am a monster. Maybe it's love of another kind, maybe it's a vague feeling that has no name in the category and history of passions, but I love your uncle and I love him because of the very description with which my mother has tried to get me to detest him."

At this point she was interrupted by Doña Blanca, who cried out:

"Clara, Clara!"

Lucía and Clara both shuddered. Although it was impossible that

Blanca las hubiese oído, imaginaron por un instante que milagrosamente las había oído y que iba a terciar en la conversación por estilo terrible.

–¿Qué manda usted, mamá?– dijo Clara temblando.

–Agua. Dame un poco de agua. ¡Me ahogo!

Las dos amigas acudieron a la alcoba a dar agua a la enferma. Entonces notaron con pena y sobresalto que la fiebre había crecido. Las palpitaciones del corazón de doña Blanca eran tan violentas que se hacían perceptibles al oído.

–¿Qué siente usted, señora?– preguntó Lucía.

–Una ansiedad... una fatiga...– respondió doña Blanca –, el corazón me late con tanta fuerza...

Lucía posó suavemente la mano sobre el pecho de doña Blanca. Entonces notó con pena que los latidos de su corazón habían perdido el ritmo natural; eran desordenados y anormales; pero no dijo nada por no asustar a la paciente y a su hija.

El cuidado que requería doña Blanca no consintió que prosiguiese el diálogo entre Clara y Lucía.

28

Tantos años de pesares y de tormentos habían ido destruyendo la salud de doña Blanca. Su tristeza sin tregua, su oculta vergüenza, con la que de continuo tenía que verse cara a cara, sin poder hallar alivio comunicándola y confiándose a una persona amiga; sus luchas de compasión y de desprecio por su marido y de amor y de odio por el comendador; su horror del pecado que creía sentir sobre ella y que le pesaba como lepra asquerosa e incurable; su orgullo ofendido; su temor del infierno, al que a veces se creía predestinada, y su preocupación incesante por la suerte de Clara, a quien amaba con fervor y a quien en ocasiones aborrecía, como vivo testimonio de su más grave falta y de su más imperdonable humillación, habían influido lastimosamente sobre todos los órganos de aquella vida corporal.

Doña Blanca hacía mucho tiempo estaba sujeta a frecuentes paroxismos histéricos. Había momentos en que le parecía que se ahogaba; un obstáculo se le atravesaba en la garganta y le quitaba la respiración.

Doña Blanca would have overheard them, they imagined for an instant that through some miracle she had indeed heard them and that she was going to join in the conversation in a terrible way.

"What can I do for you, Mamá?" asked Clara, trembling.

"Water. Bring me a little water. I'm suffocating!"

The two friends entered the bedroom to give water to the sick woman. They then saw with sorrow and concern that the fever had risen. The palpitations of Doña Blanca's heart were so violent that they could actually be heard.

"What do you feel, Señora?" asked Lucía.

"Anxiety ... fatigue," replied Doña Blanca. "My heart is beating so rapidly."

Lucía gently put her hand on Doña Blanca's chest. Then she noticed with yet more sorrow that her heartbeats had lost their natural rhythm; they were irregular and abnormal, but she kept that to herself so as not to alarm the patient and her daughter.

The care that Doña Blanca required did not permit the continuation of Clara and Lucía's conversation.

28

So many years of grief and torment had been wrecking Doña Blanca's health little by little. Her sadness without respite; her hidden shame, which she had to face continually, unable to find relief by sharing it and confiding it to a friend; her struggles with compassion and contempt for her husband and love and hatred for the commander; her horror of the sin that she believed she felt hovering over her and weighing on her like a loathsome, incurable leprosy; her wounded pride; her fear of hell, to which at times she thought herself predestined; and her incessant preoccupation with the fate of her daughter, whom she loved passionately and whom she sometimes detested, as living testimony of her gravest transgression and of her most unforgivable humiliation, had pitifully affected all the organs of that bodily life.

For a long time Doña Blanca had been prone to frequent bouts of hysterics. There were moments in which it seemed to her that she was suffocating, that an obstacle would lodge in her throat and prevent her

Entonces le daban convulsiones, que terminaban en sollozos y lágrimas. Después solía calmarse y quedar por algunos días tranquila, aunque pálida y débil.

El carácter violentísimo de aquella mujer, exacerbado por la continua contemplación de una desgracia, que hacía mayor su melancólica fantasía, la impulsaba a tratar a su marido, a su hija y a muchos de los que la rodeaban, con un despego, con una dureza cruel, de la que en el fondo del corazón, que era bueno, se arrepentía ella al cabo, no siendo fecundo este arrepentimiento sino en nuevos motivos de disgustos y de amargura. La energía de las pasiones había así, poco a poco, fatigado materialmente el corazón de doña Blanca, excitándole a moverse con impulso superior a sus fuerzas. No padecía sólo de las palpitaciones nerviosas de que daba muestras en aquel instante. Tal vez (los médicos al menos lo habían afirmado) doña Blanca tenía una enfermedad crónica de aquel órgano tan importante.

A pesar de su cansancio, tal vez el excesivo ejercicio había agrandado y robustecido de una manera peligrosa aquel activo corazón.

Como quiera que fuese, doña Blanca hacía tiempo que estaba harta de vivir.

La única idea, el único propósito, el solo fin que en su vivir estimaba era el de cumplir un deber terrible: el evitar que su hija heredase a don Valentín.

Cuando su hija le prometió con solemne promesa entrar en el claustro, y cuando después supo, de boca del padre Jacinto, y más tarde de los labios del mismo don Fadrique, el rescate de Clara, si bien le rechazó y le juzgó inútil ya, se tranquilizó, creyendo su propósito cumplido en cualquier evento, y considerándose desligada del mundo; sin nada que hacer en él sino atormentarse, y sin razón alguna para desear, estimar y conservar la vida.

El reposo relativo del espíritu de doña Blanca cuando pensó haber hallado la solución de su difícil problema, la hizo caer en una postración, en una atonía peligrosa. Por otro lado, no obstante, su imaginación fecunda en atormentarla le ofrecía mil motivos de aflicción y de ira. La generosidad del comendador humillaba su orgullo, y por más que trataba de empequeñecerla o de afear y envilecer sus causas fingiéndoselas vulgares, absurdas o caprichosas, dicha generosidad resplandecía siempre y la ofendía.

from breathing. Then she would undergo convulsions that ended in sobs and tears. Afterwards she usually calmed down and remained quiet for several days, although pale and weak.

The exceptionally violent character of that woman, exacerbated by the continual contemplation of a misfortune made even greater by her gloomy fantasy, drove her to treat her husband, her daughter, and many of those around her with an indifference, with a cruel harshness, of which – in the depths of her heart, which was good – she repented in the end, this repentance serving to bear fruit only in new motives for annoyance and bitterness.

The energy of the passion had thus, little by little, materially fatigued Doña Blanca's heart, prompting it to beat with an impulse in excess of its strength. She did not suffer only from the nervous palpitations that she exhibited at that moment. Perhaps (the doctors at least had confirmed it as such) Doña Blanca had a chronic disease in that important organ.

Despite its exhaustion, perhaps excessive exercise had enlarged and strengthened that active heart in a dangerous way.

Whatever the reason, Doña Blanca had been tired of life for a long time.

The only idea, the only aim, the sole end that she held dear in her existence was fulfilling a terrible duty: preventing her daughter from being the heir to Don Valentín.

When her daughter solemnly promised her that she would enter the cloister, and when she subsequently learned from Father Jacinto, and later from the lips of Don Fadrique himself, of Clara's ransom, Doña Blanca, although rejecting it and finding it useless now, breathed more freely. And it was because she believed that her aim had been realized in any event, and she considered herself detached from the world, with nothing to do in it except torment herself, shorn of any reason whatsoever to desire, esteem, and preserve life.

The relative repose of Doña Blanca's spirit when she thought that she had found the solution to her difficult problem caused her to fall into a state of prostration, into a dangerous atony. On the other hand, however, her imagination, productive in tormenting her, put forward a thousand reasons for grief and rage. The commander's generosity humiliated her pride, and for as much as she tried to belittle it or to discredit or debase his motives by pretending that they were trivial, absurd or capricious, said generosity always shone through and offended her.

La voluntad de doña Blanca era de hierro; pocas personas más pertinaces y firmes que ella; pero su espíritu vacilaba y no se aquietaba jamás. La fuerza de cualquier encontrado pensamiento bastaba a descontentarla de lo que había hecho, y no bastaba a hacerla cambiar y a moverla a hacer otra cosa. No producía sino nueva mortificación estéril.

Así es que doña Blanca percibía vivamente la presión que había ejercido sobre el alma de su hija; que, sin querer, acaso la había hecho infeliz; y que su hija iba a encerrarse en un convento, no devota, sino desesperada. Las rudas acusaciones del comendador durante la fatal entrevista, acusaciones contra las cuales se había ella defendido con valor y tino, terminada aquella lucha de palabras, acudían a su mente con mayor fuerza, sin que las dijera el comendador, sin que se pudieran rechazar merced al calor de la disputa, y labrando en su ánimo como una honda llaga.

El ardiente amor que el comendador le había infundido, siendo causa de que ella se humillase, se había convertido en espantoso aborrecimiento; y sin perder este carácter, sin volver a su ser primero, porque ya no era posible, porque su alma tenía mucha hiel para poder amar, habíase recrudecido en su seno durante la entrevista con el hombre que le inspiraba.

Todos estos dolores, tribulaciones y combates espirituales, no es de maravillar que produjesen en doña Blanca una enfermedad aguda, sobreexcitando sus males crónicos.

Poco después de la conversación entre Clara y Lucía, de que acabamos de dar cuenta, visitaron a la enferma los dos médicos mejores de la ciudad. Ambos convinieron en que su dolencia era de cuidado. Ambos reconocieron cierta alarmante alteración en la circulación de la sangre, que por fiebre sola no se explicaba. El corazón tenía una actividad enfermiza y un excesivo desarrollo. El pulso era vibrante y duro. El lado izquierdo del pecho de la enferma se estremecía con las palpitaciones. Un vivo carmín teñía las mejillas de doña Blanca, de ordinario pálidas.

Los médicos auguraron mal de éstos y otros síntomas: la principal dolencia estaba complicada con otras muchas. No hallando, pues, remedio eficaz por lo pronto, recetaron algunos paliativos, y entre ellos la digital en pequeñas dosis.

Doña Blanca's will was made of iron; there were very few people more obstinate than she, but her spirit vacillated and never quieted down. The force of any contrary or conflicting thought sufficed to displease her and make her dissatisfied with what she had done, although it did not suffice to make her change and prompt her to do something else. It produced only another barren mortification.

Thus it was that Doña Blanca had a clear grasp of the pressure that she had exerted on her daughter's psyche, and that she had perhaps unintentionally made her unhappy, and that her daughter was going to shut herself up in a convent, not as a devout novice, but as a novice in despair. The commander's harsh accusations during the fatal meeting, accusations against which she had defended herself courageously and adeptly, came back to her mind with greater force once the war of words had ended, without the commander having to say them again, without her being able to reject them in the heat of dispute, though they did work their way into her spirit like a deep wound.

The ardent love that the commander had awakened in her, which became the source of her humiliation, had changed into a frightful loathing; and without losing this character, without returning to its original state, because that was no longer possible, because her soul overflowed with too much bitterness to be able to love, the rage had erupted anew in her bosom during the meeting with the man who inspired it.

What with all these woes, tribulations, and spiritual battles, it was little wonder that Doña Blanca should suffer an acute breakdown, greatly aggravating her chronic ailments.

Shortly after the conversation between Clara and Lucía, which we have just related, the two best doctors in the city paid a call on the sick woman. Both agreed that her condition was cause for concern. Both detected a certain alarming irregularity in the circulation of the blood that could not be explained solely by the fever. Her heart, excessively enlarged, evinced an unwholesome activity. Her pulse was vibrant and hard, and the left side of her chest quivered with the palpitations. A vivid carmine tinged Doña Blanca's ordinarily pale cheeks.

These and other symptoms augured ill for the doctors; the primary ailment was complicated by many others. Unable, then, to pinpoint an effective remedy for the present, they prescribed a few palliatives, and among them digitalis in small doses.

Aunque disimularon bastante la gravedad y el carácter poco lisonjero de sus observaciones y pronósticos, dejaron a las dos amigas en extremo afectadas.

Todo aquel día permaneció Lucía al lado de Clara, auxiliándola en sus faenas y cuidados; pero ya no era ocasión propicia para volver a las confidencias.

Si bien Clara no volvió a hablar del estado de su alma, sin duda pensaba en él, según lo preocupada que estaba. Lo que antes de confiarse a Lucía había ella percibido en imágenes vagas y como borrosas, había adquirido, en su propia mente, mayor ser, consistencia y determinada figura al formularse en palabras. Así es que, en medio del afán y del dolor que por su madre sentía, Clara se atormentaba con la idea de aquella inclinación hacia un sujeto, a favor del cual, por extraordinario hechizo, se trocaban en causas y motivos de simpatía y afecto todas las razones que para aborrecerle le daban.

Lucía, por su parte, también estaba meditabunda y triste en extremo. Su taciturna tristeza, dado su carácter regocijado, parecía superior a la pena que pudiera sentir por el mal de doña Blanca, y aun al mismo disgusto que los devaneos mentales y los dolores fantásticos de su amiga debieran causarle.

Don Valentín, combatido por los opuestos sentimientos de la compasión y del terror que su mujer le inspiraba, seguía viniendo con frecuencia a informarse del estado de la paciente: pero, en vez de entrar en el cuarto y asomar la nariz a la alcoba, se quedaba fuera y asomaba sólo al cuarto la nariz, preguntando a su hija:

–¿Cómo está tu mamá?

Clara respondía: –Lo mismo–; y don Valentín se iba.

Fuera de la criada de más confianza, que ya venía a traer un recado, ya a dar algún auxilio indispensable, nadie más que el padre Jacinto entraba en la habitación donde se hallaban Clara y Lucía.

Al anochecer subió de punto, llegó a su colmo la agitación febril de doña Blanca. El padre Jacinto estaba acompañando a las dos amigas y asistiendo con ellas a la enferma.

Ésta, que había estado por la tarde soñolienta y postrada, empezó a dar señales de vivísima exaltación: se quejó de que le dolía la cabeza; mostró

Although they masked to a great extent the gravity and not very sanguine nature of their observations and prognoses, they left the two friends affected to an extreme.

That whole day Lucía remained at Clara's side, helping her with her tasks and watches, but it was not a propitious time to go back to sharing confidences.

Despite the fact that Clara did not speak again of the state of her soul, from her patent preoccupation there was no doubt that she thought of it. What she had perceived in vague and as though fuzzy images before confiding to Lucía had assumed, in her mind's eye, greater substance, consistency, and actual form when put into words. Thus it was that, in the midst of the anxiety and grief that she felt for her mother, Clara tormented herself over being well-disposed toward an individual in whose favor, by an extraordinary bit of magic, all the reasons she had been given to detest him were transformed into causes and grounds for sympathy and affection.

Lucía, for her part, was also pensive and extremely downcast. Her taciturn sadness, given her cheerful temperament, seemed in excess of the pain she could feel on account of Doña Blanca's illness, and even in excess of the chagrin that her friend's nonsensical ravings and fantastic sorrows ought to have caused her.

Torn between the opposing emotions of compassion and terror that his wife inspired in him, Don Valentín continued to come frequently to inquire about the patient's condition, but instead of entering the antechamber and peeking around the bedroom door, he stayed outside and only poked his nose in the outer room, asking his daughter:

"How's your mother?"

Clara would reply:

"No change."

And Don Valentín would leave.

Except for the most trusted maid, who either brought a message or came in now and then to give an indispensable hand, no one but Father Jacinto entered the room that Clara and Lucía were in.

At nightfall Doña Blanca's feverish agitation worsened and reached its highest point. Father Jacinto was accompanying the two friends and tending the sick woman with them.

The latter, who had been drowsy and prostrate in the afternoon, began to show signs of intense overexcitement: she complained that her head

en el semblante cierta movilidad convulsa; pronunció frases sin orden ni concierto. Lo que más repetía era:

–Vete, Valentín. Déjame, no me atormentes– . Sin duda la enferma tenía la alucinación de ver a don Valentín, que allí no estaba.

Así permaneció doña Blanca hasta cerca de las diez. Entonces se agravó el mal: el delirio se declaró; estalló con ímpetu.

El cerebro sintió por completo la reacción del mal que la infeliz tenía en las entrañas. Los pensamientos todos, que durante años la atormentaban, y que hacía más de treinta horas habían cobrado mayor brío, se barajaron en tumulto; se rebelaron contra la voluntad, se hicieron independientes de ella, rompieron todo freno; y, buscando y hallando maquinal e instintivamente palabras adecuadas en que formularse, salieron del pecho en descompuestas voces.

Doña Blanca se incorporó en la cama; miró con ojos extraviados a Lucía y a Clara y al fraile, y habló de esta manera:

–¡Vete, Valentín! ¿Por qué quieres matarme con tu presencia? Mátame con un puñal... con una pistola. Échame una soga al cuello y ahórcame. No seas cobarde. Toma la debida venganza.

–Sosiégate, doña Blanca– interrumpió el fraile, a quien ella se dirigía como si fuera don Valentín –. Sosiégate; tu marido está fuera... Idos, muchachas– añadió, dirigiéndose a las dos amigas –. Dejadme solo con la enferma, a ver si logro que se sosiegue.

Clara y Lucía, como si estuviesen allí clavadas, no se movieron. Doña Blanca prosiguió:

–Ten valor y mátame. Tu honra lo exige. Es necesario que mates también al comendador. Está condenado. Se irá al infierno y me llevará consigo.

–¡Madre, madre, usted delira!– exclamó Clara.

–No, no deliro– respondió doña Blanca –. Y tú, necio– añadió dirigiéndose al fraile –, ¿Eres ciego? ¿No la ves?– y señalaba con el dedo a su hija –. ¡Cómo se le parece! ¡Dios mío! ¡Cómo se le parece! Es un retrato suyo. ¡Apártate de mi vista, vivo testimonio de mi vergüenza!

Clara, llena de horror y de ansiosa curiosidad a la vez, oía a su madre y pugnaba por comprender todo el arcano tremendo. Al sonar las últimas palabras, que iban dirigidas a ella, se cubrió Clara el rostro con ambas manos.

hurt; she betrayed a certain convulsive twitch in her face; she articulated disordered, disjointed utterances. What she most repeated was:

"Go away, Valentín. Leave me, don't torment me."

The sick woman no doubt was hallucinating and thought she saw Don Valentín, who was not there.

Doña Blanca remained in this state until close to ten o'clock. Then the illness became aggravated, and delirium took hold, breaking out violently.

The overwhelmed brain reacted outright to the illness ravaging the poor woman's insides. All the thoughts that had been tormenting her for years, and that for more than thirty hours had taken on renewed vigor, jumbled up in tumult; they rebelled against her will; they declared independence from her; they loosed every restraint; and, mechanically and instinctively, seeking and finding apt words in which to be formulated, emerged from those same insides in disordered utterances.

Doña Blanca sat up in the bed; she stared with vacant eyes at Lucía and Clara and the friar, and spoke as follows:

"Go away, Valentín! Why do you want to kill me with your presence? Kill me with a dagger ... with a pistol. Put a rope around my neck and hang me. Don't be a coward. Take proper revenge."

"Calm yourself, Doña Blanca," interrupted the friar, to whom she was speaking as if he were Don Valentín. "Calm yourself. Your husband isn't here. Leave, girls," he added, looking at the two friends. "Let me be alone with her to see whether I manage to quiet her."

As if they were riveted there, Clara and Lucía did not move. Doña Blanca continued:

"Be brave and kill me. Your honor demands it. You have to kill the commander too. He's damned. He'll go to hell and take me with him."

"Mother, Mother, you're delirious!" exclaimed Clara.

"No, I am not delirious," responded Doña Blanca. "And you, you fool," she added, speaking to the friar, "are you blind? Don't you see her?" and she pointed to her daughter. "How she resembles him! My God, how she resembles him! She's the very image of him. Get out of my sight, you living testimony to my shame!"

Filled with horror and anxious curiosity all at once, Clara listened to her mother and struggled to comprehend the full meaning of that tremendous mystery. On hearing the last words, which were directed to her, Clara covered her face with both hands.

–Bien puedes estar satisfecha– continuó doña Blanca –. Te tenía olvidada; pero al cabo se acordó de ti e hizo un gran sacrificio. Ya pagó de antemano lo que has de heredar de mi marido. Te rescató de Dios para entregarte al mundo. Quédate en el mundo. Tú no puedes ser monja. La mala sangre del comendador hierve en tus venas. ¿Cómo dudar que eres hija maldita de aquel impío?

Clara, al oír estas últimas palabras, dio un grito inarticulado, y cayó desmayada entre los brazos de Lucía.

Lucía sacó a Clara fuera de la alcoba, sosteniéndola por debajo de los brazos y tirando de ella.

Doña Blanca, entre tanto, no pudiendo resistir más la honda emoción, extenuada, rendida, cayó de nuevo en la cama, con temblor convulso y rigidez de los tendones, lo cual fue cediendo con lentitud y dando lugar a un desfallecimiento profundo.

El padre Jacinto acudió entonces a donde estaba Clara, que Lucía había recostado en un sofá.

Clara volvió en sí del desmayo; exhaló un suspiro y rompió a llorar con desatado y copioso llanto.

–¡Clara, amiga querida!– dijo Lucía.

–Cálmate, niña, cálmate– exclamó el.padre Jacinto.

–¡Dios santo y misericordioso!– dijo Clara –. Tu mano omnipotente me hiere y me sana al propio tiempo. ¡Pobre madre mía de mi alma! ¡Cuán infeliz has sido! Y él... ¡ay! Él... no puede ser impío y perverso como tú supones... ¡Ahora comprendo por qué y cómo yo le amaba!

29

La enfermedad siguió su curso ascendente. Tres días después de la escena que hemos descrito, doña Blanca estaba tan mal que no había esperanza de salvarla.

Su hija y Lucía la habían cuidado, la habían velado con el mayor cariño y esmero.

Los accesos de delirio se habían renovado con largas intermitencias de postración.

La cabeza de doña Blanca se despejó al cabo por completo; pero su estado era digno de lástima: la respiración, corta y anhelante; la voz,

"You can certainly be satisfied," continued Doña Blanca. "He had forgotten you, but in the end he remembered you and made a great sacrifice. He's already paid in advance what you are to inherit from my husband. He ransomed you from God to hand you over to the world. Stay in the world. You can't be a nun. The commander's bad blood bubbles in your veins. How can there be any doubt that you are the accursed daughter of that infidel?"

When she heard these last words, Clara uttered an inarticulate cry and fell into Lucía's arms in a swoon.

Lucía took Clara out of the bedroom, supporting her under the arms and tugging at her.

Meanwhile, Doña Blanca, unable to withstand the deep emotion any longer, wasted and exhausted as she was, fell back on the bed with convulsive trembling and stiffness in her tendons, which condition slowly abated and gave way to profound enervation.

Father Jacinto then came out and went over to the sofa on which Lucía had reclined Clara.

When she regained consciousness, Clara heaved a sigh and burst out crying, shedding unrestrained and copious tears.

"Clara, my dear friend!" exclaimed Lucía.

"Calm down, child, calm down," urged Father Jacinto.

"Holy and merciful God!" said Clara. "Your omnipotent hand wounds and heals me at the same time. My poor mother! How unhappy you have been! And he ... oh, he cannot be the ungodly and perverse person you make him out to be. Now I understand why and how I loved him!"

29

The illness continued on its upward spiral. Three days after the scene we have described, Doña Blanca was so unwell that there was no hope of saving her.

Her daughter and Lucía had tended to her, had watched over her with the utmost solicitousness and care.

The outbursts of delirium had returned with long intermissions of prostration.

At length Doña Blanca's mind cleared completely, but her condition was worthy of pity: she gasped for breath; her voice had become hoarse;

alterada y ronca; imposibilidad de estar acostada: necesidad de estar incorporada.

Los médicos declararon al padre Jacinto que había sobrevenido un grave impedimento a la circulación de la sangre en el mismo corazón; y que si crecía el impedimento se seguiría la muerte.

El padre dejó percibir a Clara aquel terrible pronóstico, con la mayor delicadeza que pudo, y confesó y administró a la paciente.

En aquel momento supremo, a las puertas de la eternidad, doña Blanca depuso la dureza de su genio, su orgullo y su amargura, y no guardó en el alma sino la fe vivísima, que hizo renacer en ella las esperanzas ultramundanas y abrió el manantial de las más puras consolaciones.

Doña Blanca llamó a don Valentín, le abrazó y le suplicó que la perdonase. Don Valentín, muy afligido y lloroso, y no menos humilde, contestó que nada tenía que perdonar; que él era el culpado, pues no había sabido hacer dichosa a una mujer tan santa y tan buena.

El rostro macilento de doña Blanca se tiñó entonces de ligero rubor. Sus labios exhalaron un triste suspiro.

A Clara la llamó a sí doña Blanca; le dio un beso en la frente, y le dijo al oído con acento apenas perceptible:

–Di a tu padre que le perdono. Tú, hija mía, sigue los impulsos de tu corazón. Eres libre. Sé honrada. No te cases si no le amas mucho. Mira no te engañes. Lo sé todo... Me lo ha dicho el padre Jacinto. Si le amas y merece tu amor, cásate con él.

Pocos instantes después exhaló doña Blanca el último suspiro, diciendo con ahogada y sumisa voz:

–¡Jesús me valga!

El dolor de Clara fue profundo. Silenciosamente lloró la muerte de su madre.

Lucía lloró también y trató de mitigar con su afecto el dolor de su amiga.

El padre Jacinto, acostumbrado al espectáculo de la muerte y familiarizado con ella, cerró piadosamente los ojos y la boca de la difunta, que se habían quedado abiertos, puso sus manos en cruz, y la extendió en el lecho.

El débil don Valentín, cuando vio muerta a su mujer, sintió por un lado una pena muy viva, porque todavía la amaba; pero, por otro lado,

and it was impossible for her to lie in a supine position, which forced her to sit up in bed.

The doctors informed Father Jacinto that a grave obstruction to the circulation of blood had supervened in the heart itself, and that if the obstruction increased, death would follow.

The priest acquainted Clara with that terrible prognosis as gently as he could, and then he heard the patient's confession and administered the last rites to her.

At that supreme moment, at eternity's door, Doña Blanca laid aside her harsh temper, her pride, and her bitterness, and preserved in her soul only her deep-rooted faith, which brought about the rebirth of otherworldly hopes and opened the fountain of the purest consolations.

Doña Blanca sent for Don Valentín, embraced him, and begged his forgiveness. Don Valentín, visibly distressed and teary-eyed, and no less humble, replied that he had nothing to forgive, that he was the blameworthy one, seeing as how he had failed to make such a good and saintly woman happy.

Doña Blanca's haggard face blushed slightly, while her lips heaved a sad sigh.

Doña Blanca then called Clara to her, kissed her on the forehead and whispered to her in a barely audible voice:

"Tell your father that I forgive him. And you, my daughter, follow the dictates of your heart. You're free, released from the promise you made me. Be honorable. Do not marry him if you do not love him very much. Watch you don't delude yourself. I know everything. Father Jacinto told me. If you love him and he is deserving of your love, marry him."

Only moments afterward Doña Blanca sighed for the last time, exclaiming in a faint, submissive voice:

"Jesus, save me!"

Clara's grief was profound. She wept silently over her mother's death.

Lucía wept too and tried to mitigate her friend's grief with her affection.

Accustomed to the sight of death and familiar with it, Father Jacinto piously closed the deceased woman's eyes and mouth, which had remained open; he then set her hands in a cross and laid her on the bed.

When the weak Don Valentín saw his wife dead, he felt, on the one hand, acute grief because he still loved her; but on the other, according

según aseguran malas lenguas, que siempre están de sobra, advirtió
cierto alivio, cierto desahogo, cierto infame deleite en su alma, como
si le quitaran un enorme peso de encima; como si le libertaran de la
esclavitud. Tan opuestas pasiones, batallando dentro de su nerviosa y
débil constitución, le hicieron romper en risa sardónica. Después se
asustó de sí mismo; se creyó peor de lo que era; tuvo miedo del diablo;
tuvo vergüenza de que Dios, que todo lo ve, viese la sucia fealdad de
su conciencia, y se compungió y amilanó. Acudieron entonces a su
memoria los amores pasados, los dulces días de la ilusión, el tiempo
en que su mujer le quería; todo ello enterneció por tal arte aquel pecho
nada varonil, que el desgraciado se deshizo en lágrimas, dando sollozos,
gemidos y hasta gritos, moviendo a gran compasión el verle y el oírle.

El padre Jacinto llevó a don Fadrique la noticia de la catástrofe.

Don Fadrique, retirado en su cuarto, aguardaba siempre con ansiedad
noticias de la enferma. Esta vez, al mirar al padre Jacinto, el comendador
leyó en su rostro lo que había ocurrido.

—Ha muerto— dijo el comendador.

—Ha muerto— respondió el fraile.

El comendador no replicó palabra. Inmóvil, de pie, callado, sintió
un dolor mezclado de remordimiento. Dos gruesas y amargas lágrimas
rodaron por sus mejillas.

—Te ha perdonado— dijo el padre Jacinto.

—¡Ah, padre!... yo no me perdono... Me sería menos insufrible en la
memoria el recuerdo de una afrenta no vengada... de una vileza en que
yo hubiese incurrido... de una mancha en mi honor... En cualquiera otro
caso me sería más fácil conciliarme conmigo mismo. Aunque Dios me
perdone... yo no me perdono.

30

A los seis meses de la muerte de doña Blanca, en pleno invierno, se
reunían todas las noches en torno del hogar, en el piso alto de la casa
del mayorazgo don José López de Mendoza, a más de su mujer y de su
hija Lucía, el comendador don Fadrique, el viudo don Valentín, Clara y
a veces el padre Jacinto.

to gossips who are never in short supply, he noticed a certain relief, a certain ease, a certain infamous delight in his soul, as if an enormous weight had been lifted from him, as if he had been freed from servitude. Such contrary passions, battling in his nervous and weak constitution, made him break into sardonic laughter. Afterwards he became frightened of himself; he thought himself worse than he was; he feared the devil; he was ashamed that God, who sees everything, would see the despicable ugliness of his conscience; and he felt remorse and quaked with fright. Then he recalled past love, sweet days of illusion, the time when his wife loved him, and all of it moved his far from manly heart in such a way that the wretched creature burst into tears, sobbing and moaning and even wailing, which aroused much pity in the people who saw him and heard him.

Father Jacinto took the news of the catastrophe to Don Fadrique.

Having retired to his room, Don Fadrique still anxiously awaited news of the sick Doña Blanca. When he looked at Father Jacinto this time, the commander read in his face what had happened.

"She's dead," said the commander.

"She's dead," responded the friar.

The commander said not a word in reply. Standing perfectly still, he felt sorrow intermingled with remorse. Two big, bitter tears rolled down his cheeks.

"She forgave you," said Father Jacinto.

"Alas, Father! I don't forgive myself. Other things would be less unbearable in my memory – the recollection of an unavenged affront... a vile act that I might have committed... a stain on my honor. In any other circumstance it would be easier for me to be reconciled with myself. Even if God forgives me, I don't forgive myself."

30

Six months after Doña Blanca's death, in the depth of winter, there was a gathering every evening around the fireplace of the top floor of the home of the *mayorazgo* Don José López de Mendoza. Besides Don José himself, his wife, and his daughter Lucía, the other habitués were the commander Don Fadrique, the widower Don Valentín, Clara, and now and then Father Jacinto.

El joven don Carlos de Atienza había estado dos o tres veces en Sevilla a ver a sus padres; pero en seguida se había vuelto. Tenía abandonada la Universidad; no pensaba en los estudios ni en la carrera. Habíase consagrado enteramente a idolatrar, a consolar, a adorar a Clarita, a quien ya veía sin dificultad, de diario.

Don Fadrique y el padre Jacinto iban y venían a Villabermeja; pero estaban más tiempo en la ciudad.

La donación de los bienes de don Fadrique se había hecho en toda regla y con el posible sigilo.

Don Fadrique vivía modestamente de su paga de oficial retirado. Habitaba, no obstante, en Villabermeja, la casa del mayorazgo, alhajada con los preciosos muebles que trajo cuando vino.

El carácter de don Fadrique no había cambiado, pero se había modificado. Su optimismo natural sufría interrupciones frecuentes. Negra nube de tristeza ofuscaba a menudo el resplandor de su abierta y franca fisonomía.

Aquel dolor por la muerte de doña Blanca se había ido mitigando en todos aquellos corazones, Clara la recordaba con ternura melancólica, y el comendador con cariño y con penoso arrepentimiento a la vez.

Sólo don Valentín, que comía como un buitre, y que había engordado, y no hallaba quien le riñese ni quien le dominase, se creía en la obligación de llorar cuando menos ganas tenía. Entonces, la consideración de aquello a que se juzgaba obligado, y el ver que no le salían de adentro la aflicción y el lloro, le compungían de nuevo y producían en él el prurito y el flujo. Don Valentín era un mar de lágrimas dos o tres veces por semana.

Clara, viendo ya a todas horas a don Carlos y a don Fadrique, había penetrado la diferencia de los afectos que a ambos ligaba, y cada día los hallaba más compatibles. El comendador le inspiraba cada día más veneración, ternura y gratitud por su sacrificio generoso. Don Carlos le parecía cada día más agraciado, bello, enamorado, ingenioso y poeta.

Pasaron así algunos meses más. Vino la primavera. Llegó el verano. Solemnizóse el primer aniversario de la muerte de doña Blanca con llanto y con misas y otras devociones.

El escrúpulo de faltar a la promesa de ser monja se borró al fin de la mente de Clarita. Su madre, al morir, la había absuelto de la promesa. El

Young Don Carlos de Atienza had been to Seville two or three times to see his parents, but had returned posthaste. He had abandoned the university and gave no thought to studies or a profession. He had devoted himself entirely to idolizing, consoling, and adoring Clarita, whom he now saw daily without difficulty.

Don Fadrique and Father Jacinto traveled back and forth to Villabermeja, but spent most of their time in the city.

The transfer of Don Fadrique's assets to Don Casimiro had been made with all the legalities and with the greatest possible secrecy.

Don Fadrique lived modestly on his pay as a retired naval officer. He continued to reside, nonetheless, in his brother's house in Villabermeja, which was appointed with the exquisite furniture he had brought with him upon returning from his travels.

Don Fadrique's character had not changed, but it had become tempered. His natural optimism underwent frequent disruptions. A black cloud of somberness often obscured the brightness of his frank features.

Although the grief over Doña Blanca's death had gradually lessened in all those hearts, Clara remembered her with melancholy tenderness, and the commander with affection and painful remorse at the same time.

Only Don Valentín, who ate like a horse and had put on weight, and who had no one to scold him or dominate him, thought himself obliged to cry when he least felt like it. Then, consideration of what he believed he was constrained to do, and awareness that the affliction and weeping did not come from inside, stirred remorse anew and triggered the urge and the flow. Don Valentín turned into a sea of tears two or three times a week.

Clara, now that she was seeing Don Carlos and Don Fadrique all the time, had discerned the difference of affections that bound her to both, and with each passing day she found them more compatible. Also with each passing day the commander inspired in her more veneration, tenderness, and gratitude for his generous sacrifice, while Don Carlos seemed to her ever more graceful, handsome, in love, and ingenious, as well as more of a poet.

Thus did several more months go by. Spring came. Summer arrived. The first anniversary of Doña Blanca's death was solemnized with tears and with masses and other devotions.

Scruples about not keeping her promise to be a nun were finally erased from Clarita's mind. Her mother, on her deathbed, had released her from

amor inspirado y sentido la excitaba a no cumplirla. El bueno del padre Jacinto, confesor de Clarita, le aseguraba que la promesa era nula.

Clarita al cabo la anuló, haciendo otra promesa dulcísima para don Carlos. Le prometió darle su mano, confesándole al fin que le amaba.

Una alambicada cavilación había detenido a Clara en dar el sí a don Carlos. Clara juzgaba probable que don Casimiro muriese sin sucesión y que alguna parte de los bienes del rescate viniese a ella; pero hasta esta duda, que si bien delgada y sutil, la mortificaba, se disipó del todo.

Nicolasa, o mejor dicho, la señora doña Nicolasa Lobo de Solís, esposa legítima de don Casimiro, dio a luz un robusto infante.

Cuando el comendador, al volver un día de Villabermeja, trajo esta noticia, fue Lucía la primera persona a quien se la comunicó.

–Calle usted, tío– exclamó la muchacha –. De seguro que el niño de don Casimiro será un escomendrijo; parecerá un gazapillo desollado.

–No, sobrina– contestó el comendador –; el recién nacido Solís es fuerte como un becerro.

Así era la verdad, según hemos sabido después. El primogénito de los Solises parecía, no un becerro, sino un toro.

Don Casimiro era el varón más bienaventurado de la tierra. Estaba lleno de satisfacción y de orgullo de verse tan amado de su mujer, y de tener por hijo a un Hércules tebano, sin pensar en el Saturnio y sin mirarse como Anfitrión, pues ignoraba la mitología.

El tío Gorico, desde el casamiento de Nicolasa, había empezado a pugnar porque le llamasen don Gregorio; habíase jubilado del oficio de Abraham y del de pellejero, y no se empleaba más que en beber aguardiente y rosoli, y en ponderar la ventura y la grandeza de su hija, sus virtudes y la vida beata que daba a su ilustre esposo.

Después del bautismo de la criatura, iba el tío Gorico de casa en casa, refiriendo el júbilo de su yerno, quien ya se volvía hacia la cama donde estaba Nicolasa, ya hacia la cuna donde estaba el niño, y ya se paraba a igual distancia de la cama y de la cuna, y exclamaba, levantando las manos al cielo:

–¡Dios mío! ¡Dios mío! ¿Qué he hecho yo para ser tan dichoso?

the promise. The love that she inspired and felt induced her not to keep it. The good Father Jacinto, Clarita's confessor, assured her that the promise was null.

Clarita retracted it in the end and made another promise, the sweetest of them all, to Don Carlos. She promised to give him her hand, confessing at length that she loved him.

A complicated apprehension had caused Clara to put off saying yes to Don Carlos. She considered it likely that Don Casimiro would die without issue, and that some part of the ransom assets would revert to her, but even this misgiving – which, although tenuous and subtle, mortified her – was completely dispelled.

Nicolasa, or rather Señora Doña Nicolasa Lobo de Solís, lawful wife of Don Casimiro, gave birth to a robust baby boy.

When the commander brought this news one day upon his return from Villabermeja, Lucía was the first person he told.

"Go on, Uncle!" exclaimed the girl. "Don Casimiro's child must be a runt for sure. He probably looks like a skinned little rabbit."

"No, Lucía, he doesn't," said the commander. "The newly born Solís is as strong as a baby bull."

Which was the truth, as we learned afterwards. In fact, the Solíses firstborn seemed more a grown bull than a baby bull.

Don Casimiro was the most fortunate man alive. He brimmed with satisfaction and pride at being so loved by his wife, and at having for a son a Theban Hercules, without thinking of Saturn and without viewing himself as Amphitryon, for he was ignorant of mythology.[91]

Since Nicolasa's marriage, Tío Gorico had begun to push to be called "Don Gregorio." He had retired from his Holy Week role as Abraham and from his trade as a tanner, and all he did was wile away the hours drinking brandy and rosolio, and pondering his daughter's good fortune and rise on the social scale, as well as her virtues, and the blessed life that she provided for her husband.

After the child's baptism, Tío Gorico went from house to house, recounting the jubilation of his son-in-law, who first would direct his steps toward the bed in which Nicolasa lay and then toward the cradle in which the baby lay, only to stop midway between the bed and the cradle and exclaim, raising his hands to heaven:

"Dear Lord! Dear Lord! What have I done to be so happy?"

En efecto, la dicha pudo más que don Casimiro, y pronto se hundió en la sepultura.

Aunque sea adelantar los sucesos, se dirá aquí que la viuda llevó una vida retirada, sin recibir ni tratar, durante un año, sino al platónico Tomasuelo, y que tuvo dos gemelos póstumos, los cuales, si el primogénito merecía llamarse Hércules, no merecían menos pasar por Cástor y Pólux.

La rectitud de la conciencia de doña Blanca y sus severos fallos, hallando un leal y decidido ejecutor en don Fadrique, daban así sus resultados naturales, proporcionando pingüe herencia a aquellos mitológicos angelitos, vástagos lozanos de la familia de Solís.

Como quiera que fuese, toda persona delicada y noblemente orgullosa no repara en las bajezas y bellaquerías del vulgo de los mortales y en la utilidad que proporcionan: no acepta jamás, sino en sentido irónico y de burla, la picaresca sentencia de la fábula:

> Tómelo por su vida: considere
> que otro lo comerá, si no lo quiere.

Así es que don Fadrique se reía de las consecuencias de su desprendimiento, y no por eso dejaba de aplaudirse de haberle tenido. Lo que a él le importaba era que su pura y hermosa hija no disfrutase de nada que no fuese suyo o por lo que en compensación no hubiera él dado lo equivalente con usura.

La boda de Clara y de don Carlos de Atienza se celebró al cabo en un bello día del mes de octubre de 1795, año y medio después de morir doña Blanca.

Los padres de don Carlos vinieron de Sevilla para asistir a la boda.

Los desposados se quedaron a vivir en la ciudad donde ha sido la escena de nuestra historia.

Durante el año y medio, que tan rápidamente hemos recorrido, el comendador había vivido, ya en Villabermeja, ya en la ciudad en casa de su hermano; pero más en la ciudad que en Villabermeja.

El afecto hacia Clara le atraía a la ciudad; pero como Clara andaba muy distraída en sus amores y era muy dichosa, no consolaba tanto las melancolías del comendador como su rubia sobrina.

Too happy by half, as that happiness undid Don Casimiro and soon sank him into his grave.

Although it may constitute getting ahead of events, we shall note here that the widow led a secluded life for a year, without receiving anyone but the platonic Tomasuelo, and that she delivered posthumous twins, who, if the firstborn deserved to be Hercules, deserved no less than to pass for Castor and Pollux.

Doña Blanca's rectitude of conscience and its severe judgments, finding a loyal and resolute executor in Don Fadrique, thus brought about the natural results that provided a rich inheritance to those mythological little angels, robust offspring of the house of Solís.

Be that as it may, any refined and nobly proud individual pays no mind to the base and rascally deeds of the lower order of mortals, nor to the gains and advantages that accrue from them. He never lends credence, except in a mocking, ironic vein, to the tongue-in-cheek import of the saying:

> Take it, my word!, and make haste,
> For another will not let it go to waste.[92]

Thus it was that Don Fadrique smiled at the consequences of his generosity, but nevertheless he still gave himself a pat on the back for having practiced it. What mattered to him was that his pure and beautiful daughter not enjoy anything that was not hers or for which, by way of compensation, he had not given the liberal equivalent.

The marriage of Clara and Don Carlos de Alienza finally took place on a lovely day in the month of October, 1795, a year and a half after Doña Blanca's death.

Don Carlos's parents came from Seville in order to attend the wedding.

The newly married couple elected to stay and live in the city that was the scene of our story.

During the year and a half that we have covered so rapidly, the commander had divided his time between Villabermeja and his brother's house in the city, but more in the city than in Villabermeja.

His love for Clara drew him to the city, but as Clara was very absorbed in her husband and was very happy in her marriage, she did not console the commander's bouts of melancholy as much as did his fair-haired niece.

Ésta era la que llamaba al comendador cuando se tardaba en volver de Villabermeja; la que más le escribía diciéndole que viniese, y la que le enviaba recados con el mulero y con el aperador para que dejase la soledad bermejina.

Como Lucía estaba enterada ya de todos los secretos de su amiga Clara, y como tampoco ocurrían cosas importantes, no había motivo ni pretexto para acudir a cada momento al tío, preguntándole, como en otro tiempo, qué había de nuevo. En cambio Lucía, libre ya de los cuidados en que la suerte de su amiga la había tenido, sintió despertarse en su alma la más viva curiosidad científica. La astronomía y la botánica, que antes la enojaban cuando había secretos de Clara que ansiaba penetrar, la entusiasmaban ahora extraordinariamente, y nunca se cansaba de oír las lecciones que su tío le daba, excitado por ella. No había lección que no le pareciese corta. No había misterio de las flores que no quisiese descubrir. No había estrella que no quisiese conocer.

La discípula ponía en grandes apuros al maestro, porque si se trataba del movimiento de los astros, de su magnitud, de la distancia a que se hallaban de la tierra y de otras afirmaciones por el estilo, ella quería saber la razón y el fundamento de las afirmaciones, y don Fadrique hallaba disparatado y hasta absurdo enseñar las matemáticas a una sobrina tan guapa, tan alegre y graciosa; y, por el contrario, si se trataba de flores, Lucía quería que le explicase su tío lo que era la vida y lo que era el organismo, y aquí el comendador hallaba que no había ciencia que respondiese a las matemáticas y que explicase algo. Sin querer se encumbraba entonces a una filosofía primera y fundamental, y Lucía le escuchaba embebecida, y, como vulgarmente se dice, metía también su cucharada, porque de filosofía habla, en queriendo, y no habla mal, toda persona de imaginación y viveza.

En suma, Lucía se iba haciendo una sabia. Mientras más aprendía, más iba creciendo su afición y su empeño de saber. Las lecciones y conferencias duraban horas y horas.

El comendador se acostumbró de tal suerte a aquel dulce magisterio, que el día en que no daba lección le parecía que no había vivido.

Sus días de Villabermeja fueron disminuyendo, y alargándose cada vez más los que pasaba con la discípula.

Siempre que volvía de Villabermeja, el comendador traía a su discípula

The latter was the one who kept in touch with the commander when he took a long time in returning from Villabermeja, the one who wrote him most telling him to come, and the one who sent him messages with the muleteer and the overseer so that he would forsake his Villabermejan solitude.

Inasmuch as Lucía was now privy to all the secrets of her friend Clara, and given that no important matters were afoot, there was no reason or pretext for her to continually seek out her uncle, asking him, as before, what was new. On the other hand, freed now from the concern in which her friend's fate had engrossed her, Lucía felt her spirit being stirred by the most intense scientific curiosity. Astronomy and botany, which earlier had irritated her when she longed to uncover Clara's secrets, now filled her with the greatest enthusiasm, and she never tired of the instruction that she prodded her uncle into giving her. There was no lesson that she did not want to prolong; no mystery with regard to flowers that she did not want to discover; and no star that she did not want to know. Many a time the pupil put the teacher in a tight spot, because if the lesson dealt with the movement of the stars, their magnitude, their respective distances from Earth, and other facts of this kind, she wanted to know the reason and the basis for the facts, and Don Fadrique thought it crazy and even absurd to teach mathematics to such a pretty and such a cheerful and charming niece; and if, on the contrary, it had to do with flowers, Lucía wanted her uncle to explain to her what life was and what an organism was, and here the commander found that there was no science corresponding to mathematics that would explain anything. Without meaning to, he would then ascend to a plane of basic, fundamental philosophy, and Lucía would listen to him in fascination, and, to cite a popular expression, would also "put her two cents in," because when it comes to philosophy anyone with imagination and a quick mind can, if they wish to, engage in oral discourse and hold their own.

In short, Lucía was turning into a learned young lady. The more she learned, the more her inclination and determination grew. The lessons and lectures lasted for hours on end.

The commander became accustomed to that sweet pedagogy in such a way that the days on which he did not give a lesson it seemed to him that he had not lived. He took to spending less and less time in Villabermeja and more and more time in the city with his pupil.

Whenever he came back from Villabermeja, the commander would

libros de su biblioteca, flores y plantas de su huerto, y pájaros que cazaba vivos. Lucía gustaba mucho de los pájaros, y, merced al comendador, no había ya casta de aves en toda la provincia, ora de paso, ora permanentes, de que Lucía no tuviese un par de muestra en su pajarera.

Notado todo esto por Clara y don Carlos, daba ocasión a bromas inocentes, pero que turbaban algo al comendador y que ponían a Lucía colorada como la grana.

Los novios hablaban a Lucía con cierto retintín de su excesivo amor a la ciencia.

En fin, aunque el comendador y Lucía no se hubieran dado, ni hubieran querido darse cuenta de lo que les pasaba, Clara y don Carlos les hubieran hecho reflexionar, pensar en ellos mismos y despejar la incógnita.

El comendador y Lucía, a pesar de la diferencia de edad, estaban perdidamente enamorados el uno del otro.

Lucía admiraba en su tío la discreción, la nobleza de carácter, el saber y la elegancia natural del porte y de los modales. Le encontraba hermoso de varonil hermosura, y no le parecía posible que hubiese otro tal hombre como él en todo el mundo.

A don Fadrique le parecía Lucía tan bonita, tan buena y tan inteligente como Clara, que era todo cuanto él podía encarecer la alabanza, allá en su pensamiento. La alegría de Lucía concordaba además muchísimo mejor con el carácter del comendador que la seriedad un poco triste que Clara había heredado de su madre.

El comendador, que al fin no era una criatura inexperta, conoció pronto que amaba a Lucía y que de ella era amado; pero, pensando en su edad y en el idilio de don Carlos, no se atrevía a declarar su amor, si bien le manifestaba con su constante solicitud en servir a Lucía.

Ella no atinaba, entre tanto, a comprender la timidez del comendador, a quien juzgaba enamorado.

De aquí que se dijesen toda clase de requiebros y finezas, que literalmente podrían tomarse por efecto de amistad tiernísima, pero que ocultaban el fervoroso espíritu del verdadero amor.

Don Fadrique, a más de sus años, creía tener otro inconveniente, que en su delicadeza no le permitía aspirar a ser amado por Lucía. Este

bring his pupil books from his library, flowers and plants from his garden, and birds that he bagged alive. Lucía liked birds very much, and, thanks to the commander, there was now no species of bird in the entire province, whether migratory or permanent, of which Lucía did not have a few specimens in her aviary.

All this had been noticed by Clara and Don Carlos, which gave rise to innocent jokes, but jokes that disconcerted the commander and made Lucía turn scarlet.

The engaged couple would speak to Lucía with a touch of irony about her excessive love of knowledge.

In a word, even if the commander and Lucía had not realized, nor had wished to realize, what was happening to them, Clara and Don Carlos would have made them reflect, come to grips with their feelings, and face the truth of the matter.

Despite the difference in their ages, the commander and Lucía were hopelessly in love with each other.[93]

Lucía admired her uncle's discretion, the nobility of his character, his learning, and the innate elegance of his demeanor and manners. She thought him handsome, with manly handsomeness, and it did not seem possible to her that there was another man like him in the whole world.

Don Fadrique thought that Lucía was as pretty, as good, and as intelligent as Clara, which in his mind represented the height, the zenith of praise. Lucía's cheerfulness moreover harmonized very much better with the commander's character than the somewhat gloomy seriousness that Clara had inherited from her mother.

The commander, who after all was not an inexperienced youth, soon recognized that he loved Lucía and that he was loved by her, but, thinking of his age and of Don Carlos's idyll, he did not dare to declare his love, although he showed it with his constant solicitude in obliging Lucía.

She, meanwhile, was at a loss to explain the timidity of the commander, because she believed that he was in love with her.

Hence the fact that they exchanged all manner of compliments and kindnesses that, taken at face value, could have been the result of a most tender friendship, but that concealed the fervent spirit of true love.

In addition to his age, Don Fadrique in his sensitivity believed that another obstacle stood in his way, one that would not allow him to aspire after Lucía's love. This other obstacle was his poverty, but

otro inconveniente era su pobreza; pero Lucía, precisamente por esa pobreza y por el motivo que la había causado, amaba y admiraba más al comendador. El descuidado desdén, la alegre calma y el nada trabajoso ni lamentado abandono con que don Fadrique se había desprendido de más de cuatro millones, valían más de mil en la poética y generosa mente de Lucía.

Ésta llegó a veces a preguntar a su tío (sabido es que tenía el defecto de ser muy preguntona) que por qué no se casaba.

Cuando el tío le contestaba que porque era viejo, Lucía le aseguraba que era mozo o que estaba mejor que los mejores mozos. Cuando el tío contestaba que porque era pobre, Lucía afrmaba que la paga de oficial retirado era más que suficiente; que además la chacha Ramoncica estaba poderosísima con lo que había ahorrado, e iba a dejarle por heredero; y que, por último, podía casarse con una rica.

Todo esto lo decía Lucía con mil rodeos y disimulos; pero el comendador, si bien lo comprendía, juzgaba aún que ella podía engañarse y tomar por amor otros sentimientos de respeto y afección casi filial; por donde no hallaba justo ni honrado prevalerse tal vez de una alucinación de aquella linda muchacha para lograr lo que consideraba una felicidad para él.

En esta situación se hallaban Lucía y el comendador la noche en que se celebró la boda de Clara y de don Carlos en casa de don Valentín.

El comendador estuvo alegre, aunque hondamente conmovido, en aquella solemne ocasión en que una persona tan querida de su alma se unía con lazo indisoluble al hombre que debía hacerla dichosa.

Don José y doña Antonia se volvieron temprano a su casa.

Lucía permaneció al lado de Clara hasta más tarde. También se quedó con ella el comendador.

Juntos y solos volvieron ambos a la casa. La noche estaba hermosísima: la calle silenciosa y solitaria, el ambiente tibio y perfumado, el cielo lleno de estrellas y sin luna.

Lucía iba callada, contenta, pensando en la ventura de su amiga.

No estaba don Fadrique menos soñador e imaginativo.

El tránsito de una casa a otra era cortísimo; pero, sin reflexionar, le alargaron ellos, parándose en medio de la calle y contemplando la bóveda inmensa del firmamento, como si quisiesen interrogar a las

Lucía, precisely on account of that poverty and the reason that had caused it, loved and admired the commander all the more because of it. The offhand disdain, the cheerful calm, and the not at all difficult nor lamented abandon with which Don Fadrique had divested himself of more than four million in assets, were worth more than one billion in Lucía's poetic and generous mind.

The latter at times ventured to ask her uncle (it is well known that great inquisitiveness was a shortcoming in her) why he did not marry.

When her uncle replied that it was because he was old, Lucía assured him that he was not, and that he was in better shape than the best young fellows. When her uncle replied that it was because he was poor, Lucía declared that the pay of a retired naval officer was more than sufficient, that moreover Chacha Ramoncica had saved loads and loads of money, and she was going to bequeath it to him, and that, lastly, he could marry a rich woman.

Lucía said all this with a thousand circumlocutions and dodges, but the commander, although he understood it all, still believed that she might be deluding herself and taking for love other feelings of respect and affection that were almost filial. For that reason he considered it neither just nor honorable perhaps to avail himself of that pretty girl's delusion in order to attain what he viewed as happiness for himself.

Such was the state of affairs between Lucía and the commander on the evening that Clara and Don Carlos's wedding was celebrated in Don Valentín's house.

The commander was jovial, although deeply moved, on that solemn occasion, when a person so dear to his heart was united by an indissoluble bond to the man who should make her happy.

Don José and Doña Antonia returned to their home early.

Lucía stayed at Clara's side until later; the commander also stayed with her.

Uncle and niece returned home together, just the two of them. The night was exceptionally lovely, the street silent and deserted, the atmosphere balmy and aromatic, the sky dotted with stars, but moonless.

Lucía was quiet, contented, thinking about her friend's good fortune.

Don Fadrique was no less dreamy and lost in thought too.

The distance from the one house to the other was very short, but unconsciously they prolonged it, stopping in the middle of the street and gazing at the immense vault of the firmament, as if they wished

eternas luces, que allí fulguraban, sobre la suerte de los recién casados y sobre la propia suerte.

Lucía, dando un suspiro, dijo al fin:

—¡No lo dude usted... serán muy felices!

—Alégrate sólo y no estés envidiosa— respondió el comendador —; tú hallarás también un hombre que te merezca, que te ame y a quien ames tú con toda la energía de tu corazón.

—No, tío, no me amará— replicó Lucía —. Yo soy muy desgraciada.

Y Lucía suspiró de nuevo. El comendador, a la dulce y escasa luz de los astros, vio entonces que corrían dos hermosas lágrimas por las mejillas de Lucía. La luz de los astros se quebraba en aquellos líquidos diamantes y daba reflejos de iris.

El comendador no fue dueño de sí mismo. Acercó su rostro al de Lucía y puso los labios en una de aquellas lágrimas. Luego exclamó:

—¡Te amo!

Lucía no contestó palabra. Echó a andar hacia su casa; llamó, abrieron, y entró seguida del comendador.

Al llegar a la escalera, se volvió y le dijo:

—Buenas noches, tío. Adiós, hasta mañana. Mamá me estará aguardando.

El comendador puso la cara más afligida del mundo, viendo que tan secamente respondía la muchacha, o, mejor dicho, no respondía a su repentina y vehemente declaración.

Ella se apiadó entonces, sin duda, y añadió sonriendo:

—Hable usted mañana con mamá...

—¿Y qué?...— interrumpió don Fadrique.

—Y pida usted la licencia a Roma.

Dicho esto, muy avergonzada, pero muy satisfecha, Lucía subió a brincos la escalera, y dejó al comendador no menos contento que ella iba.

Cuando supo Clara que Lucía y el comendador habían decidido casarse, se alegró en extremo.

Don Carlos de Atienza compartió la alegría de su mujer, y recordando que debía una especie de satisfacción al comendador, el cual se había creído aludido cuando le oyó leer el idilio contra el viejo rabadán, compuso otro idilio en defensa de un rabadán no tan viejo y en alabanza del amor de los rabadanes.

Este segundo idilio, que viene a ser como la palinodia del primero, se

to question the eternal stars that glittered up there about the fate of the newlyweds and perhaps about their own.

Heaving a sigh, Lucía said at length:

"Have no doubt. They will be very happy!"

"Just be glad and not envious," responded the commander. "You too will find a man worthy of you, who will love you and whom you'll love with all the might of your heart."

"No, Uncle, he won't love me," said Lucía. "I am most unfortunate."

And Lucía again sighed. By the soft and scant stellar light, the commander then saw two beautiful tears streaming down Lucía's cheeks. The starlight danced on those liquid diamonds and returned prismatic, rainbow reflections.

The commander lost his self-control. He inclined his head to Lucía's face and put his lips to one of those tears. Then he blurted out:

"I love you!"

Lucía did not utter a word in reply. She continued on to her house; she knocked; someone opened the door; and she went in, followed by the commander.

When she reached the stairway, she turned around and said to him:

"Good night, Uncle. Good-bye, until tomorrow. Mamá must be waiting for me."

The commander pulled the most aggrieved face in the world, seeing that Lucía responded so matter-of-factly, or rather, that she did not respond to his sudden and vehement declaration.

She then took pity on him, no doubt, for she added, smiling:

"Speak to Mamá tomorrow and – "

" – and what?" interrupted Don Fadrique.

"And ask Rome for a dispensation."

Having said this, a very embarrassed yet very satisfied Lucía bounded up the stairs, leaving the commander no less pleased than she was.

When Clara learned that Lucía and the commander had decided to marry, she was overjoyed.

Don Carlos de Atienza shared his wife's elation, and, recalling that he owed an apology of sorts to the commander, who thought that the poet had alluded to him in his recitation of the idyll against the old shepherd, he composed another idyll in defense of a not so old shepherd and in praise of the love of head shepherds.

This second idyll, which serves as a kind of palinode to the first one,

conserva aún en los archivos de Villabermeja, de donde mi amigo don Juan Fresco me ha remitido copia exacta y fidedigna, que traslado aquí para terminar. El idilio es como sigue:

En la vid con sus pámpanos lozana,
relucen cual topacio los racimos.
Quita lluvia temprana
al alma tierra la aridez estiva,
y los frutos opimos
medran con nuevos jugos en la oliva
y en el almendro que entre riscos brota.
Recobra el claro río
el caudal que perdiera en el estío;
y el áspera bellota
se madura y endulza entre el pomposo
follaje, donde el viento
para las gentes de la edad primera
con fatídico acento
la voluntad de Júpiter dijera.
No como en primavera
el campo está de flor matizado;
que el labrador cansado
en las flores cifraba su esperanza,
y ora en cosecha sazonada alcanza
el premio de su afán y su cuidado.
Embalsama el membrillo con su aroma
los céfiros ligeros;
y en el limón y en la madura poma,
y en los sabrosos peros
el oro luce y el carmín asoma,
que brillaron en rosas y alelíes;
mientras, por celos de su flor, empieza
a romper la granada su corteza,
descubriendo un tesoro de rubíes.
Con la otoñal frescura
nace la nueva hierba, y su verdura
la palidez de los rastrojos cubre.
Serena está la esfera cristalina,

is still preserved in the archives of Villabermeja, from where my friend
Don Juan Fresco has sent me a reliable, word-for-word copy, which I
transcribe here to conclude this story. The idyll is as follows:[94]

On the lush, tendril-laden vine
Clusters of grapes glitter like topaz.
Early rains brings relief
To the arid estival earth,
And the abundant fruits
Thrive with new juices in the olive
And almond trees that sprout on crags.
The clear river regains the
Flow that it lost in summertime;
And the bitter acorn
Ripens and sweetens amid the splendid
Foliage, where the wind,
For the peoples of primeval times,
Spoke in a fateful voice
The will of Jupiter.
Not like in springtime,
The fields are dotted with flowers;
And the weary plowman
Pinned his hopes on those blooms
And now in a ripe harvest reaps
The reward for his industry and care.
The quince with its fragrance embalms
The light zephyrs;
And on the lemon and on the ripe apple
And on the delectable pears
Gold gleams and carmine peeks through,
As they glittered on roses and wallflowers;
Meanwhile, jealous of its blossom, the pomegranate
Begins to burst its rind,
Revealing a treasure of rubies.
With the autumnal freshness
The new grass comes up, and its greenery
Blankets the pale, stubble-strewn land.
The crystalline celestial sphere is calm,

y hacia el rojo Occidente el sol declina
en una hermosa tarde del octubre.
Filis, la pastorcilla soñadora,
bella como la luz de la alborada,
abandonando ahora
su tranquila morada,
va de las Ninfas a la sacra gruta;
y en vez de flores por presente lleva
un canastillo de olorosa fruta,
con que a vencer la resistencia prueba
que hacen a sus amores
las Ninfas que en el suelo
a Cupidos traviesos y menores
dan vida y ser contra el Amor del cielo.
No bien el antro con su planta huella,
donde reinan las sombras y el reposo,
con terror religioso
se estremece la tímida doncella.
Su presente coloca
de las silvestres Ninfas en el ara.
Y las altas razones de prudencia rara,
que pone el Numen en su fresca boca,
con esmerada concisión declara:
«Ninfas, no os ofendáis de mi desvío,
no deis vuestro favor a los zagales
que cautivar pretenden mi albedrío.
Son como los rosales,
que lucen mucho en la estación florida
y dan amarga fruta desabrida.
De su orgullosa mocedad el brío
apetece y no ama;
y con enojo en sus palabras leo
que poética llama
ni ennoblece ni ilustra su deseo;
y que el conato, que imprimió natura
en todo ser viviente,
no se acrisola allí ni se depura
del cielo con la luz resplandeciente.
Ya sé que los Cupidos,

And the sun falls away toward the red west
On a beautiful late afternoon in October.
Phyllis, the dreamy shepherdess,
Lovely like the light of dawn,
Forsaking now
Her peaceful abode,
Betakes herself to the sacred grotto of the Nymphs;
And instead of flowers, as an offering she carries
A little basket full of fragrant fruit,
With which she will try to overcome the resistance
Put up by the Nymphs who on Earth
Breathe life and existence into lesser, mischievous Cupids
Against the Amor of heaven.
No sooner does she set foot in the cavern,
Where darkness and repose reign,
Than the timid maiden shudders
With holy terror.
She sets her offering
Upon the altar of the sylvan Nymphs.
And with polished concision
Declares the sublime reasons that the
Numen of inspiration brings to her fresh lips:
"Nymphs, do not be offended by my indifference;
Do not bestow your favor on the young shepherds
Who seek to captivate my will.
They are like rose bushes,
Which dazzle in the season of bloom
Only to yield a bitter, unsavory fruit.
The vigor of their haughty youth
Bespeaks longing and not love;
And with annoyance I read in their words
That poetic flame
Neither ennobles nor enlightens their desire;
And that the hankering, imparted by nature
To every living being,
Is not purified, not cleansed
By the resplendent light of Heaven.
Well do I know that the Cupids,

vuestros hijos queridos,
dan a la tierra su virtud creadora;
mas el Amor, que en el Empíreo mora,
esa misma virtud en ellos vierte,
y difunde doquier su vida arcana,
vencedora del mal y de la muerte.
Pues bien; la que se afana
los misterios ocultos y supremos
por saber de este Amor, ¿lograrlo puede
con un zagal sencillo y sin doctrina?
Las que tesoro tal gozar queremos,
¿no es mejor que busquemos
al varón sabio a quien el Dios concede
el vivo lampo de su luz divina?
Por eso, Ninfas, a mi Irenio adoro:
como en arca sagrada
guarda dentro del alma inmaculada
del Amor el tesoro;
y arde su llama bajo el limpio hielo
con que el tenaz trabajo de la mente
corona ya su frente,
como corona el cano Mongibelo.
Así Irenio recobra por la ciencia
lo que roba del tiempo la inclemencia.
¡Cuánto zagal con incansable mano
toca el rabel en vano
por carecer de gracia y maestría;
mientras que Irenio, con su blando tino
y su plectro divino,
produce encantadora melodía,
y hace sentir al alma lo que quiere,
no bien la cuerda hiere!
Si el zagal inexperto
persigue al perdigón en la carrera,
o le pierde o le coge medio muerto:
mas la diestra certera
pone Irenio prudente
en el oculto nido,

Your beloved children,
Confer their creative virtue upon Earth;
But Amor, who dwells in the Empyrean,
Bestows on them that very same virtue,
And diffuses hither and yon its arcane life,
Conqueror of evil and death.
And therefore, she who strives to grasp
The supreme, hidden mysteries in order
To know of this Amor, can she do so
With a simple, unschooled young shepherd?
We maidens who wish to enjoy such a treasure,
Is it not better that we should seek out
The wise man on whom God beams the
Brilliance of his divine light?
For this reason, Nymphs, I adore my Irenaeus:[95]
As in a sacred coffer,
He keeps safe within his immaculate soul
The treasure of love;
And its flame burns beneath the pure frost
With which the persistent labor of the mind
Already crowns his brow
As it crowns the snow-covered Mongibelo.[96]
Thus does Irenaeus recover through knowledge
What inclemency steals from time.
How many young shepherds with tireless hands
Play the rebec in vain
For want of grace and mastery,
While Irenaeus, with his soft touch
And his divine plectrum,
Produces an enchanting melody
And makes the soul feel what it wants
As soon as he plucks the cord!
If the inexpert young shepherd
Pursues the partridge on the run
Or loses it or traps it nearly dead;
The prudent Irenaeus puts
His sure right hand
Inside the hidden nest,

do el pájaro reposa con descuido,
y su pluma naciente
sin destrozar, sus alas no fatiga,
y le aprisiona al fin para su amiga.
Ni resplandece menos el ingenio
del doctísimo Irenio
en componer cantares,
y en referir historias singulares.
Cuando me alcanza de la rama verde
la tierna nuez, la alloza delicada,
elige lo mejor, sin tronchar nada.
Cuando algún corderillo se me pierde,
él le busca y a casa me le lleva;
y de continuo me regala y prueba
su cariño sincero,
o haciendo con esmero
de los huesos de guinda
ya un barquichuelo, ya una cesta linda
o enseñando a sacar a mi jilguero
el alpiste menudo
de entre mis labios con su pico agudo.
Tan sólo me perturba y me desvela
que Irenio a veces con el alma vuela
por donde de su amor terreno dudo,
pero si Irenio de verdad me amara,
mayor triunfo sería
el lograr la victoria,
no de pastoras de agraciada cara,
sino de la poesía,
de la ciencia, del arte y de la gloria.»
Irenio, a Filis escondido oía;
y apareciendo y dándole un abrazo,
dijo con modestísima dulzura:
«Éste amoroso lazo
que labra mi ventura,
en vano, Filis, explicar pretendes
con tus alambicadas discreciones.
¡Ay, candorosa Filis! ¿No comprendes

Where the bird reposes unconcerned,
And catches it for his damsel
Without crushing its new feathers,
Without injuring its wings.
Nor does the genius of the
Learned Irenaeus shine less
In composing ballads
And in telling unusual stories.
When from the verdant branch he
Picks for me the green walnut, the tender almond,
He selects the best one and harms not the tree.
When a lambkin wanders from my sight
He searches for it and brings it back to me;
And he constantly pleases me and
Proves his sincere love,
Either painstakingly making
From cherry pits
Now a little boat, now a pretty basket,
Or teaching my goldfinch to pluck,
With its pointed beak, a minute
Seed from between my lips.
It only disturbs me and keeps me awake
That at times Irenaeus should fly off with his soul
To a place where I doubt his earthly love,
But if Irenaeus truly loves me,
A greater triumph it would be
To gain victory,
Not over shepherdesses with pretty faces,
But over poetry,
Over knowledge, art, and glory."
Irenaeus, hidden, was listening to Phyllis;
And appearing now and embracing her,
He said with the most unassuming gentleness:
"This loving bond,
Wrought by my happiness,
In vain, Phyllis, do you try to explain
With your subtle argumentations.
Alas, innocent Phyllis! Do you not understand

que, a pesar del saber que en mí supones,
amor no te infundiera
tu rabadán si muy anciano fuera?
Cuando mi amor al del zagal prefieres,
por viejo no, por rabadán me quieres.»

Madrid, 1876

That, despite the knowledge you suppose in me,
Your head shepherd would not inspire
Love in you were he very elderly?
When you prefer my love to that of the shepherd boy,
Not because I am old do you love me,
But because I am the shepherd man."

Madrid, 1876

NOTES

1. Carmen Bravo Villasante's *Biografía de Don Juan Valera* (Barcelona: Aedos, 1959) continues to be one of the most thorough and complete biographies of the author. Two other useful works are Cyrus DeCoster's *Juan Valera* (New York: Twayne, 1974) and Alberto Jiménez's *Juan Valera y la generación de 1868* (Madrid: Taurus, 1973).
2. For an excellent discussion of the intersection between Valera's life and work, see Henry Thurston-Griswold's *El idealismo sintético de don Juan Valera: teoría y práctica* (Potomac, Maryland: Scripta Humanistica, 1990). Although very little has been written on *Commander Mendoza* itself, studies that deal with some aspects of the novel include Teresia Langford Taylor's *The Representation of Women in the Novels of Juan Valera: A Feminist Critique* (New York: Peter Lang, 1997), Manuel Camarero's *Antología comentada de la literatura española, siglo XIX* (Madrid: Castalia, 1999), 324–330, and Guillermo Carnero's *Historia de la literatura española, siglo XIX* (Madrid: Espasa-Calpe, 1996).
3. See Sherman Eoff's "The Spanish Novel of 'Ideas': Critical Opinion" in *PMLA*, 55, (1940): 531–558; Manuel Olguín's "Juan Valera's Theory of Art for Art's Sake" in *Modern Language Forum* 35 (1950): 24–34; and the above cited article by Henry Thurston-Griswold.
4. In like fashion, Noël Valis has examined the integral role played by deceit in Valera's later novel *Juanita la Larga*. See for example her article "The Use of Deceit in Valera's *Juanita la Larga,*" *Hispanic Review* 49, no. 3 (1981): 317–327, as well as her critical introduction to Robert Fedorchek's translation *Juanita la Larga* (Washington, DC: The Catholic University of America Press, 2006), xi–xxiii.
5. In an article written for the Madrid periodical, *La Opinión*, on June 26, 1886, ten years after the publication of this work, the eminent author and literary critic Leopoldo Alas (Clarín) confirms this idea stating that the reason the public didn't like Valera's second novel, *The Illusions of Doctor Faustino*, was simply because they didn't understand it.
6. For more on this topic, see my "Images of Paternity in the *Quijote,*" *Hispanófila* 132 (2001): 43–52.
7. Paul Smith examines Valera's use of the illegitimacy motif and the May-December romance in "Juan Valera and the Illegitimacy Motif," *Hispania* 51 (1968): 803–811.
8. See Ana Baquero Escudero's "El perspectivismo cambiante en *El Comendador Mendoza* de Valera" (Alicante: Biblioteca Virtual Miguel de Cervantes, 2005), 28–33.
9. *Commander Mendoza* came out in book form in June 1877, but it had first appeared serially in the fortnightly periodical *El Campo*, between 1 December 1876 and 1 May 1877.
10. *The Illusions of Doctor Faustino* came out in 1875. More than half of the action takes place in Villabermeja. As will be the case with *Commander Mendoza*, the narrator of the novel merely "records" what his friend Don Juan Fresco tells him.

11. *Santiago*, in Spanish, patron saint of Spain.
12. A compilation of writings against Christianity and the Catholic Church; an 1820 Spanish translation (from *citar*, to "cite" or to "quote") of *Le Citateur* published in Paris in 1803.
13. *Chacha*, an abbreviation of *muchacha* (girl), normally means "nursemaid" or "servant," but here, with Victoria and below with Ramoncica, it is used as an affectionate honorific.
14. Greats of the Golden Age of Spanish literature: Francisco de Quevedo y Villegas (1580–1645), poet, satirist, and novelist; Tirso de Molina [Fray Gabriel Téllez] (1579–1648), outstanding dramatist, author of the earliest literary version of the Don Juan legend in *El burlador de Sevilla* (*The Trickster of Seville*); Pedro Calderón de la Barca (1600–1681), another leading Golden Age dramatist, best known for his masterpiece *La vida es sueño* (*Life is a Dream*).
15. María de Zayas y Sotomayor (1590–1661), a novelist, and Eugenio Gerardo Lobo (1679–1750), a poet.
16. All Spanish editions of *El Comendador Mendoza* give the year 1747, but the treaty ending the War of Austrian Succession, also known as the Treaty of Aix-la-Chappelle (*Aquisgrán* in Spanish), was signed in 1748.
17. A river in northern Italy.
18. Henri IV (1553–1610), king of France 1589–1610, entered Paris on March 22, 1594, to defeat and dethrone the usurper "shadow" king, Charles X. To his troops he said: "My friends, you are French. The enemy is before you. Have at them! And if you lose sight of your colors, follow the white plume on my helmet: find that and you find the path to honor and to glory!"
19. Conqueror of the Midianites. Judges, 6–8.
20. Contributors to the monumental *Encyclopédie* brought to fruition by Denis Diderot (1713–1784) in 1772.
21. La Isla [Island] de León (La ciudad de San Fernando), popularly known simply as "La Isla," site of the Naval Academy, in the Andalusian province of Cádiz.
22. Admiral Sir George Pocock (1706–1792).
23. Historic fort at the entrance to the harbor of Havana.
24. Luis Vicente de Velasco e Isla (b. 1711), who died on July 31, 1762, defending the castle.
25. General George Keppel, third Earl of Albemarle (1724–1772).
26. The reference is to the Spain-France Family (*i.e.*, the Bourbons) Pact [*El Pacto de familia España-Francia*, 1761], entered into by Carlos III (1716–1788).
27. José Gálvez, marquis of Sonora (1720–1786), Inspector General of New Spain [Mexico] and Secretary of the Indies.
28. Valera confuses the first given name: it was *José* [Antonio]. In 1776 Carlos III named him Inspector General of Peru and Chile, as well as of the River Plate region.
29. Indian leader in Peru whose rebellion of 1780 protested the inhumane conditions of forced labor in mines and mills. Sometimes referred to as Tupac Amaru II, he was the great-grandson of the first Tupac Amaru and had been baptized José Gabriel Condorcanqui. He was captured and executed with savage brutality, and every member of his family was also executed or imprisoned.

30. Valera combines two histories here. Tupac Amaru II was killed by being drawn and quartered; it was his namesake who was beheaded. See: Jacobs, James Q. Tupac Amaru: *The Life, Times, and Execution of the Last Inca.* www.jqjacobs.net/andes/tupac_amaru.html

31. Étienne Bonnot de Condillac (1715–1780), French philosopher who held that all knowledge comes from the senses and that there are no innate ideas.

32. Most accounts give 1781 as the year of the death of Tupac Amaru II.

33. It is worthwhile recalling that the full title of Voltaire's philosophical novel is *Candide, ou l'Optimisme*.

34. A possible reference to the 1783 Treaty of Paris, when Spain recovered Florida (which it had lost to England in the 1763 Treaty of Paris).

35. It is well nigh impossible to fix the equivalent in British or American currency of a *real* in mid to late eighteenth-century Perú. However, starting in 1732 the Mexico Mint began issuing [*reales*] coins of the Pillar type that were of .917 silver weighing 3.38 grams, which means that a few million of them made the Commander a man of some wealth.

36. Tippoo Sahib (1749–1799), Indian leader and sultan of Mysore from 1782 to 1799.

37. A card that is the second highest trump, hence the name of the game.

38. A card game in which the objective is to win the four kings or the four queens.

39. A kind of gazpacho that is made with bread, egg, tomato, pepper, garlic, salt, and water, these ingredients being diced into small pieces and whisked or blended to a purée.

40. Pancakes of flour, egg, and honey with the consistency of a wafer.

41. Pancakes of flour and beaten eggs that are coated with honey after being fried in olive oil.

42. *Señorito* would be the salutation given to a young man, or relatively young man, whereas *Señor* would imply a more advanced age.

43. The original reads *como garbanzo en olla*, that is, "like a chickpea in a stew."

44. The primary meaning of *Tío* with the first name is "Uncle," but in some places in Spain (and in small towns in particular) it is a title of respect accorded a married man or one getting on in years.

45. Valera, very much taken with the Holy Week traditions of his native Andalusia, gives other detailed accounts of scenes and floats in *Doña Luz* and *Juanita la Larga*.

46. For "Thriftiness." The Spanish word is *Ahorro*, but Rafaela uses the popular pronunciation and converts the silent h into the plosive j, *i.e.*, *Ajorro*.

47. A possible reference to Ángel de Saavedra, Duke of Rivas (1791–1865), Valera's friend and patron, author of the groundbreaking romantic drama *Don Álvaro, or the Force of Fate* (*Don Álvaro o la fuerza del sino*).

48. A time-honored social custom in a number of Valera's novels, the *tertulia* was a gathering that pretty much began at set hours on set days, and with pretty much the same habitués, or *tertulianos*.

49. Made with the fibrous part of a pumpkin.

50. Juan Meléndez Valdés (1754–1817), Neoclassical poet, one of the greats of eighteenth-century Spanish literature. He wrote eclogues, odes, and moral and philosophical poetry, even a denunciation of war in "The Old Man's Farewell" (*"La despedida del anciano"*).

51. The Greek goddess of flowers and personification of spring; the spouse of Zephyr[us].
52. I have translated Valera's rhymed verse into prose so as to avoid a transfer that would result in a stilted, artificial English rendering, but the text remains set in short lines in approximate measure with the original.
53. André Chénier (1762–1794), French poet who supported the constitutional monarchy, for which reason he was condemned to death and guillotined.
54. Friar Luis de León (1527–1591) and Garcilaso de la Vega (1501–1536), two of the greats of the Spanish Renaissance.
55. The diminutive *Carlitos* suggests that the commander views the poet's remarks with a touch of pique or slight disdain.
56. In this instance the diminutive *Clarita* clearly connotes affection.
57. Vicente Espinel (1550–1624), poet and author of the picaresque novel *Life of the Page Marcos de Obregón* (*Vida del escudero Marcos de Obregón*, 1618). He hailed from the beautiful Andalusian city of Ronda, famous for its dramatic gorge and historic eighteenth-century bullring.
58. Saint Hilarion (*c*.291–*c*.371) lived for more than fifty years in a mud-brick shelter, subsisting on figs and vegetables, and bread and water; Saint Pachomius (*c*.290–*c*.346) was the first monk to establish a communal life and a written rule.
59. A Spanish Inquisition garment worn by a confessed heretic, of yellow for the penitent, of black for the impenitent (from the Spanish San Benito, or Saint Benedict).
60. By abandoning the familiar you [*tú*] Doña Blanca does more than coolly distance herself from her husband: she heightens the haughty, unforgiving nature of her character and speaks to him as if he were an underling who needs to be admonished.
61. No longer observed in the Catholic rite, it was the week that preceded Holy Week, when statues and crosses were covered with purple cloth.
62. Similar to the rhythm or cadence of the Gregorian chant or the monotonic delivery intoned by a priest in a high mass.
63. Caius Sempronius Gracchus (153–121 B.C.), Roman reformer and orator.
64. Boys would use a board or plank and a pair of horns to play at bullfighting.
65. Lucius Annaeus Seneca (*c*.4 B.C.–A.D. 65), Roman philosopher.
66. Greek Stoic philosopher (*c*.280–*c*.207 B.C.) and head of the Academy in Athens.
67. Marcus Atilius Regulus, Roman general in the First Punic War, waged against Carthage, 264–241 B.C.
68. "It is not being pious, but impious, to tolerate sins."
69. David (Psalms 41:8): "The deep calls out to the deep." Solomon (Ecclesiasticus 20:9): "There is success in evil things." Amos (3:6): the full quote is: *Si erit malum [in civitate] quod Dominus non fecerit?*, "Shall there be evil [in a city] which the Lord has not done?"
70. The meaning of the Latin precedes. Ecclesiastes 3:14.
71. 22:1 "A good name is better than great riches."
72. The original is *A mal Cristo mucha sangre*.
73. A mountain range in southwestern Spain. The famous Despeñaperros pass crosses it, linking Castile and Andalusia.

74. Valera uses the word *confesado*, and if we take it at face value, Father Jacinto, who earlier agreed to the secrecy of the confessional, has violated the secrecy and sanctity of the confessional as far as Clarita is concerned.

75. A reference to university students who subsisted by begging for soup (and food in general), for which reason they carried spoons in their hat bands and sang their thanks, as do present-day student music groups in Spain (*la tuna*) who serenade in public dressed in colorful, medieval garb.

76. Gonzalo Fernández de Córdoba (1453–1515), known as *El Gran Capitán*, a general who served with great distinction under the Catholic monarchs Ferdinand and Isabella.

77. "Wise as serpents."

78. Celebrated Greek painter (367? –315? B.C.).

79. Famous Greek sculptor (*c*.500–*c*.432 B.C.).

80. Treatise [*Examen de ingenios*, 1557] by Juan Huarte de San Juan (1529–1591).

81. Greek philosopher and mathematician (*c*.582–*c*.500 B.C.).

82. Olympic athlete of ancient Greece, famed for his strength.

83. In Greek legend, a deformed, scurrilous officer in the Greek army of the siege of Troy. Achilles knocked him to the ground with his fist and killed him (Homer's Iliad).

84. The original is *Quien roba a un ladrón tiene cien años de perdón*, literally, "Whoever robs a thief will have one hundred years of forgiveness."

85. In the original: *Para vuestra dama, mucho; / para vuestra esposa, poco*. Literally, "For your mistress, [too] much or high; / for your wife, [too] little or low (on the social scale)."

86. In some respects this Nicolasa/Tomasuelo friendship foreshadows the one between Juanita and Antoñuelo some twenty years later in Valera's *Juanita la Larga* (Washington: The Catholic University of America Press, 2006.)

87. *Ave María Purísima* in the original, literally, "Hail Mary most Pure or Immaculate." A form of greeting when knocking on a door or when entering a house. It was also the phrase spoken by Catholics to a priest to begin one's confession, and the priest would respond *Sin pecado concebida*, *i.e.*, "Conceived without sin."

88. There are numerous appellations for the Blessed Virgin Mary in Spain. This one is the patron saint of Lucena (a town in the province of Córdoba) as well as of the Andalusian countryside. Araceli means "altar of the sky," from the Latin *ara* (altar) and *c[a]eli* (of the sky).

89. Doña Antonia's skills in dressing out swine is yet another instance of affinity between *Commander Mendoza* and *Juanita la Larga*, for she is clearly a precursor of Juana la Larga, Juanita's mother, who will excel in the preparation of nearly every imaginable victual.

90. "As death was appeased, death healed the broken spirit."

91. Saturn was the Roman god of agriculture; Amphitryon was the husband of the virtuous Alcene, whom Zeus seduced by assuming Amphitryon's form, which resulted in the birth of Hercules.

92. The original is: *Tómelo por su vida; considere / que otro lo comerá si no lo quiere*, literally, "Take it, by Jove; bear in mind / that another will eat if you do not want it."

93. The May-December romance comes at the denouement of this novel, but Valera will take it up as a full-blown theme nearly twenty years later in his *Juanita la Larga*.
94. Again, I have rendered Valera's rhymed verse into prose, like the first idyll, and for the same reason given in chapter 7.
95. A Father of the Church and one of the most important theologians of the second century (*c*.125–*c*.202).
96. Mount Etna in Sicily. Locals called it *Gibellu* or *Gibello*, hence "Mongibelo" (the *Mon*- from the Italian *montagna* or *monte*).